Forevermore & Other Stories

The **Toby Press S.Y. Agnon Library**
Jeffrey Saks, Series Editor

Books from this series

A Book That Was Lost: Thirty-Five Stories

To This Day

Shira

A Simple Story

Two Scholars That Were in Our Town and Other Novellas

Two Tales: Betrothed & Edo and Enam

A Guest for the Night

The Bridal Canopy

The Orange Peel and Other Satires

A City in Its Fullness

In Mr. Lublin's Store

Forevermore & Other Stories

And the Crooked Shall Be Made Straight (forthcoming)

The Outcast & Other Tales (forthcoming)

Illustrated:
From Foe to Friend & Other Stories by S.Y. Agnon
A Graphic Novel by Shay Charka

FOREVERMORE & OTHER STORIES

S.Y. AGNON

EDITED AND ANNOTATED BY
JEFFREY SAKS

ILLUSTRATIONS BY
YOSL BERGNER

The Toby Press

Forevermore & Other Stories
by S.Y. Agnon
Edited and Annotated by Jeffrey Saks

These stories, published in arrangement with Schocken Publishing House, Ltd., are available in Hebrew in the Collected Writings of S.Y. Agnon—*Kol Sippurav shel Shmuel Yosef Agnon,* © Schocken Publishing House, Ltd. (Jerusalem and Tel Aviv), most recent edition 1998-2003. Original publication data for each Hebrew story and translation appear as part of the annotations to this volume.

The Toby Press LLC
POB 8531, New Milford, CT 06776-8531, USA
& POB 2455, London W1A 5WY, England
www.tobypress.com

ISBN 978-1-59264-399-8

Printed and bound in the United States

מוקדש לנות ביתי
לאילנה גילה תחי׳

Contents

Illustrations by Yosl Bergner

Foreword

Writing in Prose What Was Sung in Praise

S.Y. AGNON, well past the prime of his life and capped by his large black yarmulke, looking somewhat ridiculous in his white tie and tuxedo tails, ascended the stage to receive his Nobel Prize exactly fifty years ago. At the time he was the first Israeli and, to this day, the only Hebrew author so fêted. At the Nobel Banquet, standing before the King of Sweden and reciting the customary blessing prescribed by the Talmud upon being in the presence of royalty, Agnon declared that he felt compelled to explain who he was and from whence he—and his art—had sprung. What resulted, however, was a most remarkable description of Jewish history (and presumably his place within it) and the impact of the arc of that history on Hebrew literature and Jewish storytelling. In telling his life's story he hearkened back nearly two-thousand years and said: "As a result of the historic catastrophe in which Titus of Rome destroyed Jerusalem and Israel was exiled from its land, I was born in one of the cities of the Exile. But always I regarded myself as one who was born in Jerusalem."

Agnon went on to explain that as a descendent of the Levites, the Temple choristers, he felt the destruction of Jerusalem most profoundly:

> In a dream, in a vision of the night, I saw myself standing with my brother-Levites in the Holy Temple, singing with them the songs of David, King of Israel, melodies such as no ear has heard since the day our city was destroyed and its people went into exile. I suspect that the angels in charge of the Shrine of Music, fearful lest I sing in wakefulness what I had sung in dream, made me forget by day what I had sung at night; for if my brethren, the sons of my people, were to hear, they would be unable to bear their grief over the happiness they have lost. To console me for having prevented me from singing with my mouth, they enable me to compose songs in writing.

If taken at face value (and so little in Agnon should be taken at face value), he is declaring that his literary gift and artistic output are some form of divine compensation and source of consolation for the tragedies of destruction and exile. Destined to be a singer of the Temple Psalms, but prevented from his destiny by the vicissitudes of history, he has been divinely tasked to write in prose what was formerly sung in praise.

In the Nobel speech (included as an appendix to this volume) as well as in a variety of other places in his writing—both in the guise of autobiography as well as outright fiction—he described that his very first composition came to him almost prophetically as a statement of poetic longing and lamentation for his beloved father, travelling on business to the regional fair, absent from the happy home in Buczacz in which young Shmuel Yosef Czaczkes (Agnon's birth-name) was raised. This theme, that writing and storytelling becomes a balm for pain, runs throughout Agnon's work. One need not be steeped in the working of Jewish midrash to understand that a little boy's longing for his father might also be read on the national plane of Israel's pining for its Father in heaven. This type of multi-layered writing (and reading) is at the core of Agnon's genius, and why a writer who—on the surface—is so steeped in the "old world" of eastern European Judaism, can be simultaneously read and understood as one of the greatest modernist authors. In almost every case, if reading any of the stories in this collection leads you to think Agnon has merely piously retold an old ḥasidic tale, you are not fathoming what is written between the lines, nor are you hearing the ironic tones which almost always accompany the work.

Perhaps no selection better demonstrates these themes than our title story, "Forevermore," among Agnon's most enigmatic works, and the object of continual fascination for critics. It contains a compelling "story within a story" as the hero's modern life in Jerusalem resonates with the ancient history that exercises such a pull on the present. It is the story of a compulsive academic, searching for the "truth" that eludes him in his scholarly pursuits. Adiel Amzeh, that cloistered scholar, has been at work for twenty years attempting to unravel the secrets of an ancient city, now reduced to dust and ashes, and to uncover it he is willing to pay with his own life—a sacrifice he makes in the present in order to recover the past. "Forevermore" is an (unstable) allegory with meaning for today's readers and contemporary Jewish history, and part of that meaning is encased in the symbolism of books, writing, the nature of the artistic calling of an author, and the relationship of all these to the "historic catastrophe," and personal and national pain, alluded to in Stockholm in 1966.

"Forevermore" is a heroically tragic tale (at least it can support one such reading), and Amzeh's encounter with the lost text he seeks can be read as a meta-reflection on Agnon's view of books and reading, their power in our lives and the lives of nations and cultures, and their ability to harness their power to experience pain and draw consolation:

> And when Adiel Amzeh read the story, he shed many tears. How great is the true writer, he thought, who does not abandon his work even when the sword of death hangs over his neck, who writes with his very blood, in his soul's own script, what his eyes have seen!... Yet learning bestows a special blessing on those who are not put off easily. Yes, Adiel Amzeh would ask himself for what and for whom he was working. But Wisdom herself would take hold of him and whisper: "Sit, my love, sit and do not leave me." So he would sit and discover new things which had been unknown to all the learned men of the ages until he

> came and revealed them. And since there were many things and learning is endless and there is much to discover and investigate and understand, he did not put his work aside and did not leave his place and he remained there forevermore.

This collection of stories, we hope, will demonstrate to you the reader that Agnon was indeed one of the "great, true writers"—like that encountered so powerfully by Amzeh—and that you will appreciate Agnon's artistry, richness, and sophistication. I am often asked, usually by Israelis demonstrating their natural chauvinism for the most decorated Hebrew author, how anyone could possibly understand Agnon in translation? – How could that Nobel committee have recognized his greatness without encountering him in the original? It is hoped that this volume, and others in the Toby Press' Agnon Library, will help answer these question. For readers unfamiliar with the complex weaving of Agnon's texts with the mastertexts of biblical and rabbinic literature, the annotations will help him or her encounter the "Jewish bookshelf" and gain an appreciation for how Agnon distilled millennia of Jewish scholarship and storytelling, recasting it into the mold of modern literature. Since this series' aspiration has been to even the playing field for the English reader without littering the pages with footnotes, major references, terms or quotations that are candidates for glossing or explication are not flagged by special markings in the body of the text, but can be found referenced by page number in the annotations. It is the reader's choice in any given instance whether or not to seek elucidation there.

The history of Agnon translation—along with its challenges, successes and failures—is a long and interesting one, and is deserving of a full telling at some other time. While a number of the translations in *Forevermore & Other Stories* are original to their publication here, many of the selections in this volume appeared in an array of publications over the years, almost none of which are readily available to readers without access to microfilm or a university library. As we collect these stories between two covers in honor of the fiftieth Nobel Prize anniversary, we are grateful to the many translators who worked over the years to bring Agnon to English-reading audiences (many of the translators are no longer with us; some of them are "identity unknown"!). In almost every case, each story has been revised to one degree or another for accuracy or to update out-fashioned style (the earliest translation collected here was published in 1931). However, it was not possible or prudent to impose a unified style on works by such a wide variety of translators working across continents and over many decades.

ACKNOWLEDGEMENTS

For their help with the wide variety of research questions that presented themselves in the course of my work on this volume, as well as finessing elements of the translations, I am grateful to: Haim Be'er, David Curwin, Hillel Halkin, Avraham and Toby Holtz, Rafi Weiser and Hillel Weiss.

My special thanks to Audrey and Yosl Bergner for permission to reprint some of Yosl's wonderful illustrations of Agnon's stories (and to Neal Lehrman for his role in bringing this about).

This volume's dedication to Ilana Joy does not presume to express fully that which is felt forevermore in the heart of her "Agnon scholar."

Jeffrey Saks
Series Editor, S.Y. Agnon Library
The Toby Press
Ḥanukah 5777 / 2016
50th Anniversary of Agnon's Nobel Prize

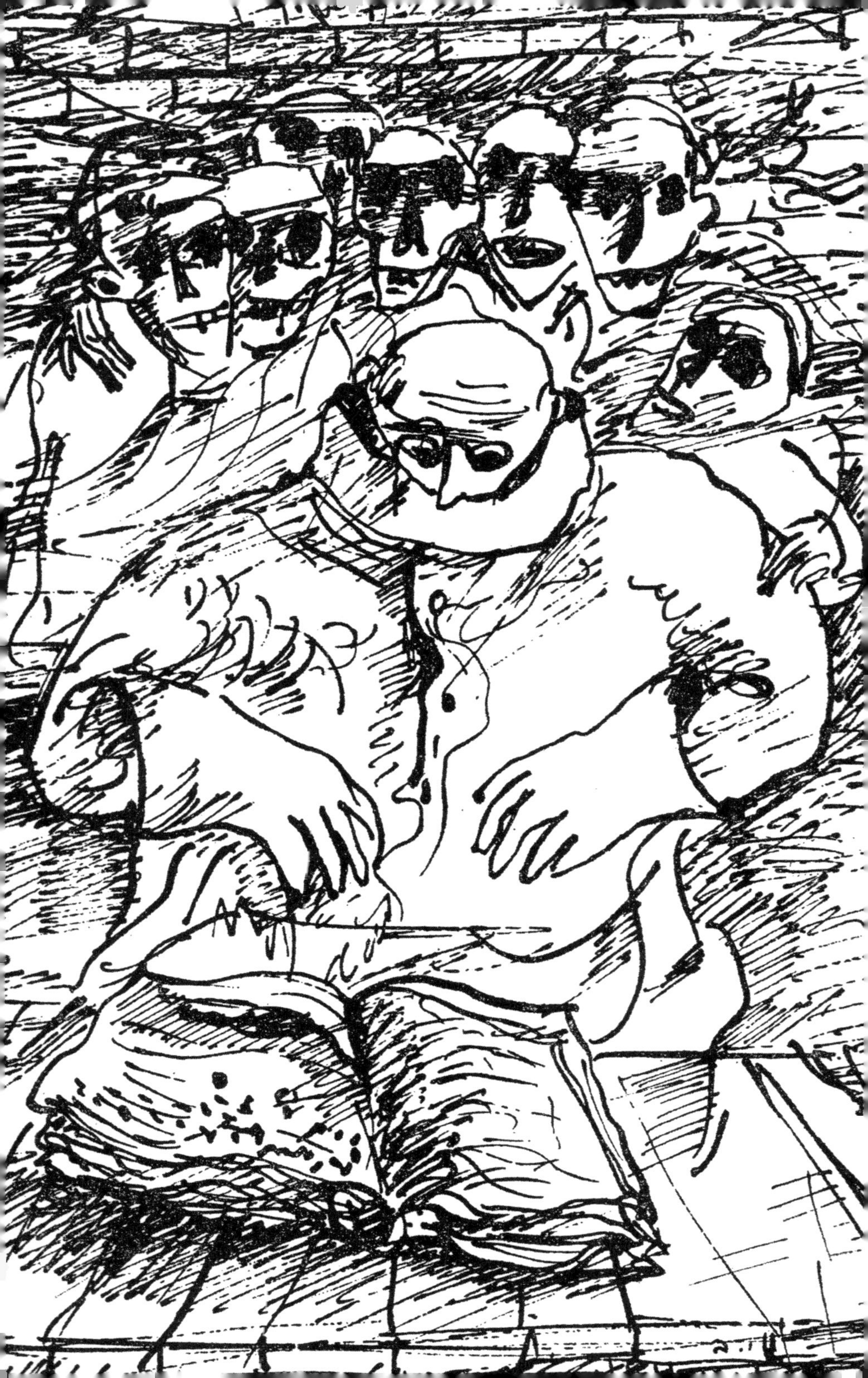

Forevermore

I

FOR TWENTY YEARS Adiel Amzeh worked on his history of the great city of Gumlidata, the pride of mighty nations until it was reduced to dust and ashes by the Gothic hordes, and its people enslaved.

After he had gathered all his researches together, examined and tested them, sorted, edited, and arranged them, he decided that his work was finally ready for publication and he sat down and wrote the book he had planned for so many years. He took the book and made the rounds of the publishers but without success. He looked about for patrons and benefactors but had no luck. During all the years he had been occupied with his research he had not taken the trouble to ingratiate himself with the learned men of the universities—nor with their wives and daughters—and now when he came to them seeking a favor, their eyes shone with such cold anger that their glasses seemed to warp. "Who are you, Sir?" they said to him. "We've never seen you before."

Amzeh shrugged his shoulders and went away, disappointed and dejected. He understood that in order to be recognized he would have to become friendly with them and he had no idea of how to go about it. Many years of painstaking research had made him a slave to his work from dawn till night, neglectful of all worldly cares. When he left his bed in the morning, his feet would carry him to the desk, his hands would pick up pen and paper, and his eyes, if not pursuing some obscure vision, would plunge into a book or into maps and sketches of the city and its great battles; sometimes he would add to what he had written, sometimes he would erase many days worth of writing. And when he lay down to sleep he would go over his notebooks again, sometimes in despair, sometimes with a sense of satisfaction. And sometimes laughing over his own mistakes that would make him ponder and rework things. Years passed and his book remained unpublished. You know, a scholar who is unable to publish his work often benefits from the delay, since he can reexamine his assumptions and correct his errors, testing those hypotheses whose ingenuity may take them far from historical reality and truth. So Adiel Amzeh revised and refined his work and brought it to the purest state, without, however, finding a publisher for it.

II

Finally, when he had despaired of ever seeing the results of his work in print, his luck took a turn for the better. Gebhard Goldenthal, the richest man in the city, informed him that he would publish the book. How did it happen that the name of a humble scholar had reached the ear of this famous man? And why would such an eminent personage want to publish a work which was sure to bring no profit? Some said he felt so uneasy about his great wealth that he had decided to become a patron of learning because his wealth gave him no inner satisfaction. He closely followed the world of scholarship and somehow had heard the story of Adiel Amzeh's book. According to another explanation, Gebhard Goldenthal secretly believed that his ancestors were among the unhappy people who were driven out of Gumlidata, that they had belonged to the city's aristocracy and that one of them had been an army general, the head of the palace guard, who fought valorously until the Goths destroyed the city. Of course, this was obviously untrue since Gumlidata was destroyed during the first wave of the Gothic invasions, and no person can say with any certainty that he is a descendant of the exiles of Gumlidata.

But whatever the reason, Gebhard Goldenthal was ready to publish Adiel Amzeh's book, even though printing this kind of work would involve many extra expenses. Several colored maps were necessary, requiring many expensive inks: one for a general view of the city, another for its temples, a third for each of its gods—Gomesh, Gush, Gutz, Guach, and Guz; one for the founding mothers of the city, one for their offspring, another for Gomed the Great, one for Gichur and

Amul—the twin pillars of prayer—and one each for all the remaining holy men, the priests and priestesses, not to mention the temple prostitutes of both sexes, the whores of noble lineage and those who were plebeian on their fathers' side, and the dogs—for each and every one a different color, to denote position and function, harlot's pay, or price. Add to all these the Goths and their allies, the Gazaens and their dwarfs, their carts and wagons, their weapons and battle defenses, and you can see how much money was needed to print such a work.

Nevertheless, Gebhard Goldenthal was ready to publish the book and make it a fine volume with beautiful printing and good paper, carefully detailed maps, expensive binding—perfect in every respect. His staff had already consulted with illustrators, engravers, and printers, and all that remained was for the author and publisher to meet, for in all his business affairs Gebhard Goldenthal would allow his staff to take care of the preliminaries—but the final arrangements had to be conducted between the client and the head of the business himself. If the client was unknown, he would be invited to Goldenthal's office; if the man was recognized in his field, he might be invited for a cup of tea to Goldenthal's home; and if he was important, he would be invited for dinner. Adiel Amzeh, who was more than a nobody but not well-known enough to be considered important, was invited by the rich man for a cup of tea.

So it was that one day Adiel Amzeh received an invitation for afternoon tea at the home of Gebhard Goldenthal. He was asked to be prompt and to come at the designated hour since Mr. Goldenthal was soon to leave for abroad and was pressed for time.

An author who for years has searched without avail for a publisher is not likely to be late for an appointment with the one he has finally found. Almost before he put down his publisher's invitation, he took out his best suit of clothes—untouched since the day he received his doctor's degree—shook it out and pressed it. He hurried to the barber, and from the barber to the bath; from there he ran to a shop where he bought a new tie, and from the shop back home to look over his book again. By morning of the day of his appointment, he had made all his preparations for his visit to the publisher. Never in his life had he experienced such a day as this. Adiel Amzeh, who for the sake of a city's destruction had put aside all personal affairs, who cared nothing for clothes or any human vanity, was utterly changed. He had become like most celebrated learned men who neglect their work for the sake of the honor they receive from others who know nothing of learning and scholarship. He sat and stared at his manuscript, rose and inspected himself in the mirror, glanced at his watch, examined his clothes, and rehearsed his gestures.

This is the regimen of all who wish to meet with a rich man. You must preen yourself and be careful of your demeanor and graces: the rich, even those who honor learning, prefer to honor it when it comes wrapped in a pleasing mantle. Yet that same love of learning which had used up so much of his energy and strength, furrowing his brow and bowing his shoulders, had touched his face with a special kind of radiance that one doesn't find except among those who are truly devoted to seeking wisdom. It's a pity Goldenthal did not see him then; had he done so he might have realized that a pleasant and happy face can be shaped from things other than money. But you see, my friend, for the sake of a little moralizing, I have gone and given away the ending at the very beginning of my story.

Well, Amzeh sat for a while, then got up, sat down again, rose again—all the time thinking of the future when the printer would take up his manuscript and transform it into attractive pages; he thought of how he would correct proofs, add and delete, omit and include certain passages; of how the printer does his work and how his book would finally be published and received. Sitting there dreaming he might have missed the appointed hour, except that all the years he had devoted to his work had sharpened him in his external affairs as well. When the moment came for him to leave for his appointment, he jumped up from his chair, picked up his house key, and made ready to leave and lock the door behind him. He stared at himself in the mirror once more and glanced about his home, astonished that his house had not changed as he had. There ought to have been some transformation, he thought, for this would have been only just for a man who was about to undergo a blessed metamorphosis.

III

At that moment, he heard the sound of footsteps and suddenly became alarmed. Perhaps Mr. Goldenthal had to leave before the appointed time and someone was coming to tell him the interview had been postponed. Amzeh stood transfixed and could hardly catch his breath; his reason was gone, only his senses functioned. His entire body seemed to become one big ear. As he listened intently to the footsteps, he realized that he was hearing the slow shuffling of an old woman. In a moment, his rationality returned and he understood that a gentleman like Goldenthal would not send an old woman to deliver a note canceling their appointment. When the sound of the old woman's footsteps came closer, he recognized them as those of a nurse who visited him once each year in order to collect journals and illustrated magazines to take to the inmates of the lepers' hospital where she worked. It was difficult for Amzeh to put the old woman off by telling her he was busy and asking that she come the following year; he had high regard for this nurse who devoted her entire life to those whose existence was a living death. But it was equally hard for him to tarry on her account, for if he was delayed, with Mr. Goldenthal about to go abroad and no one knowing when he would return, then the publication of his book would also be postponed. I should mention another factor as well, which might seem absurd but perhaps was decisive. To a man whose home is his whole universe, every unnecessary article in the house can cause annoyance. So it was with our scholar. When his mind was occupied with Gumlidata and he strolled through its ruins carrying on long conversations with the temple dogs about their price, he would occasionally raise his eyes and notice a pile of dusty old magazines. Now that the old woman had come, here was an opportunity to get rid of them; if he didn't act now, they would accumulate and gather dust for another year.

At the very moment when he was deciding what to do, whether to get rid of the superfluous volumes or to devote all his efforts to his own book, the old woman knocked on the door. He opened it and greeted her. The old woman understood immediately that he was worried and preoccupied, like a man uncertain whether to take an affirmative or negative course. "I see, Herr Doctor," she said, "that I have come at an inconvenient time. I'll leave and go about my business."

He was silent for a moment and didn't answer her. When she finally turned to go, he realized how tired the old woman must be from her long walk. After all, the lepers' home was far from the city, and she had to come on foot. She was unable to travel by bus for fear that if recognized she would be thrown off—most people are still terrified by the sight of someone who works with lepers.

"I'm sorry," Amzeh said to her as she was about to go, "but I can't take care of you the way I would like. I have been invited to afternoon tea by Gebhard Goldenthal, the famous industrialist whose name you have probably heard." (As a matter of fact, forty years previously Gebhard Goldenthal had courted the nurse and wanted to marry her, but she refused him because she had already given her heart to God's maimed, the poor prisoners of the lepers' home.) "I have a very important matter to discuss with Mr. Goldenthal," Adiel Amzeh went on. "I'll be back in an hour or so. Please sit down until I return, and later I'll fill your basket with books and journals and pamphlets and anything else I have about—they take up so much room here I can hardly breathe."

"I would like to sit here and wait for you, Herr Doctor," the old woman answered, "but I can't leave my good people for more than a short while. They are used to me and I am used to them, and when I'm away from them I miss them as much as they miss me. They are used to receiving all their needs from me. I'll go now, Herr Doctor, and if God grants me life and peace, I'll come back next year."

But Amzeh was unable to let her go away like that, without an explanation of why he was in such a hurry. Without thinking about how little time he had, he began to explain: "Perhaps you have noticed my appearance today. For many years you have been coming to visit me and you have always found me with slippers on my feet and a cap on my head, unshaven, my collar open, my hair disheveled. Today I'm dressed in a good suit and wearing shoes and a hat and a nice tie. The reason for the change is simple: for twenty years I have worked on a book and it is finally ready for publication. Mr. Gebhard Goldenthal has decided to publish it, and I'm now going to see him. He's waiting for me and for my book."

The old woman's face glowed. "You mustn't delay a moment, Herr Doctor. Hurry, hurry, don't wait, an hour like this doesn't come every day, don't put off even a minute what you have waited many years for. It is good that you found Mr. Goldenthal. He's an honest man. He keeps his promises. I, too, in my poor state owe him a debt of gratitude. I remember when I began to serve in the lepers' hospital, the rooms were full of dust and broken beds and chairs, the roof was caved in, the walls tottering and moldy. If he hadn't given us money to put the place together again, to buy new beds and equipment and make all the necessary repairs, it would have been impossible to get along there."

After the old woman had recounted all of Gebhard Goldenthal's good deeds, she let out a deep sigh. "Are you unhappy?" Adiel Amzeh asked her. "Unhappy?" she replied with a shy smile. "I've never been unhappy." He was quiet for a moment. "You are unique, Nurse Eden, you are the only one in the world who can make such a declaration," he said.

The old woman blushed with confusion. "I really should correct what I just said, Herr Doctor. I have had great unhappiness, but not on my own account." Her face turned scarlet and she lapsed into silence.

"You stopped right in the middle of what you were saying, Nurse Adah," Amzeh said, "and perhaps at the crucial point. I'm certain it would be worthwhile to hear."

"Worthwhile?" the old woman cried, stammering in her confusion. "How do we know what is worthwhile and what isn't? I'm an old woman whose grave is waiting for her—let me boast once that I told the whole truth. I flattered myself falsely when I said that I've never been unhappy. On the contrary, I haven't known a day without sorrow, a sorrow greater than that of my good people who suffer more than any other creatures in the world. For the merciful God who inflicts suffering on man provides him with the strength to withstand his woes; but if one is healthy and without physical disability, then he has no special allotment of strength, and when he looks on those who suffer and on their pain he is tormented and has nothing with which to withstand his sorrow. And especially someone like myself, who has to look after the suffering ones. I'm always afraid that I won't fulfill my obligations, that I don't do the right thing for the good people. A healthy person cannot know the inner needs of the sick. Since I don't leave them for a moment, my suffering does not leave me.... But I'm talking too much. I've forgotten that you are in a hurry. Now I'll be going. I hope, Herr Doctor, that your business will bring you a full life and peace. Only it's too bad about the poor people who must see me return empty-handed, without any books."

"Why is it too bad?" he asked, facing her. "Have they finished all the books? They've read them all?"

"They've read them dozens of times," answered the old woman.

"What kind of books do they have?"

"Oh, I can give you the names of all of them."

"All of them? Surely you're exaggerating."

"No, there aren't very many. I've been there so many years, every article and every book is familiar to me."

The old woman then recited the name of each book in the hospital library. "Not many, not very many at all," Amzeh said after she had finished. "I. can imagine how happy they must be to receive a new book. But," he went on, jokingly, "I'm sure you have forgotten one or two, and perhaps they were the best books of the lot. For that's the way we are —we always forget the most important thing. Isn't that so, Nurse Adah?"

The old woman smiled. "I have no love of dialectics. But I must say for truth's sake that there isn't a book in our library that I haven't mentioned—except for one, which is hardly worth discussing, since it isn't read anymore."

"Why isn't it read anymore?"

"Why? Because it has decayed with age, and on account of the tears."

"On account of the tears?"

"Because of the tears, yes, because of the tears that every reader of the book sheds on its pages after reading the awful tales it contains."

"What are these terrible stories?"

"I don't know what they are," the old woman answered. "Whatever I know I've told you already. It's an old, worn-out book, written on parchment. They say it was written more than a thousand years ago. Had I known you would ask, I would have made inquiries. There are still old men in the hospital who can tell the story, which I remember many years ago the old men before them used to tell with tears—the same story that is in the book. But they say that even then, years ago, the old men already had difficulty in reading the book because its pages were torn and the words blurred. The manuscript is a heap of moldy, decayed matter. They even tried to burn it. In my time one of the caretakers was all set to destroy it, but I asked him to return it. I told him that a book which had found shelter with us mustn't be treated like a rag. I believe, Herr Doctor, that a piece of work done by an artist gives joy to the creator as long as it endures."

"Tell me, Nurse Adah," Amzeh said, mulling over the old woman's words, "perhaps you have heard something about the contents of the book. What do your old men say about it? I'm sure if they say anything at all, they must know more."

"I've heard that all its pages are of parchment," the old woman answered. "As far as what is written in it, I've heard that it contains the history of a city which was destroyed and disappeared from the face of the earth."

"A city which was destroyed and disappeared from the world!" Amzeh repeated excitedly. "Please tell me, Nurse Eden, perhaps you have heard the name of the city?"

"Yes, I have heard the name. The name of the city is Gumlidata. Yes, Gumlidata is the name."

"What? What? What?" Amzeh stammered, his tongue caught in his mouth. "Have ... have ... you heard the name correctly ... ? Gum ... Gum ... Gumli ... lidata ... you said. Please, my good nurse, tell me again, what is the name of the city you mentioned? Guml ... ."

She repeated what she had said. "Gumlidata is the name of the city, and the book is an account of its history."

Adiel Amzeh grasped a table in front of him, leaning forward so that he would not collapse and fall. The old woman noticed his sudden paling and moved to help him. "What is the trouble, Herr Doctor," she said staring at him, "are you ill? Is it your heart?"

He straightened up and pulled himself together. "It's nothing, my good nurse," he began with a smile, "there's nothing wrong with me. On the contrary, you have given me new life. Let me tell you about it. For twenty years I have devoted myself to the history of this same city. There isn't a piece of paper which mentions the city's name that I haven't read. If I were king, I could build the city anew, just as it was before its destruction. If you want, I'll tell you about the historical trips I have taken. I have walked in the city's markets, strolled in its streets and alleys, seen its palaces and temples. Oh, my good nurse, what headaches I've suffered from the walks I've taken there. And I know how it was destroyed, who took part in the destruction, the name of each and every tribe that helped reduce it to ruins, how many were killed by the sword, how many died of starvation and thirst, and how many perished from the plague that followed the war.

"I know everything except one detail—from which side Geditons's brigades entered the city, whether from the side of the great bridge which was called the Bridge of Valor, or whether they entered secretly by way of the Valley of Aphardat, that is, the Valley of the Cranes… the plural of crane in the language of Gumlidata is *aphardat;* the word does not mean ravens or chestnut trees or overshoes as is claimed by Professor Alpha, Professor Beta, or the true private advisor to the court, Professor Gamma, whose pictures you may have seen in the magazines when they were given honorary titles and medals by the empire. In point of fact, 'raven' in the language of Gumlidata is *eldag* and in the plural *elgadata,* since when the letters 'd' and 'g' come together in the plural they reverse their order. I don't know the words for chestnut trees or overshoes in the language of Gumlidata. I really don't know what they are."

Suddenly his expression changed, his voice dropped, his lips twisted, and he let out a hoarse, stuttering laugh. His knees began to shake and he pinched his mouth. "I'm surprised at you, Nurse Adeh," he said, "after all, you are an intelligent woman. You should be more careful about what you say. How can you believe something which doesn't make any sense. How can you say that your hospital possesses a book containing the history of Gumlidata. Gumlidata was destroyed in the days of the first Gothic invasions. And you say that a book from these ancient times has come down to our day, and the old people in the hospital have read it. Now really, my dear nurse, how can you reconcile this kind of nonsense with simple reality? How could a book like this ever get to the hospital… to the hospital which you, my dear nurse, serve so well.… How? How?

"Pardon me, my dear Adinah, if I tell you that this is a very doubtful story. A gelded goat has got in your grange: you have heard a silly old folk tale and it has enchanted you with its romance. Or perhaps you have confused Gumlidata with… with… I don't know with what city you might have confused Gumlidata. What did you hear about this manuscript? How did it get to the hospital? You have made me curious, my dear lady, very curious for more information. I feel just like a psychoanalyst. Aren't you surprised at me, the author of a book myself, being so curious about someone else's book? It's not enough that my house is filled with books, I must go looking for others. Let me tell you, just between us, all these books in my cabinet are not there for reading, they're there for effect. And if you want, I'll tell you the real reason: self-preservation.

People, see the books and start talking about them, and I don't have to discuss my own work with them. Please tell me, though, how did this history of Gumlidata ever get to your hospital?"

"I haven't read the book," answered the nurse Adah Eden, "and when it was taken out of the reading room some time ago I forgot it. I don't devote much time to books generally. When I come to your house for books, it's not for myself, of course, but for the sake of my good people, in order to ease their suffering. Sometimes books can do that. As for the parchment pages, I remember how surprised I was when I first saw them about forty years ago—like most nurses, I had to know everything about every article I saw where I worked. An old man noticed that the volume of parchment interested me and he told me what he had heard about the book. I still remember a little of what he said. If old age hasn't confused my memory, I'll try to pass on his story. May I sit down and tell you what I heard?"

Amzeh was suddenly embarrassed. "My God!" he cried out in confusion. "How could I let you stand all this time! Sit down, do sit down... here, on this chair. Not that one, this chair over here.... it is the most comfortable one in my miserable house. Please sit down and tell me your story."

The old woman sat down in the chair that he brought her, gathered up the folds of her dress, clasped her hands together, and, taking a deep breath, began. "As far as I can remember, this is the story. After the Gothic hordes had conquered the great city of Gumlidata and reduced its strength to dust, they found the tyrant ruler of the city, Count Gifayon Glaskinon Gitra'al, of the house of Giara'al, just as he was scheming to flee. He moaned and wept and pleaded for his life, asking that he be made a slave to their nation and their king, Alaric. The Goths allowed him to live, and carried him off with them as a slave. He had with him a chronicle which contained stories of the city's might and valor, stories that might be read to Alaric the King, so he should hear of the glory and greatness of Gumlidata's grandees. On the way he was struck with cholera, and the Goths left him for dead and went on.

"He wandered about in the fields until some lepers, who were following the soldiers for scraps of food and clothing, came upon him. They took pity on him, released him from his chains, and nursed him until he revived. He soon realized who his saviors were and began to groan and curse, declaring that death was better than life with the lepers. For in those days a leper was looked upon as a dead man and anyone who came in contact with an untouchable was himself considered to be infected. They tried to comfort him by saying that if he went away he might fall into the hands of the Goths and their allies who would surely kill him, or else he might be waylaid by roving packs of wild beasts who would surely eat him alive; but if he stayed with them he would be saved from the punishments of both men and beasts and have food to sustain him. They took him to their camp and gave him a noisemaker to carry, so that if he were approached by a healthy man he might warn him away by shaking the noisemaker, and they hung a small cup about his neck, for merciful people would sometimes throw scraps of food to the lepers.

"He lived with them for some time, eating what they ate and drinking what they drank. He saw how well they treated him and began to repay them in kind. On long winter nights he would read to them from his book, entertaining them with stories of the great city of Gumlidata and tales of his ancestors, the tyrant counts who governed over Gumlidata and its dependencies. In time, both the Count and his benefactors died. No trace remained of them except the book. Men live and die, but their instruments remain and live on.

"The Count's friends died, but their place was taken by a new generation, whose lot was no better than that of their forebears. They discovered the book and read it from cover-to-cover, joining their tears to those of the first generation. After many generations the world began to change and people began to realize how great was the suffering of the lepers, how difficult and terrible their ordeal. Not only was their sickness a great tribulation, but they were forced to live in forests and deserts and wander about in search of food. And there were times during the hard winter days when they had no sustenance and were unable to beg for food and they simply died of starvation. Eventually, benevolent groups were formed and a shelter established for the lepers, where they were brought together and their needs taken care of. That is the story of the place where I serve as a nurse, and that is the story of the book the lepers brought with them. Herr Doctor, I doubt whether there is anyone else in the world who knows more than I have told you about these sheets of parchment. But you want to leave. I hope you aren't late for your appointment."

"No, I'm not late for my appointment," answered Adiel Amzeh. "In fact, this is only the beginning of my appointment. Take a little more time, sit a little while longer, and we'll fill our hands with books and take them to the good people. Sit where you are, Nurse, sit a while and forget about my book. My book is used to waiting." Amzeh went over to the cabinets lining his walls and began to take books down. When he had accumulated a large pile, he tied them into packages. He took down more books, muttering: "They'll enjoy them, they'll enjoy these books." Several times he repeated the process, searching and ransacking his shelves, whispering and muttering all the time, "What more can I give?" If the old woman had not stayed his hand, he would have taken all his books from their shelves, with all his possessions, and given them to her.

"You take a bundle and I'll take a bundle," he said when he finished, "and we'll deliver them to your patients. As for Mr.... as for Mr. what's-his-name... Mr. Goldenthaler, Gebhard Goldenthal, who is waiting for me to come, well, I'm sure he will find something else to occupy himself with. And now, my dear Adah Eden, let's hurry so that we arrive before the sun sets, and you will open the gate for me and take me to see the book—the book of which you have spoken. What's the matter, Nurse? Why do you make such a face? Don't you think they'll allow me to enter? I swear on my mother's grave that if they don't let me in, I'll lie down on the steps of the hospital and won't move an inch until they say I can enter.

"Are you unhappy? Are you sorry about something? If it's because of me, don't be sorry. This is the most glorious day of my life, sweeter than any day I have ever lived, and what you have told me is sweeter than anything I have ever heard since... since... I'm really confused now, I don't know since when. Look, look, it's already going down. I mean the sun, the sun. The sun is more beautiful when it sets than when it rises. For twenty years a man must be hidden in wisdom's shadow in order to be able to utter such a simple piece of wisdom."

IV

They went out of the city, the two of them walking together, Amzeh in long strides, the old woman with short steps. He chattered as he walked;

she managed every so often to bring forth a word which sounded more like a sigh. Everyone who passed by and recognized her stepped aside, and she avoided them as well. She knew these people were afraid of her and was careful not to arouse any unnecessary terror, for something is more frightful when one runs away from it. But Adiel Amzeh was not conscious of the passers-by avoiding them as they went along. He turned to his companion suddenly. "Do you remember whether I locked the door?" he asked. He put down his package and saw that the key was still in his hand. "I'm carrying the key with the package and am not conscious of what I'm doing," he said with a laugh. "It's because of the heaviness of the burden I have to bear." For a minute he was silent. Then he cried out, "My God!" with a mixture of impatience and reproach, for at the edge of his consciousness he saw himself reading the book of Gumlidata in the hospital and a mumbled jumble of words confused his reading. Because of this book, too, he had forgotten his own book which he had worked on for twenty years, and he had forgotten Mr. Goldenthal who had agreed to publish it. After a while, they arrived at the lepers' hospital.

I don't know through which gate they entered or how much time it took before he was granted admittance. And I can't describe the condition of the book itself, which was so covered with pus that even the lepers felt a loathing for it. I don't know all the details and have no love for suppositions. Let me put aside the doubtful and come back to what is certain.

Amzeh, then, came to the house of the untouchables and after much argument he finally was allowed to enter. He went in and they tied him in an antiseptic apron which reached from his neck to his feet. They took the book out of the chest it was stored in, and gave it to him with a warning not to touch it. Amzeh stared at it until his eyes seemed to occupy half his face. He looked at it for a long time, then jumped up quickly to open it. They took hold of him and told him to wait. He was fitted with a pair of white gloves, carefully tied, so they would not slip. Then they warned him again not to touch the book unless his hands were protected with gloves. They described to him the dire fate of the foolhardy ones who had taken the warnings lightly, telling him both fact and fabrication to scare him, so that he should not fail to take the disease seriously. I don't know whether he heard them or not. This I do know: his eyes grew so large they seemed to cover his entire face—and half his neck as well. When they saw that they would not get rid of him very quickly, they left, providing him with a table and chair in the hospital garden among the trees which are known as the "Trees of Eden," after Nurse Eden, with one of the hospital functionaries to stand by him. Adiel Amzeh sat there and painstakingly read every letter, every word, column, and page which the book contained, the assistant standing by his side and turning the pages as he progressed. They were still afraid he might be so excited that he would not exercise the necessary restraint. The book had been infected by the hands of many untouchables, and it seemed almost as if it were not written on parchment, but on the skin of a leper, and not ink but pus had been used to inscribe the words.

What more can I say? After he had carefully gone over every sentence in the book, he found the answer to the riddle that had troubled him for many years: how Gumlidata had been conquered, from which side of the city the first bands of the Goths had entered. For Gumlidata had been surrounded by a solid wall of stone and protected on all sides by bristling natural fortifications. And so, within a few short hours, Amzeh solved the problem that had caused him so much trouble during his years of exhaustive research. For your sake, my friends, and for the sake of the whole House of Israel, let me tell you the story the dead words told our scholar. I'll try to summarize what was written there at great length.

The book of parchment told the story of one of the Hun women, a young girl named Geldag or Eldag, who one day left the camp of the Huns, the allies of the Goths, and rode about on a wild ass. She reached the cisterns behind the city of Gumlidata where she was caught and brought to the city. The servants of the tyrant, the old Count Gifayon Glaskinon Gitra'al of the house of Giara'al, grandfather of the young Count Gifayon Glaskinon Gitra'al Giara'al, noticed her and brought her for a gift to their master. She was horrified by the old man and his city, disgusted by his groaning and drooling, his soft bed and his strange manners, and nauseated by the smell of the city and its sacrificial altars. She tried to flee at once, but was caught and returned to the Count. The same thing happened three or four times; each time she was caught. Finally, she saw that escape was impossible and she sat brooding how to gain revenge on her captors.

At about the same time the girl was held captive, the Goths, with Gaditon the Brave at their head, rose up and waged war with Gumlidata. The city's inhabitants held the Goths in great terror, for they knew that every place the barbarians conquered they slaughtered and burned, and if Gumlidata was vanquished, their future was annihilation. The tyrant Count saw that his city was doomed, and he fell into a deep melancholy. Had it not been for Eldag, the Hun girl, who had changed her manner and begun to show him hidden and daring ways of love he had known with no other woman or lad, he probably would have died of sorrow before the Goths had a chance to behead him.

When the court guards saw that Eldag had changed her attitude toward the Count, they ceased watching her as carefully as before. Eldag took advantage of the guards' carelessness and began to take long walks through the city, wandering everywhere. She even visited the city wall near the Valley of the Cranes, which most people avoided for fear that it might collapse. Years before, an earthquake had struck the city and shaken the wall in several places. The citizens of Gumlidata were careful not to bother Eldag, for they knew that only the power of her charms had saved their king from melancholy. So enamored of the girl was their king that he had his tailors make her a mantle as a gift, a kind of priestly garment called *izla* normally worn by a queen, woven with bands of calves' eyes arranged in the shape of the Valley of the Cranes.

One day Eldag remained in the king's garden, playing with her wild ass among the tall trees. This ass was one of many animals in the garden, each of which had suckled at a woman's breast, for there was a strange custom in Gumlidata. If a woman conceived and it was not known who the father was, her relatives waited until she gave birth and then took the infant and brought it to these animals to be suckled. They looked for an animal that had recently given birth, and left the infant to be suckled, taking the animal's young to the human mother for suckling. If they could not find the young of a wild animal, they brought her the young of a tame one. They were most careful about the children of the noblewomen, *Givyatan* in their language, for if a noblewoman had given birth and the father was unknown, the infant was killed and the young of an animal was brought to the mother, so that her noble blood would not be mixed with the blood of the common people.

So Eldag played with her pet in the garden among the tall trees. She was quite unafraid of animals, having spent most of her life with them: her father, Gichul the Clown, was the owner of a dancing bear. A young ass saw them and, growing jealous, began snorting and hee-hawing, as though he were being slaughtered. Eldag heard the young animal's cries. "An ass always sounds like an ass," she said with a laugh, "even if it has been suckled by a duchess. What is it you want? Do you want this mantle which covers my heart? Come and I will wrap round your neck an ornament more beautiful than any that has been worn by your noble wet nurse." The young ass heard her and came close. She took the izla from her bosom and tied it about the animal's neck, and made him bow his head as if in thanks, as she had seen Gothic noblemen do when they received gifts from their ladies.

Suddenly the girl was overwhelmed with a deep longing for her home, her family, and her people, whose camp was far away, who were all free, with no walls or locks and bolts to restrain them. She was filled with rage and her anger turned against the ass who reminded her of her former happiness. She was angry at the ass because he was more faithful than she was: even after she had placed the izla around his neck, the ass continued to protest. She grabbed him by the ears in order to strike him. The calves' eyes, woven into the mantle, shone before her. Her heart began to beat wildly. She tried to gain control of herself so that she would not cry out and give away her plan. She forced herself to smile and dragged the ass to the city wall near the Valley of Cranes; there, she found the place which had collapsed during the earthquake and had not been completely repaired. She broke through the opening and pushed the ass with the mantle around his neck outside. And Eldag was happy, for she knew that if the Goths saw the ass, they would understand he had been sent as a sign that they should enter the city through the Valley of Cranes. She controlled her joy and returned to the old Count, assuming a happy countenance for him, his court, and his city. So charmed was the population by Eldag's grace and beauty that they forgot about the fierce Gothic soldiers who were besieging their city.

The ass went out of the city and reached a. nearby forest. His nose sniffed the odors of trees and flowers and he began to snort loudly like a wild ass who has returned to his home. The noise was heard by some

Gothic soldiers. They were surprised to see the ass with the mantle around his neck, for they had never seen an animal adorned like this. They brought the animal to Gaditon, their general. Gaditon the Brave saw the mantle. "Is there a place known as the Valley of the Cranes?" he asked his soldiers. "Is there one of our people in Gumlidata?" Gichul the Clown heard of the matter: He groaned and he grunted and he groveled on his gut in the grass for Eldag who was gone. "If this is not my daughter's work," he said, "I am not her father. The glorious girl was gone from me, but now I know she's in Gumlidata." The Goths sent soldiers to inspect the wall near the Valley of Cranes, and when they saw the place through which Eldag had sent the ass, the Goths entered the city. They set the city on fire, killing everyone in their path: old and young, infant and aged, male and female. Not a man or woman was left alive except little Eldag, the Hun girl, who was released from her bondage, and the grandson of the old Count who was made a slave....

All this was written on the last page of the book as a kind of epilogue by the city's scribe. And when Adiel Amzeh read the story, he shed many tears. How great is the true writer, he thought, who does not abandon his work even when the sword of death hangs over his neck, who writes with his very blood, in his soul's own script, what his eyes have seen!

Adiel Amzeh read many other things in the book. There were pages which supported some of his theories, and there were other pages which completely contradicted what he previously thought. It seems he had relied too much on earlier scholars, even though he realized that much of what they wrote was confused. Adiel Amzeh remained at the hospital throughout the summer, reading the book.

When the days grew colder and the land was covered with frost, he had to stop working outside. He took a room at the hospital and had a heater brought in. He sat there studying the text, joining letter to letter and word to word until he could read whole passages without trouble. And if he discovered something unusual he would read the passage aloud to the patients in the great hall. "My friends and brothers," he would say, "listen while I read to you." And he would read to them about the people of the great city of Gumlidata, who had been a mighty nation, full of greatness and grandeur, proud-eyed and joyous, until the Gothic hordes conquered them and reduced the city to dust and ashes. He would tell them about Gomesh and Gush and Gutz and Guach and Guz, the gods of Gumlidata; and about its infants, offspring of their loins, about its great temples, its priests and priestesses, the *Gorgani,* the *Gnogani,* and the *Gechoni*—each one named according to its function. He would also tell them about the *Galmudi* and the *Golanae,* which were the dogs and the temple prostitutes, affectionately called *Golshani* and *Golshanae.* And sometimes Adiel Amzeh would tell them about his new theories.

He had thought out many new hypotheses and some of them he had written down. But his book never reached the hands of the living, for it was forbidden to remove any article or letter or book from the lepers' house. Nevertheless, in some way or other, some of his new ideas became known to his colleagues. When a true scholar discovers a thing that is right, even if he himself is isolated and hidden away in the innermost chambers of his house, something of what he has found reaches the world. Many times, when Adah Eden had brought from his house the scientific journals which he received regularly, he would read his ideas in articles signed by others. He was shocked that something which he had worked on so long and hard was now published under another scholar's signature. "If this kind of thing can happen," he would ask himself, "then why do I work? I ought to be satisfied with what the others say."

Yet learning bestows a special blessing on those who are not put off easily. Yes, Adiel Amzeh would ask himself for what and for whom he was working. But Wisdom herself would take hold of him and whisper: "Sit, my love, sit and do not leave me." So he would sit and discover new things which had been unknown to all the learned men of the ages until he came and revealed them. And since there were many things and learning is endless and there is much to discover and investigate and understand, he did not put his work aside and did not leave his place and he remained there forevermore.

– Translated by Joel Blocker
Revised by Robert Alter

Nights

A SEA-BLUE NIGHT CLOAKED THE CITY IN SILENCE. My house stood hidden in its secret bower of shadows. My heart was calm within me, its pulse steady in my veins. At last Jaffa lay at rest. The angry sea was quiet again. No sound could be heard apart from the dull groans of a cricket within the walls of my house. I sat on my doorstep, my head full of thoughts and my eyes shut that I might see what cannot be seen with open eyes. Yet the tears stabbed my eyes like desert thorns. What was the matter with my eyes that they cried all the time? My eyes were roses forever wet by the dew of my tears. I rose and took the flowers that I had set by the doorstep on the night of Salsibylla's visit. I lifted them to my eyes and said, I set you against my eyes for you to bloom from the fragrance of my tears.

A cool, moist breeze blew suddenly through the garden. The branches of the trees shook one against another. Was it the echo of forgotten words that I heard or simply the clamor of my thoughts? Be still, I told my heart, I want to hear.

The lily brought me by my little neighbor's dove stirred suddenly in its glass. For my neighbor Ruḥamah has a dove who brought me a flowering bud when it came to feed from my hand. Now the lily stirred in its glass, for I had forgotten to water it. But I said: This is no time to water your flowers, Ruḥamah. This is a time to be in bed. I shall sleep and dream of Salsibylla.

I was still talking to myself when Salsibylla came. My heart leaped in my throat and the words hid in my mouth so that I could not speak. How in my excitement could I speak to her? She looked at me and I at her. Yet though I am a brave man, I dared not look at her face but at her feet alone. How beautiful were your feet, Salsibylla, your shoes were their vases. I fell at her feet and my forehead touched the cool hem of her dress. For a long while I lay at Salsibylla's feet while she looked down on me. When I rose she was gone. But the sky was full of stars and there was a sweetness in my heart.

2

Forlornly stretched the days in which Salsibylla's footsteps were not heard. Though I called her name, she did not come. Nothing came to me but the echo of my own voice. Despairingly I took my head between my hands and said, Salsibylla has not come; if you have the power of thought, O brain of mine, think of how she might be brought to me. Yet when I pressed my head with my fingers to make it think, the hair between my fingers turned white. I thought of Dansa, who was dead, and of the curl of her hair that was tied to my heart and that was still as black as it had been on the day that she gave it to me. How could the hair of a young man like myself have turned white? If Sibylla came tomorrow, she would not recognize me.

At one end of my table lay a virgin's skull in which a candle shone. Flickering shadows fled from its flame, which cast a light on the flowers that were waiting for Salsibylla. A blue lily swam in clear water and good odors filled the house.

I stood over the flowers and put my mouth to them. I gathered every flower in the house and opening a window I cried, Salsibylla, Salsibylla. How I wished to hold Salsibylla's hands and cry upon them. Might my tears melt the clasp of the hands that had given me their blessing and shut tight.

Was that a sound I heard around the house? The house stood hugged by its shadows. I went to look.

3

I let myself be carried on the sea-blue night and on its waves of blue. What hope is there left you, my soul, that makes you run as you do?

The streets were still and the sand was very white. It played with my shadow, relinquished it, and played with it again. Clad in moonlight I stood in the spot outside of town where the seven sycamores grew. The shadows of their leaves dripped softly on the sand, whose dunes turned to dark silhouettes.

I sat in the sand and called out, Salsibylla, Salsibylla. A snail peered from its shell, overwhelmed by the blue of the night. All of a sudden it shivered. Did it fear the roar of my voice or had the night itself cast its wild spell over it?

Time passed, yet Salsibylla did not come. And still I did not despair or surrender my hope, for I hoped that she might come for my kiss to rest a second time upon her eyes. So dear to me did she seem, such love did I feel for her name, that I took my knife and carved her name on a tree so that I might see it before me. As I stood there a glowworm came and sat on the letters that I had carved on the tree so that I saw her name lit before me. When I saw it lit before me, I rejoiced. Never did I think that the glowworm might be shining for its mate to come and fetch it, for I thought only of Salsibylla and myself.

4

On the doorstep of my house I found my little neighbor Ruḥamah. She stood erect, her hair wet from the droplets of the night. She was like a wet rose, for her hair was red and her body stirred beneath its thin dress.

Hello, said Ruḥamah.

Hello, I said. And though Ruḥamah was still so little that the tree from whose wood her bridal bed would be made had surely not yet grown, I took her hand in mine and felt it tremble there.

She stood silently, then suddenly said: Ḥemdat.

My heart leaped, for since the day that Yael had left me no one had called me by my name. Yet I steadied myself and I asked: Aren't you sleepy yet, Ruḥamah?

No, she said.

Isn't it time you were in bed? I asked.

I was in bed, she said.

Then why did you get up again, Ruḥamah? I asked. And why don't you go back to bed? Is this an hour to be out?

My dove woke me, said Ruḥamah. Ever since its mate left it, it can't sleep at night.

And does your mother know where you have gone? I asked.

Does the sky know where its stars go? answered Ruḥamah.

Her words alarmed me. Hush, Ruḥamah, I said. Hush. Don't talk of fallen stars, lest they make our own stars go astray. Let me bring you? home, for the night stars are cold and you are all hot and shivery. Go home before you catch cold.

But Ruḥamah would not heed me. Tell me, Ḥemdat, she said, what are you going to do now?

Sleep, I said.

Ruḥamah looked at me in disbelief.

Perhaps I'll stay up for a while, I said.

And what will you do while you stay up? she asked.

I could not answer her question. I thought of Salsibylla whom I was waiting for that night and said nothing. At last I said, blushing as I spoke: I will tidy up and put my house in order for a guest that I am expecting.

Is it Yael? asked Ruḥamah.

My alarm grew but still I did not breathe a word. How beautiful the night is, I said. I think I will sit by the window in my room and look at the sea.

Ruḥamah's mouth twisted with grief. She looked at my hand and her knees shook. For whom are those flowers in your hand? she asked.

They were the flowers that I had taken to bring to Salsibylla.

Ruḥamah lifted her mouth and her lips grew red. Give me a flower she said.

But I would not give her any of the flowers in my hand, for how could I give her a flower that was meant for Salsibylla?

The woman who had sold me the flowers that day had stuck a rose in my lapel. I took this rose and gave it to Ruḥamah. Ruḥamah took it from me and laid it against her heart. Yet the rose was not at rest there, for Ruḥamah's heart throbbed. And I knew that the rose longed to return to the place whence it was taken.

I stroked Ruḥamah's hair with the palm of my hand. Her hair was red and warm. She came closer until she stood very close, trembling like a rose on the day of the reaper. An invisible hand took a rose from a woman's dress and laid it on a man's heart. And that man was me. I took little Ruhamah in my arms and lifted her until her mouth touched mine. The dew of her kisses dripped from warm lips and my soul shook with cold.

5

After that I was left undisturbed in my room and there was silence all around. Only occasionally a blind man came to knock on the door of the house to ask for something to eat. God will give you something to eat, the servant woman would tell him and refuse to give him a thing. The blind man recognized her voice and cursed his blind eyes for bringing him back again to the same place.

I pitied him for having to repeat his mistake in his blindness. What a mercy God in heaven had done me when he gave me eyes to see.

From now on I would err no more by straying after other women and after Yael Ḥayyut.

I sat on the veranda of my house to rest from the exertion of my thoughts before going to see Salsibylla. The sun set and shadows dropped over the house. Hail, evening shadows, I said. Hail, well and trees of the garden. Hail, scaly lizard. Your jeweled armor will avail your heart not against the evening breeze.

As I sat I looked to see where the sun would set and where the birds would spend the night. And when I heard the birds call as they winged to their roosts and saw the sun's rays disappear in their wings, I knew that night had drawn near. I shall rise now, I thought, and go to Salsibylla. The dusk wove darkness around the boughs of the trees and the evening star quivered in the sky. A light, chill sorrow brushed my brow. Dear God, how great you are and how hard are the thoughts you have given to men. The hours passed and still I did not take my customary walk to the end of town and beyond, for I was waiting for Salsibylla.

The evening shadows grew suddenly damp. I took my coat and covered myself while waiting for Salsibylla to come. Then I went to get the flowers from my room. I kissed them and placed them on the doorstep again after wiping the dust from the step. Then I lit the lamp so that Sibylla would see that a light shone in my house.

I sat on the veranda as before with open ears so that I might hear Salsibylla when she came. I heard a woman's footsteps. You are late Salsibylla, I thought. But I was far from being angry in my heart, for I rejoiced at the coming of Sibylla.

The light is on in your house, yet you sit in darkness, exclaimed my little neighbor Ruḥamah, reaching out her trembling hands.

I'll bring the lamp outside, I said, rising from my chair. And if that is not enough for you I will light still other lamps, until we can count the fish in the sea by their light.

I went to fetch the lamp and Ruḥamah came with me. When I reached out to trim the wick my hand touched hers, and in my fear I dropped the lamp and it broke. I could hear the beating of Ruḥamah's heart as we sat in the dark.

Ḥemdat, said Ruḥamah. It is you who stand in front of my house at night.

That's not true, Ruḥamah, I said. That's not true.

Evil neighbors told my mother that they saw you walking up and down. And my mother too heard the footsteps of a man all night long.

Your mother must be joking, I replied. Who ever heard of a man standing all night before the window of a small girl?

Ruḥamah's face grew pale. Yet Ruḥamah mattered not to me. How can you say that I stand before your window, I went on, when you know I go for walks outside of town? But I did not mention Salsibylla now either, though when I thought of Salsibylla my heart stirred.

Go home now, Ruḥamah, I said, raising my voice. Go home.

She did not heed me and she did not go. Then I opened the window facing out on the street so that the stars might see that my heart was not drawn to this girl, for my heart belonged to Salsibylla.

Ruḥamah stood silent and flustered. I pitied her, as I pitied all living things. Did I not even pity the cricket that chirped all night in my wall because it could not sleep?

Come, I will sing you a lullaby, I said. And I have a song for you too, O snake. I, Ḥemdat, have kissed the eye of the snake. The eagles in heaven know and are wroth, for the eagles cannot best the snakes. Another winter has passed and I have not written one song, for the eagles would not give me the feathers from their wings until the angel of song gave me a golden feather from his.

Ruḥamah looked at me and trembled. I took her hand in mine and said, The earth has turned over a second time. Now go to bed.

I walked Ruḥamah back to her home at the end of the next-to-the-last row of houses in Neve Tzedek. I did not even notice that she tricked me by taking me by a roundabout route. On the way she told me that she was studying the violin. When she sat by herself and played, all her aggravation fell away. How it aggravated her that her mother watched her all the time to make sure that she did not come to see me.

Do you think, Ḥemdat, she said, that there is something between me and my teacher? I want you to know that the last time he gave a recital I loosened his violin without telling him, so that as soon as he started to play the strings came apart and the audience began to laugh. Have you seen how yellow his fingers are? That is because he doesn't stop smoking from morning to night. I'm always afraid that he will touch my hair and make it smell of smoke.

She bowed her head. Do you think my hair smells of tobacco? Touch it and you'll see that it doesn't smell one bit.

Ruḥamah, I said. I touched your hair just the other day.

She bowed her head still more and I could see that she was sad. I touched her hair and said, What lovely hair you have, Ruḥamah. It's a lucky man who gets to stroke your head. Your hairs are like the strings of a violin upon which I shall play. I shall play a new song, the song of the golden fish brought by a mermaid to the royal streams of the king. When the king saw her, he stroked her hair. Do you know what the mermaid did? She shaved it all off, lest someone come and stroke the same hair that had been stroked by the king. And she laid it at the king's feet.

Ruḥamah lifted her mouth to me and her lips trembled violently. I covered her mouth with my hand. An inspiration came to me and I said, Now that you have heard the story of the golden fish, let us be as silent as fish and not talk any more until I have brought you home, Ruḥamah.

We reached the row of houses where Ruḥamah lived. I opened the door of the house and I said, Sleep well, Ruḥamah, and wake well in the morning.

Ruḥamah bowed her head. Her shoulders shook and she vanished into the fastness of her house, where darkness covered her. I started back, accompanied by all the stars on my way, for at home I would wait for Salsibylla. How blessed was each hour spent waiting for her. Salsibylla, my bride, my beloved, I shall await you to the end of my days.

I had kissed many girls in my life. I had kissed Dansa, who was dead, on her merry chin. Now she lay in the grave, her curls amid the earth's clods. How vestal had her dreamy eyes been on that holy night when I kissed them. I had kissed Wilma. Like a snail her mouth clung to mine, her kisses like a flock of bees too busy making honey to sting. I had kissed Thea, whose eyes were as golden as a serpent's eyes in the sun. I had gone from girl to girl, and from maiden to maiden, although I loved only one.

That one was you, Sibylla. Yet because I feared that idle tongues would wag with your name, I kissed many girls so that none should know that I loved only you, Salsibylla.

When I had finished speaking to Salsibylla I took the knife from my pocket and looked at my lips in its blade. Then I kissed their reflection, for the name of Salsibylla was upon them all day long.

I had not gone far when the night watchman stopped me and said: Why is it that you are not asleep, sir?

I cannot fall asleep I said. But I said nothing about Sibylla, for I did not want him thinking of her.

Yes, sighed the man. Those who want to sleep cannot, while those who can do not want to. And in his foolishness he advised me to see a doctor and have a sleeping potion prescribed. If I truly wanted to sleep, I laughed to myself, I would go fetch a teardrop from the eyes of the princess who must slumber in her hidden cave until her lover comes for her or die if he does not. Whoever gathers one of her tears-falls instantly asleep.

6

I returned to my room and lay there until the sun was low in the west. When it was about to set I looked up and saw that the walls of my room had the reddish hue of a violin. The last of the sun's beams were stretched across the room like the strings of a violin, and within the violin I sat and listened to the melody it played for Salsibylla. I heard Sibylla's footsteps ascend the stairs to my room and I jumped up to greet her. But when I saw her I stood astounded, for she looked like Ruḥamah. Then I understood my mistake. It was Ruḥamah.

Ruḥamah bowed her head and said, You stroked my hair, Ḥemdat.

I nearly scolded her for saying this, because it was a lie that I had stroked it. Still I kept silent to see what she would say next. What concern was it of mine if she had such thoughts about me?

But I did not bring you my hair, Ruḥamah went on. I kept it for a remembrance, because your hand touched it, and I put it away for safekeeping.

Then I noticed that she wore a black kerchief and that her head had been shaved. You look like a young man, Ruḥamah, I joked, who has shaved off his beard and left the bristles behind.

Ruḥamah removed her kerchief and I ran my hand over her scalp. Oh, said Ruḥamah. My hair has pricked your hand.

I compared you at first to a young man, I said. Who shall I compare you to now? To an orange in an almond grove, for your head is like an orange and your face is like an almond's buds.

I sat with Ruḥamah in my room. She looked all about her, at the green curtains and at the dead virgin's skull, and wondered at everything she saw. Are you a doctor, then, Ḥemdat, she asked, that you keep a skull in your room?

No, I am not a doctor, I said. I like to look at the skull and to see the holes of its eyes, which remind me that no man has eyes in the back of his head to see what is behind him.

I thanked God for having given me the wisdom to answer Ruḥamah so wisely. Surely she understood that I meant the green eyes of Yael Ḥayyut, upon which I would look no more because they were behind me. Ruḥamah looked at the bed in the corner. What is that feather doing on the blanket? she asked. I looked and saw a white feather lying on the blanket of my bed. Why, it's a feather from your dove who was here today, I said.

We sat in my room and talked about many things. There were so many of them that I can no longer remember a single one. At last I rose to walk her home, for I did not feel right about letting her walk home by herself at night. I opened the door and saw that the stars had changed places, and I urged Ruḥamah to hurry. She rose from her chair and looked again about the room. Why, there's a feather from my dove on your bed, Ḥemdat, she said. And I marveled that she should mention it again.

After I had brought Ruḥamah home I did not return to my room but went for a walk out of town. I walked over much sand until I came to the sycamore tree on which the name of Salsibylla was engraved. I sat under the tree to wait for her. I rejoiced that Sibylla had not come yet, for it was not for Sibylla to wait for Ḥemdat but for Ḥemdat to wait for Sibylla.

I saw that a glowworm was sitting on the letters in which the name of Salsibylla was written. I rejoiced to see her name lit. So greatly did my heart stir with gratitude within me that I dropped to my knees and touched my head against the tree on which the name of Salsibylla was engraved. A painful thorn pierced my forehead. Yet I did not pull it out. I took the glowworm and placed it on the thorn in my forehead so that my forehead burns like a torch to light your way to me. Have you heard of the giant who had one eye in the middle of his forehead? I, I am that giant. And have you heard of the seven girls whom that giant surely kissed? Surely he kissed them because he saw them with fleshly eyes as mortal men see. Yet when the eye grew in his forehead and fell on the king's daughter, he no longer looked at other women or even saw them. You are the king's daughter and that giant is me.

I shut my eyes tight so that I might see nothing else until she came. Then Salsibylla came to me and placed her hands on my eyes,

Salsibylla, I said, have you seen the skull of the virgin on my desk?

I have seen it, she said.

Then put your fingers in my eyes, I said, until their holes are as deep as the holes of that skull and you can see right to my heart.

Salsibylla laughed when she heard me and her laughter clung to my tears. I am sorry to have woken you from your sleep, Ḥemdat, she said. Did you want to sleep?

Salsibylla, I said. Have you heard the story of the old king who would not sleep?

No, I have not, she said.

Then I will tell you about him, I said.

Do tell me, she said.

So I told Salsibylla the story of the king who waited for his queen to come and sit beside him on the royal throne and did not sleep at all, lest the queen come unannounced and he fail to see her when she came. And many were the ladies-in-waiting who stood by him all day and all night to hold up the lids of his eyes with pincers of gold. And the king grew old in his waiting until he could see no more.

Salsibylla looked at me and said, How red your eyes are, Ḥemdat.

My eyes are red from the light of my dreams, I replied.

Why do you not sleep, Ḥemdat? she asked.

Was it in vain then that I told you the story of the king? I asked

Salsibylla was unable to answer. Her silence perturbed me and I said:

Salsibylla, there is something that I wish to ask of you.

You may ask, she said.

I mustered my courage and said, Suppose I asked permission to touch your hair, would you permit me to touch it?

You may do whatever you please, she replied.

Yet I did not touch her hair lest I stain it with my blood, for the blood was alive in my hands. Nor did I speak to Sibylla of myself. But Sibylla knew what was in my heart, for my heart shone bright within me.

Then Salsibylla asked:

What is it about your heart, Ḥemdat, that makes it shine so brightly?

I lowered my head to my heart and felt shame that my heart shone with the brightness of light. It must be, I said to Salsibylla, that there is a glowworm in my heart. Woe is me that my light has struck your eyes.

More than that I did not let her approach me, lest she touch my heart and be consumed with me. And I wept over the great light within me until the morning sun kissed my tears away.

7

After that I returned to my room and sat there all day thinking of great and wonderful things. And I considered and saw that it had not been wise of me to talk to Salsibylla about Dansa, Wilma and Thea. And I prayed in my heart that she understood that all three were only a parable.

Do you know, Sibylla, I said, who is the one I call Dansa? She is the symbol of my youth that is fled and gone and buried.

And who do you think Wilma is, Sibylla? I asked. If I compared her kisses to the sting of bees, it is because in our pursuit of pleasures we forget their sting.

And who is Thea whose eyes are like a serpent's in the sun? There is no need for me to tell you, for she is the symbol of the glittering love that harbors serpents in its midst.

When I was weary of so many thoughts I rose to go to the sea to watch the waves and rest from my exertions. I reached the shore and watched the sun sink into the sea and the fishermen return from their work crunching shells beneath their feet. Let me gather some sea-shells, I said, and place them in my yard and on the stairs of my house so that I shall hear Salsibylla's footsteps when she comes. Perhaps something of the sound of her footsteps will remain in the shells.

I gathered a large number of different shells and filled my pockets with them. When my pockets were full I removed my hat and even my coat and filled them with shells too.

I was still gathering shells when little Ruḥamah appeared with her large violin. I looked at her astounded. Why was she not with her classmates in school? So I said: Where is it that you are coming from, Ruḥamah, and where is it that you are bound?

Ruḥamah looked at me and saw that I was without my coat. Shame on you, Ḥemdat, she said, standing there as naked as a sleepwalker.

Indeed I am dreaming, I answered Ruḥamah, and we only dream in our sleep. Take care of your violin, I said to her, so that its strings do not come loose. The violin stirred in Ruḥamah's hands but Ruḥamah said nothing.

Ruḥamah was very pale. Since the day she had shaved off her hair and donned a black kerchief on her head her pallor had increased. Yet when I looked at her she blushed. A pin flared like fire in her hair when I looked.

Ruḥamah laid her violin on the shore and helped me to gather shells. To keep them from getting confused with mine I put her shells to one side. And because it pleased me that she did not ask why I was gathering so many shells, I chatted with her about this and that. I told her of various things I had seen and of my room that hummed toward evening like a violin. I told her about the fisherman who stood deep in water at night and how if one of them heard a mermaid's voice he would never come home again. Don't leave your violin on the shore, I said, because the mermaids may take it to play.

Ruḥamah listened carefully. I knew that my nakedness without a coat did not upset her and that she had only mentioned it to engage me in talk.

You weren't home all last night and you haven't eaten all day, she said to me. Let me buy you two or three fish and grill them for you over a fire.

I thought of the fisherman's daughter who had once grilled and eaten fish with me on the mat before the hearth while her father had fished all night. Meanwhile Ruḥamah went and bought live fish.

I'll grill two of them for you, she said, so that you'll have something to eat.

I see the fish, but where are the fire and the spit to grill them with? I asked.

Ruḥamah took the gold pin that held the tie that she wore around her neck and skewered a fish with it. While she did this I took the fish that she had not skewered and whispered to them, Salsibylla, Salsibylla. Then I threw them back into the water and said:

Go tell my secret to the mermaids.

Ruḥamah did not see what I did because she was busy making a fire to grill the fish. And when she could not find enough wood for the fire, she took her violin and cast it into the flames. I watched it going up in smoke and listened to it play as it burned.

8

Then came great and wonderful days. A glad sun shone down on the world and the heavens rejoiced with great joy, for there was a celebration in the heavens above and I too was invited. Yet I did not ascend to the heavens, for I was with Salsibylla on earth.

Do you know, Salsibylla, I said, that there is a great celebration today?

Yes, she said, I know.

And can you see what the angels are doing? I said. For the angels were drinking from the wine of paradise and dancing until the sky shook.

I was still talking when Salsibylla laid her head on my heart and said: We have much to celebrate today.

You have spoken wisely, Sibylla, I answered. We have many good things to celebrate. Is there no one to give me a glass of wine with which to mark our celebration, Salsibylla?

Someone there is, my brother, said Salsibylla. And as she spoke she placed her mouth upon mine and I drank of the choicest wine.

Drink your wine in good cheer, she said.

I lifted Salsibylla as one lifts a glass and I cried: To our life.

To our life, replied Salsibylla.

We sat up all night. For it was a night of celebration with us.

Shall I tell you more of kind Salsibylla? Or shall I sit by myself and keep silent the better to remind myself of those wonderful days?

– *Translated by Hillel Halkin*

Ḥemdat the Cantor

DAWN ISSUED OUT of the darkness and shone upon the universe. The dew of the morning opened its eyes and gazed cheerfully at creation. A chill wind rustled bringing with it the cold. The wagoner slackened his grip upon the reins and the horses pulled the cart at their ease. I wrapped myself in the blanket Father had given me and laid my head upon my shoulder. Sleep overcame me and I fell into a doze. Suddenly Father's wife came and sat in a treetop, whistling like a bee-eater. I came closer to her for I was whistling Always she screeched like a hawk and now she was whistling like a bee-eater. She mocked at me saying, It seemed that you had gone to Jassy and here you are back in Vasleu. I began to weep and awoke.

The morning star burst forth and rose. The birds of the air gave voice and from the marshes a frog croaked. Some creature followed by another, gave a fearful leap, both vanishing in the mist that rose from the ground. The orb of the sun soared high in the heavens, as the sound of tumult and confusion came closer. Men, women and children came up hurrying, running. Some carried great melons in their arms. Other balanced small casks on their heads. Yet others held wicker-baskets in their hands out of which a thin trickle of blood dribbled, from the fowls slaughtered in atonement, for all our sins and the sins of all Israel. To every Jew there were three or four Gentiles, on foot and on horseback, in portly carriages or in upright carriages, in red wagons or in green carts.

Some were cracking the whips they held, others were greeting them. And before these had the time to return the greeting of those other carriages came up with horses and ponies trotting and neighing. The wagoner guided his horses and brought them to a standstill in a wood.

All was now quiet. Tranquility rested on all about us. The wild apples gave forth their scent, and the river glistened like a field of wheat after the rain. The sky reflected the glow of the sun, though I had yet sought the moon and the stars when I had set out from Vasleu.

The wagoner climbed down from the wagon, repeating the morning benedictions. He caressed his horses and signaled to me, saying, Nu! Nu! But when he saw I did not comprehend he interrupted his prayers, saying,

Why do you stare at me like a cock at *Bnei Adam*, and compel me to cry out? Do you want me to take you back to Vasleu for the half *yarmelik* your father gave me? If so, wait until after the Day of Atonement and if I find other passengers I will take you back to the wife of your father.

Is this Jassy? I asked him.

What did you think it was? he said to me. Perhaps Ashtoret Karnaim?

I told him that I did not know.

Where should you know from? Did you learn in your prayer-book where Jassy was? Jassy is a town not mentioned anywhere in the Bible, so take your feet and get down.

I took my bundle, wrapped my blanket about it, alighted from the wagon, and took my leave of him, wishing him that he be inscribed for a good year. He returned my blessing, asking my pardon, saying that if he had vexed me I should forgive him. For every Jew, he said, was worthy that he enter upon the Day of Atonement with the reproach of no man against him. Finally with the whip in his hand he pointed out a synagogue, gazing at me meanwhile as one does upon a friend, about to observe a precept, which he himself is not able to do. For he, too, had not yet recited the morning prayer.

I entered a small house of prayer, one of Jassy's one hundred and ninety nine synagogues and houses of prayer. I loosened my bundle, extracted my prayer-book and phylacteries and stood to pray.

Because of the tumult in the synagogue the voice of the cantor could not be heard. For at the time a corpulent man was standing there holding a tray of honey cakes and everyone was coming up to take one, saying, If God forbid, it be decreed that I should require the charity of flesh and blood, may this morsel which I have taken from your hand suffice. Opposite him stood another man, his eyes like two turgid flasks, pouring brandy. All drank and congratulated each other with all the blessings which one repeats on the Eve of the Day of Atonement. I, too, snatched a slice, regretting that I had not yet finished my prayers and must refrain from drink. But failing any other alternative, for regret I substituted confidence that in the second minyan, too, good cheer would not be wanting. But seeing that every laudable quality must be strengthened I wound up my phylacteries as one wraps some article and lays it aside for another occasion. Tomorrow would be the Day of Atonement and it were better for my prayers to be said on that holy day with devotion and in a tranquil spirit than to be gabbled in haste.

Every laudable quality is profitable, confidence most of all. I pronounced the blessing over the cake and took a morsel. I had scarce finished the slice when another *gabbai* stood over me, his function like that of his predecessor. Another came up pouring brandy, but as I was busy eating I did not press forward. The people there thought that it was because I was well-mannered and I found favor in their eyes. They threw me one slice and two slices and someone held out one glass and then another. The *gabbai* seeing that they were all busying themselves about me was filled with zeal. He took two slices and offered them to me but as both my hands were engaged, one with cake the other with the glass I could only stare at him in desperation. Seeing that I tarried he scolded me, saying, Perhaps you wish me to chew it for you. I thought that it were better that I should eat it than he. While I was thus occupied his companion approached bringing a large glass. I drank and I ate and I drank until the floor beneath and the ceiling above began to dance together. Had I not been busy eating I would have joined them in their dance.

But I was not diverted from my chief purpose and when I sobered up from the wine I asked one man, how I could find, for instance, Ḥemdat. The man was deep in his glass and was fearful lest his wine go down the wrong way. He stared at me with two red eyes, like the glasses into which wine is poured for children on the Passover Feast and began to cough and splutter and did not reply. And it was well that he did not for if he had I would have drowned in spittle.

I noticed an old man there, standing with a long stick in his hand, that reached up to his beard and I knew that he was a Hasid of Ruzhin, for their sticks are as high as their beards. Now I liked the Hasidim of Ruzhin exceedingly for once Father had been found worthy to sing before the Saint of Ruzhin and Father was wont to say, To me it appeared that he, may his merit protect us, looked at me.

The old man became aware of me and asked, What do you seek, young man? I told him. You are a stranger, he said to me. I am a stranger, I replied. He smiled and said, Did I not recognize you were a stranger here, else, had you been from Jassy, you need not ask. So we must first greet you and then we shall reply to your question.

He extended to me the tips of his soft fingers, two or three of them, scarce touching the tips of my own, after the fashion of the Hasidim of Ruzhin who are very ceremonious in their manners and delicate in their limbs and their fingers are soft. And when they offer a greeting they do not grasp the whole hand but touch and yet do not touch. They are concerned for their own hands and concerned for that of their fellows. He looked down into his beard to see if there was no crumb there and asked me, What need have you of Ḥemdat. Father sent me to him, I replied. Had this day not been the Eve of the Day of Atonement it would have been profitable to hear who is the Cantor of Vasleu and why he saw fit to send you to Ḥemdat. But I am engaged and today even he is engaged and even you are engaged, so we must hurry and not tarry, and reply to your question.

The old man put his stick aside and said: Now you wish to go to Ḥemdat and you do not know where he dwells and so you ask me. But if I were to tell you, for example, Turn left or turn right, ere you had gone outside you would be unable to distinguish between your left hand and your right, and all my trouble would have been in vain. But I will advise you. When you reach the street the first person you chance to meet ask him and if he is not deaf or blind or a fool, he will show you the way.

As he was about to leave he called me back saying, Can I rely upon you or must we repeat what we have already said? I nodded my head affirmatively. He stroked my cheek and said, I see that you are a clever lad and have understood what I told you. And so, go out into the street and whoever you chance to meet will show you. And as he spoke the old man took his tallit and his tefilin under his arm and with his stick in his hand, with the dignity of one who had done his duty both to God and man, his stick preceding him as if it knew before whom it went, he strode out.

I went out into the street and found a man suffering from none of the blemishes above mentioned and I enquired of him. Follow your nose until you reach the camp of the gypsies, said he to me. Thence go to the horse-market, and thereafter to the potter's market. Nearby, before and not after it, stands a princely mansion. That is the residence of Michael Daniel. Nearby, after it and not before it, on the left hand, you will remark many windows. These are of the Petersburg Hotel, which the apostate, may his name be blotted out, built with his money. Take yourself thence towards the right and behold, before you are twenty synagogues built together. Make your way through there and there, friend, they will tell you where Ḥemdat is to be found. For you asked after Ḥemdat, did you not, friend?

I followed my nose but reached none of the places he had told me. Again and again I questioned passers-by. Some replied similarly, others otherwise. And to ensure that I reach my destination and not err, they counseled me saying, As you have asked me, ask of others also. So I betook myself, and went along the roads they had shown me, at every step stopping because of the horses, because the people of Jassy are wont to multiply carriages and horses, and their city is as filthy as a sty. People were travelling to and fro, and one must divine the wish of the horses, else they break one's head.

I was no longer heedful of my destination as if I had not come hither but to extricate myself from the carriages and from the horses. But I gazed at the passers-by to enquire of one of them how to come to Ḥemdat.

Suddenly a tall, thin man stood before me, with sunken cheeks and bushy brows, his head inclined a little to the left, with tufts of hair, like spools of thread jutting out of his chin. His eyes were smiling. Here is clearly a good man who will bring me to Ḥemdat. But before I could open my mouth he put forth a white hand, holding his fingers as if he were taking a pinch of snuff and offering some to a friend and began. Fortunate indeed are you in this city. For just now have I written a ditty, and you, my dear friend, O glory of light, give ear to my speech, in my song delight.

> When in the streets of Jassy you tread
> The bones of your body guard well
> Keep looking about you rightward and left
> Lest, God forbid, you can see it with dread
> A horse and a cart coming at you pell-mell
> Leaving all your kindred bereft.
>
> When in the streets of Jassy you tread
> Guard your face well, son of man
> Like a cow or calf do not stare, do not stand
> For the heart of a carter is very low-bred
> And turned against the pedestrian
> Whom he flays like a dog with the whip in his hand.
>
> Aye he flays like a dog with the whip in his hand
> So keep looking about you, rightward and left
> For the heart of the carter is very low-bred
> So look to your ways O man do not stand
> Gird tightly your loins and be deft
> As the roads and the streets of Jassy you tread.

When he had concluded the song he twitched his bushy eye-brows at me and looked at me with great affection. I asked him, Perhaps you could tell me, sir, where Ḥemdat lives? He slapped me on the shoulder and said, My very dear friend, whoever you are, I'm not your servant, and you're not my sir, but since I like you, may I pay my respects, without mincing words as I speak my next? Though of iron your guts or even of brass, in the street do not stand to be struck by the outstretched hand, for every drayman upright in his seat, like a destroying angel, on a place of honor, his whip in hand like a drawn sword, and right and left he keeps flaying so that loud is the sound of every blow, and all of a sudden, havoc and ruin, stretched on the ground your body is strewn, and you're making your bed in mire and muck, and you're in despair, and you've lost your pluck. Lucky indeed he is who without stumbling removes from the drayman's hand and the horses' hooves, and though your guts be of iron and your bones be thick, turn, run, my friend, and help yourself quick.

I turned left where I should have turned right, and right where I should have turned left. Thus I forgot where and how I had been told to turn. Everyone I asked replied similarly or a little otherwise, or placed me in the hands of a friend, and that friend in the hands of his friend. I despaired of ever reaching my destination, walking hither and thither until of a sudden I revealed twenty synagogues.

I found a Gentile woman standing there washing the floor. I said to her, Perhaps you know where is the house of Ḥemdat the Cantor? She stared at me as Gentile women are wont to stare when they see a young man and called out, Mrs. Beadle! Mrs. Beadle! A Jewish young man here is enquiring after something! An old woman came forth and shouted, What are you braying like a mule for? I am not braying like a mule, the Gentile woman shouted back. I only said that a young man was enquiring after someone.

The old woman came up to me saying, What do you want of the Gentile woman? So I told her.

You found no one else to ask only this woman? How should she know where Ḥemdat is? She comes from the village! And even if she did know would you find Ḥemdat at home?

I asked her, Where is he?

Am I a prophet that I should know? She replied, Either he is in the bathhouse or sitting before the barber or sitting with his choristers rehearsing the prayers with them.

Her neighbor overheard us and said, You are seeking Ḥemdat? Why, then, do you not go to him?

The wife of the beadle said to her, Why do you send him to Ḥemdat? Is he in his house?

Just as it is possible that is elsewhere he may be at home. Betake yourself, my son, to the courtyard standing before you and you will find a gateway opening upon five courtyards, facing each other. By the door of Yachnes the Physician, turn to the courtyard on the right, thence to the courtyard of Shatnez the Tailor, thence pass through and walk until you come to Ḥemdat. But I cannot warrant that you will find him at home. For it is the eve of the Day of Atonement today and perchance he is preparing his choristers for the service of tomorrow. Oh, however, one prepares it is never enough!

The old woman wiped her eyes and followed me with a long Oi! I took my leave thinking, All of them know where Ḥemdat is, but I who need him do not! How many hours have already gone by, how many will yet pass ere I find him?

A sweat of fear covered my face and my heart was sore with deferred hope. The driver had spoken truly. Jassy was a city not mentioned even in the Admonition. I moved my bundle from my right hand to my left and from my left to my right, and passed through from courtyard to courtyard until I reached the door of Yachnes the Physician. I found an old man sitting before the barber and though I had never seen him before I knew that he was Ḥemdat. My soul was linked up with his and I stood and stared at him. When he had finished shaving he rose from his chair and moistening his fingers with spittle began to curl his side-locks until they were like two corkscrews. He stuck his fingers into them, stroked his beard with his hand and put on his hat. The barber looked at me and said, Take your rump and sit. Another man sprang up and set before the barber. I addressed myself to the old man, saying, Is your honor Rabbi Ḥemdat? What difference does it make, he replied blithely. I told him who I was and what need I had of Ḥemdat. He said to me, I am not Ḥemdat, but what is the difference? But you require Ḥemdat and so I will bring you to him. But first tell me, How comes it that a Jewish lad does not know Ḥemdat. I replied, I am not of this place. He asked, Where do you come from? I told him. He said to me, How comes a Jewish lad to go forth to another city on the eve of the Day of Atonement? Certainly you have fled from your home without the knowledge of your father and your mother and are worthy of being taken by your two ears and brought back to them. Is that not so my young fellow?

I said to him, With the permission of my father I came hither. He said to me, And your mother what did she say? I said to him, I am orphaned of my mother. The old man said to me, You have reminded me of my grief. I, too, am an orphan but not only of my mother, but of both my mother and my father. And so you said that with the permission of your father you set forth. What did your father see to send you out of his house on the eve of the Day of Atonement? I said to him, The wife of my father sent me to slaughter her atonement offering. I took the fowl and went to the slaughterer but the fowl fled. When I returned to the wife of my father without her atonement offering she swore I would never have atonement until she had rooted me out of the world. So Father forestalled her and sent me to Ḥemdat for Father in his youth was of Ḥemdat's choir.

The old man listened shaking his head in wonder. Then he rose and said, Though a man live long he will never hear all the new things that come to pass in this world. Now, my son, we have reached the house of Ḥemdat, or, more precisely, we have already passed it and must return three or four houses, though in truth, they are all one house. And though they seem not so, they are owned by one man. Indeed were it not the Eve of the Day of Atonement, when it is not meet to speak evil of any man, I would tell you who he is. Now, my son, look and see. Here is the house of Ḥemdat, here in this place which I show you.

At that hour Ḥemdat sat before his table, reciting grace. His face was flushed and there were crumbs of food in his beard. His belt was loose, lying on his knees and the aroma of viands of the Day of Atonement filled the house, mixing with the fragrance of diverse drinks.

I lay down my bundle and eyed the master of the house in doubt and suspicion. There was indeed reason for doubt, for he that sat at the table was unlike the old man who I had thought was Ḥemdat. And even when the likeness of the old man I had thought was Ḥemdat had faded and I heard the voice of Ḥemdat as he recited the benediction, I still doubted whether he was indeed Ḥemdat. When he had finished the grace, he rose from his chair and poured out a glass for himself. He noticed me and said, You have come to call me. I realized that he confused me with another lad. I took out the letter of my father and extended it to him. He took the letter, placing it beween his coat and his shirt, upon his heart and asked, Who are you, my son? I told him who I was and reminded him of the letter. He asked me, Have you eaten?

My walk had consumed the food I had eaten while the smell of drink sharpened my wits. I said to myself, If he will invite me to eat I will not refuse. He called his wife and said, Have you anything to give him? His wife said, God be with you, Ḥemdat! What talk is this. A Jewish child is hungry and you ask, Have you anything to give him! And even had I not, would I let him go hungry? Let him wash his hands and eat!

She placed before me a wheaten loaf made in the shape of wings. I washed my hands and dipped my benediction slice into the honey. She brought me a dish full of fish and then meat pasties, floating in a congealed sea of gravy. Ḥemdat sighed and poured me a glass of brandy, saying, For the sake of fellowship I will pour one for myself, too, and we shall drink to health. He poured a glass for himself, picking two or three raisins from the loaf to sweeten his drink. And seeing that they did not suffice he stretched out his hand and took a piece of fish, and drank afterwards as one does with fish and sweetened his drink with two meat pasties. And because he avoided eating in pairs, he took a third and meantime said, Would we not eat, were something to eat brought to us.

If you wish to eat, said his wife, Wash your hands and I will bring you food. Ḥemdat replied, Easy is it for you to say, Wash your hands. But I must go to my choristers and they will invite me to eat with them and I am a weak man and cannot refuse. Said she to him, Then eat first, and you will have more strength to eat with them. Said Ḥemdat, A woman who brings her mind into concord with that of her husband at times can give good counsel. Have you anything that does not oblige the washing of hands? Such as a cake, or a roll, or a filled cake, or a rusk or a loaf kneaded with eggs, or a cake with apple filling, or a loaf baked with honey, of the kind we ate on the New Year, or those wine-cakes with plums, or ginger sweets, or any sort of cake that does not require the washing of the hands.

Said his wife, In all my days I have seen none so slothful as this man, who is too lazy to wash his hands, while the Day of Atonement loaves lie before him! Said Ḥemdat, You think that we should wash our hands? She smiled and said, Am I a rabbi to be asked questions? Ḥemdat replied, Go and talk to women when they cannot reply to the purpose. Said his wife, Did I not reply to the purpose? You said, If something to eat was brought before us I would eat. And I replied, Wash your hands and I will serve. Said Ḥemdat, What measure of eating is there? According to you one must sit all day and eat and eat. Have you ever seen such a woman. She wishes to show off her cookery and tempts me to eat. And this old fool does her bidding.

Said his wife, Remember your Creator, Ḥemdat, and do not cause strife within your own household! The Day of Atonement is upon us. It is proper that one should bring peace upon his house and not quarrel. Said Ḥemdat, God forbid. Who seeks to quarrel? I merely wished to speak my mind. And you bid me to wash my hands. I have bidden nothing, said his wife, but give you good counsel. Said Ḥemdat, Good counsel maketh the marrow fat. I will go and wash my hands. May my trouble not be in vain. Said his wife, So may we fear the retribution of judgment as you have cause to fear for this trouble. Wash your hands! The day does not stand still. Said Ḥemdat, Shah! Shah! I run to do your bidding. He rolled up his sleeves and washed his hands. He blessed the bread, cut a generous slice, and of all that his wife placed before him left nothing but a morsel for the poor and bones for the cat. As he washed his hands again for grace he sighed, saying, Food without drink is like drink without food.

He rose and brought a little cask. He poured and drank and poured again. When he had emptied the cask, he said, If one eats one feels it in one's stomach. And if one drinks one feels it in one's head. What is the remedy? To eat and drink together. Regarding what do I say this? Regarding that woman who sees that I drink and brings nothing to sweeten the drink.

His wife said to him, You have eaten fish. You have eaten meat pasties. What else shall I give you? Said Ḥemdat, The Day of Atonement approaches. Must I sit here and think of the needs of my flesh? Bring whatever you have. Perhaps a sweet-meat or a dessert or a little carrot. His wife said, Blessed be he that remembers what is forgotten! She went and brought for him. He rose and stood by the door where there was a cask, full of apple-cider. He took a ladle and drank, licked his lips and repeated, Not bad! Not bad! Worth examining its taste! Again he filled the ladle and drank, like a man pouring the contents of a vessel into another that is empty. When he had eaten and recited grace, he rose from the table and raising his belt from the floor, put it on. And while so doing he remarked, Strange! Only yesterday it was long and today it is short. Now, my son, we will go and see what the band of my choristers do. He kissed the mezuzah, took me by the hand and we went out.

I walked side by side with Ḥemdat thinking, How much I had asked Father to allow me to go to Ḥemdat and now that I have come to him he does not question me. What would happen if suddenly Ḥemdat forsook me and I must return to my stepmother? I recalled my dream, when she had said to me, You went forth to Jassy and what are you doing now in Vasleu? I began to fear and reminded Ḥemdat of Father's letter. Ḥemdat silenced me looking straight ahead as if he saw something new. He placed his hand on my shoulder and said, Do you see, my son? Here they sell mead. He shuffled the slippers on his feet, put forth his hand towards the mezuzahh and entered.

The publican hurried towards us, exclaiming, A Happy New Year, Cantor! A Happy New Year! For us and for all Israel, Ḥemdat replied. He glanced at the casks in the cellar and said, Jacob Psanter met me in the bath-house and praised some mead he had drunk, I do not remember where. The publican sprang up and said, Mr. Psanter is a constant frequenter of my house. I would not exaggerate to say that he scarce moves from here. Before dawn he came to me together with the King of the Gypsies and his wife and concubines, saving your honor, and they ate and drank until the time came to recite the Thirteen Attributes of Mercy. Would that all they wished me in their cups come to pass! Said Ḥemdat, Can one depend upon him. The publican said, There are none so wise as men of experience.

Ḥemdat said to him, Bring us not into trial or contempt. Said the publican, Not every day does such a trial occur. So he hastened and brought a full flask. Ḥemdat looked at the flask and poured me a glass, examined the glass, saying, Its appearance is good. Drink, my son, drink! I said, I cannot drink. Said Ḥemdat, What sort of talk is this. Must an old man drink in your stead? I looked up at him, beseechingly, and reminded him of the letter of my father.

He fingered his clothes and said, Your father is a great stylist and can write well. Once, at Purim, he sent me a poem. All the scholars of Jassy licked their fingers over it and said that even the Malbim would not be ashamed of it. Indeed it is profitable to see what your father writes. He poured himself a last glass repeating the blessing, Who hath created souls.

When we had made our exit, a woman came up and stood before us, wringing her hands and shrieking, Never would I have thought that the Cantor would cause me such shame! Tilshi, what is it that I have done to you that you gabble like a hen? Ḥemdat enquired of the woman. Perhaps you, my son, know what this Tilshi is babbling against me? Tilshi replied saying, If the Cantor wishes to tune his throat for his prayers, must he go to my enemies? Ḥemdat said, Have you not become reconciled today? Tilshi answered, What else could I do. The Day of Atonement is upon us. But may all the curses I have called down upon him, and all those with which he has cursed me came to pass upon him and his wife and his children and his children's children, unto the end of all generations. Shah! Shah! Shah! Ḥemdat said, Because of a mere drop I have drunk with a Jew, all this wrath? Let us go into Tilshi's and restore peace in Israel. Pour glasses, and if I will not drink the son of the Cantor of Vasleu will. Tilshi's face brightened. She ran and brought a full flask. When he had drunk, Ḥemdat raised himself from his stool, kissed the *mezuzah* and shuffling the slippers on his feet, went out.

On our way he said to me, We did not do wisely in drinking without having a snack with our drink. A man who drinks and does not eat is like one who eats and does not drink. Come, my son, nearby dwells Bar Bar-Jonah, the Sefardi. Perhaps there we shall get a morsel of meat, for his father and his father's father before him already conducted themselves like Ashkenazim save for the grilling of meat upon coals. And now I will tell you something. Should you be hungry and seek food, wherever you descry smoke coming out of a chimney, know that thence you will not go out hungry. If you have eaten your fill but wish to do yourself well, go to the Sefardim. Sometimes I leave a religious repast thinking that I shall not eat again till the morrow. But as soon as I come to one of their eating houses, all the food within me is digested and I am as if I had not dined at all. We have here Ḥakham Ezra Hacohen Mareli, who derives his lineage from Eli, the Priest. What shall I tell you, my son. All my life I have grieved over the verse, And the custom of the priests with the people was that when any man offered sacrifice, the priest's servant came while the meat was boiling, and so on—all that the fork brought up the priest took for himself. I said, Could it be that Eli's sons, sons of the High Priest, grabbed like tipplers and gluttons. But once I chanced to be in the eating house of Ezra Hacohen Mareli and I began to excuse them, I went down into a gloomy cellar and stood in a haze of grilling meat. Ḥemdat called out into the void of the cellar. A Happy New Year, Mr. Bar Bar-Jonah. Out of the cellar came the reply. May you merit many good years, Ḥakham Rabbi Ḥemdat. May blessing rest upon you, Ḥakham Rabbi Ḥemdat. Said Ḥemdat, I myself cannot drink and who is it that can, but seeing I have entered I will taste something. That meat on the skewer is it perchance mutton? Bar Bar-Jonah replied, You have guessed well, Rabbi. It is mutton. And it is for the well-being and the enjoyment of Rabbi Ḥemdat that it is prepared. Said Ḥemdat, What have I with the mysteries of the Merciful One? But if you have here the meat of a kid bring us a chicken's peck.

Mr. Bar Bar-Jonah asked Ḥemdat. And with what shall we fill the glass of Ḥakham Rabbi Ḥemdat? Ḥemdat replied, To bring out the flavor bring us a needle's eye full of cider. And you, my son, Ḥemdat addressed me affectionately, You, doubtless, would like plum juice. The landlord hurried bringing in one hand a flask full of cider and in the other a bottle of plum juice. Ḥemdat poured himself a large glass of plum juice, next to it a small glass of cider, and between one glass and the next ate of the skewer.

Mr. Bar Bar-Jonah asked Ḥemdat, What says your honor of the plum juice I have served? Said Ḥemdat, Bring another bottle and I will ascertain its quality. What is its price?

The gift varies with the quality of the man, said Mr. Bar Bar-Jonah, the rich pay in silver, the wise in good words. Said Ḥemdat, If it be not too much trouble, bring two or three drops of common brandy lest we become proud because of these fine drinks. When he had served them Ḥemdat poured a glass for himself and another for the landlord. He grasped his hand and drank his health. Then closing his eyes he said, I will tell your honour a fine tale I have heard. Mr. Bar Bar-Jonah lifted his hand to his lips and kissed the fingers. Said Ḥemdat, This was told to me by Rabbi Abramtchi Zefati, of the Holy City of Safed. The secret of preparing brandy was in the power of the evil spirits, the Merciful One save us. But there was one spirit who observed the sufferings of Israel and the exile enduring without end. So he rose and revealed to them the secret of distillation. And that spirit was found worthy and was raised up and became a holy angel. Your life, Mr. Bar Bar-Jonah, *Lechaim*!

As we came up out of the cellar Ḥemdat glanced up at the heavens and said, The time for the midday meal has come. I should not have stopped at Mr. Bar Bar-Jonah's, but I did not wish to deviate from my habit. Let us hasten, my son, and go!

He turned at the end of the street entering a gloomy alley and thence to an open courtyard. He pricked up his ears and said, Here dwell the members of my choir. Come, let us go in. What letter have you brought me from your father. Had I not forgotten my eye-glasses I would read it now. Come, my son, here by these steps, we go up to the women's gallery of the Furrier's Synagogue. Give me your hand and I will lead you. Have you ever in your life seen such stuttering stairs? Can you see anything?

As he had forgotten his eyeglasses I served as his eyes and led him from step to step and at every step I would repeat, One! One and one! One and two! One and three! Ḥemdat looked at me and said, Your voice, my son, is pleasant. Why has your father sent you to me? Is there not peace between you and your step-mother? That is the error into which Cantors fall. For if a householder serves them with tea and sugar they think that they are as sweet as sugar both to him and his wife. And when they chance to marry the widow of such a householder they think the gates of Eden have opened for them. But they know not that tea and sugar are in the hands of men and a wife is in the hands of Providence. Your mother, rest her soul, was the daughter of a scribe and while she lived your father saw life. Now I will reveal to you, my son, I arranged the match between your father and your mother. How came it? Together we happened to be in Buczacz and your father had not yet taken a wife. I said to him, Shimshi, Buczacz is a fine town, is it not? He nodded his head and said, Yes. Said I, How fine are the folk of Buczacz! He nodded his head and said, Yes. Said I, If its men are so, perhaps its women also. And perhaps, Shimshi, even their daughters. For as our sages have said, As a woman is, so is her daughter. The face of your father was red, for at that time he had looked upon a maiden, the daughter of Rabbi Michli, the Scribe of Buczacz. She was your mother, rest her soul. But Rabbi Michli was poor and was unable to give any dowry. So I said to him, to your father, Of what profit is money, be it even a thousand dinars of silver. If I pray before the pulpit on a thousand Sabbaths I earn a thousand pieces of silver. Your mother was a good woman and protected your father like a rampart. This rampart that rears itself up suddenly before us whence has it come? I whispered to him and said, It is a door. It is a door, cried Ḥemdat astonished. Praised be the name of God that Ḥemdat can see without eye-glasses. Push and we shall enter. I pushed and we stood in the midst of the company of Ḥemdat Cantor's choristers.

Throughout the year Ḥemdat prayed without a choir to accompany him. Said Ḥemdat, What need have I of such a company? One sigh uttered during one's prayers is of more avail than all the choirs and singers. But for the New Year and the Day of Atonement he would prepare a number of choristers according to the custom of many congregations where men versed in music assisted the Cantor. But when Ḥemdat approached the pulpit he disregarded them entirely. It was said that they themselves were the cause for as soon as he began the prayer they forthwith burst into tears and were unable to accompany him. But others said that he was the cause for he changed from one melody to another, in harmony with his heart and soul. Thus all the melodies he had taught them were in vain. But if it were thus or otherwise, many were there who called themselves the choristers of Ḥemdat. And these choristers were wont to prepare a repast on the Eve of the Day of Atonement to which Ḥemdat would come. I heard that at first it was held in the house of the bass for he was their senior and his wife served in the house of Michael Daniel who ate seventeen courses at one meal, not reckoning those coming before the meal, and after the meal, and during the meal. Once there fell a quarrel between the bass and the tenor and the bass threw the tenor out of the house. So they resolved to hold the repast in a place where everyone could consider himself master. What was the cause of the quarrel? Once when they had entered to partake of the repast and the meat pasty and then the meat of the fowl of Atonement the tenor said, I fear we have not done our duty by the meat pasty of the Eve of the Day of Atonement made of the flesh of the fowl of Atonement. The bass mocked at him. The tenor grew angry and said, You mock at the precepts of the Torah. The bass grew angry and said, Not at the precepts of the Torah do I mock but at the ignoramus who does not know that the precept of the pasties is one thing and that of the flesh of the fowl of atonement another. For if you come to mix all the precepts of this day you might fill the meat pasty of Purim with clappers and of Hoshana Rabba with beaten willow branches. But the Holy One, blessed be He, loves Israel and all that He has ordained, He has ordained for the good of Israel that they eat and be happy and rejoice. And if that ignoramus does not know that is written in the Torah let him not open his mouth about the meat pasty which my wife has made and let him not eat. The tenor took a meat pasty and threw it in the face of the bass. The bass took the whole dish and broke it over the face of the tenor. Then the tenor rose and struck the bass. Then the bass rose and threw the tenor out of his house, and the choristers were troubled from their feast. So the bass gave them another on the Rejoicing of the Law. When they went into the repast and they placed before them roast goose, the tenor opened his mouth and said, What I have seen recalls a story. It is the tale of a Saint who sat down to a Fifteenth of Shvat feast. They brought before him roast goose. The Saint noticed in the goose that the slaughterer had not recited the benediction devoutly. The compassion of the Saint was quickened on account of the bird for it had much meat and was exceedingly fat. He uttered one word, The goose raised itself out of the dish, shook off the garlic that was on it, stood on its feet and walked. That same bass mocked him. The tenor grew angry and said, You mock at deeds of the Saints! The bass also grew angry and said, Not at the deeds of the Saints do I mock but at that Gentile who talks and knows not of what he talks. When did this matter come to pass? Was it not on the Fifteenth of Shvat! And if it came to pass on the Fifteenth of Shvat, how could that goose stand up on its legs and walk? Why? Because there is an hour in Shvat and the same in Tevet, when if at that hour a goose is slaughtered, the slaughterer does not live out the year, unless he eats of the goose. And therefore the slaughterer takes the feet in order that he may have a plea before the goose to say, For my own need I slaughtered you. Said the tenor, If the goose had no feet, how did it walk. Said the bass, Surely it raised its wings and flew. One said walked the other said flew until the bass made the tenor fly out of his house. So they ordained that the repast be served in the Prayer House of the Furriers, for most of the choristers were furriers. And then the bass could tell no one to leave for there they were all masters.

A company of black heads and bald heads, of bearded and beardless, with curled side-locks and Jassy side-locks, were seated about a table each with a plate before him and a glass in his hand. No one heeded our entry.

One bearded man, whose voice betrayed that he was the bass, looked up and called out, Welcome Cantor! Ḥemdat stirred himself, took some snuff and sneezed. The company of his choristers came up to him one with a glass in his hand another with some sweet meat. Ḥemdat passed his hand over his eyes saying, Where are my eye-glasses? Said they to him, Does the Cantor not know the blessing over the wine by heart? Ḥemdat smiled and said, Oi, you are drinking wine. He took a glass pronounced the benediction and drank, and extended his hand to every one of them, saying, May it be His will that all our prayers on the Holy Day coming, be favorably received. They all replied, Amen, so be it! One placed before him a stuffed neck, another a piece of liver, a third some other portion to sweeten the wine. Ḥemdat gazed at them with goodly eyes and said, Were today not the Eve of the Day of Atonement, whose precept it is to eat and to drink, I might ask if it were not better to sit and to rehearse the liturgy that your tongues stumble not. Eat lads, eat, so that you may enter upon the fast with appetite. What is that roaming there in the gravy? He stretched out his hand drew out a piece of chicken and ate standing. They said to him, Let the cantor wash his hands and eat with us. Said Ḥemdat, The time for the midday meal has come and I must eat in my own house. Said they to him, Ere you come to your own house you can eat yet twice. Said Ḥemdat, Not exactly twice. Said they to him, If not twice, then at least once. Ḥemdat closed his eyes, wrinkling his brow like a man trying to make a reckoning. But meanwhile they brought him water to wash his hands and each of them offered him the tails of his garment on which to dry them.

When he had eaten and drunk, he rose from his chair, saying, Ḥemdat, Ḥemdat, you waste your time, when you should sit with your wife at the midday meal. He dipped his hands in the last water, recited grace and left.

On our way he said to me, If I did not hasten to my house I would bring you to the market and show you kinds of melons the like of which you have never seen. How time has flown! I recall how I used to swallow melons as a man eats cherries. What is it your father's custom to drink before the fast? You do not know? A man must heed the deeds of his fathers, so when he grow old, he may do likewise. Before today I took an important melon and I cannot remember where I left it. Either in one prayer-house or another or perhaps in a certain study hall. It were a pity if it were eaten without devotion.

Ḥemdat's wife came out to greet him staring at him with suspicion. Ḥemdat saw her and said, Why do you look so darkly at me? Said his wife, You have filled your stomach and now I must seek some man from the street to eat your meal? Ḥemdat replied, May this son of my companion testify if I have tasted more than a man takes as a matter of courtesy. Do you not know that any dish not prepared by you is tasteless to me? The countenance of the old woman brightened and she said, Let us eat and we shall see.

We sat down and ate the midday meal. Because of the multitude of dishes and drinks I cannot recall what we ate and what we drank. When he had recited grace, Ḥemdat rose from the table and walked back and forth. He took a prayer-book and turned its leaves. He took a bottle of drops and sniffed at it. He filled his box with snuff and sneezed. He examined his kittel and laid it out on the bed. He gargled his throat with liquor, and came and sat down, and laying his head on the table, dozed. After a short while he woke and went whither he went. He washed his hands and pronounced the blessing. Meanwhile the clock struck. Ḥemdat said, The day does not stand still and we have many acts to perform before the onset of the great and awesome day. Lord of the World, may you have compassion upon us, and not look at the evil of our hearts! Take a prayer-book and we shall go to afternoon prayers.

Ḥemdat took the memorial candles and we went to pray. When he came he handed the candles to whomever he handed them to and walked up to the reading desk, which was crowned with many plates for each and every local charity. He took out his purse, dropping a coin here and a coin there, leaving not a single plate in to which he did not place an offering. When he had prayed and suffered stripes we returned to his house.

The house had changed completely. The scent of purity pervaded it, and on its floor there was not a speck of dust. A clean cloth was spread on the table and the wife of the Cantor was clad in her Day of Atonement garments—a long white dress, reaching below her feet, a white kerchief on her head down to her eyebrows, her voice like that of a child who has been pacified after weeping, and on her heart some old silver jewel fashioned of tablets. She walked on tip-toes holding her head back to restrain the tears. Ḥemdat sat and was silent, as if he had chanced upon a place that was not his and he did not know whether he was welcome to the master of the house.

Ḥemdat blessed the bread and took the spoon, his tears dripping into the soup. And with every spoonful that he raised he sighed and new and fresh tears welled up in his eyes. He tugged off an olive-sized morsel of meat from the chicken, dipped it in the sauce of boiled prunes and ate a piece of pudding, the size of an olive. He raised his eyes, staring through the window. Finally, he thrust away his plate, washed his hands in the last water, and taking a prayer-book, turned its leaves and sighed saying, When I recall that I am seventy years old and that every day I eat and every day I drink and every day I look to my own welfare and I see no betterment in the world, I am sad, my son, I am very sad. Oh, my son, I grieve for Israel. Distress grows but there is none to stand in the breach. We cannot say that we have no saints, but they are bereft of their power. Oh, Lord of the World, if you have deprived the saints of their power, do Thou because of Thy might and Thy exceeding compassion. Ḥemdat closed his eyes and began to chant, "When the Lord restored the captivity of Zion," with tears streaming from his eyes. When he reached the benediction, Who buildeth Jerusalem, he began to weep and to hawk and to groan. His face grew red and his eyes started out. I thought to myself, If his voice is so hoarse, how will he conduct the service on the Day of Atonement. I was sorry for the old man and wept too. He saw that I was weeping and he stroked my cheek and said, Weep, my son, weep. The tears of a boy who has not sinned are acceptable before Him, may He be blessed. May it be His will that He see your tears and have mercy upon us.

When he had risen from the table he put on new socks, and took counsel with his wife what clothes he should wear and what he should leave behind, for the heat in the synagogue was great and his tallit was thick. Then he filled his box with snuff and taking several handkerchiefs, put some of them in each of the pockets of his garments, binding a new handkerchief about his neck. Then he put on his kittel, tied on his sash, and took his tallit and prayer-book. He blessed his wife and said to me, Come let us go. When he came to the mezuzahh, he stopped and said, When I recall that there I stood a year ago in complete confidence that this year we should dwell in the Land of Israel and now the year is past and I still stand here, I am ashamed before my Creator. Do not weep Malka! God will grant us life and make us worthy and will bring us up soon to his City. She did not weep but looked after her husband saying, Ḥemdat, your kerchief is loose about your neck. In the name of God, be careful, lest you catch cold, God forbid. Said Ḥemdat, The holiday of Sukkot approaches. I have faith in God that He will grant me to observe the precept of dwelling of properly dwelling in the sukkah. And as he spoke he turned his head back towards his wife and looked upon her with good eyes. He placed his lips upon the mezuzah, and kissing it walked out.

On his way he entered the bath-house to bathe before the onset of the Day of Atonement. The bath-house was crowded, men coming and going, one doffing his garments, another descending and immersing himself in the water, a third emerging and drying himself, all hurrying and rushing as in a panic, no man taking note of anyone in his haste. Ḥemdat took off his clothes, descended, immersed himself in the water, saying as he entered, The smell of a thousand Jews, no evil eye befall them. When he had ascended and donned his garments he took his things and hurried to the synagogue. One man stopped him by the way to greet him. Ḥemdat nodded uttering not a word. It was clear that he was in another world.

The synagogue filled until no room remained and yet it went on filling and filling. Straw was scattered on the floor and large, thick candles flickered on every table and in every window. And in the windows by the candles, countless children stood. The women's gallery, too, was crowded with worshippers, who, throughout the year prayed in other synagogues or did not pray at all, and on the New Year and Day of Atonement came to pray with Ḥemdat, besides a number of Gentiles of high station who came to listen to the service. And as the synagogue was crowded with men the gallery was crowded with women, over their heads a myriad of lamps, lighting over against the candles that stood on the tables and in the windows. Ḥemdat wrapped himself in his tallit down to his feet. He wiped his eyeglasses and opened his prayer-book.

What I relate here may seem idle. But in all truth this is no exaggeration but things as they came to pass Ḥemdat began to grow less and less and it seemed that he was shrinking and shrinking, his stomach as if disappeared and he was like a bundle of clothes over which a tallit had been spread. Thus he stood motionless, until of a sudden he was impelled from his place and began to falter with outstretched hands to the pulpit, all making room for him, and weeping and saying, May it be His will that your prayer be accepted in compassion. And he answered, Amen, and said, In complete repentence! And when he came to the pulpit he gripped it with his two hands, and cried out, *Oi*! as if it were all-devouring fire.

A sudden awe fell upon the entire congregation and all rose and stood and trembled. Ḥemdat stood before the pulpit, surrounded by his choristers, but disregarding them. Thus he stood, silent, his knees alone trembling like a hero girding on his strength though his knees betray him. He took hold of the pulpit and struck his head upon it. The windows quivered and candles flared up and from one end of the synagogue to the other a sigh rose, reaching up to the gallery, and from the gallery to the street and from the street it returned to the synagogue. Children stood and wept and even men and women joined them. Ḥemdat raised his head, his eyes closed and compressed, groping in the air, his eyeglasses swimming in tears.

The *Gabbai* rose and opened the Ark, took out several Scrolls, handing them to the elders of the synagogue. The elders took the scrolls and stationed themselves to the right and the left of the Cantor. Ḥemdat removed his eye-glasses and placed them on the pulpit. He covered his face with has tallit down to his heart, and he began to give voice, every time in a melody sweeter than the last. Then I understood what Father meant when he said, He who has heard the *Kol Nidrei* of Ḥemdat, knows what *Kol Nidrei* is.

And after *Kol Nidrei* he began to recite. And may forgiveness be granted to the entire community of Israel, the first time in supplication then in confidence then in confidence and assent.

I gazed straight ahead and was astonished. It seemed to me, at first, that here stood a being with six wings, but it appeared it was but a son of Israel wrapped in his tallit, his right hand on his ear, the thumb of his left, supporting his chin. While I stood thus bewildered Ḥemdat stretched forth his hands again and cried, "And as Thou hast borne this people from Egypt unto this day, I recalled all the trials with which my fathers had provoked the Holy One, blessed be He, in Egypt." My heart filled with compassion for that old man, who endeavored to pray for a people such as this.

The memorial candles flared and as in one voice was heard, And God said I have forgiven, as you have spoken. Thus once, thus a second time, thus a third. And the hands of the Cantor were raised above and a voice spoke out of the Cantor's throat, And God said, I have forgiven as you have spoken. Stirred, fearful, I stood looking at this Jew, this old man, so humble, emissary of a congregation, to whom the Holy One, blessed be He, had granted the strength and the courage thus to pray before him.

Once again the candles flared and emitted a brighter and yet a brighter light. The good smell of wax rose from the candles and from the straw spread on the floor, like the smell of honey and the smell of the fields. Silence filled the synagogue, and from out of the silence came the sound of a sigh restrained. Ḥemdat raised himself and pronounced the *Shehecheyanu* benediction in a loud, joyful voice, like once rejoicing that God has vouchsafed him life to perform precepts and good deeds. And all the people repeated the benediction together with him in a joyful undertone. And indeed they were worthy of their joy at that hour, for they were as if created anew, because of their rejoicing in the precepts of God, and because Ḥemdat, their emissary, has stirred their hearts by his prayer which he had prayed for them before God. For Ḥemdat prayed in awe and fear and feeling and with a broken heart, for Israel the holy nation, who sought to return to Him with a whole heart.

– *Translated by Isaac Halevy-Levin*

And Solomon's Wisdom Excelled

AND SOLOMON'S WISDOM EXCELLED the wisdom of the children of the East, and all the wisdom of Egypt. For he was wiser than all men... He also uttered three thousand proverbs and his songs were one thousand and five." Some of our rabbis explained that "three thousand" refers to three teachings of proverbs, while others maintain that Solomon himself spoke three thousand proverbs on every verse, and to every proverb gave one thousand and five meanings.

Why did Solomon himself not record his wisdom, but confine his writing to three books? Rabbi Yehudah the Ḥasid explains that, had Solomon written down all his wisdom, people would have busied themselves solely with that, diminishing their study of Torah. They would, moreover, have come to rely on this wisdom and neglect Torah study and practical commandments. The truth is that Solomon's wisdom – indeed all types of wisdom – is hinted at in the Torah, either in part or by example.

Rabbi Levi ben Gershom says that he included these proverbs in the Book of Proverbs and the songs in the Song of Songs. Thus the beginning of the Book of Proverbs explicitly states: "The proverbs of Solomon, son of David, king of Israel; to know wisdom and instruction." This means that those proverbs alone concern these matters, while the rest of Solomon's proverbs did not.

Hence these books were not written down, even though they were transmitted under divine inspiration. When he says, at the beginning of the Song of Songs, "The Song of Songs of Solomon," he refers to the choicest of Solomon's songs.

Rabbi David Kimche observes that many books were lost during Israel's periods of exile. Among them were the books Solomon composed regarding knowledge of nature, of which it is written: "And he spoke of trees," explaining their nature and curative powers. In the same way, he penetrated the world of the beasts, fowl and fish; everything which exists beneath the cycle of the moon. From this he composed books, though they are no longer extant.

The rabbis have left me space in which to elaborate. Not that I come, heaven forbid, to take issue with them. But, just as one text lends itself to numerous readings, so each reading may be understood in various ways. Thus, when it is written that, "He uttered three thousand proverbs," this must be taken literally. Similarly, that "his songs were one thousand and five," must also be taken at face value. But, perhaps, only three books have come to us, because Solomon himself hid the rest.

Yet why would Solomon have wanted to hide them? When he was a young man and the divine inspiration was upon him, he composed the Song of Songs – a song greater than all other songs, the choicest of songs – combining both love and fear of heaven.

There was a certain crowd in Jerusalem, however, of good-for-nothing intellectuals who would take the holy words out of context and twist the plain meaning. Of these people Solomon observed: "Little foxes that spoil the vineyards." To which vineyard does he refer? To none other than the vineyards of the Lord of Hosts, of the House of Israel. What did this crowd of intellectuals say? "Look at Solomon! The people of Israel are building the Temple and he busies himself writing love songs!" These words reached Solomon. He placed his left hand beneath his head like a man examining his deeds. His songs came before him and he saw that each was whole, without blemish or fault. He despaired of mankind and wished to flee. Thus said Solomon: "Flee, my beloved."

So why did he not flee? Because all Israel had set him on the throne of David, his father, and needed him to consolidate the kingdom and to judge Israel. His stomach turned when his songs fell into unworthy hands and left them prey to criticism. He decided, with the aid of the Divine Presence, to hide the remainder of his songs. This is referred to in the verse: "In the cover of your presence you hide them from the plots of men; you hold them safe under your shelter from the strife of tongues." And further in the same verse: "You shall be hidden from the scourge of the tongue."

Solomon went up to the mountain of myrrh and the hill of frankincense, as it is written: "Before the day cools and the shadows flee, I will get me to the mountain of myrrh and to the hill of frankincense." How do we know that he wanted to hide his songs? From the following verse: "You are fair, my love; there is no flaw in you." What is it that is fair and without blemish? It is the Song of Songs. Said Solomon: Until the day of the wicked cools off and they flee like shadows, I will bury my words in the dust, just as one would say: "He put his mouth into the dust."

When Solomon reached the mountain of myrrh and the hill of frankincense, he came upon the daughters of Jerusalem gathering myrrh and frankincense. Solomon feared that they would place his songs on a rock, like a bundle of myrrh.

He went to the fig tree and found it putting forth its green figs. Solomon feared that his songs would be gathered in with the first fruits. He went to the apple tree; he saw young men, their love awakened. He descended to his garden to the bed of spices; he saw the shepherds with their flocks. Solomon became afraid lest the shepherds find his songs. He went down to his grove of nut trees, but even there he did not hide his songs. And why not? Because the nut does not cover its roots during planting.

Solomon finally went to his vineyard at Ba'al Hammon, for thus we find that, "Solomon had a vineyard at Ba'al Hammon. There he built wall and on it erected a tower of silver. He hired out the vineyard to keepers to guard it." Since he saw that it was well-guarded he went and hid his songs – one thousand and four of them – in the ground. When the fifteenth of Av came and the daughters of Jerusalem went out to dance in the vineyards, Solomon's songs arose from the ground and were heard between the vines. The young maidens stood and listened. Their lips dripped like honeycomb as their love was aroused. Of this moment Solomon wrote: "I charge you, O, daughters of Jerusalem, by the gazelles and by the hinds of the fields. Do not stir up nor awaken love." The young girls heard Solomon's oath and hid their songs in their hearts. Because they were hidden, so they became silent and since they were silent they were forgotten, and as they were forgotten no one remembered them.

When he grew in greatness, Solomon observed and took to heart how most men were distracted by alien matters and fell into the net cast by the evil inclination. They were ensnared by its temptations which spread beneath their feet, putting darkness in place of light and light in place of darkness. Solomon considered how he might guide those who had strayed, by showing evil to be loathsome and by arguing for the truth. Thus stirred, he composed the Book of Proverbs, for within a proverb, man balances a proposition and its opposite.

Israel began to attend to Solomon's proverbs, to know wisdom and instruction, understand words of insight, parables and interpretations. They became God-fearing and saved themselves from the judgment of hell.

Yet there was in Jerusalem one crowd of deceitful miscreants who loathed divine instruction and were sick of Solomon's regal rebukes. About them he remarked: "You have ignored my counsel and would have none of my reproof." This same group retorted: "What is it that the son of David comes to teach us? To know wisdom and instruction and understand words of insight? What can he teach us? To persevere in the study of Torah, which only weakens our ability to cultivate the world?"

There was another group in Jerusalem who were reckoned among the most important and honored, since they were supported by public funds in gold dinars. Of what did their wisdom consist? Their studies revolved around new interpretations concerning, for example, the question as to why an egg is sharp at one end and blunt at the other and not the reverse. The same people busied themselves with divine mysteries, enquiring into why the stars went round in circles, for, if they moved in squares, they would not be such a bother to the Holy One, blessed be He who, each night, places them in the firmament, since it is far easier to place things in a square than on a circle. These same people studied Torah in any way that came to mind, switching round the verse "In the beginning…," for that which came after the beginning of creation.

Since they were wise in their own eyes, these people were also considered wise in the eyes of others. No one could address them without appending titles of greatness and honor. These wise men noted that from the day that the Book of Proverbs was published, "Wisdom cried aloud in the street and raised her voice in the market." They became apprehensive that people would rise against them, having perceived that all their so called wisdom was just nonsense. They thus began clucking their tongues against Solomon and his book.

The people of Israel noted their criticism and reasoned: if these authorized scholars, who are supported from public funds in golden dinars, look down their noses at Solomon's book, can we be wiser than they?

When Solomon heard this he thought: For whom do I toil and deny myself? He said: "He who has knowledge, spares his words." He decided to hide the rest of his three thousand, nine hundred and nine proverbs. About that moment Solomon, in his wisdom, said: "The wise hide their wisdom." Thus it is stated: "He prepared many proverbs." He prepared them, but he did not publish them.

As he grew much older and gained wisdom and knowledge, Solomon surveyed everything that happened beneath the sun; and beheld that everything was vanity and a striving after wind. Said he: "I built Israel a Temple in order to atone for all their iniquities. I showed them the right path and brought peace to the land. I arranged for ships to bring gold and sandalwood, precious stones, vessels of silver and gold, dresses and weapons, spices, horses and mules. I distributed money in Jerusalem like pebbles. All Israel rejoiced and was glad. All they have to do is to study Torah and wisdom. And what do they do? Against my advice they put fools in prominent positions and gather around them to hear their words of folly. They are enticed by their vain words, like fish caught in a wicked trap."

When Solomon saw that this was indeed so, he railed against what was happening and called out: "Vanity of vanities, all is vanity." Eventually he gathered all his words in a book, the Book of Ecclesiastes to reprove mankind for their iniquities.

What did Solomon's enemies say? If the baker admits his dough is bad what more proof is needed to discredit it? If everything is vanity, so, too, is Solomon's book. Moreover, if this were the only thing that Solomon said, we would laugh. But he also said: "What profit is there for man in all his work?" All mundane work, whether it be of community leaders, Temple administrators, treasurers, financiers, princes, and merchants, are also vanity of vanities. It makes no difference if, after all this, a man feigns piety by saying: "Fear God!"

Solomon responded by saying: "Then I saw that all toil and all skills come from man's envy of his neighbor." I composed the Song of Songs to proclaim Israel's love of the Holy One, blessed be He, and His love for them. My people were immediately angry with me. I wrote the Book of Proverbs to make straight the hearts of Israel, giving them sage advice as to how to control their speech – and they immediately ignored my advice. Now that I have devoted myself to the pursuit of wisdom and to knowing the way of the world – and collected my words for Israel's good – they have immediately begun crying: "Vanity of vanities"!

Finally Solomon said: "Beware of making many books." Indeed he had hidden those he had already written, namely two thousand, nine hundred and eight proverbs and one thousand and four songs. Since they were hidden they were lost, and since they were lost they perished.

Come and see how evil is perpetrated by twisted and devious people, who have little understanding of Torah, who lack knowledge, who are misdirected, arrogant and narrow-minded. If not for them we would have merited the rest of Solomon's books, three thousand proverbs and one thousand and five songs. Alas for our great loss and for those same crowds who are still active among us.

– *Translated by Mordechai Beck*

The Garment

A CERTAIN TAILOR WAS SITTING, working on a garment at the end of the day. The garment was intended for the minister and the weave was among the finest to be made in the minister's workshop. The tailor was old and his eyes no longer served him well. His hands, too, were weak. The sun was setting and the work still unfinished. While it was day and the sun shone, the tailor was bothered by things that seemed to him impossible to do without; as the day passed and the hour drew near to bring the garment to its owner, it became clear to him that he had no need of them. But there was a need to bring the garment to the minister.

Just as people usually realize too late what they should have realized initially, so the tailor finally realized what he should have known beforehand. This realization brings its owner no pleasure, but only grief and regret. The tailor began to think—if it weren't for those things that bothered me unnecessarily, I could have presented myself to the minister and collected my fee for the garment. Thinking about the minister and all the benefits he had derived from him, his thoughts returned to the garment. He took off his spectacles, wiped them and, replacing them on his eyes, examined what was missing. The buttons were secured and even the items that lent extra beauty to a garment were in place. But the garment itself still lacked something. Only with it would the garment be complete: without it, it would remain incomplete.

Grief and regret for the lost day made his fingers careless and the needle shake in his hand. More difficult than grief and regret are thoughts. At another time thoughts could have helped. But now, with evening falling—when the garment lay unfinished in front of him—they could only be a hindrance.

He stood and poured himself a glass of brandy and lit a light to brighten the darkness. The glass uplifted his spirit but the light revealed what was amiss with the garment. The hour, too, was pressing, since the time to bring the garment to the minister had already arrived. The tailor looked at the garment in his hand and looked at the window. The day was becoming dark and disappearing, and the night was about to fall, and if he didn't bring the garment to the minister the minister's people would fetch him and the garment. Fear descended upon him. Even the brandy that had initially elevated him now filled his limbs with heaviness. His eyes felt sleepy, and inside his frail body even his old bones began to slumber. The tailor forgot the minister and the garment, and let his head drop on to his chest and he sat as one curled up in his mother's womb, with nothing before him and nothing behind him, and nothing at all.

How long was he curled up like this? How long are an old man's forty winks? He rested his head a short while and then awoke. He awoke and saw the unfinished garment. He was gripped by a fear that the minister's men had come, taken the garment from him, and humiliated him. Unlike the minister, who was compassionate and kind to craftsmen, his servants were hard and cruel and showed no mercy to those who fell into their hands.

His strength returned and he picked up the needle and sewed—one stitch here, another there. If he had sewn during the day, when it was bright, every stitch would have been in the right place. Now, by the light of the candle, the tailor's fingers fumbled. If he hadn't spoiled that which he had mended, then neither had he mended that which needed to be mended. He put aside his needle and looked at the light and thought to himself: whose end will come first—that of the light or that of the man? The tailor finished with an "Oi" and said: Whatever has to happen, let it.

He didn't say this in so many words, since he knew how hard and cruel were the minister's servants, and that if they arrived he'd die of fright. When some time had passed and they had not arrived, he breathed more easily. He rubbed his hands and said—before they come, I'll mend something.

He picked up the needle again and threaded it anew. Since there was not enough time to mend the whole garment, he placed the garment in front of him, and examined which repair to do first, as each mend would reduce the amount that still had to be done.

He steadied his hand and commenced work. A noise was heard, the noise of feet and the cracking of whips. Even someone from whom nothing is demanded would be frightened by such a noise, how much more so someone who anticipates a visit.

There was a kick at the door and the minister's servants entered. Because of their voices the candle trembled and went out, and the tailor was left in the dark, until he disappeared and nothing could be seen of him except for the needle between his fingers, which turned hither and thither sewing the wind. The servants cracked their whips and shouted: "Thread, son of a needle—are you ready?" Even though he had been summoned by the minister they still made fun of him, as though it was inconceivable that the minister should commission work from such a man.

The tailor took the garment and stood with a heavy heart and a downcast face, aware that the garment was not of a standard befitting the minister. Even though he was ready to go, the minister's servants still hurried him along, prodding him with their whips and saying: "Get up and go, get up and go!" They hardly gave him time to put on his overcoat, though it was unbecoming that someone be brought before the minister in his work clothes.

The servants of the minister brought the tailor to the minister's house and put him in the place where such people are kept until the minister decides that he has time to see them. The place was small and cramped to a degree that it would have amazed you to find in a house as wide, high and grand as the minister's, a room so narrow and cramped.

The tailor sat and thought: the minister's affairs are many and even though he ordered a garment from me and sent his servants for me, he could have given me a little extra time. Since he has now left me some time I'll check the garment and complete it.

The tailor stretched out his hand and felt around for the needle and thread, in the manner of tailors who are used to going about with their needles and threads. He searched in his clothes and found nothing. Don't be surprised if he found nothing since, when he left for the minister's house, he had changed his clothes.

The tailor sat and fretted, because now that he had time to do the mending he could not do it, since he lacked a needle and thread. The suffering in the grave is nothing by comparison. Since no choice was left to him he had to depend on the minister's beneficence.

The minister's mercies are many but his servants are hard and cruel. Mercenaries of a good minister, they carry out their duties in a rage. While the tailor was sitting, the servants entered and said to him: "Eye of a needle, thread your legs and move, the minister wishes to see you." The tailor was dragged along to the minister by the minister's servants, who pushed him and beat him and raged at him and called him Son-of-a-Needle, Thread-of-a-Spider, and other insulting and frivolous names.

Since the servants already knew that the minister would not be favorably disposed to the tailor, they allowed themselves the liberty of mocking him. The tailor thought to himself; I'll tolerate this for a while, until they bring me face to face with the minister. His heart groaned. And what complaint will the minister make when sees the garment? The strain of the journey and the insults of the minister's servants gave him no rest. Yet imagining bad thoughts is harder than the thoughts themselves. He felt pressured and followed the imaginings of his heart: Did I not wish to do something? But what it was he did not know.

They brought him to the place where such people are taken and left him standing there. He stood alone, not knowing why. Presently his thoughts left the garment, the minister, and himself. This seemed to be for the good, allowing his mind to rest. But the truth was it wasn't good, for what was the good of moving someone from place to place, without bringing him to the place he thought he was going to—even if it was where he would receive his punishment—since the threat of punishment is more dreadful than the punishment itself. The tailor was forced to see what was around him, and pricked up his ears to hear what was being said. The windows were sealed and he could see nothing so that, even when things reached him, he could not comprehend them.

After many hours, the minister commanded his servants to fetch the tailor. They went and brought him. The minister saw the tailor's fallen countenance, his lowly spirits and lifelessness. But surely a few days beforehand, when he gave him the material to make the garment, he had been happy, as though the whole world had fallen into his lap. He said to him: "Are you the tailor whom I requested to make me a garment? Show me what you've done." The tailor began to stammer: "My lord minister, the garment is almost complete. But your servants came suddenly and snatched me from my workshop, just as I was sitting sewing the last stitch—took me away and brought me to you. If they would only have left me for a little while longer I would have completed it to your satisfaction."

The minister stared at him in surprise. "How many days was the woven cloth with you, without your managing to finish the work?

The tailor began to squirm before the minister, telling him about the many distractions he had had. He was a member of the "Society for Clothes-for-the-Indigent," and second beadle at the tailor's synagogue, and one of the worthies of the craftsmen's guild. And sometimes, because of the needs of the community, he neglected those of his own. And thus he rambled on until the minister stopped him and said: "In short, you didn't spend all your time on the garment." The tailor turned to him and said: "If the minister would return me the garment for a short while I could complete what it lacks and return it whole and beautiful. The minister, who has many garments, can afford to give one up." To this the minister replied: "Take the garment and do with it as you said."

The tailor left the minister with the intention of returning immediately to his work. In truth the garment lacked only one thing, and there was no need to make his eyes bad at night. Still he had obligated himself, he had to put his hand where his mouth is, and demonstrate to the minister that he was a person of his word.

He returned home and entered his work room. He lit a light and spread out the garment. Again he noticed what he had seen beforehand—that it lacked something. If only the servants of the minister had not come he would have been able to complete it, without having to suffer embarrassment. He could have made the minister happy and would not have had to return to work on the garment. But what was past was past and what needed to be done was still undone. At that moment his wife was standing in the kitchen preparing supper. The smell of the cooking wafted to him. He raised his head and thought to himself, I will not be far from the truth if I declare that my better half—may she be worthy of life—is cooking kashipani. Kashi is a tasty dish as is pani, how much more so when they are cooked together! Were it not for the garment I would go and eat immediately.

Though his sadness prevented him from eating, it seemed to him that it was only because of his craving for kashipani that he imagined that his wife was cooking it. And even if she were, it was necessary to clarify for which meal she was preparing the kashipani—for supper or lunch. This was his wife's custom: on a laundry day she would prepare lunch the night before, in order to be free to do the laundry. And for supper, radishes and onion would suffice. If what had happened had not happened he would have been satisfied with a small repast; after what had happened it was only right to comfort himself with the choicest foods.

He stopped thinking about the garment and thought about food. The fragrance of the pot, which has neither body nor—it goes without saying, hands—grips your nostrils and pulls you after it. He reframed from going to the kitchen immediately, since he wished to give his wife the satisfaction of showing him the pot and saying to him: See what I've cooked for you. This old lady—the Good Lord should be her help—still had youthful ways. Truly one could say of her that she was a woman of valor. With one hand she prepared supper and with the other lunch, not like him who had not even managed to do the one thing that he was obliged to do.

Hunger began to trouble him, and the enticing smell of the food drew him away from his work. He realized that as long as he hadn't inspected the food he would have no peace. He lay out the garment and stuck a needle in the place which needed mending, so that on his return the garment would be ready, and he stood up so as to go to the kitchen. As he stood, the garment caught in his clothing, dragged after him, and fell. He bent down, lifted it up and scolded himself; not enough that it won't be ready, I'll also have to go back and check which place needs mending! I won't tarry now because of it, but I'll go and see what's being cooked. It would have been better if man were created without a need for food and drink. But since he was created thus, it is just as well that his food stands ready before him. If it were not for food and drink you wouldn't have enough strength' to hold a needle and thread. The word thread here stands for work, which is to say that if man did not eat and drink he'd have no strength to work. Work! Man works in order that he'll be able to eat and he eats so that he'll have strength to work. Thus it is every day until a day comes when he has no food, no drink, no work and nothing at all.

What makes me think such thoughts? Since the day I emerged from my mother's womb, has it ever happened that I had so many? I am amazed by researches whose every minute is filled with thoughts; what use to us are thoughts? Not only are they a waste of time, they also divert your mind from the essential thing. Just as I, for example, by being so absorbed with my thoughts, forgot about the garment. While you are not hungry, the world says: Don't eat. While I, on the contrary, say: anticipate hunger with food. Because if you eat because you are hungry you can't appreciate fully the taste of the food. Now let us pour a small glass before starting the meal, so that we don't begin eating because we are famished. There is a great advantage in strong wine; it lessens the hunger yet increases the appetite.

The tailor went to a box of bottles in a corner. He found the box but not the key, as it was in his clothes while he was working. What's this? thought the surprised tailor to himself. Have I sat working in the Sabbath clothes in which I went to the minister? Now, my dear friend, let's take off those clothes and wear something else, otherwise tomorrow when you need respectable clothes, you'll find them creased. How will you be able to present yourself to the minister increased clothes?

He took off the Sabbath garb, hung it on a nail, put on his work clothes and took the key to the box. His wife's voice was heard saying: "Yisrael, come and wash your hands for your meal." The tailor smiled and said in an affectionate manner: This bad woman feels that I want to pour myself a glass of strong wine and has called me to eat. I know that she hasn't yet set the table nor served the food. It's right that I teach her a lesson and that I drink first and let her wait, so that she knows that she cannot make a laughing stock of me. And just in case she did lay the table and has served the main dish, I shall set aside the wine and go to the kitchen. If the table is laid that will be all for the good, and if not I will take my revenge by drinking a double quantity.

He went to the kitchen and found the table laid, but not yet with the food. His wife had already brought out the pot from the oven and as she stirred it the fragrance arose. The tailor went next to the pitcher of water, rinsed his hands and made the appropriate blessing. Sitting down, he cut a slice of bread and made the blessing, dipping the slice into the salt, eating it and declaring: "I'd like to know what my dearest has cooked for me. Tasty morsels for kings she has certainly not prepared, nor has she stirred herself to make my favorite dish."

Said his wife: "What, for example, are your favorite foods?"

Said he to her: "It seems to me that it's about time you knew."

His wife humbled herself before him and said: "How could I know? A man enters the world of ministers where he smells the fragrance of good foods that I am incapable of preparing."

Said he: "Am I to be suspected of lusting after the tables of ministers? It is enough for a person like me whatever my mistress cooks for me."

Said she: "If that is so then behold the kashipani is all ready for you."

Said he: "You cooked kashipani for me but I didn't smell it."

Said she: "How insensitive is this man to smell; he cannot distinguish the fragrance of cooked kashipani. This comes from your use of tobacco, which destroys the sense of smell."

Said he: "And am I alone in my habit of inhaling the smell of tobacco? The whole world does it."

Said she: "I would do nothing to prevent you from inhaling the smell of tobacco; I merely pointed out the dire consequences. Now go and eat."

He took the spoon and said: "Yes I will, for I'm dying of hunger, but can one eat your food if it is boiling hot?"

Said she: "For this reason the Holy One Blessed be He, created the mouth so that a person might blow on his food."

Said he: "It's easy for you to speak, for you have nothing to do. Whereas I took a break in the middle of my work in order not to make you wait, while you sit me down and talk philosophy!"

His wife answered him thus: "While you've been talking the food has cooled."

Again he stuck his spoon in the pot and, as it reached his mouth, he pointed it towards his wife with an angry look and said: "You say cool and I say freezing."

Said his wife: "Wait and I shall warm it."

Said he to her: "And what shall I do in the meantime—sing hymns? I can see that it was decreed that I should not enjoy a hot meal."

Said his wife: "Eat a small amount and I will add to it from what is on the oven." Again he inserted his spoon and ate rapidly, in order to leave more space in the pot.

His wife said: "Easy, easy. Before you begin, the pot is already empty. I'll fill your plate now, on condition that you don't gulp your food."

After two full plates of kashipani, his belly began to expand. He took a pinch of salt and placed it on his tongue, took a piece of bread and kneaded it. A doubt came to him: Did he or did he not say the grace after meals? He said to himself: if you ask me what food you ate, I could tell you exactly. If you asked me whether or not I said grace I don't know what I'd say. What should be done now—to recite grace or not? If I do, and I had already done so, I would have made an unnecessary blessing, and if I don't say the blessing—but how could a Jew fill his stomach and not say the grace after his meal? He decided to ask his wife whether she heard him say grace. His eyes began to shut sleepily. He rubbed his eyes and thought to himself: if I drank a glass of brandy I'd blame the glass, or if I hadn't drunk I wouldn't be falling asleep, since strong drink opens the guts and stays in the stomach. Wonder of wonders—that both brandy and bread are made from grain: you eat too much bread and your limbs feel heavy, you drink strong brandy and your limbs feel heavy. But this heaviness is not because of the drink, this drowsiness comes from... what did I want to say? My mind is fatigued from too many thoughts. Nevertheless this thought that I just had, I'll pursue to the end, or perhaps I'll leave it till tomorrow and return to the garment.

He lifted his head and was surprised that he had spent time at the dining table when he should have been doing his work. He heard the noise of running water and realized that his wife was washing the dishes, showing that little time had elapsed since he caught himself napping.

Meantime he again put his head on the table and drowsed until his wife awoke him and brought him to bed.

After an hour or so he awoke. He saw where he was. He said to himself: what a way to start! I went to sleep without saying Shema and stood up after my meal not knowing whether or not I'd recited grace. And what about the garment? In any case, now is not the time for work. I will thus sleep and gather my strength for the work tomorrow. But I need to wash my hands and recite Shema. How amazed I am by those righteous ones who rise every night to mourn for the destruction of Jerusalem. Still, if they are righteous, why is Jerusalem still rubble—for the Holy One blessed be He loves the prayers of the righteous and does their will. Again I dozed off, or perhaps I'm still awake. While analyzing whether or not he was awake or asleep, sleep overcame him and he fell into a deep slumber.

In the morning he went to the synagogue. His prayers did not come easy to him, because of his wandering thoughts, and because of the prayer leader who was in a rush and swallowed his words. The tailor's thoughts were about nothing in particular and not worth dwelling upon, but still they disturbed him. In truth, even righteous individuals struggle with their thoughts but, precisely because they are righteous, God has pity on them and saves them, which is not the case of a simple tailor when the Holy One blessed be He appears to turn His eye from him.

The tailor stood in prayer and thought: Now that I'm free from the whips of the minister's servants, if I wish I can raise my voice, and if I wish, I can pray quietly, but is my prayer a prayer? Even a minor servant of the minister holds a greater fear for me than I have for the Holy One blessed be He. It would appear that the bigger something is, the smaller the fear. This I saw yesterday: I was more afraid of the minister's servants than of the minister himself. The tailor was suddenly fearful of these thoughts which were certainly heretic.

He enfolded himself in his tallit and tightened the straps of his tefilin until they hurt. But neither the bodily pain nor hiding his face in the talit helped, and were as nothing compared to his alien thoughts.

He returned to his prayer and meditated: Oh, that I would finish my prayer and be free of such thoughts! How strange. When I'm working no such thoughts come to me. Yet here, in a holy place, a person has to be free of such thoughts—how much more so when he is wrapped in his talit and tefillin, and has his prayer book in his hand. However, He who gives thoughts to my heart, makes within me all that He desires. When did I fall under this spell? From when I left the minister in order to mend the garment. Yet, the garment I have still to mend. Why have I not mended it?—again because of thoughts—at first about the mending, and then, regrets over my not doing anything. Man's thoughts are many, but the most important thought he never reaches.

Now, the service is ending and the mourners are reciting the mourner's *kaddish* after the concluding prayer. Yet it is as if I hadn't started praying. The mouth moves, but if you asked me whether or not I had prayed, I couldn't say yes. It's just like yesterday with the grace after meals. Now all I have to do is take off my talit and tefilin and return to my house and my work. That which I didn't complete during the morning prayers I shall finish at the afternoon prayers. The Holy One Blessed Be He did righteously with His creatures in not sending them His servants after each prayer to examine how good it was.

Who knows where his thoughts would have reached if his neighbor had not stopped him to say that it was time to tell the head of the Craftsmen's Guild to resign. It was a similar story with the senior beadle at the Tailor's Synagogue, except that the former could be thrown out immediately, while for the latter it was necessary to wait till Simḥat Torah. Either way there is a need to begin to deal with it. The tailor was drawn by his companion and amazed that he knew how to connect one thing with another until a third thing emerged. Between this one talking and that one listening they left the synagogue. It was a pleasant day. It's possible that the day before was also pleasant but yesterday he had been involved in his work and had not noticed whether or not it was pleasant. Among other things the tailor felt a certain weakness in his heart. He wasn't hungry. Nevertheless, a taste of something would be the right thing at the right time. Thus it was here that he came upon an inn.

They found a number of people there. This surprised the tailor. The sun had not yet wiped its eye from sleep and people were already sitting in an inn. Was there nothing for them to do? But, by the same token I could ask myself—what am I doing here so early in the morning? Still, my own behavior I can explain; for them there is clearly no excuse.

What are they drinking? From the shape of their glasses they're downing mead. He turned to his neighbor and asked: "What is your opinion of this drink?" His neighbor said to him: "If you want mead, let it be mead. No one need insist on a certain food or drink, whereas regarding this good-for-nothing—the beadle of the Craftsmen's Guild—who holds the needle and pricks with it—it is necessary to remain obstinate until he is ejected. I don't wish him harm—he should live as long as he wishes, even a million years—as long as he gives up his position for someone more suitable. As for mead, it's necessary to examine at the outset which to choose, one which is sweet or one which is sharp. To me both are fine, except that the sweet one needs to be supplemented by onion and pepper-flavored crackers, and the sharp variety with honey droplets. Either way the choice is in your hands. What's good for you is good for me."

The tailor thought to himself: see, he says the choice is in my hands. If it were up to me I'd sit at home and mend the minister's garment. Since he reminded himself of the garment and his desire to mend it, he became morose. His companion looked at him and asked: "Why are you sad?" He replied: "Who said I'm sad? I'm not sad." He said to him: "I have a good sense of smell and I can smell your sadness. Still, whether or not you're sad, let's have a toast. To life, my friend! To life! May it be His will that we be joyful. Just as it says: 'And you shall surely be joyful.' A Jew has to be joyful, both because he's a Jew, and also because he's not a non-Jew, and also the opposite, which is to say because he's not a non-Jew and because he's a Jew. 'Who can compare with your people, Israel?' See, my friend, even after a thimbleful I'm already happy. Is it because of the drink that I'm joyful? No, I'm happy because of the essential thing, which is sitting together. Now my friend—my beloved—let's return to the main item, which is the reason we came here. So what then is your opinion? I can see that your ears are in another place. Where did you leave them? By the way, what's with the garment that the minister left with you? The minister has many garments, and if he's short of one he won't go naked. You're sad again. To life! To life! To life!"

Two friends mulling over public events. Sometimes it seemed to the tailor that he was wasting his time, and sometimes he felt that he was engaged in something that could not be bettered. In the meantime, his sadness did not leave him, in the way of people who have it within their grasp to do something and don't do it, and most of the day had passed. When the tailor stood up to go to his house, he was ashamed to find himself in the road with his talit and tefilin under his arm—for what reason, people would ask. But to leave his talit and tefilin in the inn would be the way of drunkards, who leave them there as a pledge. When the tailor left the inn, it was already time for afternoon prayers. He thought about returning to the synagogue and joining the *minyan* at the afternoon service, and to make up for what he had missed in the morning prayers. Another idea came to him, to return home and pray by himself, since people can sometimes focus their prayers precisely because they pray alone, while in the synagogue people talk and confuse a person in his prayer.

He walked in the direction of his house, thinking to himself, I shall recite the afternoon and evening prayers and then take the garment to mend. As he continued on his way, his heart began to worry him— how he had wasted a day's work. It was true that he had engaged in work for the public good, but his heart was not satisfied. He was amazed—he had busied himself with a religious duty and should by rights have been happy, but in the end he was filled with grievances. So absorbed was he that he became confused and strayed from his path.

In the meantime the sun had set and the time for the afternoon prayer had passed. He stood where he was and prayed, filled with all sorts of thoughts—among them calculations regarding money—how much had he spent on mead and onion and pepper-flavored crackers? These thoughts began to disturb his prayer since he felt that the inn-keeper had made a mistake and had taken more than his due.

He stood and thought about how many drinks he and his companion had drunk and how many crackers they had eaten. He realized that the innkeeper had indeed been at fault, but by making an error, not in his own favor but in favor of his guests. The tailor was upset that he had suspected the man, but there was some satisfaction in his sorrow. Yet, when he felt the joy at the profit he had made unjustifiedly he was again saddened. In order not to yield to temptation he made up his mind to return to the inn-keeper and pay him the excess. He quickened his prayers, swallowing a number of words, to the point where the evil inclination was unable to come and talk him into reaping a benefit from his ill-gotten gain.

He had in the meantime prayed the afternoon service, when it was quite definitely night. He glanced at the moon and the stars that were preparing to come out. Couldn't they wait? Couldn't they stay in the firmament, even for a short while longer? On a fast day when everyone yearned for them, they stayed put until the soul expired, while today when you didn't need them, they were suddenly hasty.

In order to placate the Creator the tailor thought of commencing the evening prayer immediately and to mend whatever went awry in his afternoon prayers, just as he had asked beforehand to make up in the afternoon prayer what he had skimped in the morning prayer.

He remembered his wife, who had been waiting for him since breakfast, and now it was time for supper. Uprooting himself he went to his house.

He reached his house. His wife saw him and greeted him with a sour look and began to scold him with harsh words, that because of him her face was black from standing next to the oven so that the food did not grow cold. He realized that she was right. His evil inclination however would not relent. He said to her: "You sit in your house like a real madam and everything is given to you while, in order to support you, I wander around like a stupid dog. And when I return home tired, worn out and depressed, you put on a show! You want to know where I was?" And immediately he began to invent lies in order to justify himself until he worked himself into a state and entered his room.

He saw the garment and began to scream: "You caused all the troubles that have befallen me!" His anger got the better of him and he threw the garment to the ground. Dust fell on the garment and it became dirty.

On the following day, he remembered what he had done. He picked up the garment, shook it and brushed it. As he was busying himself with the garment, he crossed in front of the window, where one of the minister's servants was passing. The tailor had a shock and was gripped by fear. He took the garment and hid it without looking where he hid it, concerned only to remove it from the sight of the minister's servant. By hiding it and not looking where he hid it, no improvement was made to the garment and the dirt on it was left uncleaned.

After the servant left, the tailor took out the garment and again cleansed it and shook it until he forgot that it was lunchtime. His wife came and said to him: "Go and wash your hands and eat!" But he didn't listen. Again she spoke to him and he didn't listen. She went and brought his food to his work room. He sat and ate, with his eyes on the garment. He didn't pay attention to his food or see how good it was, how much fat was in it, since his wife had given him all the meat he had not eaten the day before and added to it today's portion, which she made fat and good.

While he was eating, a drop of sauce fell on to the garment. The tailor jumped as though he had been pricked by a needle. The table shook and the entire plate spilt. And where did it spill? On the minister's garment! The tailor slapped himself in the face, hit his head against the wall and cried: "Woe is me! Prepare me a grave and shrouds!" His wife heard and came running. She tried to calm him down and said: "Everything is not yet lost. I'll take the garment to the river and wash it."

The tailor cried in his anger: "Who asked you? If it's still washable, I'll clean it myself. Bring me soap and I'll go to the river."

The tailor took the garment and went to the river. He laundered the garment in pure water and left it on the river bank to dry, saying to himself: It is good that the minister did not set me a time. The garment will dry and I shall return with it to my house and take an iron and iron it extremely carefully.

A fish came and swallowed the garment. The tailor jumped into the water and chased after the fish. He pursued him. The fish waited in the water and then vanished. Now, no one could ask about its whereabouts, because it is the nature of fish not to speak.

As long as he was not far out in the river the tailor was able to keep above the waves, but as he went further, the waves overcame him. Moreover, he got tangled in the water weeds. In the water he struggled hard, either to save himself or the garment. In the meantime, clumps of weed surrounded him. Some grasped him and others pricked him. As he pulled himself away from the weeds so the waves slapped his head. He was overcome by panic. One thing remained stubbornly inside his head—that the minister had given him a garment and it was lost. This knowledge sustained him, but not for long. On the contrary. On dry land one's strength is not great, how much less so then, in the midst of a rushing river with strong and powerful waves—many and cold—which cut his old flesh like a knife.

Due to his great grief he forgot about the garment, and something else began to engage him—this was the calculation that he had made concerning the innkeeper, during his afternoon prayers, when he realized that he owed him money. Eventually he lost his clarity, and lost all his strength. He had plunged deep into the mighty waters and found no way for his hands and feet to exit. After many days the water vomited him out on to the dry land. After many days his body was found. They wrapped him in his shrouds and brought him to his grave.

What he found in his grave we don't know, but it's possible to guess that a lot of good he didn't find. It's true that the Holy One blessed be He is compassionate, but his servants who are destructive angels are evil, hard, bitter and violent—in the upper world, as in the lower.

As regards the garment which the tailor did not finish, and moreover made dirty, and even lost—the minister has many garments and is able to give up one, whereas the tailor who lost the garment which was made from the cloth of the looms of the minister's workshop—what will he answer, and what will he say when they ask him, "Where is the garment?"

– *Translated by Mordechai and Penina Beck*

The Father of the Ox

THERE IS A SPOT IN JERUSALEM which is known by the Arabic name of Abu-Tor, which means "the father of the ox." And the spot goes by this name on account of something that happened there once upon a time. If you like, I shall tell you the story.

Once upon a time there was an old man in Jerusalem. An old, old man he was, yet as innocent as a child. Now this old man had neither child nor wife, but he had a little house and he had a field and he had an ox. This ox had ample strength and a tender heart. He felt sorry for his owner and used to serve him like a slave serves his master. He would plough his field for him and fetch him up water from the spring; and when it was necessary the old man would hang a basket with money round his neck and would tell him, go to the market and fetch me my food. And the old man wanted for nothing with him. I can only hope that we, too, may never lack for anything either in this world or the world to come. And the neighbors used to call the old man Abu-Tor, or Father of the Ox, all because of the ox he had.

Now one day enemies came to town. When enemies come to town, they do not come peacefully but in order to rob and pillage and kill. So they robbed and looted and they killed. All those who were not killed ran away, and those who did not manage to run away went and hid themselves. Our old man also went and hid himself in a cave.

The ox came and stood at the cave-mouth and lowed. Abu-Tor put his hand out of the cave and stroked his ox's horn and whispered to him, be quiet, my child, be quiet, for if the enemies hear you, they'll come and kill us both. But the ox went on lowing and stayed where he was. Do you want to tell me something? said Abu-Tor to him. The ox lowed again. One lowed and the other groaned, but neither could understand what the other was saying; like the proverb they have in Jerusalem, the ox has a long tongue but can't get a word out. So Abu-Tor whispered again, What do you want, my child? Thereupon the ox lay down in front of him, and in his own fashion indicated what his mouth couldn't say. Abu-Tor began to pull his thoughts together and use his wits and think. One thought leads to another, and between unaware and well-aware the thoughts sometimes lead to the truth at last. Abu-Tor finally understood what his ox wanted and said to him, maybe you have found me a better place than this cave, my son, and you want to hide me there. The ox nodded with his horns and stretched out his head. Then Abu-Tor knew that the ox was lying there so that he should get on its back, and ride away with him to some spot where he could hide himself properly from the sword of the foe.

The old man gathered his bones together with his flesh and crawled out of the cave and climbed up and rode off on the ox's back. Once he was up there, the ox dashed off with him to the field of battle. When the old man saw the soldiers at their work, his soul simply dropped away from him. But the ox looked at him like a friend looking at a friend and clicked his tongue. If we were to translate this to human speech, it would mean, my soul for yours, my master, if I don't aim at your well-being. And right away the ox began goring with his horns, and went on goring till he had killed quite a few of the enemy. Those he didn't kill he wounded; and those he didn't wound began to shiver and shake and quiver and quake and ran away for all they were worth. Once they ran away, they didn't come back any more.

When the old man saw all that the ox had done to the enemy, his soul returned. He raised his head and stretched his neck and cried, brethren, my brethren and townsfolk, come out of your hiding places and see the victory that God has wrought upon our foes for us. The townsfolk heard this and came out of their hiding places, out of the dens and the fens, the cellars and the attics tall, and the holes in the wall, and every kind of wary spot, while the breath in them was still fresh and hot.

When they saw what a great victory Abu-Tor and his ox had achieved for them, they rejoiced very much indeed. And I only hope that we too may soon rejoice like them when the Holy One, blessed be He, places our enemies in our hands. They brought bundles of myrtle to wreathe the horns of the ox and went ahead of him with flutes and dancing and singing, until they had conducted him and the old man back to their home. And they called the spot "Abu-Tor," after the old man and his ox. And the place is still there, and so is its name.

2

Now Abu-Tor had a certain neighbor, such a neighbor as does not deserve to come up among decent folk. One day he married a fresh wife, in addition to those he already had. He invited all his friends and prepared them a feast. He slaughtered a sheep and roasted meat for them. When there are plenty of eaters the meat wastes away almost without being noticed. One takes a double portion and eats for all he is worth, the others do exactly the same, and the meat vanishes between hand and mouth. So he went out and slaughtered them another sheep and yet another. They sat eating like that for all the seven days of the marriage feast. One sheep followed another, and the third followed the second, and what happened to the sheep happened to all the other meat producers. But though they spent a long time over the eating, we shall make a long story short. In brief, he went on slaughtering and slaughtering and slaughtering. He had already slaughtered a whole flock of sheep on their account, nor did he spare his knife from the various other kinds of beasts which admit to being eaten. There was no ram or ewe or goat which he did not slaughter, yet the bellies of the guests were still lacking.

When the host saw that they were still craving meat, he said to himself, I shall go and see whether I can find some creature alive in the cowshed for me to slaughter for them. As he went, he came across the ox. He took him by the horns. The ox innocently supposed, this neighbor of mine wants to make a fine impression on his guests through me, because I saved him and the whole city from death. I shall not display any false modesty about myself, but I'll go with him. But this neighbor of ours was thinking, this fleshy brute here can fill the throats and bellies of the gluttons who have gathered against me. In brief, one pulled the other by the horns and the other let himself be pulled and went along. The ox thought to himself, these human creatures are pleasant folk. When a man has a celebration in his home he promptly remembers those who love him and brings them to take a leading part in his pleasure, for he did not realize that he was merely being led as an ox to the slaughter. While our nameless neighbor did not think about anything, his heart throbbed and his hands were hot. Why make a long story of it? Before ever they reached the place of the feast, the man stopped and did his foul deed.

Next morning, Abu-Tor got up early. He rose and took his basket and wanted to hang it round the neck of his ox, as he always did when he sent it to market to fetch him food; for he had not been invited to that wedding feast I was telling you about, and he was hungry. He looked for his ox but could not find it. He stood and called, ox, ox, but there was no reply. He lowed like a cow, but there was no reply. He looked here once and there twice and elsewhere seven times, then he looked here seven times and there once and elsewhere twice. But, just as the ox swallows the grass of the field, so the field had swallowed all trace of the ox. So he went around calling out, have you seen my ox? But there was nobody who could tell him anything. Then he went back home and stretched himself out on his straw mattress, with grief groaning in his heart; and every now and then he stood up and went out to look for his loss. But what the belly has devoured you will never find again in the land of the living.

Two or three days passed, and then Abu-Tor went out to seek his lost ox once again. As he walked along he came to a huge pile of rubbish. He looked and saw two horns whose points were just sticking out of the rubbish, and recognized that they were the horns of his ox. So he jumped on top of the pile and began tugging away until he got them out of the rubbish. Then he began peering and gazing and staring and lamenting and weeping, ox of mine, where did you go, your horns, oh your horns, to whom did you show? The horns wherewith your people did gore are now flung as though worthless upon the floor. Arise now, awake and put on your horns, for then God will help you laugh all foes to scorn. And so the old man wept and moaned and implored the Merciful One to have mercy and let the ox restore his horns to his head.

Meanwhile the day grew dark, and the world as well. Abu-Tor looked in the gloom at each severed horn and kept on thinking and wondering, why did those horns see fit to part from their possessor? He did not know that it was the ox which had parted from them, leaving behind nothing more than those horns. At last Abu-Tor rose and went back home and lay himself down on his bed. His eyes closed and he fell asleep.

Suddenly he started up from his slumber, because he heard a sound of howling. And so it was one night and a second night and a third night, until seven nights were passed.

3

Now Abu-Tor had a Jewish friend and comrade. He went to him and told him how night after night for seven nights past he had heard a howling. And the Jew said to him, I am not astonished the way that you are. You are astonished because of that howling sound; but I am not astonished, because these are the nights when we say our *Seliḥot,* our midnight penitential prayers before our New Year; and then we blow on the ram's horn. But what does astonish me is that you say this howling has gone on without interruption for seven full nights. Yet there cannot be seven days without a Sabbath among them, and on the Sabbath we don't blow the ram's horn.

What do you advise me to do? said Abu-Tor to the Jew. What do I know? answered he. But here among us we have a certain sage, Doxistus the Scribe by name, who is not permitted to practice his craft because he used to write charms made up of Bible verses in order to cure sick people. Let us go to him because he can achieve many things. Maybe he will see his way to tell you something. So Abu-Tor took the horns of his ox, and together with his Jewish comrade paid a visit to Doxistus the Scribe.

Doxistus put one horn to his mouth and a howling sound was heard. He did the same with the other, and a howling sound was heard. Then Doxistus said to Abu-Tor, did you hear the howling? I heard it, said he. They slaughtered me, they slaughtered me, is what the horns are moaning and howling, said Doxistus. Then the scales fell from Abu-Tor's eyes and he said, my neighbor so-and-so married a fresh wife and invited ever so many guests. Maybe he slaughtered my ox for them, in order to feed his flesh to his guests. What do you think, oh wise Doxistus? Tell me.

Doxistus shook the tufts of his beard, nodding, and said to him, I am of your mind, Abu-Tor. And may all Israel and I myself among them merit speedily and soon to enjoy the flesh of the Wild Ox Behemoth at the great feast which the Holy One will at some future time make for those who fear Him, as surely as those ill-willed ones enjoyed the flesh of your ox. At this, Abu-Tor beat his head against the wall and slapped his face and head with his two hands and began to cry out, woe is me, woe is me, that worthless scoundrel of a godless one, that demon of scoundrels, he slaughtered, alas he slaughtered my ox and with his flesh he fed those accursed sons of the accursed. I swear by my ox that, ere I depart from this world, I shall exact full vengeance of that whore-son lecher.

But Abu-Tor did not know what he should do or what vengeance he should take, for the other was a brawling evil man of violence, while he himself was old and weak. In the meantime one day passed and two days, and then three days and four days; and thought has its own term just like a worm, crawling a long pace and slow, but not telling him what he had to do.

A few days later, Abu-Tor went and stood at the door of his house. Another neighbor of his passed by and saw that his face was fallen and his mood was low and his knees were trembling, and he seemed just like a man who is busy mourning. You are sad, said he, has any mishap befallen you, God forbid? My ox has vanished, answered Abu-Tor. Your ox has vanished, yet you do not search for it? said the neighbor. I have been everywhere, said Abu-Tor, but I have not found it. Not found it, you say, what is the meaning of not found it? How can I find it, said Abu-Tor, when it is dead. Dead? asked the neighbor. What manner of death did he die? What manner of death? replied Abu-Tor. A dog came and ripped him open. And once again Abu-Tor began lamenting and weeping, my ox, most staid, my life and aid, my strength and my exalted horn, what is my sin for which you are torn, that you should be food for the son of a cur, and I must be left as empty as air!

The neighbor thought his own thoughts and parted from the old man. Then he met the man who had slaughtered the ox and said to him, it seems to me that Abu-Tor must be out of his mind. Why? Because he said that some dog must have ripped open his ox. Have you ever seen a dog ripping an ox open and killing it? When the one who had slaughtered the ox heard this, he thought, if Abu-Tor says that a dog has ripped his ox open, that means he knows who slaughtered it. His heart fell into his slippers and he began to fear for his own self. He began to think a little this way and a little that way, what shall I do for the old man and how can I appease him? Then he stood up and went to pay him a respectful visit and show him honor.

4

So the man sat with Abu-Tor, conversing like one neighbor with another; such as, here is the father of so-and-so may his mother bury him, who is a such-and-such, and there is this woman may devils suckle her breasts, who is a this-and-that; and all about pots which sound *knock knock* even when they have no food in them, and about the turban of Quarrel, the constable, who has got the leprosy, and about the slippers of Preacher, the mufti, which have gone down to hell with their owner. In this way the man sat talking about one thing and another, the way a good neighbor converses with his neighbor. Finally he stopped all that talk and said, it seems to me that we don't see your ox about. You don't see him? said Abu-Tor. Where is he? said the other. He has gone off to wed him a wife, said Abu-Tor. The other looked at him smoothly with his eyes and asked him, for weal or woe? For woe, said he. And who is the woman? said the neighbor. Your daughter, answered Abu-Tor. Then the neighbor knew that Abu-Tor intended harm to his daughter. And he was fonder of this daughter than of all his other children, because her mother had conceived her in a field of crocus, and so they called the girl Crocus.

Now he said to Abu-Tor, permit me to ask you a question, why my daughter when he could wed a cow, a handsome cow of good stock? And if that is not enough for him, I shall give him two cows, two handsome healthy cows which have never borne the yoke. You smile at me, old man. It seems to me that I am saying good and proper things to you. Then Abu-Tor answered, now consider. You yourself do not possess even a single horn, yet do not rest satisfied with one wife but have taken a third and a fourth. So it simply stands to reason that my ox who has two horns will not rest satisfied with two wives. Then the slaughterer of the ox said to Abu-Tor, the father of the ox, what is your opinion, neighbor? If I give him three cows or four or even five, will he let my daughter be? And is your daughter such a trifle in your eyes, said Abu-Tor, that you want to buy her off with only five cows?

Why prolong the agony? Before they left one another, the neighbor had given Abu-Tor seven fat cows with seven whole calves, the smallest of which was worth at least as much as his daughter Crocus. But as Abu-Tor was not yet satisfied, his neighbor added so much land and so many fields. If you suppose that he gave them merely for grazing, you are wrong; for he gave them to him in perpetuity, meaning for good and all.

That is the tale of Abu-Tor and his ox so fine, on whose flesh and whose skin a many did dine, leaving nothing thereof save his horns that day, may the Lord raise our own horn for ever and aye.

Ascents and Descents

"The Blessed Holy One sits and fashions ladders"
(Midrash)

I

REB ḤANNAN ABBA WAS A VERY RICH MAN. He had a shop selling bolts of wool, silk, velvet, and satin, from which he made a fine living. He and his wife dealt with the merchandise, and the Holy One would bless all their efforts with success.

Outwardly, the shop was nothing to look at. The building was as unimpressive as were its appurtenances. There was not even a sign or a shingle at the entrance. All the unknowns could put up fancy signs with their names on them, but Reb Ḥannan Abba would stick with tradition. If it had been ordained in heaven that customers should find their way to him, they would get there on their own. A name wouldn't matter. What are we and what are our lives that we should be called by names in this world? The earth is the Lord's, and the fullness thereof. The shop itself too—the building was not his, but rather rented from others. Had Reb Ḥannan Abba wanted, he could have built himself a grand hall. But he said to himself, "No, let a Jew get rent for his shop!"

In short, the business was on an even keel. The shop was filled with merchandise and customers and clerks. Twice a year, Reb Ḥannan Abba would travel to the fair, and upon his return he would be followed by many wagons full of abundant merchandise, aside from what arrived in the interim, each type of merchandise in its season.

II

Once, Reb Ḥannan Abba went off to the Leshkowitz fair. It was a summer day, and Reb Ḥannan Abba set out with a happy heart and a joyful countenance and a wallet filled and brimming. The way was filled with travelers, some in coaches and some on horseback, and twice as many afoot as there were people who made the Exodus from Egypt. Reb Ḥannan Abba sat in a bounding carriage, its interior covered in cloth, with his bookkeeper and two advisors seated to either side of him, a book open in front of him, and a snuffbox resting on his lap, for him to sniff and to bring others enjoyment from its aroma. The advisors sat and chatted about matters of merchandise and merchants, about cities and fairs and the changing times—that is, how things are different now from the way they once were, when once a person could make a fortune worthy of Koraḥ and scoop up gold nuggets effortlessly. And the bookkeeper sat and listened in amazement at the good old days. Reb Ḥannan Abba gave a heartfelt sigh that contained a sort of directive to the blessed Lord, like that of a person who cites the verse "May the Lord be blessed each day." Today too, the blessed Lord had not allowed His steadfast beneficence toward him to flag. "If only I can prove to be so worthy before Him all my days."

III

Evidently he was not so worthy. At a certain point he exited the carriage to see to his bodily needs. To be discreet, the carriage went some distance ahead and waited for him. When he came back and stepped up into the carriage, he said to them, "Go!" and off they went. And since they had been delayed a bit, they moved at a hurried pace. He arranged his cushion beneath him and took a pinch of tobacco to sniff and set about to open a book. Suddenly he felt in his breast pocket.—The money was not there. His face went white, trembling took hold of his bones, and with all of his strength he managed not to cry out in distress. Nevertheless, he did not return to the place where he had lost his money. He knew that in a place where there are passersby, it would be impossible for him to find it, especially given that the passersby were many and his purse was large. And so that no one could sense what had befallen him, he pretended that nothing at all had happened. For if word got out that he had lost his money, his good name would be lost, and he would lose his credibility with the vendors. So obviously he did not talk about what happened. And when he got to the fair he turned away from all the merchandise. He said, "These are not the sort of goods I'm looking for." The experts sidled up to him and whispered in his ear, "Reb Ḥannan Abba, such merchandise doesn't come along but once in a jubilee. Is this wool? This is silk. *Silk*! Top quality." He touched it with his fingertips and at once let it fall from his grasp. "These are not the goods I'm looking for." In that fashion he rejected each and every bit of merchandise. For his purse was empty; there was no money in it. They stayed a few days until it was time to go back. When departure time arrived, he settled accounts properly with his advisors. Back home, in his own town, he would pay them for their efforts or their time. "With God's help, if not Leshkowitz then Oniph, and if not Oniph then Leipzig. Leshkowitz is not lacking anything, God forbid, but what I was looking for I didn't find, and what I did find I didn't like. A person makes plans, but for now, thank God, I have goods in my store, and the Leipzig fair is not far off. If I'm not mistaken, the fair will take place this year during the month of Shevat, as it appears in the synagogue calendar," said Reb Ḥannan Abba in jest, as if the makers of synagogue calendars needed to know about fairs. "Perhaps the days will pass and we will not have sold our merchandise." In short, Reb Ḥannan Abba did not buy anything but what the major vendors forced on him against his will. They said, "Reb Ḥannan Abba comes all the way to Leshkowitz and leaves with no merchandise?" They loaded him with bolts of wool, silk, velvet, and satin so that he wouldn't forget to come back to their stores the following year. "Other shopkeepers could make do with this merchandise for a few years, but for a merchant like Reb Ḥannan Abba this is just the sash on the robe." The carriage drivers hitched up the horses, arranged the carriages, and Reb Ḥannan Abba headed home with his people. The carriages were light, but his heart was heavy.

IV

On the road, when he arrived at the place where he had lost his money, Reb Ḥannan Abba said to himself: "I'll go and see the place where I lost my money." He alighted from the wagon and told the driver to move on.

When Reb Ḥannan Abba arrived at that spot, he saw his purse lying before him, and all of his money was there. No one had touched the money. Reb Ḥannan Abba picked up the purse, put it in his pocket, and went back into the coach. From this point on, he spoke to no one. Instead, he sat and buried his face in a book. The others in his entourage asked him: "What's going on, Reb Ḥannan Abba?" Reb Ḥannan Abba stared at them with tears in his eyes. He was speechless.

In the midst of his weeping, Reb Ḥannan Abba fell asleep, and he dreamed a strange dream. It seemed to him that it took place on a Friday afternoon. His wife handed him his clean white garments to take with him to the bathhouse, to bathe and dress for the Sabbath. He took the garments and entered the *kloyz* to order some liquor from the *shamash*. He left his shirt with him, and he went wherever he went. When he returned, they said to him: your shirt has been stolen, and the thief has been caught! He went to him and found that he was sprawled out, his limbs spread-eagled. His skin was scorched, slippery as an eel and coated with oil. It seemed as though his head were missing. Reb Ḥannan Abba asked: "What's this?" They answered him: "They threw the thief into a vat of boiling oil and he got burned." Reb Ḥannan Abba enjoyed hearing this but was distressed. He enjoyed the fact that they had captured the thief and punished him appropriately, but he was distressed that he took pleasure in such a violent act. While he was still standing there, someone came in and cried: *Kolibris!*

Reb Ḥannan Abba woke up. He looked about him to see whether all of his possessions were in their proper places, washed his hands and got up. Several times that day he said to himself: "You saw a good dream, you saw a good dream." In fact, he had seen a kind of fish in his dream, and just as with the fish in the sea the water covers them and the Evil Eye has no power over them, so too, he realized: "The Evil Eye has no power over me either." And he understood the meaning of "*kolibris*," for he had seen among the novelties of the fair a kind of small colorful bird called a *kolibri*—a hummingbird.

V

When they arrived home, his wife and the whole household came out to greet him. They hugged him and kissed him, and they asked how he was doing and what he had done at the fair. Had he found nice lodgings there, and a hot meal each day, and had he purchased a large volume of goods, and where had he made his purchases, and had such-and-such a dealer come with all his wares, and had a particular thief been apprehended and punished? And all the while, they cast their eyes about to see what gifts he had brought back from the fair. Reb Ḥannan Abba stood there speechless. He did not hear their questions, and he obviously gave no answers.

He suddenly realized that he had brought no gifts from the fair. He whispered to the bookkeeper, asking him to go and buy some. He said to him, "I am confident that you know what they're hoping for." And once the bookkeeper had permission to make purchases, he didn't rest until he had found the very best. He was sure that he was doing his master's bidding. May God grant long life and health, and an appropriate occasion for donning fine accoutrements would certainly not be lacking.

VI

And, thank God, everyone was healthy and well. And were it not for the machinations of the serpent, they would all have lived long lives, all the way to the coming of Messiah. But come see: from the day that Reb Ḥannan Abba returned home, it was as though there was an evil eye upon everything he did. The merchandise that had been in his shop sold quite well, actually, and what the dealers at Leshkowitz had heaped on him also did not go without buyers. Buyers were not in short supply. If only there was enough merchandise. The forgiving of debt was not common in those days, however, and if circumstances forced a Jewish shopkeeper into bankruptcy, he was not to be given any synagogue honors. And thus Jews were warned not to plunder their fellows' assets, except for a few corrupt folk who took merchandise on credit and afterward their children inherited the business and said: "Father was out of his mind, and his debts cannot be collected."

But other expenses put a dent in his assets. Reb Ḥannan Abba's wife was used to traveling to Hungary to wine and dine at the best spots. And his daughter-in-law would go with her. Jews did not yet make their way to the spa towns, but that custom began to spread among the people, and some women from wealthy families would go there. The older woman was satisfied with the delicacies Hungary offered, but her daughter-in-law, who wore a fancy hat even on Rosh Hashanah, was not satisfied with that, and she told her husband flat out, "If you don't allow me to travel to Franzensbad, I'm not going to immerse myself in the *mikveh*." What could he do? His father paid her travel expenses, and since a young woman should not travel alone, they said, "Let her mother-in-law go with her." In any case, the spa known as "Salvation Springs," is nicer than the Hungarian wineries and dineries. And what about the money? Reb Ḥannan Abba, thank God, had money to spend. As the saying goes, a rich women can afford to give birth even twice a year. They made travel garments, and they sewed marvelous clothes, and they prepared hats, and they bought jewelry, as was befitting at that time and place. Today's jewelry items are here today, and tomorrow they end up in the trash. At one time, a man would buy his wife a string of pearls and a silver pendant that she would wear on Shabbat and holidays all her life, and not only that, but she would bequeath them to her daughter, and that daughter to her own daughter. But what do people crave today? All sorts of loops and knots and the feathers of non-kosher birds—whatever is the latest fashion. It's a miracle that his daughter did not ask for such bizarre things.

VII

In truth, he was not particularly pleased with his daughter, either. She had a husband, and he was an ordained rabbi. You see, Reb Ḥannan Abba used to say, everything that the good Lord made in His world He made well. He had given him a son and a daughter, and at first he had expected his son to be a rabbi, but he had chosen a different path. And what he didn't succeed at with his son he got to set right with his daughter. He had married her off to wonderful young man ordained as a rabbi. That ordination had cost him money, with the usual scribes and attendants needing to be paid. And it would be best to set him up in a rabbinic position, or else he would wind up engaged in commerce, in which he had already begun to dabble. Matters of this world have an attraction, after all. But there are more rabbis than there are towns. It is a saying among the common folk, "If you want to get the rabbis settled, chop down the forests and build cities and towns." They asked around and found that there was a town by the name of Spinovky in which the position of rabbi was open. Open and not open, that is, because while there was no rabbi there, the last rabbi's widow laid claim to certain benefits, although she could be placated without much expense. When it comes to money, one can arrive at a compromise with a woman. During her husband's lifetime, how much had this poor woman ever received? He used to say, "If it weren't for the fact that I fast every Monday and Thursday, I would long ago have died of hunger."

However, this town had one rich man, and that rich man had a son-in-law, and that son-in-law was an ordained rabbi, and he began to issue rabbinic judgments even though his teacher cried out like a whooping crane, "Was it for issuing rabbinic judgments that I gave you ordination?! It was just to keep you working away at your studies!" The rich man thought of making him the head of a rabbinic court, like the case about which it said, "The jackal bears offspring and casts the obligation to feed them on the residents of the town?" But it was only the rich man who wanted this. Those who were dependent upon him said yes, and those who were not dependent on him said no. So what did he do? He went to the governor and paid him off. The governor dropped hints that the tests for army service were coming up. If they listened to him, all would be well and good, but if not, the whole town could expect to be taken into the army. A matter of life and death. They lowered their heads and said, "Let him be the rabbi until we can't stand him anymore. Do we really need his instructions anyway?"

But the people Israel are not bereft. That wealthy man had a brother-in-law, who was not a poor man either. The two detested each other. They were bitter enemies. From the time that they had begun to divide up their father-in-law's property, not a single day passed without strife. And he too was friendly with the government authorities. He went to the regional governor. The governor ordered the *mikveh* closed down. He said, "Let your rabbi come up with a dispensation to do without the *mikveh*." From Spinovky they sent a delegation to Reb Ḥannan Abba, telling him, "Reb Ḥannan Abba, it is a great mitzvah to rescue an entire community. If your son-in-law were to come spend one Shabbat with us, everyone would immediately start pursuing him." Their words entered his heart, and discord entered as well. And once it was in, it did not come out.

VIII

Reb Ḥannan Abba's daughter-in-law saw another world at Franzensbad. A person comes to Salvation Springs and he is not really ill since he is on a hiatus from his work and freed from worries, and the money for his expenses is already set aside, so of course he follows his heart, and even if he generally tends to pinch pennies, here he turns into a spendthrift. After all, it is for his health that he has come, so he needs to stuff his body. And the body, which is delighted from eating and drinking and bathing and oiling and other pleasures of life immediately takes on the view that all the world's pleasures are for oneself. At once, he is set upon by all sorts of cravings he had never before known. And if he arrives alone, once he sets foot someplace where no one knows him, the Evil Impulse claims him as its own.

Reb Ḥannan Abba's daughter-in-law did not, Heaven forfend, stumble into transgression, but life's luxuries did lead her astray. When she got home, her city had become too small for her, and everything she had seen at Franzensbad insinuated itself into her mind more and more. If she saw beautiful things, or if she saw a lovely dress, she craved them right away. One day she wanted silk and needlework for a dress, and the next, satin with ivory buttons for a coat. Her father-in-law was out of town, having gone off to Spinovky with her brother-in-law to deal with rabbinic affairs, and her husband was basking in her glow and telling her, "You have such good taste!" She sewed herself a new garment, made herself new shoes, put together a new hat, and she did not overlook her daughter: that baby girl had to stand every day like a mannequin one uses to examine all sorts of clothes. Having clothed herself in high fashion, her face flush from eating and drinking, she came and rendered judgment on her husband's clothes. These were as long as the length of our exile, and those were the color of the eyes of a mouse who had fallen into an oily dish. All of them should have been replaced back during Creation. Not long passed before there was no room for more clothes in her closets. So she made plans to build more closets for them. When the closets were installed in the house, she found that their color did not match the color of the clock, and the table and chairs were yet another color. She sent for the carpenter and ordered new ones. When she saw the room in all its glory, she thought, "A room full of such fine things cannot be without carpets." The maid said, "Such heavy carpets! I can't lift them to beat the dust out. If you don't put an assistant at my disposal, I'm going to flee from here." The mistress of the house said, "I am not too pleased with that maid either. There is nothing worse than hanging onto a domestic servant for too many years. During the first year, when she mentions something in the house, what does she say? 'The mistress's....' The second year, what does she say? 'Our....' From that point on, she says, 'My....' But until the new one is up to speed, you don't get rid of the old one." And thus she came to have two maids, because the new one managed to avoid doing the work by herself. Reb Ḥannan Abba's wife saw this and her eyes filled with grief. For the sake of keeping peace in the house, however, she said nothing. Why should people say, "A mother-in-law resents her daughter-in-law?" Let Reb Ḥannan Abba do what is appropriate.

But Reb Ḥannan Abba was far from home. All that time, Reb Ḥannan Abba stayed with his son-in-law in Spinovky in order to set him up with a place in that town. He had already rented him a large house and brought his fine furniture and cabinets filled with many books, and put a helper at his disposal, and hired two roustabouts to protect him from his enemies. He also bought his daughter a fine wig made of silk strands and all sorts of expensive garments made of silk and of sable and beaver skins like those that the notables among the rich and their eminent wives in this country of ours are accustomed to wearing. And a maid sent over a young woman from the house, one who knew how to bake and cook, and they would serve meals and throw parties for his friends, with thick borscht and potatoes on Saturday nights, and goose gizzards and mead on Rosh Hodesh. The house was full of "Litvaks" and brilliant yeshiva students and wheelers and dealers and advisors, peace-makers and middlemen. The fire of controversy burned larger in the town, and Reb Ḥannan Abba stoked the fire with cash and currency.

IX

That rich man had a brick factory that was his main source of income. Reb Ḥannan Abba made his life miserable by building another one to compete with his. He delivered him a double punch: not only did he do damage to his antagonist's income, but he also gained allies among the workers. The brickworks were built, and they produced bricks. The market was flooded with bricks, but no one built and no one bought. Unless a new Tower of Babel were to be undertaken, the bricks would sit there until they disintegrated. The wealthy man made the rounds of the gentile officials, and anyone who planned to build would of course order bricks from him. As for Jews, either they had inherited a house or they lived in their neighbor's home. The brickworks stood, and the workers performed their tasks, and bricks were added day by day, and fees and property taxes would be constantly charged anew. Reb Ḥannan Abba said, "Since the mikveh is closed and the Jews are distraught about there being no immersion, I'll build a bathhouse. He hired an engineer and started to build. The townspeople stood by, astounded, and Reb Ḥannan Abba said he wouldn't let his enemies get even a hair from their heads wet. And in his town, the idle folk said about him that a promissory note signed by Reb Ḥannan Abba wasn't worth a cent. Such an outrageous lie! Reb Ḥannan Abba was as generous as ever. Go look at the young men sitting in the *beit midrash* with yarmulkes on their heads. Who gave them the velvet for those yarmulkes? Why, Reb Ḥannan Abba! And who knows how many people from good families down on their luck clothe themselves in garments from him?

X

To get even with his enemies, Reb Ḥannan Abba's son wrote an article against the young man who was rough and tumble, neither pious nor humble, who made of the social order a jumble, and with just a word and a mumble set himself up as rabbi and preacher, with his father-in-law as his teacher in being mean and cruel when establishing his rule over wise man and fool, even youngsters still in school; birds of a feather flocking together, they gave truth short shrift and forsook the divine gift, giving evil a lift and leaving our people adrift, and sent off the article to a journal, whose editor even added a bit to it himself. A good while later, the article made the rounds of the entire town, and anyone anxious to read a bit of good writing would pick it up and read it and give it to his children as a guide to fine composition and an incentive to love the Hebrew language.

A good while after that, the poet was asked to come see the town's governor. The members of his household inquired, "What business do you have with the town's governor?" The poet smiled and said, "Well, the emperor's jubilee year is almost upon us. Perhaps the governor will ask me to write a paean to the emperor." He dressed in finery, took a handsome walking stick in hand, and went to the governor, greeting him in elegant language. The governor pulled out a printed page in Hebrew and asked him, "Are you the author of this article?" Filled with pride, the poet replied: "Yes, sir, it is I." The governor was immediately filled with rage and replied, "You fool! You have insulted a most prominent citizen. You have loosed your tongue against my friend!" At that moment, the poet stood like a baby slapped on the mouth by an angel and made to forget every language on earth. Before the governor's wrath had abated, he had him sent to prison. "Why is he so late returning?" his surprised mother asked. They sent the servant to inquire. He came back and reported, "He has been arrested." They reported this to Reb Ḥannan Abba in Spinovky. Reb Ḥannan Abba went to see the governor and arranged for his son to be released on bail. The son got out of jail. His family got together to encourage him to run away to America. His father gave him all the cash he had on hand, and he ran away. Because of his shame, he left and fled to the wide world, and his wife returned to her father's home.

XI

And still, Reb Ḥannan Abba's home was filled with all kinds of dealers who stayed with him and received travel expenses and salary and gifts. He, for his part, was burdened and troubled too, with travels from here to there, and from there to somewhere else, and his business was neglected, and his employees did whatever they wanted. One stole whenever the opportunity presented itself, and another was cheating customers, and no one thought to order merchandise for each new season. Whether his son-in-law would triumph was in doubt, and even if he did, how would he make a living? He couldn't depend on Reb Ḥannan Abba. The shop stood abandoned. Blow at it and it will fall over. Customers had no faith in Reb Ḥannan Abba anymore, and they were slipping away, one by one.

It was a waste to be paying clerks who were eating up his revenue, and they did nothing but sit around and let dust gather on the merchandise.

But his employees ran away before he could fire them. First, the bookkeeper left the shop. He oversaw the accounts, and he realized that this man had no money with which to pay salaries to clerks and managers. So he left for the big city, where he went into partnership with a young yeshiva student who had come to the end of the time his father-in-law would support his studies, and they opened up a shop. The bookkeeper had the wisdom and experience, and the young man had the money. After a while, the young man too had wisdom and experience, and the bookkeeper too had money, and he went into business for himself and his fortune soared higher and higher. He married a proper wife, too, the daughter of a prosperous family. Each morning she would cook him a buttery porridge, and he grew fatter and fatter, with a round belly already distinctly noticeable. And because he had been raised in a respectable Jewish home, that of Reb Ḥannan Abba, he too behaved properly, taking part in public affairs. He had already been appointed a *gabbai* of the synagogue, and when it came time to choose new *parnasim*, he would obviously be elected a leader of the community.

After the bookkeeper left, the shop manager left as well. Ever since Reb Ḥannan Abba had become caught up with matters of rabbinic posts and turned his attention away from commerce, this person had begun to cultivate the customers, and when he opened a shop across from his employer's shop, most of the customers came to him.

The same was true of his assistant. He brought in merchandise and opened a shop, taking with him an old yardstick so he could use it to mislead the country folk into thinking he was an old shopkeeper, and with that yardstick he performed some real magic.

The employees rose higher and higher, while Reb Ḥannan Abba sunk lower and lower. The shop was empty; there was no merchandise in it. Yet still the landlord did not toss him out. As long as no one else came along to rent it, Reb Ḥannan Abba sat chewing on his beard and gnawing the yardstick, looking over the cabinets and the empty crates and the tables full of dust. How quickly the time had passed when the cabinets were full of merchandise and the tables were full of coins. If it weren't for the splinters he took from them for cutting his fingernails, there would be no use for them at all. And what of the brick factory? It had emptied out of workers and had become a haven for criminals. And the bricks? A third were stolen, a third sank into the ground, and a third were disintegrating, dirtying the street. And Reb Ḥannan Abba had already received an order from the governor to erect a fence around the place.

XII

While Reb Ḥannan Abba was preoccupied with the rabbinate business, he slept one night in his brick factory and overheard two workers talking about a shoemaker who had won a thousand silver guldens in a lottery. The simple shoemaker had never seen such a coin in his entire life, and yet in an instant he had acquired a fortune! Did the winning numbers come to him in a dream? No! He pulled them out of thin air and won! There are those who say that that year was the emperor's jubilee, and that he calculated and decided to bet on his age and the number of years of his reign.

When Reb Ḥannan Abba heard the story, it came in one ear and went out the other. Now that he was sitting alone it occurred to him to try his luck at the lottery. It was possible that salvation would come upon him that way. So he said and so he did. He put two pennies down on the three numbers that correspond to the three initial Hebrew letters of the verse "He lifteth up the needy out of the dung hill." The attendant came back and returned his pennies, for it turned out that the lottery form had already been sealed and sent to Vienna. But the Lemberg and Berlin lotteries were still open to receiving orders. Reb Ḥannan Abba had not put much thought into it, even though he certainly wanted to win at the lottery. Once the attendant had gone, he promptly stopped thinking about it. Now that he had come back and told him such and such, he felt a pang in his heart as if he had lost something precious. He got up and took out two silver gulden—one for the Lemberg lottery and one for the Berlin lottery—for if he should win, he might as well win a lot. What's the point of winning a few pennies?

It may be hard to believe, but that very week, the three numbers, 40–10–1—the numbers corresponding to the three initial Hebrew letters of the verse "He lifteth up the needy out of the dung hill"—were the winning numbers of the Vienna lottery. Those were the winning numbers—and yet no person had bet on them, so no one won. If he had only placed the bet and sent the money by telegraph, he would have won. From then on, he never missed a bet. If certain numbers came to him, he would bet them on the lottery. If it happened that the list of numbers in his city had already been sent, he would send his own bet by telegraph. And how much would he bet? As much as you were permitted to bet in the lottery. And what he did with large amounts of money, his wife did with small amounts of money. Reb Ḥannan Abba would sit in his store and think, "King David, may he rest in peace, wrote the book of Psalms, and there are 150 psalms in it, and there is not one psalm that does not have a nice verse to generate promising numbers on which to bet in the lottery."

XIII

Neither Reb Ḥannan Abba nor his opponent was victorious. If you saw the two of them fighting, it was certain that a third would come and defeat them both. It happened that a righteous man once wanted to appoint his son to the post of rabbi in that town. Not that it is proper to offer instructions to Jews, but the income that would accompany it, even if somewhat small, would be proper. There is a small Hasidic *kloyz* in Spinovky made up of the most arrogant people in town, and he was the administrator of the funds collected for the Land of Israel, and since there was no one in town who did not have relatives in the Land of Israel or who was not expecting himself to set off for the Land of Israel, they bowed their heads before him and said, "You are our rabbi." The men in town who had kicked out the grandfather of that righteous man from the town one Sabbath eve at dusk, even though his little fingernail was worth more than all of their descendants put together, were no longer around. The generations have steadily declined, and now we have neither the self-sacrifice of the early mitnagdim nor the modesty of the early ḥasidim.

They came and offered Reb Ḥannan Abba another rabbinical post. Well, actually not another rabbinical post, but something like it. It turns out that there was a rabbi who had received permission from the emperor to perform marriages in an adjacent city, since the rabbi of that other city had no license to do so, and he continued to have this right for several years. Now, he was ready to sell his right to perform marriages there for a small amount of money. Reb Ḥannan Abba realized that he did not have the money to purchase a bona fide rabbinical post, so he sold everything he could and he paid the rabbi money to vacate his position. Reb Ḥannan Abba's son-in-law travelled there and began conducting marriages and took a share of the rabbinical fees. Would that the fate of all of the enemies of Zion be like the lot of this one! The young rabbi wanted to dwell in peace, but rabbinic anger pursued him. The rabbi in that adjacent city died and went the way of all flesh, and they appointed another rabbi, who was wealthy and learned in languages. He went and acquired the right from the emperor to conduct weddings. In truth, there weren't many weddings in the town. The Jewish youths did not have a lot of money to support themselves, and so they were leaving for America, and the Jewish women would sit and bemoan their spinsterhood.

In any event, a conflict broke out in town. They said, "Is it possible that there could be two kings wearing the same crown?" The rabbi of the adjacent town cried out, "This one has come to sojourn," and instructed him not to show his face where he did not belong. The young rabbi brought that rabbi to court, with a claim based on the principle of the poor person who was examining a cake and someone else came along and took it from him and the principle of the poor person who was gathering olives at the top of a tree and another claimed the ones beneath him. In short, he and his wife were sitting among scorpions, and Reb Ḥannan Abba and his wife were sitting in an empty store with no merchandise and no customers. And yet still the owner of the store was not trying to evict them. So long as someone else did not come along to rent it, he was free to sit there in his store. As soon as another tenant came along, Reb Ḥannan Abba would have to surrender the premises.

XIV

The Master of Mercy does not strike first at people themselves. The Holy One, blessed be He, waited until Reb Ḥannan Abba was preoccupied with his possessions, and then he cast a pall over his wife's mind. His wife sat alone all day in a corner of the house in silence, not speaking to anyone. Several times a day she would jump up and go to the attic and rummage around there. They say that she had hidden a stocking full of gold jewelry there, but then it was stolen and she lost her mind. The doctors ordered that she be taken outside of town to get some exercise. But before they could find a wagon driver to take her in his carriage, before they could find the money to pay him, she abandoned the world of suffering and breathed her last, dying of sorrow. The townspeople came to perform their last acts of kindness toward her. While they were still attending to her funeral, several businessmen got together and raised some funds to rent a small store for Reb Ḥannan Abba so that he could provide for himself with dignity. How does the rabbinic saying go?—Righteous women die before their husbands so that they shouldn't suffer disgrace as widows.

When a man is wealthy, he can mourn properly over the dead as he wishes, but as for a poor person, concerns about making a living can drive him away from his mourning and cause him to forget the one he has lost. When he got up from his mourning, Reb Ḥannan Abba tried his luck a second time and rented a small store. He didn't bring his merchandise from afar, nor from the big cities; he didn't travel to fairs, like the wealthy merchants; rather he purchased fabric in his own town, and he paid for it with his own labor. Reb Ḥannan Abba bought merchandise from a local shopkeeper in town. Formerly that shopkeeper had been a clerk in Reb Ḥannan Abba's shop; now, he was the biggest shopkeeper in town. Reb Ḥannan Abba purchased his merchandise from him, and the shop was registered with the local government in the name of the man's wife. Every evening he would return the store key to him, and every morning he would pick the key up again. That man did not deal harshly with him; when a customer asked for merchandise that he did not have, Reb Ḥannan Abba was free to acquire it elsewhere. And so it was that Reb Ḥannan Abba would get merchandise from his former clerks; sometimes from this one, and sometimes from that one. When the customer left, Reb Ḥannan Abba would go and either bring the owners back their merchandise or bring them payment for it.

Reb Ḥannan Abba saw no blessing in this store. The world had become clever. Whoever had money in his pocket would go to the wholesaler; whoever did not have money in his pocket would go to Reb Ḥannan Abba. In short, the only buyers who came to him were the poor and destitute and penniless, whose promises were as worthless as a garlic peel. The merchants stopped providing him with merchandise, telling him that he was too generous with other people's money.

He became too impatient to sit in the store. He was miserable if customers came in, and he was miserable if they did not. Reb Ḥannan Abba would spend time in the *beit midrash* studying a chapter of Mishnah. At a yahrzeit or some other celebratory gathering in the *beit midrash,* they would seat Reb Ḥannan Abba at the place of honor and give him a double portion. Reb Ḥannan Abba would cut a small slice of bread for a blessing, and that would suffice for his morning meal, and he would leave the rest for the evening. During the day, you can deal with hunger pangs; but not at night, when hunger disturbs your sleep. When one doesn't sleep, melancholy—God save us—can overtake one.

The One who prepares sustenance for all His creatures prepared Reb Ḥannan Abba's sustenance. Whenever there was a celebratory meal in the town, whenever a *yahrzeit* was observed in the *beit midrash,* they never forgot Reb Ḥannan Abba. Sometimes a neighbor woman would strike a bargain in the market—a chicken or a duck—and she would invite him to join her. Reb Ḥannan Abba would do so, against his will, in order that people would not feel as though he were withdrawing himself from everything. And what she would prepare for him, he would divide up into many meals. Her bargains saved him from hunger, for already Reb Ḥannan Abba had stopped attending celebratory meals because of something that happened. Here is what happened: a guest came to the *beit midrash* and gave charity to the poor on the occasion of the *yahrzeit* of his father. He saw Reb Ḥannan Abba and gave him a penny. Reb Ḥannan Abba's face turned red, and he threw the coin away. He threw the coin away and stopped attending meals that were not his own. But it was already decreed on high that he would come to be dependent on others. It wasn't long before a quarrel arose between him and the shopkeeper. Reb Ḥannan Abba threw the keys in his face and stormed out of the shop.

XV

The Torah says, "And if your brother waxes poor you shall support him." When he waxed poor, they supported him.

How so? Two distinguished young yeshiva students went around among the prominent people in town and collected funds on his behalf, and the men at the *beit midrash* took it upon themselves to give him some money every week—a few pennies here, a few pennies there. They appointed someone to oversee this, and on Fridays he would discreetly bring Reb Ḥannan Abba the money. They wanted to employ him as a supervisor at the slaughterhouse, so he wouldn't be dependent on other people's generosity. However, they were so exhausted from last year's controversy that when the time came to appoint a trustee, they dropped it. They supported him, this one this way, that one that way, each one as God's blessings allowed. The young people in particular did what they could to support him. The story of what had befallen him frightened them terribly. Apart from his weekly disbursement, they gave him a portion of the money that they raised at the reading of the *megillah* on Purim, at the half-shekel collection, et cetera. On the eve of Yom Kippur they set aside a large bowl for the sake of a prominent poor person. Two prominent students stood there, speaking heart to heart with everyone, urging them to give generously. But there is no room for secrets. Everyone knew that Reb Ḥannan Abba received a portion of the money raised during the *megillah* reading, and that he was the very same prominent, secretly poor person for whose sake they put out a bowl on *erev Yom Kippur,* and they began to get used to the idea that he was poor. And so they began to treat him as though he were poor and began to give him money in public, just as they gave to all the other poor people. Once he became poor like all the other poor people, the contributions diminished, and once the contributions diminished, his town diminished for him. He got up and left for another town. He walked from one town to the next and from one village to the next, asking for handouts.

Reb Ḥannan Abba walked from one town to the next and from one village to the next, asking for handouts—God help us! In one place they would give him a few pennies, and in another, they would give him a bowl of porridge in the kitchen. In one place they would tell him, "No one is home." In another, they would say to him, "God will provide"—and not give him anything at all. Reb Ḥannan Abba took it all in with love and would simply say, "Such is God's will, may He be praised!"

Sometimes Reb Ḥannan Abba would reflect: "Why did God first raise me up and now bring me down, from the highest of heights to the deepest of depths?" But then immediately he would justify God's judgment and say, "Who am I to poke my head into matters that are beyond my comprehension?" Man is stronger than rock and can tolerate much. Reb Ḥannan Abba suffered. He suffered more and more.

Several years passed this way. "God maketh poor and maketh rich." Reb Ḥannan Abba fell lower and lower, and his former assistants rose higher and higher. Reb Ḥannan Abba got down to his last loaf of bread, while his attendants came to be eating delicacies. Reb Ḥannan Abba had already forgotten that he had been rich. It was as though all his wealth had been in a previous incarnation, and he began to behave like all the other poor people who go from door to door, arousing the mercy of others. Sometimes he would encounter another poor person and they would walk on together, in order to make themselves more noticeable, so that others would give them more. When he realized that his begging partners were deceiving him, he once again took to walking alone.

Once he entered a house and reached out his hand for a handout. The owner was the very person who had been his bookkeeper. The bookkeeper recognized him, but Reb Ḥannan Abba didn't recognize the bookkeeper—just like what happened to Joseph: "And Joseph recognized his brothers, but they did not recognize him." Rashi comments on that verse that when the brothers had last seen Joseph he had not yet grown a beard, and now his beard had grown, and his appearance was impressive and his belly was full.

Since he recognized him, he took out a gold ducat and gave it to him. Reb Ḥannan Abba sensed that the coin was particularly heavy. He looked at it and saw that it was made of gold. He returned it to the gentleman and said, "Your Excellency has made a mistake." The homeowner said to him, "No, I didn't make a mistake—and what I gave you I gave intentionally." He even went ahead and invited him to dine with him on Shabbat. And he used these exact words: "Please, fellow Jew, don't go off and dine elsewhere. On Friday night, come pray at the Great Synagogue and ask the attendant there for the *parnas,* and he will bring you to me. For God's sake, don't forget!" The poor man was happy. When a rich person approaches a poor person, the poor person is ready and willing to respond to the approach.

XVI

It was on that Friday that Reb Ḥannan Abba went to the bathhouse to purify his body in honor of Shabbat. He took off his clothes and folded them and wrapped his sash around them, and he descended to immerse himself. He rose up, dried himself off and tied a kerchief around his head, and then sat on the top level of the steam room to sweat. He took a brush broom to strike his flesh after sweating and looked around for someone to do him a favor and hit him with the broom. He saw a group of people sitting and talking. He could tell from their conversation that they were beggars. He sat and listened to them. He heard them talking about who gives a decent contribution and with whom they would be eating on Shabbat. Reb Ḥannan Abba spoke up. He told them that he had stopped by the home of the *parnas,* and that the *parnas* had given him a gold ducat and invited him to dine with him on Shabbat.

The beggars were convinced that he was mocking them and said, "You want to put one over on us! May your innards be as generous as you say the *parnas* is!" He said to them, "I didn't tell you this to boast, but rather to show you where a good man lives. I swear that everything I've told you is true!" They said to one another, "He's misleading us, and he swears falsely. Let's pick up his clothes and toss them into the boiling water." When they did that, they found the coin. They said: "Money! Who knows how much more money he has tied up in these rags?" They stood up and ripped his clothes to pieces, thinking that perhaps he had coins or bills stitched into the seams. When they were done, nothing was left but a pile of rags, and they left that poor person naked in the bathhouse.

After a while, when Reb Ḥannan Abba got up to get dressed, he found nothing but a pile of rags, not one large enough to bandage a wound. When he realized that, he began to dance with joy. The bath attendant turned to him and asked, "What are you so happy about?" And the poor man did not answer. Instead he jumped and leaped and twirled with joy. The bath attendant was certain that he had lost his mind. He led him to the wood shed, shut the door behind him and locked him in. Reb Ḥannan Abba stood naked without clothing, barefoot without shoes, and he danced and twirled with joy.

XVII

Meanwhile, Shabbat arrived. The cantor completed the service, recited kiddush over the wine, and the congregation wished one another, "A blessed and peaceful Sabbath!" After the *parnas* finished responding to the well-wishers, he walked toward the door where the paupers' bench was set, looking for the poor person who had previously been his employer, but he did not find him. The *parnas* asked the *shamash*: Have you seen such and such a man? But there was no one in the synagogue who had seen him. The beadle sent word to every synagogue and study hall in town, but no one found him. The *shamash* asked everyone, "Have you seen such and such a man?" His words reached the bath attendant. The bath attendant said, "It seems to me that I've got who you're looking for locked in the woodshed, for he was behaving like he was crazy and he's stark naked." The *parnas* heard about this and sent him clothing. They dressed the poor man, and hurried him from the prison. Reb Ḥannan Abba got dressed and came before the *parnas*. They made kiddush over the wine and washed their hands and sat down to eat.

XVIII

During the meal, the *parnas* could not restrain himself, and he said, "I am your servant; I used to keep your books. And now, do not be upset and do not be angry at me that I didn't tell you who I was."

Then they spoke to one another as friends. They recalled the days of old: the great store that was full of merchandise and customers, and the journeys to the fair in Leshkowitz, and to the other cities famous for their merchandise. The master of the house said to Reb Ḥannan Abba: "One thing I ask of you. Please, sir, do me the honor of replying." Reb Ḥannan Abba said, "Ask." And so the householder asked Reb Ḥannan Abba: "Why did you dance in the bathhouse when they took away your clothing and you stood naked without clothing and barefoot without shoes?"

Reb Ḥannan Abba's face lit up, and he was silent.

The householder said, "Speaking of which, I remember that time I was returning from the fair in Leshkowitz with you, and life couldn't have been sweeter. Suddenly, you cried out and your tears began to flow like a fountain; now, when they took away all your clothes and didn't leave you with anything, even a cloak with which to cover yourself, you dance and twirl in joy!? What's that all about? Isn't that what happened?"

Reb Ḥannan Abba responded, "The very thing that I had cried about and gotten upset about earlier I am now joyous about." The householder said, "And what is that?" Reb Ḥannan Abba said, "On that very journey when we traveled to the fair, I lost all my money on the way, and after I had lost hope and abandoned hope of ever getting it back, I found all my money in its entirety. At that very moment I said that all the transient successes had been fulfilled in me, for look, even the money that I had abandoned hope of getting back, I found again. This is because my success was at its peak, and it was impossible that it would not be followed by a descent. This is why I became upset and began to cry. Now that the wheel of fortune has spun, and my luck has turned, and I have come so low that they took away even the shirt off my back, I am certain that my salvation will come soon. That is why I was very happy and danced!

The *parnas* sat in shock. He picked between his teeth with his fingernails, and the pauper sat by his side gathering up and nibbling at the crumbs that had fallen from his piece of bread, and the children of the household sat in silence, stunned in the presence of their honored guest and the wonders of his tale. After Reb Ḥannan Abba had swallowed the last crumb, he wiped his mouth with pleasure and said, "Let me tell you a parable. To what may this be compared? To the wheel of a wagon. The edge that goes up to the top comes down again to the very bottom. The edge that comes down to the very bottom rises up again to the very top. So too, me: I lost all my money in a place where many people go to and fro, and yet no one found that money until I returned there and found it. Why? Because my success was so great and my good fortune stood for me and protected me—and that is why I cried, because I saw that already I had come to the peak of my success, and it would be impossible to go any higher, and therefore, inevitably, the moment of descent had come. Now that I have fallen so low that they didn't even leave me a single garment, I am secure in my faith in God—may His name be blessed—that my time for ascent has already come."

They say that it was not long before Reb Ḥannan Abba ascended higher and higher. Not only that, but he returned to his previous honorable status.

Salvation comes from the Lord!

– Translated by Peretz Rodman and Carl M. Perkins

The Death of the Tzadik

THERE ONCE WAS A GREAT TZADIK who departed from this world. The whole country gathered to offer eulogies. From every city came patrons and notables, personages and noblemen, rabbis and judges. The government even sent a delegation of high officials to pay their respect to the deceased, for that tzadik had been a rabbi to the Jews, and the government was a beneficent one at that time.

The coffin was brought to the town square, and holy books authored by that great scholar were placed in it. Around the coffin, people assembled in seven circles, one inside the other. In the first circle, great sages and government ministers stood with the deceased's relatives, and his relatives' relatives. In the second circle were Torah scholars without official positions, but whom everyone respected and wished to honor.

In the third circle were ordinary dignitaries and important folk. In the fourth circle were the late sage's students. The fifth, sixth, and seventh circles were populated by everyone else who had come and claimed a spot for himself, arranged according to the order of their arrival and the strength of their elbows.

The principal eulogist stood and delivered a lengthy eulogy. He spoke of the deceased through flowing tears, recited his accomplishments, and brought the audience to sobs. He linked one verse to another, one rabbinic saying to another, along the way offering a few explanations for some of the evils in the world that are so difficult to understand. People pushed closer to hear him better.

There was one man there who stood outside all the rows, because he arrived last, because he had not intended to be there, because God-fearing men and acolytes of the Divine were of no importance to him at all. Once he saw everyone rushing there, though, he came along as well. He pushed his way into the seventh circle.

He stood there thinking, "All the effort I've gone to, and it's gained me nothing! This place I'm standing in is not particularly nice, because there are six circles separating me from the person delivering the eulogy, and lots of people are standing in each row, and each one is soaking up the words first, leaving me nothing. If I made it into the sixth circle, I could hear every word of the eulogy, and maybe it would inspire me to true repentance. But standing here, so far away, not only can't I hear, but I'm getting bored." He spread out his arms and shoved the person in front of him until he had made his way into the sixth circle.

He stood there thinking, "This place is better than the last one. From here, I can make out every word of the eulogy. Even so, I ought to find out whether this is such a nice spot in and of itself or whether it's nice only because I was standing so far away before. Either way, there is a better place than this one. And which one is that? Why, the spot right in front of me. All I need to do is spread out my arms and push a little and I'll be standing right among those with the good fortune to be in front of me." He spread out his arms and jostled a little and there he stood, in the fifth circle.

Seeing himself standing there, he said, "Now that I've made it here, I can hear what's going on. Why, there are only four rows of people between me and the person delivering the eulogy. But now that I've tired myself out, I can't muster the proper concentration. Too bad for someone who pushed his way here—and not further ahead!" He looked in front of him and didn't see a way in. That's because that row was filled with the late sage's students, who stood up against each other, cramped and crowded like books forced into a bookcase. He was about to give up in despair when he was blessed with a miracle: one of the students fainted and was carried away out of the line, and he slipped into that student's place.

He thought to himself, "Those people who got places in the third row—what did they do to deserve that? If it is for their Torah learning—well, the second row is reserved for Torah scholars. If it is for their prominence—well, the first row has the very prominent personages. So it's because they're important and respected. We should inquire into just what sort of importance that is—importance that comes from others or importance that comes from oneself? If it's because *they* think they're important—well, I can tell you I'm important, too. And if it comes from others, well, I can say that in my view they're of no importance whatsoever. So what are they doing standing in front of me and not me in front of them?" He started insinuating himself between them, until he was standing right there with them.

He stood there with all the dignitaries, not considering them important or respected. He said to himself, "Who are they to be standing with me in the same line? I'm leaving them and getting into the circle ahead of me."

From the third line to the second, the distance is not far. And whoever has an arm with some force shoves and makes his way in. Not more than a short while had passed before he found himself among the wise men.

Once he stood there, his heart began to feel a grievance against the personages and noblemen standing in front of him, blocking the light and preventing him from seeing all the high officials who had come out of respect for the deceased. He said to himself, "All that effort I've gone to has been for nothing, since those potbellied fellows are blocking me and I can't see a thing! And tomorrow, when they're all talking about which officials were here, and what clothes they wore, and what symbols of honor they were wearing on their clothes, I won't be able to contradict them and say, 'Not so! They were wearing such-and-such clothes with this and that marking on them.'"

He began thinking, "If I were a rich man, or a rabbi, or a relative of the deceased, why, I'd be standing in the first row and the fellow standing back here and sweating and struggling his way from row to row would be standing and looking at me and dying of envy." But this man was not a rabbi and not wealthy and not a relative of the deceased, but simply a regular fellow who didn't know his place. His mood grew dark, and he began to press his case with his Maker, who had not given him wealth or property and had kept him from being respected and honored. He said to Him, "Master of the Universe, of all the people standing here, you couldn't find anyone but me to humiliate?" And as he filled up with audacity toward God, he also came to be insolent toward other mortals. He shoved the people standing around him and pushed his way into the first row.

Once he saw himself in the first row, he became filled with arrogance. He started speaking about himself in the royal "we," saying, "So here we are standing in the same row as all the patrons and notables, generals and noblemen, officers and rabbis." As he continued to talk to himself, his conversation brought him to boredom. He chastised himself, saying, "You worthless knucklehead, get yourself back to people like yourself!"

But that knucklehead did not relent, continuing instead to badger himself. Since he saw he couldn't get rid of himself, he stopped looking at himself and turned his eyes toward those standing about him. He began to eye the people standing around him, taking the measure of each of them and taking the measure of himself alongside them. That tired him out, and he began to perspire.

He wiped his face with the hood of his coat, looking at the bier as he did so. He saw that it stood at the center and all the great men among the Jews encircled it in respect, protecting it from being jostled. And the king's ministers stood looking at it. He was seized by envy and said, "Here I am, standing on my feet and sweating like a bear, pushed this way, while that guy is laid out in his coffin with no sun baking him and no people jostling him. If that is because he is a tzadik—well, when it comes to death, everyone is equal before the Angel of Death. If it is because of all the Torah he learned and taught—well, he got paid for his work while he was living. And woe is me, standing here. My legs are already swollen from standing, and there's no end in sight. One speaker comes down and then next goes up, and the line of people offering eulogies goes on. Oh, my head, my head! If I don't faint and collapse, I'll rot away from sweat." He summoned all his strength to stand steadfast, but he saw himself collapsed and falling down.

At that moment, the tzadik in his coffin was praying in his heart, "May my merits not be cancelled out by all the honor being given me in this world, and let neither retribution for my honor be extracted from the eulogists nor retribution be extracted from me for the honor of the eulogists, who are heaping upon me one praise after another and reciting all my deeds. He regretted that he had not issued instructions not to eulogize him, but because as his death approached he had been tied up in reviewing all his learning, his attention had been distracted from this world of illusion. He placed his trust in Him, may He be praised, before whom all a person's thoughts are exposed, that He be filled with mercy for him and not take him to task for this honor being granted him. And as he saw all the honor being granted him and all those who had come to pay their respects to him, he regretted all the money they had wasted on travel expenses and not given to poor Torah scholars so they could buy bread for themselves. After all, the student who had fainted had passed out only because he had not had a thing to eat, due to his poverty. The deceased peered out from his bier and saw one eulogist descending from the stage and another going up. He was linking one verse to another, one rabbinic saying to another, taking them out of context and applying them to the present moment. The deceased thought to himself, "If I were not concerned about wasting time that should be spent in Torah study, I would listen in to hear what is being said."

While he was thinking this, he noticed that man who pushed his way in from row to row. The tzadik said, "This means there is a person deriving some comfort from those words. So I, having derided the eulogists, will be punished for that. How hard it is to dwell among human beings! Even the thoughts in a person's own heart do him harm." He was filled with mercy for God's creatures, and he was filled with mercy for himself, for he was still present in this world. He began to long for a quick burial. He looked at the eulogists and the gravediggers and asked, "When will these fellows finish their talking, and when will they put me in my grave and fill it in? Look, it's already time for the afternoon prayers."

The tzadik thought, "What is my obligation regarding prayer? When a person dies, he becomes freed from the obligations of the Torah and the commandments. But to sit around and do nothing is impossible. He took one of his books that had been placed with him in his coffin and had a look at it. The tzadik felt sorry and said, "How am I going to fare in the next world, the world of truth, with the original ideas I've come up with in Torah study?"

The legs of the man we spoke about earlier had given out, and he was in a confused state, and his soul became more and more impatient. Not long passed before he collapsed. Once he had fallen down, it seemed to him he was dead.

Destructive angels came and took him and put him onto the tzadik's bier, which had been emptied a short while earlier, for the angels on high had already taken the tzadik and brought him before the righteous in Paradise, who had been waiting, eager to hear the sermon he had prepared, growing impatient waiting for the eulogizers to conclude their eulogies.

After the man had been placed in the deceased's bier, the gravediggers came and lowered him into the grave, covered him with earth, and closed up the grave. He lay there in the grave for a while and found no rest, for his soul was still battered about from place to place. All the time he had been alive, he had seen rows and rows in front of him. Now that he was dead, all the rows gathered together, and he didn't know what his rush had been, what he had pushed and been pushed for. He wanted to put a stop to his running, but his legs kept running on their own. And although they ran, he didn't move from the same spot. He began to be afraid, thinking he was going out of his mind, because a person does not run if he is lying down and he is not lying down if he is running.

The angel entrusted with the souls of the dead came and asked him: "Did you engage in Torah study?" He had not engaged in Torah study during his lifetime. Instead, the undeserved honor he had sought was what caused him to be laid in the tzadik's grave and buried before his time.

Three bands of angels came toward him. One said, "There is no peace," and one said, "... said God to the evil ones," and one said, "You shall lie down in pain." But the Holy One's mercy is very great in the world, so they brought him out and took him before the Heavenly Court, in case there might be one person in a thousand who would speak of his righteousness.

I do not know if they found anything to weigh in his favor, or what it might have been. After all, I was not there at the time, since it is not my practice to shove my way into the upper realms, but when I see a person pushing his way into someplace he doesn't belong, that incident always comes to mind.

–Translated by Peretz Rodman

The Mother's Voice

THIS STORY WAS TOLD TO ME by Mr. Ḥaim Naḥman Bialik, may he rest in peace. I don't remember whether he said he had read about the incident in the newspapers, or whether he was relating something he had heard.

An old widow, a feather merchant, was accustomed to leave her home daily to go out to her work. One day she left but did not return. They sought her but found her not. She had vanished without a trace.

She had a beloved only son. He left his home and business and traveled all over, asking everywhere, "Was a woman called so-and-so here? Was a woman called so-and-so here?" They said to him, "No." But then he came to one city where they said to him, "We saw her a year ago. She was going to such-and-such a place." He went there.

That day was the eve of the anniversary of her departing. A gentile acquaintance with whom his mother had business dealings happened upon him. He greeted him warmly and asked him what he was doing there. He told him. He sighed a heartbreaking sigh and said, "She was a fine old woman, it's a shame she is dead. You are doing a fine thing, my son, searching for her grave. Your mother was a clever Jewess, she knew her merchandise and she knew her business. She never tried to cheat anyone, and she couldn't abide anyone cheating her. Have you not dined today? I suspect you haven't eaten a thing. Come, let us dine." He went to the gentile's home. He brought him food and drink. He washed his hands, and ate, and drank. The gentile came and sat with him, singing the praises of the wretched woman who had died before her time and was undeservedly buried in an unmarked grave. "You see, my son, she often ate in my home, here, in this very place. She would take her bread from her basket and dip it into the water in her cup and peck at her bread like a lazy chicken, but when she said grace her strength was renewed and she would mumble and mumble endlessly. You don't find women like her nowadays."

When the son was done eating and drinking and saying grace, he got up to go. Said the gentile to him, "If you are looking for lodging, you needn't leave. Here's a bed, and here are pillows and blankets."

He listened, and sat with him till his eyes clouded with sleep. The host took his leave and departed. The Jew said the Shema, and lay upon the bed. Sleep overcame him, and he nodded off.

As he slept, he heard a voice crying. But since he was weary, he ignored the sound. He turned over and nodded off again.

The voice came again. Said the son, "It seems to me that this voice sounds just like mother's." So he listened, and he heard the voice say, "My son, you are crushing me!" He wanted to see what it was, but he could not pull himself out of bed and once again he fell asleep.

As he slept, his mother's voice returned, throbbing, "Ai, my son, you are crushing me! Ai, my only one, you are crushing me!" A trembling seized him and he tumbled out of bed. The voice now came at him from the ground. He jumped up and tried to flee. He ran to the door bur found it locked. He pushed, but it would not open. And he realized that it was locked from the outside. He opened the window and jumped out.

A policeman saw and apprehended him. He said to him, "Thief. Off to jail with you!" He said to the policeman, "Let me explain. I am the son of that woman who disappeared a year ago, and I have been searching everywhere for her. Some days ago, I was told that she had been last seen in this city, and I came here to the home of this person who is an acquaintance of mine. He brought me food and drink and offered me a bed. As I slept, I heard a voice calling from the ground, 'My son, my son, you are pressing on me.' This happened once, twice, three times, and I realized that it was my mother's voice. Fear overcame me, and I tried to flee. I found the door locked from the outside. So I stood and jumped out the window. Now, if you believe I am guilty of a crime, arrest me."

The policeman, not wise enough to be skeptical, took out his whistle and began to blow. A number of policemen came and gathered. He related the incident to them. They listened and said, "There's something going on here. There's something going on here." They entered the house. The master of the house heard and came and said to them, "Sir, what is it you are looking for?" And he opened every chest and every cabinet, but they found nothing suspicious. They asked him to forgive them. He said to them, "You are just doing your jobs, and I have no complaints against you."

Just as they were about to leave, one of them saw something unusual about the floor beneath the bed. They investigated and found the bones of a dead person, the son's mother, and they realized that the host had murdered her and hidden her there, beneath the very bed that he had offered her son.

– *Translated by Michael P. Kramer*

Three Sisters

To Berl Katznelson, blessings!

THREE SISTERS LIVED IN A BLEAK HOUSE sewing linens for others. From dawn to dusk, from the end of Sabbath to Sabbath eve their fingers never strayed either from scissors or needle. A deep sigh penetrated their hearts throughout both summer and winter. But their efforts did not produce any benefit. When they found a dry crust of bread it failed to relieve their hunger.

On one occasion they engaged in making a lovely wedding dress for a wealthy bride. Upon completing their handiwork they recalled their sorrows for they had nothing on their flesh but frail skin, and that too was growing old.

Their hearts overflowed with grief.

One sighed and said, All our lives we sit and toil for others while we lack even a piece of cloth to make burial shrouds for ourselves. The second one told her sister not to tempt Satan. She sighed as well and shed a tear. The third also wanted to say something but when she opened her mouth to speak blood splattered out and stained the bride's garment.

When she brought the dress to the bride her wealthy father left his study. He saw the stain and rebuked the seamstress— it goes without saying he did not pay her. Oh, if only the second sister had spat blood and the third had wept we could have laundered the garment with her tears and the wealthy father would not have been enraged. But nothing occurs as it should. And even if everything did occur at the proper time, that is, if one had wept after the other spat blood, there would still be no true consolation.

– *Translated by Shelly Lilker*

Earth of Israel

When I went back to Poland to visit my relatives and to pay homage at the graves of my family I met the Grave-keeper there, one of the early "Lovers of Zion" in that town, who, in his youth, had hoped to go to the Land of Israel. While he was trying to go he bought a piece of land near his town and lost his money; then he rented a field and lost his tenancy; it was even as the Rabbis used to say, "property outside Israel has no blessing." He hired gardens and the birds consumed them so he opened a shop of tools, and seeds, and fodder, and the war came and they turned his tools into weapons and fed the horses of the recruits with his grain. In the end when the land quietened and the sword returned to its scabbard the Polish government took his two sons away to the army and his wife died. His strength failed and he could not earn a living and in pity the townspeople made him the Grave-keeper.

Because of his love for the Land of Israel, from whence I had come, he was friendly towards me and went with me round the graves, graves of the righteous whom the town had thought worthy to have rest for their bodies in its earth: and he took me to the new cemetery which was full of graves, in number double that of the town's whole population, not counting the war dead who had been buried in heaps and heaps, even their names unrecorded.

The day was bright and the heat pleasant, the trees in the fields spread their shade and there was a lovely scent from the shrubs and herbs;

sometimes a breeze moved them and a berry from a shrub waved against a tombstone and the worn letters were dyed in the movement. I read the writing on the stones which anonymous poets of the community had composed in honor of the dead, who had passed on, and in honor of the living who were their descendants. I read the verse, "These are the seed, blessed of the Lord," the beloved of Israel whom their Creator blessed with a good name although they were buried in unclean ground.

Because of my love for Israel I began to grieve for those who died outside the "Land" and were not privileged to be buried in Israel, for they die twice; one death here and another in the future when the Holy One, blessed be He will open the graves and bring them up with Him to the Land of Israel. And not only that, they will not be the first to be resurrected in the days of the Messiah or taste the delights of His coming. It is worse for those who are destroyed in war whose names are unrecorded, whose mothers are childless and wives forsaken, without joy, blessing or the means of support.

From the graves came the sound of weeping, of women widowed, of children made orphans, or a childless mother, of old men and women and beggars holding out their hands. Elul, the month of compassion leading up to Rosh Hashanah, was under way: the living begging from the dead for salvation and life, and the poor begging from the living for charity that they might not die of hunger.

When I left the dead I sat with the Grave-keeper and we began to talk together of one thing and another until we came to the things which had happened at the time when I was a child being taught Torah with Rashi's commentary, and he was a clever young man familiar with newspapers and secular books; I busy making a model of the Tabernacle and its contents out of wax, and he busy selling shekels and bonds. I reminded him of the delight we had had when they brought into the town a barrel of wine from Rishon LeZion and he and all the aged Zionists of the town went out to the crossroad to welcome the barrel which they brought in on a wagon calling, "The first from Zion is here" and some other verses from the Bible. I also reminded him of the day when they first brought in oranges from Israel and all the town came to buy them; the rich bought one whole orange for the household and the poor divided shares of one orange among friends, and on each blessing the leaders of the town stood up and said, "Amen." I told him that now we, in Israel, eat oranges like potatoes – although the two cannot be compared – and that even the poor in Israel eat many of them every day, swallowing the blessing, sucking the juice and throwing away the fruit; and as regards wine, already Israel has forgotten all the blessings which we repeated over wine – "that which cheereth God and man." And what do they want now? Beer! The people's drink, which dulls the spirit, weighs down the limbs, and lowers man's brain to his belly and makes his whole body a casket for the stomach: and there is yet another drink called *gazoz* which is not a drink at all; when taken it gives no benefit, increases perspiration, and turns the blood of Israelites into water.

I told him much more, like a man telling his friend what pleases him, and he sat and listened with shining eyes and parted lips like the dumb who hear and cannot speak, opening his mouth to show that he had swallowed every word and feared that it might be stopped in the middle.

In truth I did not want to stop, for conversation about Israel was so dear to us, but when he gave a deep heart-felt sigh I stopped and asked him why he sighed; was it for the good which he had never seen – not everyone attained that – or was it for his conscripted sons – they would be released soon: he said, "I am distressed for one who has not managed to get to the Land of Israel." I said that that was indeed distressing, and we sighed together. When I got up to go he said to me that he had already reached the age of his father and he was worrying; and he asked me to do him the kindness to send him some earth of the Land of Israel, and I promised to send it. He pressed me to write it in my notebook so I took out my notebook and wrote his name, and the name of his town and his request.

2

When I returned to Jerusalem I had many things to attend to and I forgot the request of the Grave-keeper, or rather I did not forget but pushed it from my mind like a man who puts aside the wishes of his friends on account of his own affairs.

A letter came and I was reminded, and because I did not have any chance to go to the Mount of Olives to collect earth I wrote to him, "The time has not yet come."

After a little he replied and wrote to me that man does not know his day, and so on, one day here and tomorrow in the grave. For the days of man are as a shadow which passes, and there is need to think of dying suddenly – God forbid! On this account he pleaded earnestly with me for his wish. He begged this friend of his youth who had been fortunate to walk in the Land of the Living, the Holy City of Jerusalem, to collect for him a handful of earth of the Land of Israel and send it to be placed upon his eyes, as the verse says, "The earth of Israel atones for His people"; even a small bit of earth atones, and so he trusted me to do him this kindness and not to neglect it.

It was as if a little prophecy fell from his pen. Whenever I remembered it I delayed, yesterday for one reason and today for another, the most important reason being that the road to the Mount of Olives was very dangerous and it had happened that old men going to pray at the graves of the righteous had been stoned by the Arabs. I was afraid to go: so I waited and wrote to him – "there is yet time."

Then one day when I was looking in my notebook I saw that all the pages were crossed out except the one on which I had written – to so and so, son of so and so, in such and such a place, some earth of Israel, and I said to myself "as long as I have not fulfilled my promise I may not put away this notebook." While I was still thinking about this I saw people carrying someone for burial and I followed along for the requisite four cubits one must follow the bier, and while I accompanied them the others scattered and went away, and only the pallbearers were left with the dead. He had been poor, and not known to many, and mourners had not been found for him, so I joined them until they brought him to the Mount of Olives and buried him.

After they buried him I went to the side of the hill and dug and filled my pocket with earth, the finest earth of Israel.

When I returned to the City I went to a draper and got cloth of the best material able to stand the wear and tear of a journey, and I sewed a small bag of it and filled it with the earth and wrote the name of the poor fellow, his surname, and the name of his city and the name of the country, and I went to the post office.

The post office was full of Jews and all the other nationalities in Jerusalem laden with parcels and parcels, and a clerk was sitting behind the grille doing something. I got a place and waited until that person in charge paid attention and beckoned me.

While the post office clerks were attending to their business I had time to think of many things. I stood and thought – "Why all this trouble? Is the Grave-keeper short of soil in his own country that he wants a mere handful of earth of the Land of Israel?" The grass of his city reappeared before me and the good scent of wheat and rye, fruit and vegetables, and other products of the land contrasted with this parched land, toasted like burnt bones left unburied in the sun. God forbid that I should belittle the Land of Israel whose earth was dear to the righteous, but I did think that the man should be satisfied with what he had. One who has spent all his days outside the Holy Land should stand on his own, and we whose feet struggle in the dust of the Land should hold on to it.

While I was thinking thus about him his troubles presented themselves before me. He had had fields and they were confiscated; he became a tenant and was turned out; he had opened a shop and the legions had emptied it; and in the end he was made the Grave-keeper. He had had many fields and nothing was left for him, and all he hoped for was a little earth from the Land of Israel. How could I not send it? Surely now he deserved a small handful of earth for himself? At that moment I said to myself, "This is the most important thing that I have to do." I looked at the clerk in a friendly way for he would share in what I was sending, and I was astonished to see that he showed no feeling.

After an hour and a half, or more, I reached the clerk and I handed him my parcel and put money down in front of him. He took the parcel and returned it to me and said that it was not yet in order. I asked the meaning of "not in order." "Sir if you wish it well packed, it is well packed; or well tied up, it is well tied up; or well addressed, the writing is clear." He stood and treated me to an account of the law about parcels and about packing them and sending them at home and abroad; he taught me screeds and screeds, all of which were forgotten on account of my annoyance. I picked up my earth and went away deeply disappointed.

I went home with my parcel and I inspected it on all sides; I wanted to remember the rules but could not remember them: but I knew one thing – that the parcel was not in order. It came to my mind that he had feared that I might have hidden spices, or gold, or silk, or pearls in the sack as had happened with the customs agents and Abraham our father and Sarah our mother when he hid her in a chest in order that the Egyptians might not see her.

Next day I would go back to the post office. I would tell the clerk that there was nothing there except a handful of earth of Israel. He would take it at once and send it to that old man who would rejoice with great joy; and I also would be happy because of managing to keep my promise. Then I said, "How easy it is for a man to keep his word; I only need to speak the truth and immediately all harsh decrees will be removed."

I went to the post office and waited an hour or two, or more, until I reached the grille, and after the clerk had opened it a little I gave him the parcel and told him that only a handful of earth was in it and there was no need to be so particular. He took it and examined it and said, "It is not yet in order," and he began to teach me one thousand other rules about sending parcels. I saw that I could not concentrate on what he was saying and went out deeply disappointed.

I spoke to my friends about my difficulty and hoped for their help. Some of them examined it and said, "What do you mean? It is wrapped up perfectly"; others did not look at it but gave me advice about how to make parcels; some sighed and said, "It all depends on luck, and even Solomon and Bezalel would not be able to understand the mind of the clerk!" So, ideas about parcels and opinions went around without any discovery and meanwhile I did not find a friend to help me in the matter.

Anger is unseemly, and one ought to keep away from it, and yet I was unable to control my temper. Every time I saw the parcel lying before me I was angry and said that that clerk who had no love for the Land of Israel might be buried one day in its earth while an upright Jew whose thoughts were all towards Israel could not get a grain of it.

And I was not only angry with the clerk but I was angry with myself because I was included among those to whom the world seems upright and enjoyable in this time of peace; and it seems that the whole world is mistaken, and how gravely mistaken! The doubters, the hesitaters and the suspicious ones only, are the men of truth because they see the world as it really is; not like those who delight in their portion and rejoice in the world, who, because of their happiness close their eyes to the truth.

All the time that that earth did not move from my sight I thought, there it lies and serves no purpose while that Jew abroad is waiting for it so eagerly. I had forgotten that it was only a handful of earth to cover the eyes of the dead, it seemed to me as if there was nothing like it anywhere. The more I thought of it the more I loved it, and if I saw a fine tree or flower I planted them in my imagination in that earth. But how could this handful of earth reach the eyes of one longing for it? Perhaps I should go to another town or to a neighboring country and I would find a clerk who was less particular.

Even at night my heart was unquiet. Bad dreams and great terrors visited me in my sleep. I saw myself like one wandering where I was not known, and worse, that even Jerusalem itself was not my own city. The people who appeared to me like friends showed me in a dream broken steps and narrow flats and advised me to go up and hide myself there. When I got up I saw that even if I shrank my limbs and squeezed my body I was too big and could not get in. To increase my anxiety I went on reading the letter of the Grave-keeper which I now knew by heart. But in spite of that I returned to it and read that "man does not know his time," etc., and on that account he begged me "to dig a handful of earth from the Land of Israel to lay upon his eyes." and so on.

When I put down the letter from my hand the eyes of that old man glanced at me as if saying, "I had so much land and it was all taken away and now I am asking for a handful of earth of consolation, which you are denying me."

The worry and dreams and terror at night became a stumbling block. I am a man of peace; I do not exalt myself before the great or belittle myself with the lowly. I like authority and pray for the peace of the State. And already in my childhood I read with satisfaction in the prayer book the prayers for the health of the King and the health of the Princes and Princesses although pronouncing their names was much more difficult than the mystical names of the angels who are summoned by the blowing of the shofar. But from the day when I had that affair with the clerk there was confusion in my mind. God forbid that I should mingle with outsiders or lend my ear to slander about those in power. I was not at peace. While walking in the streets of Jerusalem I saw with my eyes the cemeteries in other lands, old graves and new graves, double the number of a town's inhabitants, and the city itself was full of graves not counting the Grave-keeper who was still alive. He had reached the age of his father and was of an age to worry about his end, and indeed he was distressed and worried. "When would that handful of earth from the Land of Israel reach me?" If it had not been for that clerk, who prevented it, the poor fellow would have been happy with the earth and have accepted his worries with love.

3

The thoughts of man cannot be relied upon. You think thus; He who is above has already thought otherwise. One day I found in a newspaper an account of a clerk of the post office who stole money from the post and bolted out of the country. When I read it I did not pay attention to it, perhaps because the papers continually report evil doings and if a man pays much attention to all that he would have to wear sackcloth and ashes.

After I had put aside that story in my mind a page of a newspaper fell into my hands and I read that the day before yesterday judgment was passed on the post office clerk in Jerusalem who stole from the parcels. The investigation of the accused was undertaken without him because he had escaped the country; three witnesses had established the evidence, etc., etc. Then my heart was filled with anger. Far away lived an old sick woman and her only hope was in her son. The Lord saw her distress and put it in the son's heart to send her two or three banknotes. Confusion entered the clerk's heart and he took that money for himself and that woman died of starvation. In the same way many miserably poor people were waiting for alms from kinsmen in the exile; and the Holy One saw their need and put it into the hearts of generous people to send them charity. The clerk appeared and took the money for himself, and they died of starvation. Not only did the clerk betray his duty and caused the death of the poor of Israel from famine but he shut up the mercy of the Holy One, blessed be He and caused the slander to arise against Israel that they were not caring for their kinsmen. Anger is an ugly mood and the rabbis caution us to keep far away from it. However, I admit that I was angrier with that clerk than I had been with the clerk who could not trouble himself to send my parcel: and not only that, I even began to give him credit for being so particular about sending it because he had been concerned that Israeli money should not be lost, although he himself was not an Israelite.

While thinking of that I went to the post office although I did not know why. Perhaps to look at him more kindly? Or perhaps like one who says, "What does it matter that I should traverse an additional four cubits in Israel!"

4

When I reached the post office I found no one there, it was almost empty. But it was neither a Jewish nor gentile holiday. Where were all those people who had been standing squeezed together and pushing each other? Possibly they had heard about the story and feared to deposit their money in the hands of the post office. I was greatly mistaken: the reason was that as soon as that clerk had run away they replaced him with a quick and clever clerk, a young woman who attended to everyone quickly so it was not necessary to stand in lines squeezing one another. It seemed that I despaired already of sending the earth, and yet in my heart I did not despair; either I was waiting for some miracle or was naïve enough to hope that some friend would come and help me.

For one reason or another I never left my home without my parcel so there I was in the post office with my parcel and I said to myself, "I shall try – who knows? Perhaps this moment is favorable and my parcel will be accepted." Beside the grille instead of that clerk sat a girl who looked at me kindly. She was young and pleasing, a true daughter of Israel, so she had a kind heart. Her welcoming face and pleasant voice gave me courage, but because I had been turned away already twice I began to hesitate like a man who comes to swindle the authorities. The girl asked me, "What do you want sir?" I bowed to her and greeted her and pushed the parcel to her muttering, "I want to send this parcel, there is only a handful of earth in it, a handful of earth of the Land of Israel, please ma'am, if it is possible for you to take it you will be doing a great mitzvah." The girl looked at me in astonishment and took the parcel: she looked at it all over and said, "It is well packed, a ship sails today for abroad, and in eight days the parcel will reach its destination." I thanked her for her trouble and I went out happy.

After I sent away the bundle of earth a load fell from my heart. I thought of that girl and her kind face, her efficiency and loveliness, and I praised the authorities that had placed this pleasant creature to delight mankind, as the saying goes, "When the King is good his councilors and ministers are good as well." And if the clerks are also good what does the world lack? Perhaps the world is getting better and mankind happier.

After some time I turned my mind from such good thoughts and from my parcel which I had sent: the troubles of Israel made me forget the troubles of the world.

5

Some time later the sons of the old man wrote to me a letter of thanks for the earth of the Land of Israel which their father had received just before he died; and they also wrote that from the day when he fell ill to his departure he had prayed that he might merit that the earth would reach him before he died; and truly his prayer was answered. Almost as he was expiring a messenger came from the post and brought him the parcel of earth of the Land of Israel: at that moment father was dying but he turned his face to the package and smiled as his spirit left him.

When the year of mourning was past the sons of that old man came to the Land of Israel. They came to ask how I was, and told me that during the seven days of mourning the whole city spoke of the event, of how the earth had been received in the very moment when the father departed from this world and that he had merited that his eyes should be covered with earth of the Holy Land: and concerning this their Rebbe – *long may he live*! – had said that the men of Israel possess the spark of prophecy, for what was written in the first letter was, "the hour is not yet," and in the second letter, "there is yet time," and when the time came the earth came.

I said to them that other people in Israel certainly have the spark of prophecy but in this matter what happened was that when I first received their father's letter I answered what I answered because it was difficult for me to obtain earth from the Mount of Olives: and later when I did go and get the earth I was not able to send it until they dismissed a wicked clerk and he was replaced. Then I sent the earth to their father. But the sons of the old man said, "If so, how did you know the exact time? It was possible to be a day early or a day late, and because it was not early or late, it is clear, sir, that you were directed by the Holy Spirit.

I said to them that it was not done by my design; it was the intention of the Land itself for the Land of Israel itself possesses the Spirit of Holiness. How? All the time that their father was alive the Land had waited for him and when the hour of death came near and he had not arrived it sent the handful of earth. How did their father merit this handful from the Land of Israel? Because he longed to settle in Israel. Do not people say, "If you want to know the wishes of the fathers, look to the deeds of their children."

And you have brought his thoughts into action. Happy are you that you came here with the love of your father in your hearts. May it be that you will find great satisfaction in your stay and the Land find satisfaction from you. Your father had great possessions in the Diapora and they brought him no blessing; he decided to rent fields from others and found no blessing in them; he set up a business and there was no blessing; he became Grave-keeper and in the end obtained for himself only a four cubit plot for himself. In the future he will shake off that earth and depart for the Land of Israel. This is his great merit because not all those who depart for Israel remain there. Those who did not intend to return there during life are rejected by the Land after death. But you have become worthy to settle in your lifetime and not only that, but all the Land of Israel is before you and in the future, the Holy One, blessed be He will enlarge your lot until your lips wear out saying, "Enough!"

– *Translated by J. Weinberg and H. Russell*

Yisakhar and Zevulun

When Yisakhar arrived in Gan Eden to receive his Heavenly reward, they examined his book and found it written: Yisakhar occupied himself with the Torah for a total of two days.

Yisakhar was astounded.

He said, "Is it possible that I, who all my life never budged from the diligent study of Torah, and always accepted all the burdens of Torah learning I am to be rewarded for only two days of Torah study?"

They said to him, "Yisakhar, how did you make a living in that world that you just came from?"

He said to them, "I had a brother named Zevulun, and he and I were partners. He lived by the sea and he went out on commercial ships. Since he earned enough for both of us, I sat and studied while he was working."

They said to him, "If so, then all the Torah you studied is accounted to Zevulun's credit, because if not for Zevulun's work, you would not have been able to learn Torah. And therefore, you have already used up your Heavenly reward by enjoying the delights of Torah on earth below. And as for the two days that are written to your credit – they were two days that your brother was slow in returning with food for you, and yet, nonetheless, you never flinched from your diligent study. So those two days are written to your credit."

Yisakhar asked them, "And what was accounted to my brother Zevulun?"

They brought out Zevulun's book and found written therein: Zevulun earned the merit of Torah study all his life, except for two days.

They checked the dates and found that those were the two days that Zevulun was delayed in bringing back food to Yisakhar.

Yisakhar heaved such a great sigh that his voice was heard throughout Gan Eden.

Zevulun said, "That voice sounds like the voice of my brother Yisakhar." He went and found him in great straits.

Zevulun turned to the Heavenly court: "Isn't it true that whatever reward I received comes to me only because of my brother, Yisakhar, who was always busy with the study of Torah? The truth is that it is not I who sustained Yisakhar but Yisakhar who sustained me! And on top of that, now I should take away his portion in Heaven also? God forbid that one of my father's sons should do that! Rather, let Yisakhar take my place here in Gan Eden."

Yisakhar said to him, "My dear brother, can you possibly think that I would take away your place in Gan Eden? That you should suffer while I enjoy myself here?"

Zevulun answered him, "It's not my place but your place. Whatever good they are giving me here is only in reward for the Torah that you learned."

Zevulun refused to return to his place in Gan Eden because Yisakhar was so upset, and Yisakhar refused to occupy the place because of his affection for Zevulun.

Then the Holy One, blessed be He, said, "Yisakhar and Zevulun, each of you keeps deferring to the other. Because of such love, I will enlarge your portion in Heaven." At that moment, Zevulun's place in Heaven expanded so there was room for Yisakhar, too.

And to this day Yisakhar and Zevulun sit in Gan Eden and study Torah together, basking in the Divine presence, while the Holy One, blessed be He, spreads His glory upon them. Because Zevulun supported Yisakhar, and Yisakhar supported Zevulun, the Holy One supports them both with His splendor and glory.

– Translated by Stephen Listfield

Tranquility

AN OLD MAN was a neighbor of Moses, a blameless and upright old man who feared God and turned away from evil, like Job. The Holy One had blessed him with sons and daughters, sheep and cattle, camels and donkeys; he lacked nothing except tranquility, and even at night when people rest he was disturbed and he found no peace.

When Moses was about to go up on high the second time to receive the final tablets this old man came to see him and said, "My master Moses, you know that ever since I could think for myself I have observed your precepts and have not departed from your commandments. When you brought Israel out of Egypt, before my dough had leavened I wrapped it in my clothing and carried it over my shoulder, to follow you in the wilderness, in a land not sown. Not even for an instant did I hesitate, nor did I even prepare provisions for myself. The Egyptians pursued us, but I listened to your voice and jumped into the sea, not knowing that we would pass through the sea on dry land, or that the water would cover Pharaoh's army. When the Holy One delivered Israel from the hand of the Egyptians and your heart prompted you to sing a song I craned my neck and repeated after you as a child repeats after his teacher. We walked three days in the wilderness and found no water—I sucked my thumb like a baby and I said nothing. We came to Marah and we could not drink the water there because it was bitter. I was not among those who grumbled against you saying, 'What shall we drink?'

And so it went every day: I would not quarrel with you for taking me out of the flesh pots, out of Egypt, but I would gather manna, leaving none of it over until the next morning, and I did not worry that manna might not fall the following day, that I and my household would starve to death, for I directed my heart to our Father in Heaven, as you had taught me. When you went up to receive the Torah and took so long in coming back, Israel conspired against Aaron and made a golden calf for themselves—I had nothing to do with that deed. Now that you are going up to receive the second tablets I have come to ask you to ask one thing of the Holy One on my behalf."

Said Moses to him, "What is it?" Said he, "I am not asking for wealth or for children or that my oxen be obedient at the plough or that my crops not dry out or that my barns be blessed. What, then, do I ask? A little tranquility I ask. Please, Moses, don't forget me up there. And even though my days should be as numerous as grains of sand I will never forget your kindness." Said Moses to him, "As soon as you started to speak I already decided to ask on your behalf."

Moses went up and received the final tablets. When it was time for him to go down, Moses said to the Holy One, "Lord of the Universe, there is a certain neighbor of mine, a worthy old man who is God fearing. Please, if You would like to do me a favor, find for this man a little tranquility."

Said the Holy One to Moses, "Ben Amram, you are asking for something impossible." Said Moses, "There can't be any lack of power on high! Did You not write in Your Torah, 'Is the Lord's hand shortened?'" Said The Holy One to Moses, "In six days I created everything I created, but tranquility I did not create."

– Translated by Jules Harlow

Tears

IT WAS TOLD to me by Rabbi Shmuel Arieh: In my youth I lived in the village of Koshilovitz, the same Koshilovitz which gained world renown because the Ba'al Shem Tov was a *shoḥet* there before his greatness was revealed. I met a *shoḥet* there, an old man over eighty. I asked him, Did you perhaps know someone who knew the Ba'al Shem Tov? Said he, I have never met a Jew who saw the Ba'al Shem Tov, but I have met a Gentile who saw him. When I was a young man I used to lodge with a Gentile farmer. Whenever I would pour water on a stone before whetting my slaughtering knife the farmer's grandfather, an old man of ninety or a hundred, would shake his head. I used to think it was due to his age. One time I sensed that he was doing it out of disapproval. I asked him, Why do you shake your head while I work? Said he, You are not going about your task in a nice way. Yisroelki, before he whetted his knife, would dampen the stone with tears.

– *Translated by Jules Harlow*

The Mill Owner and the Miller

Just as Rebbe Mottele of Chernobyl of blessed memory was the rebbe of the living, so too was he the rebbe of the dead.

He had a poor ḥasid in an impoverished village who would visit him regularly every year. One year he did not come, his situation was so dire.

The ḥasid would sit with his wife and children, wrapped in hunger, naked without clothing, their dwelling as dark as the grave and their stove as cold as a corpse. It was as if they were dead, but not yet buried. When his troubles grew so great he could hardly breathe, he went outside so as not to witness his family's sorrow. "If only my rebbe could see me," the poor man said, "then pity would well up inside him and he would pray that we not die of hunger."

Just then a four-horse carriage arrived. Looking up, he saw his rebbe sitting there, along with another fellow dressed in a very common manner. He ran to greet him with great joy, crying, "Rebbe, Rebbe, the Heavens have brought you here." Said the rebbe to the driver, "Tie up and feed the horses. This fellow and I are going to dine in the house of the ḥasid."

The ḥasid entered his home and informed his wife and children that his rebbe had come and would dine with them. The woman beat her head and said, "Oy, what will we give him, we have not even an olive-measure of bread in the house." The ḥasid turned here and there, looking for something that they might pawn. He noticed that his baby was wrapped in a sort of pillow. He took the pillow and gave it to his wife to hock. The woman ran all over the village until she found a villager who took the pillow and gave her a handful of flour and salt. "Better one handful of flour than two handfuls of nothing," the woman said. She returned home, made some kind of dish, and prepared a meal for the rebbe.

During the meal, the rebbe asked the master of the house about his business. The poor man sighed a loud and bitter sigh, and he and his wife began to cry.

"Why are you crying?" asked the rebbe.

"How can we not cry," the master of the house responded, "when my house is empty, and my family is hungry, and they have not even a slice of bread to satisfy their hunger, neither today nor tomorrow."

"But your father was a rich man with a comfortable livelihood," said the rebbe. "Is there nothing at all left of his wealth? I remember he had a mill where they would grind flour for the villagers."

"The mill the rebbe speaks of is now a ruin," said the ḥasid. "Three years before my father passed away, the devil incited someone to come here and build a huge mill, and he made flour finer than my fathers. Everyone left my father for the new miller, and my father's mill was abandoned."

"Take me to the ruin," said the rebbe, signaling to the one who was with him to accompany them.

He entered the mill and found it in shambles. The rebbe examined the millstone and said, "I don't know why this mill must stand idle. After all, the mill owner is a good man who earned an honest living." He looked toward the one who accompanied him and said to the ḥasid, "This man is a miller by trade. I will leave him here with you until you and your family regain your livelihood, and more." The rebbe immediately boarded his carriage and rode off.

The miller remained with the ḥasid, setting up his lodging in the mill. He removed the rubble and repaired the millstone. The ḥasid's wife smote her hands together, saying, "Oy, we ourselves have nothing to eat. How are we going to feed this fellow?"

But the man did not trouble his employers nor ask anything of them. He prepared his meals himself, and supported himself. Not more than a month or two passed before word spread that the mill was once again operating, and people began to come, some with wheat, some with barley. The mill went on grinding, and the ḥasid and his family were happy, eating and drinking and dressing like the best householders in town.

The ḥasid and his family would sit in a house filled with all the best, eating and drinking and being merry, and the tradesman would stand in the mill and produce fine flour, giving all he earned to his employers. They never saw him speak to anyone except about business, and they never saw him eat or drink. All this time, he never changed his clothes or shoes, and if they got worn, the flour with which they were covered made them seem new and white. Many times the ḥasid invited him to his home, but he would never come, sometimes because the work was mounting, sometimes because the customers were impatient. Eventually his employers got used to the idea, as if this had always been their arrangement.

Thus one year passed, and then another, and then another. The miller milled and the owners grew rich. Their house was well-stocked and their oven was well-stoked. Perhaps it was even warmer than the average person required. Perhaps the excess warmth alone would have been enough to heat the home of a Jew who was not so amply blessed.

One winter day, the ḥasid and his wife lingered about their table. The smell of cabbage rose from a pot, the meat that was cooking with it seethed in its juices, and it brought a satisfied ruddiness to the faces of the ḥasid and his wife. A fine loaf was set before them, warmly welcoming its eaters. There too was a bottle full of whiskey, to help the digestion.

"Would our rebbe come today," said the woman to her husband, "he would find a pleasant dwelling, a warm oven, and delicious food. When I think about that meal that I made for him then, my face blackens with shame. How many years have passed since then? If I'm not mistaken, it's three years to the day. The time seems to have passed so quickly."

"Such is the nature of years," responded the ḥasid. "When they are bad, each week seems like a seven-year sabbatical cycle, and each year like a fifty-year jubilee. And when they are good, they pass like…" Before he could find an appropriate analogy, he pricked up his ears and said, "The sound of a carriage do I hear."

"The neighing of horses do I hear," responded his wife.

The ḥasid tightened the sash about his waist and said, "I will go and see." "Look out the window and don't go out in the cold," his wife said to him. Because they had become wealthy and their house was so well heated, not a hint of frost appeared on the window. It was as clear as on a sunny summer day and they could see outside.

As they got up, the carriage pulled up to the house. They saw that Rebbe Mottele was sitting in the carriage. They rejoiced greatly and got up to greet him.

The rebbe knocked on the window and said, "Call the miller." "Please come in, Rebbe," they said to him. "Please come in. Perhaps the rebbe would like to warm up a bit and eat something." The rebbe shook his head and said again, "Call the miller." They said to themselves, "The rebbe is in a hurry to tell the miller something, and when he is done he will come and dine." They went to call the miller.

The rebbe looked at the miller and said, "Your clothes are all white."

The miller moved his lips and whispered, "Yes, my rebbe."

The rebbe said to the miller, "Sit in the carriage."

When he was seated, the rebbe said to the coachman, "Tell the horses we are going." The carriage began to move slowly, slowly, with the ḥasid and his wife walking behind it in case the rebbe changed his mind and would dine with them. They saw that the rebbe was sitting in a deep spiritual trance, as if he were unaware of them. The miller sat silently to the left of the rebbe.

When they left the village, the rebbe said to the coachman, "Nearby there is a cemetery. Direct the horses there."

The coachman turned the horses and drove on to the graveyard. When they arrived at the graveyard, the rebbe said to the miller, "Are you ready?"

The miller whispered, "I am ready."

He said to him, "Descend."

He descended.

He said to him, "Return to the place whence you came."

The miller entered the graveyard.

There was an open grave.

The man entered his grave in his white clothes, and the grave closed behind him.

And the ḥasid and his wife watched.

– *Translated by Michael P. Kramer*

Dessert

Ḥaim Naḥman Bialik, may he rest in peace, told me what he heard from reliable storytellers who heard from some who heard from others who heard from the Rabbi of Apta, may his memory be a blessing, about a Jewish innkeeper living in a small village. He earned a comfortable living serving passersby even though he did not charge high prices for his services. He introduced the unusual custom of greeting every guest with a pair of tefilin for his use in prayer. This allowed the guest to directly start praying, relieving him from the task of rummaging through his satchel. Upon completing prayer guests could sit down to eat.

For their convenience the innkeeper purchased pairs of tefilin and placed them in a large barrel at the entrance to the inn together with other barrels. Whoever entered the inn took a pair of tefilin, prayed and then ate. For this courtesy the innkeeper was revered in heaven and on earth.

On the day preceding the shortest Friday of the year a large number of guests arrived at the inn. Heavy rains and snow made the roads impassable, forcing the guests to remain at the inn for Shabbat. To ease their distress at being far from home the innkeeper's wife cooked a lavish Shabbat meal. To crown the meal she prepared her special after dinner dessert.

The innkeeper's wife suffered from poor eye sight, an outcome of the innumerable days she spent by the oven cooking and baking for the guests. As the day was overcast she mistook the barrel of tefilin for a barrel of prunes. Instead of prunes she put tefilin into boiling water, added sugar, various spices, cooked everything in the pot to perfection and served the dessert to the guests. They relished this dessert, heaping praise on the innkeeper's wife. Never had they experienced such a tasty dish. Even heaven was pleased with this dessert and granted the innkeeper and his wife happiness and prosperity for the remainder of their lives.

– Translated by Shelly Lilker

Shabtai

THE DETAILS OF THE AFFAIR ARE NONE TOO CLEAR, but in the main the facts are that there was a fellow in our town, Israel Coppersmith by name, who was a real master of his craft and used to make things in copper and brass, kettles and basins and ewers and Ḥanukah candlesticks and Sabbath candlesticks, tiny lamps and great lamps for hanging in the synagogues and houses of study and in the houses of decent folk, as well as lamps with holes and pipes for wicks. Some of them would be made like lions and some like eagles and some like deer and some like buds and blossoms and all the other shapes that give the eye pleasure and are bright as the moon and the stars on Sabbath eves when they light up the eyes of Jews at prayer. And while he was working he would think to himself about the secret comforts and salvations that stand and wait in the World to Come for those who keep the Sabbath, till his innards were filled with song and he would break into Sabbath songs and the pleasant prayers of the Sabbath, while the hammer answered him back, and he would raise his voice for joy that the Holy One should have given us so great and hallowed a day.

His wife would say, what are you so happy for? And Israel would answer, the Sabbath day has just come to my mind so I feel joyful—for consider the virtues of the Sabbath when a body lights the Sabbath candles and they shine bright for him in two worlds. Sure a man prepares himself a fine portion for the Sabbath; it supplies him all his needs, and besides, he who keeps the Sabbath in this world has his body preserved in the next world and is safe from every kind of mishap. And he used to grieve that his poverty kept him from properly honoring the Sabbath, since for all his toil he saw no decent recompense in this world, and when the Sabbath eve came round he had nary a coin to buy anything with. And his candlesticks stood without candles and his pots stood without meat or fish or any Sabbath dish, and his wife would be grieving and saying, Woe's me that we have nothing at all for the Sabbath.

And seeing he did not wish to treat his Sabbath like a non-holy weekday he would go where he had to and take seven bits of copper and beat them out and sink a die into them and turn them into seven coins like the Government makes. The Emperor, long life to him, Israel used to say, is a rich enough man and has a good heart towards the Jews and could never be annoyed at me making myself a couple of coins. One he would make for candles and one for raisins to be boiled into wine for kiddush and one for Sabbath loaves and one for meat and one for fish and one for dessert and one for pudding and pie, and would give them to his wife to buy Sabbath ware. Nor was there anybody who could distinguish between his coins and those the Emperor strikes. Maybe the Emperor might be able to tell which were his coins and which were the smith's, but the Emperor lives in Vienna while Israel lived in our town and from our town to Vienna lies a stretch of five hundred miles and more.

Me and you being decent folk never went and said anything about him to the Emperor, but others went and told the Emperor, Israel Coppersmith is minting counterfeit coins. So the Emperor sends for Israel Coppersmith, and that day was Sabbath eve when his wife was just about to leave for the market to buy food for the Sabbath. Before she could even start out a man sent by the Emperor came and took his coins and put them in the Royal treasury to test them and tied Israel's hands behind him and put him in iron chains and led him off to prison. The hands that had been used to prepare fine vessels were chafed by iron chains and the mouth that had been filled with sweet song was dumb for suffering.

And Israel's wife sat moaning and eating her heart out for her husband in prison and she had no candles for the Sabbath, no wine for kiddush, nor Sabbath loaves, nor meat and fish, nor anyone to weep in front of for lack of the wherewithal to usher in the Sabbath. Everybody, who knows how a woman slaves only in order to greet the Sabbath can suffer her sufferings when she stood without a single penny and her husband in iron chains being led off to a distant city and no telling when he would come back to her. She stood and raised her hands aloft and said, Lord of the Universe, was it for our own profit that we did what we did? Wasn't it for Your Sacred Name's sake we did it, because You ordered us to honor the Sabbath, and now because we have done what you commanded I must sit forlorn in my house while my husband sits forlorn in prison.

And who can tell how long the unhappy woman might have sat grieving if an old man hadn't come along just then and knocked at the door and asked, Does the wife of Israel Coppersmith live here? She opened the door and, in front of her, she saw a fine man of good appearance who looked like a king, and stood a head taller than all other men, with his eyes glowing like the light of creation, and his white beard dropping down to his middle and his voice like a man reciting the Torah and his words sweeter than honey. He sets seven coins down before her and says, Your husband has sent you money for Sabbath, so as you can get candles, and wine, and Sabbath loaves, and meat and fish for yourself.

And before ever she could ask him where he had seen her husband the old man had vanished. So she wipes her eyes and puts her kerchief round her head and goes off to the market and buys all her Sabbath ware and arranges her table with candles and wine and food and drink.

And that wasn't the only time, for every Sabbath eve while Israel was still kept in prison the same old man would come and set down seven copper coins in front of her and say, Your husband sends you money so you can prepare Sabbath. And before she had a chance to ask questions he would be gone.

We don't know how long Israel was kept. When the Government lays a hand on anyone it doesn't let go of him so quick. But God Almighty saw the sufferings of Israel and took pity on him and loosened his chains and brought him out of prison, and more still, He brought him back to his home and his wife, and more still, they couldn't bring his case to court because the coins the soldier had took from him were all vanished out of the Royal treasury and not even one single one was left. And once they were all gone nobody could come and test them and pass a judgment against him.

So Israel left the prison and came back to his home and his wife. They were both mighty glad and offered praise and thanksgiving to the Holy One who frees the imprisoned, and made a great holiday and told one another about everything that had happened to them since the arm of the law had come between them.

While they are busy speaking, Israel asked his wife, How did you keep going all this while? And she answered him, All the week through I licked the dust, but on the Sabbath my table was arranged and my candle was lit and I lacked for nothing. He asked her, How did you do it? Said she to him, Didn't you send me money every Sabbath eve so as I should get me Sabbath fare? He said to her, I don't know what you're talking about. Said she, You're a fine one for joking, Israel, why you yourself used to send me money. He stood staring at her all wondering and said, I sent you money? She told him, every Sabbath Eve an old man used to come and say, Israel sends you this to have for Sabbath needs. Then Israel said to her, I don't know anything about the whole thing. And she answered him: If you don't know anything about it then who does know?

Israel took the business to heart and said, I don't know who the old man was any more than you do. Then it could only have been Elijah the Prophet, of blessed memory. And perhaps it was him too that took my coins out of the Royal treasury so as the Emperor shouldn't find out I made the coins. But Israel's wife says to him, Don't say it was Elijah, because I distinctly heard him say, My name is Shabtai.

And we also believe the same as that woman, that the old man wasn't Elijah, because we find in ever so many places in the Talmud how it is assured us Jews that Elijah won't arrive on Sabbath eve, and so on. But on our own we hold that this was the Holy Sabbath himself, who said for love of truth, Shabtai is my name. It was out of God's love for the Jews and His wish that they shouldn't have to turn their Sabbaths into weekdays that He sent the Holy Sabbath himself to her.

– *Translated by I. M. Lask*

The Coin

IT HAPPENED THAT A CERTAIN POOR MAN was coming home from the synagogue on Shabbat evening night and saw a copper coin on the road. Said the poor man: "This is a lucky moment for some other fellow, but what am I to do, for it is Shabbat now and I can't move it. If only I had found it before dark, I would have bought two or three raisins with it and made wine for Kiddush, or I would have bought wheat bread, or other good things with which to enhance the Shabbat." He went to his home and greeted the Shabbat—without wine, and without wheat bread, and without all the other things which make for pleasure—and he recited Kiddush over a piece of black bread.

In the morning on his way to the synagogue, this poor man said: "I'll go and give the coin greetings. If a Gentile hasn't spied it and taken it, I'll find it resting in its place." When he came there he saw that it wasn't a coin of copper but one of silver. Said the poor man: "Fate is smiling on a certain man—for he thought to find a copper coin and found a silver one in its stead. The Holy One is, indeed, putting me to a difficult test." His feet led him away and he went to the synagogue.

After the services the poor man said: "Now I'll surely not find it anymore; many people must have passed that way and many must have seen it. Is it possible that they haven't noticed it, and haven't taken it? Anyway, I'll go there. If they haven't taken it, I shall see whether it really is silver, and if they have taken it, I shall be free from forbidden thoughts and won't think about it anymore."

When he reached the place, he found it resting there just as he had left it last night, and just as he had left it in the morning—except that last night it was a copper coin, and this morning it was a silver one, and now it is one of gold! If this isn't a trick of magic, then it must be the sun. For the mid-day sun is shining on the copper coin and so it looks like gold—and if it isn't gold, it must surely be silver.

The poor man mused to himself: "How many things can be bought with this money! All I have to do is to lift it up, and immediately all the luxuries of the world are mine—white bread and a bit of schnapps and a piece of herring, and other good things with which you can bring pleasure to the Shabbat and to the body. The poor man bent down once or twice, but his awe and reverence for the Sabbath prevailed—and he returned home empty-handed.

At the time of the afternoon prayer he did not return to the coin. Said he to himself: "Who knows if I will be able to withstand temptation. During Shabbat when all the stores were locked I could restrain myself, but this is not true late in the afternoon. In another hour, the stores will be opening and the odor of foods and drinks will come out of them and into one's nostrils—I fear lest I would not control myself."

But man's evil inclination sometimes is too much for him. He kept arguing with his evil inclination and his evil inclination kept arguing back to him. It said to him: "Am I asking you to take it in your hand? Just push it with your foot and move it to the side of the road, or place a stone over it so no one else will take it." After he finished his prayers, he reconsidered and went to that spot—"After all, seeing isn't sinning."

By this time it was twilight. The sun was about to set and golden sparks were coming from it. Upon reaching the coin the poor man found it resting in its place, but it wasn't *one* coin, there were many coins. Maybe they weren't real coins, but just that this one coin shone onto its surroundings just like a coin falling into a heap of refuse would brighten the entire heap. Anyway, that coin was a golden one. If only he would bend over and pick it up, he could support himself for two or three weeks. What are the real needs of a poor man? With a single golden coin, you could maintain him for a few weeks.

Said the poor man: "It is a good thing that my home is empty and I am not obligated to prepare the final third Sabbath meal, for now I am free to keep my eyes on the coins. The man was an idiot who left his money in the dirt. Did he think that they would grow and bear fruit? Were I in his place, I would guard them close to my heart, and every time that my wife and children would ask for something to eat, I would say to them: "Gourmets that you are, so you want to eat? And immediately I would take out a golden coin, and go into a shop and give it to the shopkeeper. May evil come upon me, if he bows as deeply during his prayers as he would then bow before me."

Just as the poor man was about to bend his body down in the manner of a merchant upon seeing a coin of gold, the thought struck him that perhaps here was an act of Satan. Perhaps Satan placed this money here in order to test him. Immediately, he straightened himself erect and said: "Such a prankster! He stands in the dirt and makes fun of a Jew. He does not have to pray, and his mind is unoccupied, but I have to recite the evening prayers and my mind is not free for such foolishness." Whereupon the poor man tore himself away and ran to the Synagogue.

After the services, upon conclusion of the Sabbath, he didn't wish to give any further thought to the coins. Said he: "It's enough that they mocked me all day." But when he turned his eyes away from them, they sparkled at him like coins of gold. When he realized this he told himself, "Now that the Holy Sabbath is over, I'll go see what is shining so."

He stooped and saw what no eye has seen and no hand can count. He stretched out his hands and threw all the pieces of gold into his pockets until his pockets were filled with them. Don't think that he had small pockets. Oh no, they were quite large. Don't think that the gold was light of weight, come and see what he bought with only one such coin: Wine for havdalah, and good white bread, and herring, and other delicacies that are good for the body and do not harm the soul. And he still had change to spare.

He returned home happy. While still singing the Saturday evening hymns his wife set a table of plenty for him. He washed his hands and sat down with his family to dine, and they did full justice to that small bone whose only pleasure is derived from the meal of *Melaveh Malkah*.

From this time forward, his Sabbath was never lacking in anything. Because he had kept one Sabbath in poverty, he became privileged to observe many Sabbaths in plenty.

Concerning Those Who Assemble in Laughter and Frivolousness

THIS IS THE STORY of a certain woman who, on every Shabbat, after praying and reading from the portion of the week, used to sit alone in her house and spin her thread, so as not to be with her neighbors to engage in idle matters and in gossip and slander.

Once it happened that Moses our master was walking on the Sabbath. He came upon the town of the said woman, and he saw one house enveloped by the Divine Presence. When he entered the house, he found a woman sitting at her spindle.

Said he to her: "My child, are you not aware that today is the Sabbath?"

Said she to him: "I am aware that today is the Sabbath."

Said he to her: "And do you not know that on the Sabbath it is forbidden to work?"

Said she: "I know that on the Sabbath it is forbidden to work."

Said he to her: "If that is so, why are you spinning?" Said she: "And what else am I to do now?" Said he to her: "You should be praying and reading from the *Tze'enah uRe'enah*.

Said she to him: "I have completed my prayers, and I have already read from the portion of the week."

Said he to her: "Then go sit amongst your neighbors and do not profane the Sabbath." She stood up, laid down her work and went to her friends.

On the next Sabbath, Moses our master saw that the Divine Presence had forsaken the house. He entered and discovered the woman sitting amongst her neighbors and talking with them. And what were they discussing? Mrs. So-and-So had made herself a garment worth fifty gold pieces; Mrs. Such-and-Such had been regaled by her husband with a string of jewels; somebody's son had eyes for somebody else's daughter; and somebody's daughter had eyes for somebody else's son. And so were they engaging in idle chatter and gossip and slander. Moses, when he saw this, said to her, "My child, return to your former deeds, and do not busy yourself with foolish matters."

Therefore, a person must be extremely cautious so as not to engage in idle matters on the Sabbath.

When these words were brought before the Sages, they argued that the Sabbath was not the day in question but rather the New Moon. For on the New Moon, although working is permitted, women are exempt from work, as we find in the teachings of Rabbi Eliezer: Because the women were unwilling to surrender their earrings to their husbands for the making of the golden calf, the Holy One blessed be He granted them their reward in this world, that they would celebrate the New Moon. And what reward is He granting them in the world-to-come? That they are destined to be renewed like the New Moons. Regardless of which version of the story we accept, a person should exercise extreme caution so as not to create a gathering of laughter and frivolousness.

And why were the New Moon festivals given to the women? Rabbi Yaakov ben Asher explains in the name of his brother Rabbi Yehudah: Each of the twelve New Moons was given to the twelve Tribes of Israel. When they sinned at the Golden Calf, the New Moon festivals were taken away from them and delivered to their wives, who did not involve themselves in that great sin.

– *Translated by Samuel R. Whitehall*

Introduction to The Tales of Poland

A LEGEND IS TOLD, handed down to us from our forefathers who went forth to Polin, as the Jews were accustomed to call Poland. The Jews had seen the persecutions continuing unabated and the troubles forever beginning anew, their subjugation growing more oppressive and the evil kingdom issuing decree after decree, until they could no longer bear up against their foes. They stood at the crossroads and beseeched the ancient pathways to reveal to them which way they should go to find rest for their soul. A note fell from Heaven: "*Go to Polin.*" They departed, arriving in the land of Polin, where they heaped a mountain of gold upon the king. And the king received them with very great honor. The Lord had mercy on the Jews and caused the king and his ministers to show them compassion. The king gave the Jews leave to dwell in all the regions of his kingdom, to trade throughout the length and breadth of the land, and to worship the Lord according to the dictates of their faith. He protected the Jews from all adversaries and enemies and they resided unharmed in Polin for many days. They engaged in commerce and in all manner of workmanship and handicrafts. There the Lord ordained a blessing upon them, and He blessed them in the land. They acquired a good reputation for themselves among the nations, bought and sold in neighboring lands and even minted coins. Indeed, these were the coins engraved with the inscription "Mieszko, Polish King," that is, "Mieszko, Król Polski" (as the Poles used the word "król" for king). While sojourning in the land, they came upon a forest of trees and on each tree was etched the text of one of the tractates of the Talmud. This was the Kawęczyn Forest, near Lublin. They said to one another, "Behold, we have arrived in a land where our forefathers dwelt in ancient times." And why did they call it Polin? Inasmuch as the assembly of Jews had said to the Holy One, blessed be He, "Master of the World, since the hour of our redemption has yet to arrive, *po lin* – dwell here with us in this darkness of exile, until such time as You shall deliver us up unto the Land of Israel."

– Translated by Paul Pinchas Bashan & Rhonna Weber Rogol

The Dance of Death

"The beloved and pleasant in their lifetime—in their death they were not separated" (II Sam. 1:23)

AT THE OUTSKIRTS OF A SMALL TOWN in remotest Poland stands a very old synagogue. By the side of it is a stone heap, four cubits large, with blood-red grass bursting forth from it. Weddings are not held there, nor does one hear there the voices of happy bridegrooms, and the Cohanim, the descendants of Aaron, do not set foot on this hill until this very day. The reason why this story will tell.

In days long past there lived in this town a distinguished, rich man of excellent character. He had an only daughter, a sweet and lovely girl, beautiful like the sun and pure like the moon. When she had grown into young womanhood, her father sought for her a man after his own heart, a youth excelling in the knowledge of the Law and the fear of God. Then he erected for them a splendid and magnificent bridal canopy, according to the law of Moses and Israel, by the side of the Great Synagogue. For the poor of the town he prepared a good meal, and he called many musicians to gladden the hearts of bride and groom. And since he loved his only daughter very dearly, he asked the Count, to whom the town belonged, to permit her to put on a silken gown on her wedding day, for in those days the Jews were forbidden to wear silk. For good measure, the worthy man sent along with his request a full purse for the Count and a pearl pendant for the Countess.

The Count replied with his good wishes and congratulations but withheld the permission to dress the bride in silk; he did not want to set a precedent. The men bowed their heads and the women cried and wailed, because the Count had refused the girl to dress herself in costly silk on her wedding day.

The worthy man did not protest against the Count's decree, but from the way he shook his hand, one could see that his heart was not reconciled with what had happened. He said: "My daughter is a beautiful and lovely bride even in a simple dress. Merely because of a dress one does not put off a wedding, and as to who is right, God will decide." He proceeded therefore with the wedding arrangements, set for the upcoming full moon. The expensive silk garments he sold off, donating the proceeds to marry off poor brides.

The festivities began with great splendor and beauty, with gladness and songs, with timbrel and lute, according to God's beneficence that had blessed the bride's father. A short time before bride and groom were led under the bridal canopy, the outstanding citizens of the town covered the bride's face with a veil, and the groom's friends dressed him in white and put ashes on his forehead, there where the tefilin are fastened—symbols which make the eye shed tears over Jerusalem, burnt in fire, and the heart repent by the reminder of the day of death.

Then the groom takes his place under the canopy and the bride's friends escort her to him. His friends go to greet her, they approach her and draw back again while her friends lead her three times around the groom. The Cantor, his right hand on his ear and his thumb under his throat, sings the Psalm, "And he is like a bridegroom who goeth forth from his bridal chamber." The singers sing, and women and children come from every street and corner to watch the wedding.

Now both bride and groom stand under the canopy. They notice a small cloud of dust approaching from the outskirts of town, and recognize a man on horseback. The relatives, trying to guess who the rider is, say to the bride's father; "Look, the Count is sending a special messenger to recall the prohibition of silk dresses." "No," he replied. "Because he has emphasized that a precedent should not be set, and that the decree remains valid. If this man is coming to us, he bears a letter from our Rabbi to add to our happiness." He was silent and looking at his lovely daughter, radiant in her beauty, he thought: my daughter makes a beautiful bride even in a simple outfit. But from the way he shook his hand, one could recognize that his heart was dissatisfied with the decree.

Then the groom took the wedding ring and placed it on the bride's finger pronouncing the formula: "Behold, thou art wedded to me...," and all the guests and onlookers cried: "Mazal tov!" Then the groom broke a glass, as a reminder of the destruction of the Temple. The marriage contract was read, and the women stepped forth and began to dance. They took two loaves of bread and holding them up they danced in front of the bridal pair. One sang: "The groom is like a king," while another cried: "The bride is lovely and beautiful," and all the bystanders joined in the chorus with "Mazal tov! Mazal tov!"

The bride lowered her two pure eyes to the ground. Who is riding there on the horse? The rider's shadow lies like that of a heavy rock between her and the groom. The rider arrives, and they recognize the Count. The elders of the town trembled when they saw him, but aloud they said: "May you come in peace, for you came to a celebration." They bowed and offering him honeycake and wine, they said: "Sir, let the light of your countenance shine upon us and accept our blessing. Partake also of the meat and the fish and the good meal, because we celebrate a wedding. Your servant gives his only daughter in marriage to the excellent youth who stands before you."

The Count did not pay attention to them and to their words, for when he saw the bride at the side of the tender youth, he almost dropped from his horse, because her beauty made his heart beat faster and the blood boil in his veins. His sword swayed like a drunkard touching his thighs and the iron points of his shoes. Suddenly the Count awoke, like a man overcome by wine. He drew his sword and struck the groom, wounding him fatally. Then he snatched the bride and rode off with her to his palace.

The groom collapsed with a sad smile on his lips. Quietly he stretched out his arms to take his bride to dance; but a thick, sweet moisture mounted in his throat, it contracted, and his life ebbed away.

The smile was cut off from his lips from which the tongue protruded. Silently he lifted his eyes to look at his bride, but she was gone. And the groom died, right in front of the Great Synagogue. The blood gushing forth from his throat colored his white clothes, and the bride was gone, carried away by the Count.

The girl cried, but nobody could help her. The poles of the bridal canopy dropped from the hands of the groom's friends, and terror spread among the guests. What could one do? God gave and God took away. The wedding had turned into a funeral. The friends of the groom went about their task with bitterness and a turbulent spirit; they brought spade and hoe, took the body of the groom and buried him. Where his blood was spilt they dug the grave, by the side of the Great Synagogue. They buried him as he was in his wedding attire, in the shrouds that were soiled with his life blood and with his shoes.

The earth which had absorbed the blood, they lifted with spade and hoe and buried it with him. Thus the grave became his bridal chamber and his joy was transformed into general wailing, for he and his bride were mourned for a long time.

But also the girl did not live long in the palace of the Count. She refused to abandon her belief in the God of Israel, and sad and oppressed by the burden of her grief she passed her days. Once when the Count was away hunting, she sat at the window that looked out to the town. She saw the place before the Great Synagogue where her bridal canopy had stood, and she recalled her youth, her wedding day when her groom had stood at her side in front of the synagogue. A man on horseback had come to the wedding, a messenger of our Rabbi with a letter from the famed teacher. The friends of the groom had clasped their hands and called "The groom is equal to a king!" And the friends of the bride clasped the twisted breads and cried: "The bride is beautiful and graceful!" And all those who stood around had called: "Mazal tov! Mazal tov!"

Who is riding there on a horse? It weighs on her heart like the shadow of a heavy rock. The canopy trembles and its poles fall to the ground. She stoops because her very heart turns in her. Just as she was breathing her last, the Count returned from the hunt. But she did not speak nor did she notice what was going on around her. Then she asked that they give her the bridal dress she wore on the day she came to the palace. A maid helped her put it on. She got up with much effort and began to dance, just as the Count entered, his clothes red with blood. In shock he dropped his game, for suddenly she collapsed and died.

The Count buried her among the Christians and all his servants participated in the funeral. But every night, at midnight, when the rooster crows the second time, and the stars turn in their paths on the firmament, a grave in the Christian cemetery opens quietly, and a woman, all wrapped, ascends in the quiet of the night. She covers her face with a veil, of fear of the watchmen, and she walks, bowed by grief, to the Great Synagogue. Then the dead groom who was slain there comes out of his grave. In the mystery of the night he stretches out his arms, takes his bride to his heart and together they dance the dance of death.

This is why the Cohanim do not set food on that hill, and why weddings are not held there.

Heart and Eyes

You have no doubt heard what is told of Esther, queen of Casimir, King of Poland. Her face was as pure as snow, as snow that falls on the synagogue the Sabbath we read the Song of the Sea, and her eyes were like the sun in spring, and the sweetness of her voice was like the song of morning stars throughout the land of Poland. And Casimir, King of Poland, saw her, and his soul did cleave unto Esther, and he brought her in his golden chariot to his royal city. And on its streets he sprinkled gold and sugar. And the King brought Esther to his glorious palace. And the King lived with Esther many years. He allowed his eyes no sleep, his eyelids no slumber, so as to see Esther night and day. For beauty is sweet to the sight, and no man was satisfied to behold Esther's charms only once. Her rivals—Casimir's three wives, Anna of Lithuania, Adelheit of Hesse, and Hedwig of Sagan—shuddered at the King's love for Esther, and in their jealous passion they scratched with their fingernails on the walls of the house of Esther, wicked inscriptions about the Jewish woman the King had married. For Esther was a Jewess, the daughter of a Jewish tailor. But Esther was not afraid and took no heed, for a kosher mezuzah protected the portals through which the King came to Esther. And Esther lived with her husband the King until she died. Loving her husband the King, she died.

And now I will tell you what the King did to his wife Esther, when his wife Esther died. When Esther died, the King removed her heart and her eyes, and placed them on the wall of his glorious palace, beside his bed, set in a setting of gold and gems. For there was neither graven image nor likeness of Esther. For all the days she lived with her husband the King, she found no time to sit for portrait painters. For Esther dedicated all her days to her lord, her husband the King, and so, too, her husband the King knew Esther. And the King dug a grave for his wife, for Esther, in the valley of flowers opposite his palace. And he buried her in the valley of the flowers of the King.

And Esther lay in the valley of flowers, in the grave the King had dug for her. And the King looked through his window toward the grave he had dug for Esther and gazed at her eyes and her heart that he had set in a setting of gold and precious gems upon the wall of his chambers. And his eyes never turned away from her eyes, and his heart never left her heart.

And Esther lay in her grave, as all the dead lay in their graves, but she found no rest among the dead. For one whose eyes and heart are not with her can find no rest in the grave. And Esther would rise from her grave at night and search for her heart and her eyes, which she had given to her husband the King and which the King had taken for himself. And Esther wandered from the pit of her grave to her pleasure-home to search for her heart and eyes, but she wearied to find the door. For Esther had no eyes and could not see, as the King had taken them along with her heart. Thus would Esther do every night, until her fellow Jews would rise and recite the Shema. And as they read the words of the Torah, "so that you stray not after your own heart and your own eyes," Esther would return to the pit of her grave, to return again at night to search for the heart and eyes after which she had strayed.

– *Translated by Michael P. Kramer*

The Great Synagogue

"How abundant is the good that Thou hast in store for those who fear Thee" (Psalms 31:20)

SCHOOL CHILDREN WERE PLAYING ON THE HILL: Games such as Forty Thieves and Three Brothers, the Battle of David and Goliath, and the Priest Anointed for Battle. When they had tired of these pastimes they said, "Yesterday was Tishah B'Av, the day that the enemies destroyed the Temple. Let's begin to rebuild it." They examined their tzitzit to make sure they were fit, and agreed among themselves that there would be no hatred among them—for they knew that the Temple had only been destroyed on account of the groundless hatred that had existed among Jews. Thus they commenced the task of construction. One brought a pocket full of clay, and another a bit of water. This one a stone and that one a broken brick. And until such time as they might find the magical *shamir* they decided to cut the stones with their teeth. They spread themselves out over the hill and dug, one with a stone and another with his fingers. And they sang the Passover song: "Exalted is the One who will build His sanctuary soon, quickly, quickly, in our day, soon." One of the boys was the rabbi's son. He said to his friends, "My father has a Talmud volume that contains a picture of the Temple and its vessels. I'll go and bring it, so we can have a plan for building the Temple. I'll even bring the box in which my father keeps his Sabbath hat. It is made of brass, and would serve well as the Brass Altar." His friend, the son of the gravedigger, said, "And I shall bring stones that were cut for tombstones. Once the Temple is rebuilt the Redeemer will come. No one will die any more, and there will be no need of tombstones."

As they were digging they found a piece of wood. They continued digging and found something that looked like a roof tile. They tried with all their might to dislodge it, calling out, "Please, O Lord, help us!" Their teacher heard them and came out. They said to him, "Rabbi, we have found a tile." Hardly had they finished speaking when a second tile was found. The rabbi saw the discovery and leapt upon it. Raking the dirt he found several tiles, together forming the shape of a roof. "It is divine providence!" he said. "The rainy season is rapidly approaching, and the Holy One has provided me with the means to repair the roof of my house."

Meanwhile dusk was falling. The teacher sent his students home, and until it was time for the afternoon prayer, he and his family continued to rake the hillside. They found tile after tile. They continued digging and found still more. If this was not a sorcerer's trick, it was the roof of a house. In a few more days they had cleared away all the refuse. And once they had cleared the refuse, they found a large roof. The whole town gathered to see. They surrounded the roof and said, "Such a large roof, such a large roof! There must be a palace underneath, and this is the palace roof." The elders recalled the story of a lord whose wife had run after other men. The lord had invited all of her lovers to a feast. When they had eaten and drunk, he ordered his servants to seal all the windows and doors, and they all died of suffocation. Upon hearing this story the workers shrunk back in terror. But the taskmasters stood over them, making them clear away all the dirt. Several stained-glass windows were uncovered, and they knew this to be a house of prayer. So they drove the Jews away, saying, "This is holy ground."

In the old beit midrash, between the afternoon and evening prayers, long sighs could be heard. Who knows? It could be a synagogue. After all, we have found in the responsa, the legal records of Buczacz, which borders on Jaslowitz, a tradition that Jaslowitz was a great city, a "mother city of Israel." And if it was a great city, might this not be its great synagogue? Other than many tombstones, there is no sign that here was once a great community of Jews. And the old beit midrash—how small it is. The ceiling is falling down and the earthen floor is rising. Whenever the heart is full there is no room for all who are bending in prayer. The Holy Ark is worm-eaten, the dust hanging from it is used to spread on the wound of circumcision. The wings of the two doves on the ark curtain, symbolizing the Jewish people, are plucked and fallen. There is not a penny to pay the building's upkeep. The Days of Awe are coming. The townsfolk. may they not suffer the evil eye, are fruitful. Last year there was not room for them all in the beit midrash. How will there be room for them this year?

On the hill they continued digging, and a beautiful building burst forth and rose up. And when the late summer sun shone upon the stained glass windows, all creatures were filled with the glow. Ancient days, ancient palaces.

It was not many more days before they had swept away the hill round about. Once they had cleared away the entire hill a great building was revealed. But they found that the entrance was closed. They brought the carpenter and the locksmith. The men tried, but were unable to open the door. They tried to break it open, but no tool of human invention succeeded. And as they stood near the entrance they heard a voice issuing forth from the building. They said, "This must be the spirit of one who was not given burial, wailing from within." And they fled for their lives, lest an evil spirit take possession of them and they die.

So they called on the Jews to do their work. And they came and heard the voice which issued forth from the building, and behold: the voice is the voice of Jacob. They inclined their ears, and the voice said, "How goodly are thy tents, O Jacob, thy dwelling places, O Israel." And when they put their hands on the gate, the gate opened before them.

They entered, and found the great synagogue. Was it not the greatest synagogue ever seen in Jaslowitz? The building was large and spacious, the Holy Ark full of Torah scrolls. And above it a pair of doves spread their wings, and the wings of the doves were covered with silver, and a large prayer book was written in elegant script on deerskin. Everything was in its place. Only the eternal light was about to go out.

– Translated by Laurence L. Edwards

In the Depths

"And You have made man like the fish of the sea" (Habakuk 1:14)

ASONOVKI IS A LARGE VILLAGE IN THE DISTRICT OF PODOLIA. It used to be a place where the Gentiles grew wheat and tended their flocks and the Jews lived peacefully by their side. The sons of Jacob did not covet the worldly goods of the sons of Esau, and the sons of Esau, busy since time immemorial with working their fields, let the sons of Jacob go their way unharmed.

The village belonged to the fief of the Count of Buczacz, and all the Jews in it belonged to congregation of Buczacz, from whence they received not only the exact dates on which the feasts fell each year, but also the palm branches, the citrus fruit and the myrtle for the Feast of Tabernacles, and all the various things a Jewish soul needs to keep up his Jewishness.

And yet, when the Days of Awe came round, they all left the village and went into town to pray. For it was the Law of Israel and ancient custom that on the New Year and the Day of Atonement people from the villages came to pray in the synagogue in Buczacz. As this was before the time of the ḥasidim, before there were any divisions in the Jewish camp, the villagers looked up to the heads of the congregation, whose word was law unto them.

And so, each year, on the eve of the New Year, the Jews of Asonovki got up before dawn, saddled the horses, loaded their carts, and, having said the early morning penitential prayers, set out to the town of Buczacz to converse in holiday prayer with the great congregation of that town. So they traveled, leaving their homes and worldly goods at the mercy of the Gentiles, but the Lord kept watch over their belongings, as He had done in the Land of Israel, when the people made their pilgrimage to Jerusalem three times a year.

When the villagers arrived in the town for the holy festival, they made their way to the houses of their relatives bearing presents, the best fruit, butter and cheese, healthy fowl, as heavy as fattened calves, to be eaten as an atonement for sins. They brought sweet-smelling honey, in which the piece of bread eaten after the blessing over the bread was dipped. Indeed, they brought enough honey for all bread to be smeared with it, from that day until Ḥanukah in winter, when the fat of slaughtered geese was melted down.

As they emptied their sacks, out rolled some of the wonders of the earth—roots and herbs and tree barks used in cures, and sweet-smelling beeswax to make candles with, candles for the house of the Lord and candles in remembrance of the dead. All these gifts were safely packed away in the hay which filled the carts; this hay was afterwards spread on the floor of the house of prayer. Such was the offering of the villager when he came to town, there, in the midst of his brethren to glory in the nearness of the Lord.

And the synagogue was crowded with worshippers on holy days. There was hardly room for all the townspeople and so all the villagers had to pray in the ante-room; they sat when others sat, and when all the others got to their feet to say Amen, so did they, although they could barely hear the blessings and the prayers. But after the morning prayer, when the Torah was read, it was customary to read slowly and in a loud and clear voice. Books were heaped in front of them, so that they, too, should follow the readings and be uplifted to the light of the Holy Book, instead of wasting away their lives in the darkness of the villages.

Such was the custom of these simple people for many years; each year they came into Buczacz meeting people from other surrounding villages, because on these days they all came into town to pray.

Such, then, had been the custom of the people of Asonovki. So, one day, on the eve of the New Year, as they set out for Buczacz as usual, the

Count was leaning over the parapet, and seeing the travelers, he said to his servants: "People are coming down the mountain."

And his servants answered: "They are Jews, coming to pray before their God." Then the Count said to his servants: "I tremble with sudden fear for these poor people, for if the bridge collapses under their weight they will surely fall into the depths of the river and drown." The Count chuckled as he spoke, and his servants understood. "Yes," they said, "the bridge will certainly give way under their weight and they will all be drowned in the raging currents. Indeed, they are not thin and light-boned like the Jews of the town, these village Jews are stout and bursting with health."

And the Count said, "Why do you stand around doing nothing why don't you go forth and attack the Jews as they arrive at the crossing, and by shoving their carts into the water save the bridge from destruction." And his servants said to him, "We are your obedient servants, your honor, and we shall do as you wish." And they left the Count to prepare an ambush for the people of God.

The bridge over the gorge was made of strong and heavy iron, because the currents of the river flowing underneath were swift and terribly dangerous. And there were two toll houses at the foot of the bridge, because everyone passing over the bridge either in a cart or riding a horse had to pay a toll. That was where the Count's servants lay in wait for the people of God.

As the crowded carts approached the river the Count's servants left their hiding places and surrounded them. When the Jews of Asonovki saw that the Gentiles were intent on taking their lives, a great fear seized them. Quickly they unwrapped their prayer shawls and put them on, saying, "We shall not meet our Maker in everyday clothes." And so they made themselves ready to die.

The Gentiles heaved the carts and riders into the deep river. Those that stayed in the carts were buried under them, and those who tried to jump out were crushed beneath the wheels. And the horses, blind with rage flaring up in their blood, lashed out with their hooves, lacerating in their crazed fury the breasts of their erstwhile masters, whose life-blood poured away into the river. And the people of God drowned in the dark waters.

This happened at a spot where they used to say: "Let us pause here and say the *Tashlikh* prayer, in honor of our merciful God." The waters parted to receive their bodies and closed over them, leaving no trace of a hint that the serene flow of the river had ever been disturbed.

It happened shortly after this that the commander of Demisov decided to give a big banquet, and to entertain his guests with the best fare in the land. So he commanded his servants to go to the river and bring him the best of the huge fat fish to be found there. And he sent fishermen to fish all the bays and inlets of the neighboring rivers, as the fish in one river tasted differently from the fish in another. And many fishermen went out to fish, each with his own net, and they stood fishing on the banks of the river in the middle of the night.

The sharp wind which blew during the month of the High Holy Days ruffled the river, and the fish trembled in the water, and the moon had not yet arisen and darkness clung to the reeds and the rushes. The fishermen cast their nets on the water and hauled them in empty, without a single fish. So they lowered the nets again, and this time brought to the surface the carcasses of a few dead chickens, the skull of a horse, and a cartwheel.

Suddenly, an apprentice boy said to his masters: "It seems God has sent us a very big fish today because the net in my hand feels most heavy." And indeed the net was so heavy that, try as he might, he could not draw it out of the water by himself. So his masters ran to help him. And they drew up the net, and there was a dead body in it. They saw the dead body and were afraid and crossed themselves. Then they brought it to the village to give it a decent burial.

But when they came to the priest, he said to them: "Don't make such haste to bury the dead. Can you not see that this is the body of a Christian boy who was slaughtered by the Jews, so that they could mix his blood in their Passover bread?" When they heard these words the villagers trembled with rage and wanted to go out and avenge the gruesome crime there and then. But the priest quieted them down and said, "Have no fear, brothers, this deed shall be fittingly punished, as there is justice in the land. Be patient until their Day of Atonement arrives, when the watchman of the synagogue, who is one of us, shall hide the body there and the judges shall see for themselves the proof of the crime of which we accuse the Jews."

And they said to him: "That is the right thing to do, Father." And so saying they went back to their homes and their work. And the priest started a rumor all over the countryside that the son of a Christian was missing from his home, that they had searched for him in all the villages and that he could not be found. And to the people the priest said: "Do not lift up your hand in anger until I give you the sign." And when the Jews heard what was happening and of what they were falsely accused they trembled with fear. And they said: "The Day of Atonement is near, let us take courage. Perhaps the Lord will help."

Many simple folk living in those parts, on hearing the rumors that were put about, armed themselves with hatchets and sticks and set forth to attack the Jews that night. And the people of Israel were filled with fear, and they all put on their festive garments and their prayer-shawls and went to God's House, there to wait for His will to be done. And their brothers living in the surrounding villages came, too, as they had done in the past saying: "If God has cast us off and delivered His people to the slaughter, then let us die near Him, in saintly company."

And the synagogue was filled to overflowing. And although the air was festive, hearts were sick. They opened the Ark and brought out the scrolls of the Torah, and each and everyone in the congregation kissed them and they all wept bitterly. And the cantor intoned "Light is sown for the righteous, and gladness for the upright in heart." And two old men from among the elders of the congregation stood by his side, one to the left of him and one to the right of him, and the cantor chanted the *Kol Nidrei* first softly, then somewhat louder and the third time loud and clear followed by the blessing "Blessed be the One who has preserved our lives!"

And there was a great crowd of people in the synagogue, greater than any that had been seen there since the day the house was built. The air in the hall was heavy and hot and the people became weary of their prayer-shawls and lowered them from their heads. And when they had done so they noticed that there were strangers among them who looked like villagers. And the strangers stood in their midst, silent and still, covering their faces with their prayer-shawls. Suddenly the strangers turned towards the door, got up from their places and walked, one behind the other, into the store chamber for disused books, and brought out of there the dead body of a child. They carried him in front of the Ark, waved him about like a sacrificial offering, and then walked silently out of the building carrying the body with them. And the people in the synagogue glanced at them and saw them descending the slope towards the river bed, and their hearts grew faint at the sight.

While they were wondering what to do, a huge crowd surrounded the synagogue, and called out: "Bring forth the child that you have slaughtered." And so saying they rushed in and opened the Ark and all other places where a body could have been hidden, but search as they would, they could find no dead body. And the priest went into the store house, where the body had been hidden, saying: "I tell you that this is surely the place these God-cursed people have buried the slaughtered child." And they searched the place and found nothing, and the people who had come with the priest were filled with amazement. Thus they only devastated the house of prayer without harming anybody that was in it.

While the fishermen were fishing at the command of their lord and master, he himself, accompanied by his followers, was hunting in the forest, bringing terror to the birds and animals within his reach. Finally, sated with hunting, the company returned home by a route passing the river; there the fishermen were standing along both banks, casting their nets. And as they made ready to draw them forth again the nets became taut until they were ready to burst with the weight of the catch.

Laughing gleefully, the fishermen drew in their nets with all their might; and the first net that was drawn ashore had a dead man caught in it who was shielding a small boy he had in his arms with his prayer shawl. And the fishermen screamed and the nobleman and his retinue shouted to teach other that there was not a single net did not have its dead. And they were filled with horror and dread at having caught nothing but dead bodies in their nets, and they knew that these were the remains of the Jews whom the Count of Buczacz had drowned in the waters of the Strypa.

And the thing became known in Demisov, and the gladness the Jews felt at their own salvation was turned to mourning, for the Jews of Demisov learned what had befallen their brethren from Asonovki at the hands of the Count. The next day they all set out to ransom the bodies from the hands of the fishermen. And they paid the ransom money in full and brought the dead back with them and gave them a burial in hallowed ground, burying them not in shrouds but wearing their clothes and their shoes, so as to provoke God's anger and vengeance.

Ever since that day the Jews of Demisov pray on the Day of Atonement without covering their heads with their prayer-shawls, in memory of the drowned and slaughtered who came to pray in the house of the Lord that night of Atonement.

– *Translated by Yoram Matmor*

The Goat Which Was Blessed

THERE IS A STORY OF A WIDOW whose husband left her a houseful of orphans without leaving any more for their sustenance than a milk goat. And every day, as the children were about to leave for school, their mother would give them a cup of milk and would say, "My sons, He who gives strength to all the Universe will give you strength and valor to learn Torah and bear the duty appointed by the Holy One blessed be He." And they would recite the blessing before drinking the milk, "Blessed is He at whose word all is come into being," and the goat would nod her head and bleat at them, saying "Amen" in her own way. They would stroke her head because they were so fond of her, and would say pleasant things in her presence, and would go to school to study God's Torah. When they came home from school they would take her out into the field and find her good pasture and would lead her to the brook to water her. They would tell her all manner of fine stories, like the story of the goats of Rabbi Hanina ben Dosa who brought bears on their horns, or the story of the goat which went through a cave to the Land of Israel and always brought back a great deal of milk in its udders, sweeter than honey and with the taste of Paradise. And then they would comfort her and soothe her and make her a great promise that when our righteous Messiah comes speedily and in our days, Amen, they would take her with them to the Land of Israel and feed her on carob fruit and give her the dew of Mount

Hermon to drink. And they would speak to her in this fashion, "Now you eat grass and the other growths in the ground over which we bless 'At Whose word...,' but in days to come you will eat such things as require the blessing, 'Who createst the fruit of the tree.'" And they would invent all kind of happy tales to amuse that goat, and the goat gave them milk with pleasure till they grew and prospered in Torah and in piety and became valiant in performing the will of their Father in Heaven.

But when sins increased – *the Merciful One deliver us*! – and it was decreed that the Exiles of Israel in Russia and in Poland and in Ukraine and in Lithuania should all but be lost – *God forbid* – to the world, Chmielnicki the oppressor, *may his name be blotted out,* came with all his accursed jackboot Cossacks to the town of that widow and laid the whole place waste and destroyed all the houses and killed all the Jews and made a great desolation in the town.

When the widow saw the plunderers nearing her house she put a slaughterer's knife into the hands of each of her sons and said, "When these accursed ones come to compel you to transgress the commandments of the Torah, then take each of you your knife and slay yourselves to sanctify God's holy name, and do not transgress, God forbid, even a single commandment of the Torah." And she took a knife and stood over them so that if they chose a life of shame and disgrace and denied, God forbid, the God of Israel, she would slay them on the spot.

The lady took the knives and prepared to hallow the name of Heaven. At the same time their mercies turned to that pure beast which had sustained them with her milk, and which would now fall into the hands of the accursed who would eat her flesh without reciting a blessing. The goat herself, feeling what they had in mind, stretched her throat and bleated very loudly and lay down before them. Then the oldest of them all rose and held her between his knees and took his knife, recited the blessing "On the slaughter," and slaughtered her in accordance with the Law, and said "Now the accursed will not hear your voice nor drink of your milk, nor fill their bellies with the meat of you who sustained babes of the schoolhouse." When he had slaughtered her, he poured out her blood before the house. Ere the plunderers reached the house the widow and her sons found opportunity to hide.

After the foes had destroyed the entire town they reached the widow's house. When they saw bloodshed at the door they said, "It has already been attended to and went their way to another town. Once the accursed ones had gone the widow and her sons left their hiding-places and sustained themselves on the meat of the goat which had been slaughtered in accordance with the Law by a proper kosher blade and to the utterance of the blessing "On the slaughter."

A long time passed and the land became calm. Some householders returned to the town and found it all waste and desolate, all the synagogues and houses of study being burnt, except that one house which had not been destroyed. They entered and set apart a place for congregational prayers and brought an Ark of the Torah and sacred books. And every day they prayed there and studied Torah, but with the length of Exile the Synagogue has grown old and its walls and roof are bowed close to the ground and grass has begun to grow upon it and goats leap about eating the grass. And at the hour when the Jewish people prays and says the Kaddish and the blessings, goats bleat on the roof and say Amen, in their fashion, as their mother's mother used to say Amen to the grandsires of those within.

The Light of Torah

"Night-time was only created for the study of Torah" (Eruvin 65a)

KOROLEVKY WAS A SMALL TOWN with few people—it could fit inside a man's hand. Its mortar houses were close together and bowed over, with no mark of pride in them. And were it not, *may the Evil Eye be averted from them,* for the sing-song voices of the schoolchildren, and the Jewish groans lamenting the difficulties of making a living and the burdens of taxation, one could hardly have said that this was a Jewish community at all. There was one house in Korolevky, however, that was both spacious and dignified. And built over the house was a little attic. This house belonged to Asher Baruch and Reb Asher Baruch was the rich man of the town. Both wealth and plenty dwelt in the house of Asher Baruch and his knowledge of the Torah was twined round his very vitals. For he was both a great scholar and one crowned with possessions. In him did wealth and learning find a dwelling-place together. Thus it was that his house had the marks of dignity upon it and was higher than any other house in the town. But if the master of the house was himself bowed over, it was only with the burden of the Torah.

And this is the story of that house, where the store and the kitchen were below and the attic above the house. It was in this attic that Asher

Baruch sat over the Torah and the service of God and pondered the Torah both by day and by night. His wife was a woman of valor and it was she that carried on the business and supported her household in honor, while Asher Baruch sat within his attic over the study of the Torah and the service of God. Neither would he turn the workings of his spirit to the vanities of this world, nor would he mix in trade, as was the custom in Israel in those days. Thus each night and every night Asher Baruch would sit studying by the light of his candle. As for that candle, it was neither set in a silver lamp, nor in a tin one, nor in an earthen vessel, nor was it fixed upright in a hole in the table, rather it was held erect in the fingers of Asher Baruch himself. For the study of the Torah is fatiguing to man and the urge to sleep creeps up upon those who pore over the Torah and one must be wary lest sleep or slumber should come upon him. Thus it was that Asher Baruch held the candle between his fingers, so that should he nod off the flame would reach his fingers and he would rouse himself again and rise up to the service of the Creator.

Now Korolevsky is a border-town. And there, in this town, were numbers of smugglers, as is usual. These were scoundrels who smuggled cattle from one province to another. At night-time, when no one was abroad and when there was no one left in the streets, they would go forth, crossing the border and returning with their cattle. Each night they did this, in the darkness, so that the frontier-guards would not see them. And only the light from the candle held by Asher Baruch shone through the darkness from his attic window upon them and guided them to the road leading into the town. For great, indeed, is the power of the Torah, there are no limits to it, truly. Each night and all through the night Asher Baruch sat beside his candle and pondered the word of the Torah. But the desires of man have neither rest nor slackening. And the desire for vain possessions is as wide as the mouth of Hell and thus, night after night, the smugglers went forth and stole across the border and led their cattle across. He sat waking and watching through the night and they, too, walked and watched. Late in the afternoon, as the dusk drew in, Asher Baruch would rise up from his scantly-snatched afternoon nap and would go to the synagogue to say the afternoon and the evening prayers. When he had finished his prayers, he would return to his home where he would eat and drink a little, so that he might say

Grace and fulfill the injunction concerning the hundred blessings of the day, and in order to fortify his body for the study of the Torah. Then he would rise and mount up to his attic, where he would wipe his eyes with a damp towel and his wife would bring him a measure of candles to light him through the night in his blessed study of the Torah. At that very same hour the smugglers of Korolevky would assemble and go forth in little groups and parties. Some of them would go to the frontier-guards and would sit with them, drinking brandy to put them to sleep. Others would wrap their feet in straw and bind them up with rags before they went forth to their work. This was their practice for several years and Asher Baruch aged from year to year, but he did not forsake his study of the Torah. Therein his strength remained as it had always been, for there is no strength in man for the night, save it be for study. Some slight change would seem to have taken place, for it was now his wife's practice to bring him the narrower kind of candle. She would say: "As for this Asher Baruch of mine, may his life be preserved, his hands have grown heavy with old age, his fingers have begun to tremble, perhaps thick candles are too heavy for him." But as for everything else there was no change whatever. Asher Baruch remained Asher Baruch and the light remained light, shining as well as it ever shone. And every night and all through the night, Asher Baruch sat and studied and the smugglers crossed the border and kept the frontier-guards quiet and crossed back again to the town, leading the cattle by the light shed from his candle.

Nevertheless, man's strength is not forever; for each man there is an appointed time. And so Asher Baruch went the way of all flesh. Asher Baruch died, leaving the ways of life to the living. It had been his custom to sit up, night after night and all through the night, pondering the teachings of the Torah. Nor did he cease from his study, although his flesh was weary, even on the very day of his death. But on the night of his decease he could no longer continue his study. His illness seemed to gain the upper hand and his strength was drained from him. They brought him down to his winter lodgings and put him to bed. Nor was his candle kept burning any longer. Whereupon the party of smugglers went forth and were unable to return. All the night long they strayed about the fields without finding their own town. In this way, they wandered about all through the night, until the light of dawn. When the day dawned, they saw their appointed meeting place from afar. So they went forth as was their wont and returned. Upon their return, their master's fury leaped out at them angrily: "May your guts be found dangling from without your bellies, cursed thieves that you are! Where were you all night long? I thought that you had been caught or that a wild beast had attacked you and had devoured all of my goods!" To which they answered: "What can we do, master? We wandered about in confusion all night, without finding our path. And though we sought it all night, we failed to find our own town." Whereupon they told him of the way in which they were accustomed to walk and the way in which they would return and how the light would guide them so that they would find their way. There had been a light shining in the town formerly and it was by this light that they would walk and this night there was no light there and all was darkness in the town. And they said: "It is the light of Korolevky that has gone out," prophesying a truth that was beyond them. For, in a few moments, it was heard that Asher Baruch had passed on and that the light of the Torah was extinguished in Korolevky.

– *Translated by Hilda Auerbach*

The Tale of Azriel Moshe the Book-Keeper

AZRIEL MOSHE WAS A PORTER FROM A FAMILY OF PORTERS, and was exceptionally strong and hard-working. He walked in God's ways, in the manner of simple Jews. Each morning he would rise before dawn and time his prayers with the rising of the sun. After taking off his tefilin and placing them in their pouch, he would say: "Master of the World, I don't understand the prayers that I've prayed, but You, to whom all is revealed and known, probably already know everything that the siddur contains anyway. May it be Your will to receive my prayer with mercy and pleasure." He would suddenly run to the tavern and down a shot of brandy while saying to himself, "A know-nothing ain't no better than a horse. Just as a straw-gnawing horse gets his fill of drink, Azriel Moshe, after you've prayed, you get drink too." People would mock and poke fun at him: "Wine speaks from Azriel Moshe's throat, spirits splutter in his bowels." Azriel Moshe would shake his beard and reply "What can I do! My father and mother died on me when I was young and I had no rabbi. I was destined to be like a yoked donkey or a loaded horse. I swore by my beard that if God gave me a burden to carry I would ferry it freely." He went right to the market and assumed the yoke that is earning a living. There was a corner in the market where he would stand in God's shadow, and he would scan every which way for someone summoning him to carry his things. When someone in the city died – *God save us*! – he would fetch the board and the tub for purifying the dead. Because of his beautiful beard, his peers appointed Azriel Moshe to be the Jew Mordechai in the Purim play and as Jacob our father in the productions of the Joseph story, in which roles he would cheer Jewish hearts with the joys of Purim.

Thank God, there are many, many episodes to report about Azriel Moshe – thirty reams of paper could not contain them. For example, he would use his beard to sweep the floor before the Holy Ark, like Rav Ya'akov ben Rav Yakir of blessed memory. And his wife would berate him and grab his beard shrieking, "The fiend grows himself a beard as long as the exile, but for me he refuses to produce even two hairs for a wig." But the toils of Exile sap our strength and cripple our ability to write them all down, so one cheap piece of paper's worth is all we have written. As it is small it felt right for us to record it. So here it begins:

One day Azriel Moshe was standing in the market with the rest of his friends. A man came and called them to carry his things from one lodging to another. Now this was an upstanding citizen and an educated man, his home was brimming with books: he had both the Jerusalem Talmud and the Babylonian Talmud, the *Yad HaḤazakah*, the *Arbah Turim*, the *Shulḥan Arukh*, the *Mikraot Gedolot*, books of science, philosophy, and history, aside from the prayer books for the Sabbath and Festivals, fulfilling with them the following rabbinic interpretation, "'This is my Lord and I shall beautify Him,' meaning, beautify yourself before Him with exquisite mitzvot." The books were bound with beautiful covers, and he beseeched the bearers to be careful and avoid their damage or destruction. Azriel Moshe jumped up, put his hand on his beard, and said to the man, "Let me! I'll do it!" So he took the books, put them in a sack, and bound them with rope. He then bent down to lift the books on his shoulders and started to take them to the new lodging.

Halfway there he stood, the sack still on his shoulders, and said, "Master of the World, how great is Your Torah, and still there are people who know it all. But as for me, I can't comprehend a single book, a single page, a single line, not one word. I'll eat my hat if I haven't heard it said that God assigned for Abraham our father – *may he rest in peace* – Torah and Wisdom themselves to act as tutors, letting him suck up his learning like mother's milk. Far be it from me to charge You with not treating the son of my mother like Abraham our father, but I'm desperate to know what all these books say."

He began to spurt sacred words, *Ḥumash, Rashi, Gemara, Tosafot, Midrash, Targum,* and *Targum Sheni.* He walked and whispered through the market saying *Ḥumash, Rashi, Gemara, Tosafot,* and so on. He recited the names of the five books of Moses, and the names of every portion. He then thought to himself, "So, it was God who took us out of Egypt and gave us the Passover lamb with which to eat *matzah* and *maror,* and with which to drink four cups, and there is also the fast on the Ninth of Av, when we sit on the floor and lament the Temple's destruction. That means that the people of Israel entered the land of Israel and went up to Jerusalem, remaining there until the villain Titus came and destroyed it." But he didn't know where these things were written. He began to sob inside. "Stupid me who hasn't studied! Stupid me who knows nothing!" His heart withered from the scale of his pain, and even that which he knew was forgotten. He walked like a mourner until he lowered his load.

After unloading his load and taking his fee he went into a shop, opened a bag, and bought a small piece of chalk. He stowed it at home and listed every name in the Torah on the door and the lintel: the names of the Patriarchs – *may they rest in peace,* the names of the Matriarchs – *may they rest in peace,* the names of the Priests and Levites, the Kings and Prophets. Not a name from the *Ḥumash* or *Haftarah* – Moses, Aaron, David, Solomon, and so on – was left off his walls, until they appeared to be plastered with elaborate wallpaper.

When it was time for the afternoon prayer he ran to pray with the congregation in the study hall. Between Minḥah and Ma'ariv he listened to scholars battling each other in *halakhah.* He stood in the corner, stuck his thumbs into his rope belt – his other fingers hovering above it – and absorbed every word. He listened to them say "the Rambam, the Rosh, and the Tur say this and that," and understood that these were the world's great sages. His heart bloomed and he recited their names in a whisper. When he got home he listed them and rehearsed them again and again until they flowed fluently from his mouth. The next day after prayers he did not race to the tavern but ran to the study hall to hear the words of scholars. If a book's name was mentioned he would repeat it, like a child that mimics a blessing he hears from his teacher. If a scholar said, "Such is mentioned in this *Gemara*" or "Such is brought in this book," he would focus his energies on memorizing the name and remembering the place. By the end he knew every book, and if a scholar needed one, Azriel Moshe would race to the shelf and fetch it for him. This is how he behaved each day, incrementally increasing his knowledge. On returning home he would list each name that he'd heard in the study hall. He would kiss the writing on the wall with immense joy—now knowing the names of Torah scholars, and then he would weep – feeling still ignorant of their teachings. From the many tears and kisses the writing gradually rubbed away. So what did he do? He took a sheet of paper and began to inscribe, name after name, with a pencil. Whenever free from work he would read these names.

Azriel Moshe, went on to read almanacs – the dates of the world's creation, the flood, Moses' birth, the exodus from Egypt, the building of the first Temple, the exile of the Ten Tribes, the miracle of Ḥanukah, the destruction of the Temple, the production of Gutenberg's printing press and more. The Zohar states that if a person thinks a good thought it rapidly soars to their heart – the body's essence – and then diffuses to each limb, at which point the thought and the limbs instantly blend, breeding a Divine glow. Undoubtedly Azriel Moshe became a new man. From then on his life changed. When his wife would berate him he would concentrate on the names of great men and ignore her derision, and, since he snubbed her scorn, her impulse to further curse him diminished and a peace grew between them. She even began to respect him, to praise him in front of the neighbors. Even the neighbors began to respect him and were eager to engage him in conversation. Every calendrical query – when a certain festival or *yahrtzeit* fell – was taken to him. He would stroke his beard and respond, "Wait and I'll check the calendar." He would stand, take the calendar off the peg, check it, and answer. His prestige soon spread through the city. Sometimes he would even have a scholar to dinner. He undoubtedly did not eat like gluttonous folk, who slur blessings at speed and eat greedily. He ate with composure, with a tidily spread table cloth, honoring God with a flattering tune from his throat. Between courses his guests told him stunning tales of the righteous, and he was sure to study some practical wisdom. We heard from the mouths of truth-loving men who knew him and testified that Azriel Moshe was a handsome man, and that nothing in his face betrayed him as a commoner.

See what the Holy Shelah wrote and you will be shocked. These are his words: "I have seen and received that even a complete know-nothing, etc., etc., if he reads these names (that is, the names of the sages and the names of their books), his soul desires them, and he cries for lack of understanding, then he is pleasing to God and he will merit much in the future."

Many years later, when Kings warred with one another, a horde of soldiers came to Azriel Moshe's city. Many Jews fled to the fields and forests, and the rest accepted Heaven's judgment – whomever by the sword by the sword, whomever by hunger by hunger. Israel pined away. But Azriel Moshe raced to the great study hall and filled sacks upon sacks with books, hiding them to prevent – *God forbid*! – desecration at Esau's hands. Each day in the study hall he would stir himself in his prayer shawl, and fast. He would read the names of the Sages of the Mishnah and Talmud, the names of other holy Jewish giants, and the names of the holy books, until, one day, the enemy came. He saw Azriel Moshe and his beard and panicked, as it says "All the peoples of the Earth will see… and fear you." Then and there he fled for his life. His officer said to him, "Did you complete your mission?" He said, "I saw an old man and panicked." Then and there the officer gathered his troops and stormed the study hall – it was a Monday at the moment of God's temper, and Scorpio was rising in the path of Sagittarius in the year 1847 since the destruction of the Temple. They surrounded Azriel Moshe. Azriel Moshe looked up and turned his heart to his father in Heaven, saying, "Master of the World, take my soul now while my mind is pure and my heart true, so that I will not – *God forbid* – be made to deny the God of Israel." He accepted his fate and spread out his neck for slaughter.

They grabbed him and hung him by his belt and his beard. These fiends' passions did not dull until they had plucked out his eyes, torn out his tongue, ripped off his fingers, and overturned the house. They found the books and shredded them in rage. They swept through the city to break and uproot, eradicate and kill, slay and destroy all its Jews.

Azriel Moshe hung by his beard until Elijah the prophet – *may he remembered for good* – took him down. He gathered the fragments of his fingers, revived the light of his eyes, returned his tongue to his mouth, stood him on his feet, and brought him to the cave of Rabbi Gadiel the Infant. Then and there Rabbi Gadiel the Infant rose, wearing robes of retribution, brought out a great and terrible book, took the soot of those who sanctified God while consumed by fire, and listed in true writing all that the fiends had done to Azriel Moshe. He then went out to meet him, gave him a greeting, tied him a crown of honor, and brought him to the realm of the Ten Martyrs. As he knew the name of each book, they sent him to the bookcase and Azriel Moshe stood and served before them.

Here ends the tale of Azriel Moshe the porter, Azriel Moshe the book-keeper.

– *Translated by Dov Lerner*

The Messenger from the Holy Land

At one time in the midst of my wanderings, I chanced to come to one of the cities of Poland. As I entered the city, not a man was to be seen. I went from place to place, from street to street, only to find that every shop was locked. I stood amazed, bewildered. "The day is yet young," I said to myself, "why is it that all these shops are closed and locked? Why is every street so deserted? Perhaps the government has decreed some hateful edict on the community, Heaven forbid, and all the Jews are gathered in the synagogue to pray for their very lives. No, it is more likely that they have made some miscalculation in the calendar." While I was still standing thus, undecided, I heard the dull murmur of far-away weeping. Following the direction of the sound, I finally came to a synagogue. Upon entering, I found that it was full of Jews, wrapped in their prayer shawls, crowned with tefilin, their faces flushed with deep emotion. They stood up to their knees in tears, so to speak, and beat upon their hearts crying, "Alas, woe unto us!" And whenever the cantor uttered the name "Jerusalem," they fell upon their faces weeping so bitterly that the tefilin on their foreheads seemed to glitter through the tears. Later, the *shamash* made the rounds with a large box in his hand on which was written *Eretz Yisrael*, and into it each dropped coins of silver or gold.

My hair seemed to stand on end, so astonished was I at this strange sight; and I was too breathless with excitement to inquire—What is this? And wherefore? "Will this weeping be eternal?" I wondered. "If indeed these be mortal men, then is it not written, 'Withhold thy voice from weeping'; and if they are angels, then even angels and seraphs cease from their singing occasionally." I thus stood waiting until they should finish praying, but when the prayers were over, they hastened, like eagles making for their nests, straight to the ark to bring out the books. Then immediately, some of them sat down to study the Talmud and others to study the Mishnah, and they studied aloud, with voices chastened by tears. They studied with such whole-hearted fervor, that even the words of those whose studying clearly showed them to be possessed of no great learning, flowed forth like songs and hymns of praise. And their voices seemed all the more dear to me, for I was like a man wandering through the desert who, when he hears the chirping of birds, even though far away from a settlement, finds his heart filled, nevertheless, with deep joy and pleasure in the thought that he is near civilization, gardens, and orchards.

On beholding such intense worship, I did not have the heart to ask the why and wherefore of it. And thus the hours flew by; it was already past midnight, and then ere yet the call of the cock was heard, all of them sat down on the ground and lifted up their voices in lamentation over the destruction of Zion. They sat there in awe and reverence and fear so great, that their souls seemed about to expire from anguish, when suddenly there entered an old man who brought bread and wine from which they drank "*Lechaim!*," and blessed each other with "*Next year in Jerusalem!*"

The old man went from one to the other until at last he came to me. He poured a glass of wine for me, handed me a honey cake and then stretched out his hand to receive my offering. Immediately I seized his hand and said, "By your life, I shall not let you go until you answer my question." "Ask, my son," he said, "what is it?" and I said to him, "For what reason are you all gathered here in the synagogue amid such bitter lamentation as this?" "And where should Jews gather," he answered, "if not in the synagogue?" "That is very fine," I agreed, "indeed, where should Jews assemble if not in the synagogue, but why at this particular time, is what I want to know. It is the weeping that I asked about."

The old man opened wide his eyes. "I see that you are a stranger." "Indeed I am," I retorted. He greeted me and said, "You are not from this province then?" I returned his greeting and said, "No, I am not." "Whence do you come?" he asked. I told him that I was from Jerusalem. As soon as he heard that I was from Jerusalem, he took me by the hand and went around the synagogue with me, crying, "A Jerusalemite is with us!" and then led me once more to the front of the synagogue. "A good omen! Truly a good omen!" they all exclaimed, and immediately they came forward and greeted me. And so fervid were the greetings and so profuse the handshakings that in that moment I felt called upon to render praise and thanks to Him, may His name be blessed, who gave the voice to Jacob and the hands to Esau, for if He had given the hands to Jacob there would not have been left of my own hand even a little finger. And I further commented, "Mystery upon mystery! This is indeed a bewildering puzzle. I came to a city and it was empty. I entered the synagogue and it was full." "Wait," they said, "until we have explained all this to you and you will hear more wonderful things than these." "So may it be, God willing," I replied. Then they began saying to one another, "Let us cast lots to see which of us shall act as host to him." But the old man said to them, "Why do we have to cast lots? Let that one among us entertain the guest at his table, who will give most liberally for the poor of Eretz Yisrael."

"What is this?" I interjected. "Blessed be His name that I have not fallen into the hands of pirates who would sell me for money. I am not entitled to be considered a righteous man like he of whom it is written 'because they have sold the righteous for silver.' If I had not seen your tears I would have said that you were mocking me."

"Why?" they asked. And I replied, "Many there are swollen with hunger in Jerusalem, dying for lack of something to eat, because they are penniless. Yes, there are many suffering from hunger in Jerusalem and many are dead in the cemeteries, because money was lacking, and the Diaspora has forgotten them. And if they should send a messenger to the cities of the Diaspora, he usually has to prostrate himself at the feet of every one in order to arouse pity. But no pity is aroused, for the people are hard-hearted, and as far removed from giving charity as stones. And now I come here and you actually quarrel for the opportunity of having me as your guest!"

When they heard this, they sighed heavily and said, "There is no teacher like experience. If the people of the Diaspora had been wise, they would have sent all of you back, riding in wagons and they would have crowned you with crowns of gold coins." "Have you not made the mystery great enough already, that you should add to it now?" I inquired. "I swear by Him who caused His name to dwell in Jerusalem that I will not move from this place until you answer my question." When I had thus adjured them in the name of Jerusalem, they said, "You shall be told immediately." Then the old man began, "Know thou, my son ..."–but then he paused, brought out a snuff box from his pocket, tapped it, opened it, stuck two fingers into it, took a pinch of snuff, sniffed it, wiped off his moustache and began to stroke his beard. After a while of that, he stopped a moment, began stroking his beard with the other hand, and said, "But why tell it from memory, when you can read it in the community register." Immediately he motioned to the *shamash* and said, "Run to my house where under the clock you will find a sort of stand and on the stand there rests a glass vase and in the vase lies a key. Take the key, and give it to my wife, and tell her in my name that she should go to my bed and lift up the top pillow of the bed, and then the bottom pillow which is under it, and with this key have her open the box which is at the head of the bed. There you will find a thick book—it is the register. But for God's sake, take care not to touch the bundle you find there, lest you spill it, for it is a bundle of soil from Eretz Yisrael, and I am an old man with one foot already in the grave. Then bring the register to the synagogue in order that the guest may read all that is written therein. For how can hearing compare with seeing in a case like this."

"Oh, fickle folk," I said to him, "I am beginning to think that before I hear the story I shall hear the Shofar of the Messiah." But he sighed and answered, "Would that it might be so." "See here," I said, "do you not know that he is heartsick whose hope is not realized. I am all out of strength and patience. Tell me now, and if not I shall fly from here."

At these words they all began to tremble and even he became somewhat frightened, for he immediately began and said, "Know, then, that in days of yore this city was renowned for study and wisdom, and indeed it deserved its reputation, for all its inhabitants were learned in holy lore. Even the children were expert in the most intricate laws. And if a man in the street were asked, 'How far to such and such a place,' he would answer with true talmudic insight, 'It all depends on the length of the road.' And even the interpretation of those difficult passages which puzzled the great Rabbis was as nothing in the hands of the poorest, most ill-clad wretches of our city. In the large beit midrash learned scholars would sit with their Talmud folios in their hands; all through the city it was almost impossible to hear one another talk for the din of those at study. And after they had finished the evening prayer, all the householders and students would gather together, each with a candle in his hand until the light of their candles outshone the moon. And on this regard they took great pride in their city and would say, 'This city is the very crown of beauty. There is none like it in the entire world.' And there is a story about one man from our city who during a trial with a resident from another city, lifted up his eyes to heaven and said, 'O, Lord God, you know that I come from the city of...'—we hide the name of the city, which having repented in full does not deserve to have its name besmirched—'therefore, favor me in judgment.' And there is another story about one of the residents of our city who was visiting in another city, when the time came for the sanctification of the new moon. Turning aside in contempt, and turning up his nose, he exclaimed, 'And is this what you call a moon? Truly, there is no moon to equal the moon of our city!'

"Thus many years passed. The people were prosperous and the houses were filled with Torah. But the charity box of Rabbi Meir, the miracle worker, remained empty. It became covered with a spider web as thick as a silver dollar, and filled with golden rust. And there is a story that once, when a charity collector from Eretz Yisrael came to collect the money from the charity boxes, an axe was needed to open them. And when they were finally opened, not a penny was found. But they were not hard-hearted people, who turned their backs on charity. God forbid! They merely said, 'Our land is Eretz Yisrael and our city is Jerusalem, but before we distribute money to the poor of knowledge in Eretz Yisrael whence not even one worthwhile book comes to us, we might better build for ourselves a great study hall where we shall reap glory for ourselves through worthwhile books.' And so they did. Immediately they chose a fine site, and they brought large stones from the mountains, and they mixed the whites of eggs with the whitewash in order that the building might stand forever. The workmen toiled from early morning till late at night. And if they tried to rest and refresh themselves, the elders of the city would strike them with the long stems of their pipes and say to them, 'O, you ignoramuses! The Torah wanders about without a roof and you dare make saloons for yourselves.' And they brought tables as strong as iron, which could stand up without breaking under the great pile of books, which the men would place upon them while studying. And when they dedicated the beit midrash, they began to expound on the glory of such a lodging place for the Torah. But what could they say? Were it not for the Rabbis, may their memory be blessed, who said that he who has not seen the Holy Temple before its destruction has never seen a truly beautiful building, then they might have considered their building truly beautiful—as it was, they had to remain quiet.

"When that beit midrash stood complete in all its glory, there chanced to come to the city a certain charity collector of alms, a messenger from Eretz Yisrael. He brought his belongings to the beit midrash and walked about aimlessly. But as they were all deeply engrossed in their studies no one greeted him, nor did anyone ask him whence he came or whither he was going, whether his lodging was provided for, or with what wealthy man he was staying. They did not set any food before him nor did they give him anything warm to drink. The charity collector fetched out of his bag two or three dates and a piece of bread a little bigger than a date, and though his meager repast did not fill his stomach, his sighs filled his soul to overflowing. He drank some water from the basin, took his staff and went to the Rabbi to get permission from him to speak in the beit midrash that Sabbath. The Rabbi told him that the city was full of Torah and all the inhabitants learned in holy lore, and that when a preacher came to the city they would worst him in legal discussion until he no longer had any courage to speak, and that in the end, he would have to descend from the pulpit disappointed and shamefaced. The collector, however, did not heed the warning of the Rabbi but answered him in the words of the biblical verse, 'For the sake of Zion I shall not be silent.' So he returned to the beit midrash and then printed signs announcing that a learned man who was a fine speaker had come to town from the

Holy City of Jerusalem, etc., and that the occasion would be a rare treat for the audience. He went out into the street, entered a bakery shop where he bought a pot full of paste and then went about the city posting up his signs.

"That Sabbath the entire town came to the synagogue. This learned man mounted the pulpit, wrapped himself in his prayer shawl, and standing near the Holy Ark, began to expound the praises of Eretz Yisrael and the qualities of the holy land, and the love of Jerusalem, may it be rebuilt and re-established. And he wove a fine argument about the settlement of Eretz Yisrael, delivering it quietly and without excessive zeal, and it was all seasoned in the most approved manner with the spices of the Torah. 'According to the Biblical verse, the sons of Jacob,' he said, 'took of the best fruits of the land, a little balm and a little honey, spices and myrrh.' The Torah verses inferred, he continued, 'that when a man comes to speak about Eretz Yisrael, he must not begin with great things immediately but should proceed little by little, step by step, for only in the end does it say "and take double silver in your hands."' While he was yet expounding, a voice was heard from the congregation. The messenger turned his head and listened while someone asked thus and so about his words. He answered him thus and so. The questioner countered and answered him, not so, but thus and so. The messenger brought forth proof from the Talmud, thus and so. They told him, however, that he had not gone deep enough into the matter to even fill the eye of a needle, and that if it came to a decision, it was thus and so. And they broke down his arguments and they rebutted his contentions until his face was as gloomily dark as the bottom of a pit. Thus they tied him all up with words and worsted him in the disputation. For every point he finally succeeded in explaining, they asked him seven more questions. And when he had answered the seven questions they brought up seven more to take their place until his mind was all confused and he was at the end of his arguments. But the air of Eretz Yisrael imparts wisdom, and he displayed his ingenuity by beginning to expound an Aggadah. Yet even here they kept after him and did not permit him to find shelter. What did he do? He stopped in the middle, touched his lips to the curtain of the Ark and burying his face in the Star of David, cried until the threads glistened from his tears like pure gold, and then taking off his talit, shamefacedly descended from the pulpit. He went to the back of the room and there behind the furnace tearfully paced back and forth.

"While he was standing there, all the rattle-brained youngsters began to tease him as did the boys in the story of Elisha. And not the boys alone, but all the vagabonds of the city who had looked upon him with antagonism from the moment of his coming, began to mock him. 'Just look at the fellow who considered himself worthy of the honor of speaking before great men. This is the wrong place and this is the wrong city, Mr. Almost-Rabbi. Now go, and bear the tidings to the goats in Eretz Yisrael that even outside of the holy land they eat carob fruit.' The messenger heard their mockery but did not answer, only swallowed his tears and stretched out his hands in prayer. So the Sabbath passed and he found himself without funds to continue his travels, for all the money which he had previously collected, he had already sent ahead to Eretz Yisrael, confident that the sons of Israel, 'the merciful ones, the sons of merciful ones' would not be tight-fisted, Heaven forbid. And so when they finished the morning prayer, he approached one man after another on the subject of making some contribution for Eretz Yisrael. But here this one cried and there that one cried, and though all of them gave plenty of excuses, no one gave any money. And this is how the head of the congregation answered when the messenger came to him. 'Do you see this beit midrash,' he said. 'What is more important than the beit midrash? Is it not written, "The Lord loveth the gates of Zion more than all the dwellings of Jacob"? And this means,' he continued, 'that the Lord loves the gates which are distinguished in the study of the Law, for from the day that the holy Temple was destroyed, the Holy One Blessed Be He, has no interest in this world except within the narrow confines of the Law.'

"The messenger realized that nothing was to be obtained from them, so he took his staff and bag, went up to the Holy Ark, and burying his head among the holy scrolls, cried bitterly, 'Master of the world—Dost thou not know that not for my own glory did I do this, nor for the glory of the house of my father, but for the poor of thy people, Israel, who dwell in Thy presence in Thy holy land and suffer the pangs of hunger? How many pilgrimages and hardships I have gone through! The waves of the sea have risen up against me to drown me in the deep, and robbers have sought to take my life. Yet not even once have I said to thee, "Why hast thou troubled me?" And now I have come to thy sons who are learned in thy holy law, and see what had befallen me!' And immediately he closed the Holy Ark, touched his lips to the curtain, went to the door, kissed the *mezuzah* and began to sing in a wonderful voice, the words of the Rabbis of blessed memory. 'The Lord loveth the gates which are distinguished in the study of the Law,' and he continued, 'and all the synagogues and houses of study which are outside of the Holy Land are destined to be transplanted to Eretz Yisrael.'

"At that moment all felt the earth tremble underneath their feet. They fled for their lives and stood watching from afar. They saw the walls of the beit midrash bend toward the east like a man who is about to walk. And the messenger walked before the beit midrash singing in a sad voice, 'The Lord loveth the gates which are distinguished in the study of the Law,' and he himself responded, 'and all the synagogues and houses of study which are outside of the Holy Land are destined to be transplanted to Eretz Yisrael.' He had not yet finished, when the beit midrash was moving after him, books and tables and all. He walked slowly and the place where the beit midrash had stood was now bare and naked, hiding itself in the evening shadows.

"When the residents of the city saw this, they all began to sob and to weep and stirred themselves to complete repentance. And they decreed for themselves and for their offspring and for the progeny of their offspring, until the coming of the redemption—may it come speedily in our days, Amen—that they should observe every year, a strict fast on that day. And the day of this fast we spend in penitence and supplication. And we give a great deal of charity to the poor of the Holy Land and we go to the river and pray that we may be pardoned for not having bestowed upon the messenger honor that was his due. And we fast until long after midnight when we partake of a light meal in order that we may not perish, God forbid, from the great stress of our grief and penitence. And thus we fulfill the three-fold function of fasting and prayer and charity, true penitence in body, in voice and in deed."

Immediately I tried to comfort them and said, "My teachers and masters, I testify by heaven and earth, that I have seen a beit midrash such as you have described, in Jerusalem. There the building stands on a holy site and the sons of Israel, the holy ones, study in it the holiness of our holy Law. And," I continued, "Rejoice O Israel, that even the houses in which you study the Torah, the Holy One blessed be He, brings to Eretz Yisrael, and if the Holy One, blessed be He, troubles Himself about those things which are but beams and stones and brings them to Eretz Yisrael, how much more is it likely that with Israel itself, who studies the Torah and the Commandments, He will do likewise. It is indeed as has been said, 'Even them will I bring to My holy mountain and make them joyful in My house of prayer.' May it be thy will. Amen."

– Translated by Harold I. Saperstein

The Tale of Little Rabbi Gadiel

RABBI GADIEL WAS BORN by virtue of the Torah, which his father taught the babes of Israel. And when Rabbi Gadiel came out into the world he was so small that one could hardly tell that he was human. When he came of age his father began to instruct him in the commandments and in piety. And he made him a *tallit katan* with fringes fringed of early fleece, and shaved the hair of his head while standing by the gravesite of Rabbi Shimon ben Yohai on Lag BaOmer and left him side curls, and carried him about in the pocket of his clothes morning and evening to the great synagogue to say "Blessed is He and blessed is His Name" and to answer "Amen, may His Great Name be blessed." And when the cantor said the blessing, Rabbi Gadiel would repeat after him "Blessed is He and blessed is His Name" and answer "Amen" with all his might. And Rabbi Gadiel would lift up his voice until the doorposts trembled and none would know from where came the voice because he was hidden inside his father's pocket.

And when he turned five, and came of age to begin Torah study, his father took him and set him down on the snuffbox and opened before him the five books of Torah and studied with him and interpreted for him the words of living God, until he learned the whole Torah – the Bible, Mishnah, the laws and legends, the Babylonian and the Jerusalem Talmud, midrash and kabbalah. And if his father dozed off in the middle of his teachings, Rabbi Gadiel would get off the snuffbox and sit at the edge of the pages of the book and examine the flourish and shapes of the letters, the big letters and the small letters. When his father awoke and did not see him, he assumed that the child was with his mother, and not knowing that he stood between the pages he closed the book and turned to his affairs, leaving Rabbi Gadiel to stand among the letters, studying and poring over and reviewing all that he had learned, and he was diligent in his studies and exceedingly successful in Torah and wisdom.

And so that these words might not be construed as mere exaggeration, God forbid, we see fit here to describe how small Rabbi Gadiel actually was. It happened that a vial of olive oil was set down for the Ḥanukah candles and Rabbi Gadiel fell into the vial and sat there until his father came to light the candle and only when he poured the oil into the menorah could Rabbi Gadiel jump out, his face shining, perfumed with the fragrance of good oil. And because Rabbi Gadiel was so small his father feared to put him down in public lest he be trampled on by passersby and he carried him in the fold of his clothes, and when he went to market to do trade with the nations of the world, Rabbi Gadiel would lie in the corner of his tallit and listen to the conversation of his father and the conversation of the people, what his father said to them and what they said to him, and in this way he learned the languages of Greece and of Edom and of Ishmael and all the other languages of the nations and he could converse in their tongue in an exemplary fashion.

One day several of the wickedest men of the nations of the world who were envious of Rabbi Gadiel's father came together and said: "How long will this Jew usurp us and rob us of our livelihood? The time has come to remove him from this world." One said to the other: "But for fear of the authorities we would swallow him alive." And one stood and said: "These Jews' Passover is approaching; come let us take a corpse and put it in this Jew's house and say, 'One of ours he killed, for his *matzot* he killed, to bake them in blood he killed,' and we will go and call the judges of the town and the elders of the community and they will arrest him with iron chains and lead him out to be executed and we will have our revenge on him, and moreover we will have his wealth and divide it amongst ourselves." But they did not know how to go about it. So one among them resolved in his mind and advised the others: "It is their custom on the eve of their Passover to drink four cups of wine and leave one large goblet on the table, the prophet Elijah's cup it is called. Come, let us fill a skin-bottle with blood and stir up the household on the eve of Pesach, and while the Jew and his family are confounded we will pour out the wine from Elijah's goblet and fill it with blood, and we will alert the king's guards and community elders and they will put him in shackles and arrest him in jail and sit in judgment over him and kill him and we will take our revenge on him." They all heard and said, "It is well," and they spread a rumor that "a lad of ours has been lost" and they agitated over the imaginary loss and they incited the wicked of the nations to seek vengeance from Israel.

On the eve of Pesach various knaves and scoundrels from the nations came together with axes and hatchets to kill and destroy and wipe out the seed of Israel. And because Rabbi Gadiel's father was a community elder that year they came to him first, according to the adage "Begin with the greatest," in order to upset his home and its inhabitants. Rabbi Gadiel's father and his family were reclining around the table and telling of the exodus from Egypt that night when the door opened with a great clamor and a horde of soldiers entered and set the house in turmoil. The family looked on and were afraid because fear of the nations befell them. They stood cowering, this one wailed and that one wailed, and Rabbi Gadiel, who was so small, jumped into Elijah's cup and remained hidden there undetected, and he stayed inside Elijah's cup until their priest came and secretly raised the cup and drank all the wine so that the blood could replace it in the cup.

Rabbi Gadiel remained inside this wicked man's belly and the knave was unaware of his presence because his intestines were exceedingly coarse from eating a thousand pigs and thousands of measures of drink and he could feel nothing. Rabbi Gadiel remained inside this wicked man but he did not sit and wait for his body to be absorbed in the wicked one's body and their flesh to become one; instead he reflected on the seven wisdoms and the seventy tongues so as not to reflect on matters of Torah in such a place as this.

After the Gentiles had filled the cup with blood, they placed guards around it and ran in great confusion and called the elders of the community and the judges of the town and showed them the blood and said: "See how these Jews take our lives and suck our blood to drink on their holidays?" A great anger immediately filled the community elders and they took Rabbi Gadiel's father and his mother and his brothers and his sisters and they put them in iron chains and they lowered them into a ditch and they tortured them with various tortures while they waited for the execution order to arrive from the king.

The matter was brought before the king and his ministers and Rabbi Gadiel lay inside the belly of the knave and fed off Elijah's cup and reflected on matters of wisdom and rhetoric and the fables of the nations and conversation of men. And the kingdom was a benevolent kingdom that year and they did not judge crime without investigation and examination. They investigated and examined very closely and brought all those who had been present to bear witness and chief among them was the priest. And they swore in the priest with an age-old oath and said to him: "Open your mouth and give your evidence." The priest pulled out a crucifix from his pocket, swearing on it that all his words were true and just and prepared to begin his evidence. And what did Rabbi Gadiel do? He rose into the wicked man's throat and began to poke around with his finger. The knave felt the poking in his gullet and was unable to emit a single word. His claims remained blocked up and the wicked gentleman was disgraced. The king shouted and said: "Open your mouth." And what did Rabbi Gadiel do? He began to speak from inside the knave's throat and in the knave's language and told all that had come to pass. The scoundrels all bowed their heads in shame and the king and his ministers stood shaking and aghast for they had almost spilt innocent blood and, God forbid, destroyed a large community of Israel which had done no wrong. They immediately punished the wicked and set free the imprisoned in great honor and hung the priest on a tree. Thus was he repaid by God for what he had conspired to do to the Jews.

And thus hung the priest all day until came the prophet Elijah, of blessed memory, and kicked the knave and took Rabbi Gadiel out of his belly and wrapped him in the corner of his cloak and brought him to the hot springs of Tiberias and bathed him there and anointed him in pure olive oil and immersed him into flowing streams of perfume and dressed him in a gown of light and led him into one of the caves of the just and there he sat with him and studied Torah about the prosecution and punishment of the wicked who so oppress the children of the Lord.

And Rabbi Gadiel still sits in the yeshivah of the righteous and faithfully records every crime with which the nations of the world defame the children of the Lord. And when God's day shall come, that great and awful day, Rabbi Gadiel shall go forth from his place and he shall put on garments of vengeance and shall be clad with zeal as a cloak and he shall speak to the Gentiles and show the nations and roar against them so saying: "Such and such you did, such and such you said." And they shall have no excuse, the ministers of the nations, to refute him and they shall go into the holes of the rocks and into the caves of the earth, as it is written (Isaiah 2:15), "And they shall go into the holes of the rocks and the caves of the earth for fear of the Lord and for the glory of His majesty when He ariseth to shake terribly the earth."

So ends the tale of little Rabbi Gadiel, but unended are all his deeds.

– *Translated by Evelyn Abel*

Rabbi Katriel the Cantor

There was a Rabbi Katriel, a cantor, from the remnant of a congregation of pious men in Jerusalem, men who reduced their own needs in order to increase the glory of Heaven, who sat in places of Torah, reading Scripture, learning Mishnah, laws, and legends, and meditating on the secrets of the Torah and the esoteric lore of the Sages. Recalling the righteousness and kindness of the Holy One, blessed be He, every day and hour, and sanctified His great Name in the world, with all their deeds and with their thoughts.

They lamented over His glory being spoiled among the nations, and over the glory of Israel which was taken from them. And they fanned the longing in their hearts for the glory of Jerusalem, of the Temple, and of Israel, on the day when all the exiled would re-enter the Land of Israel, and the Holy One, blessed be He, would return His holy Presence to Zion – for as long as Israel is cast among the nations, and the nations dominate and disgrace the people of Israel, God Himself suffers along with them. Therefore do these pious men place all the sorrow against their own hearts and weep before Him, may He be blessed, that He might bring around His impulses of tenderness toward His sorely-tried children, His beacons, the sheep of His pasture, descendants of His faithful Abraham, the children of his only-begotten Isaac, the congregation of his first-born Jacob. For there is no revival of God's Presence, as it were, but through the redemption of Israel.

Because Rabbi Katriel was an upright man, fearful of Heaven, clinging to the ways of God, a favorable man, a man of peace, a man of good attributes, whose house was clean of sin, who was expert in the secret lore of prayers and their mystical meanings, whose voice was sweet, whose heart was most humble, and whose body was free from all blemish: his brethren, the pious men, had found him fit to serve as the prayer leader before the Holy One, blessed be He. When Rabbi Katriel had acquired the correct age of service, that is, in his thirtieth year, they appointed him to be their representative before God the Omnipresent. And since the day he was appointed cantor, Rabbi Katriel would rise every day at midnight, bathe in the ritual bath, go up to open the door of the synagogue, and sit himself down on the ground and offer lamentation for Jerusalem, together with the other mourners for the Holy City, until all the worshippers came to pray. When the time of prayer arrived, R. Katriel would stand, wrap himself in his tallit and tefillin, and stand before the ark, free from thought of sin and proper in behavior – for he was offering up to his God the prayers of Israel. He would stand before the ark as if the Divine Glory itself were immediately in front of him, and lift up his heart and soul with sweet and pleasant sounds – on every day, in every prayer, whether weekday or Shabbat, whether major holy days or minor days of a festival, on Rosh Hashanah and Yom Kippur, on New Moons and fasts, on Ḥanukah and Purim, each prayer in its proper time, each prayer with its proper expression. For no prayer, from the time of the world's creation to the end of days, totally resembles any other. Each day, new meanings are illuminated. Each day, sparks are generated anew. Each day, new forces exert their influences. Each day, the prayers leap back to heaven, leaving only a memory. There are prayers which a man prays with joyful melody, because he is happy to deserve the honor of giving praise and thanks to the Omnipresent. And there are prayers which one prays with weeping, like a man who know his lowly state and gives his heart to weep. Sometimes one draws out his prayer, as with benedictions and praises, for a man rejoices to lay out the praises of the Omnipresent. Sometimes, one hurries in his prayer, like a man who brings a gift to a king and is eager to present it. Each and every word which Rabbi Katriel brought forth from his mouth was presented like royal pearls.

Whenever Israel performed the will of the Omnipresent, the Attribute of Mercy was extended: an abundance of blessings would descend from the high heavens, all creatures would love one another, rejoice together, and be kind to one another, and no man in the Land of Israel needed to petition for his needs, for the Jews in exile would send money to the Land of Israel. But because of our many sins, the Attribute of Judgment was extended: malediction went forth from the enemies of Israel, the wellsprings of livelihood ceased, and the Jews in exile could barely feed themselves, let alone the residents of the Land of Israel. They did not know that all their benefits came only from the Land of Israel; for they themselves possessed no merit of dwelling in the Land. They had only the merit of their brethren, the dwellers of the Land of Israel, who picked out for them clods of earth from the Holy Land.

So the livelihood of Rabbi Katriel was diminished, and he and his household were left without food or sustenance. When the time came that they had not even a piece of dry bread, nor even a sliver of carob, his sons and daughters raised their voices and cried. The wife of Rabbi Katriel said: "Katriel, my husband, how long shall we live under this oppression? Pray for us that we not die from hunger!" Feelings of tenderness for his wife and children overtook Rabbi Katriel, and he took upon himself to pray for sustenance, even though he had never in his life made a request for his own needs. And when did he plan to offer this prayer? On the evening of Rosh Hashanah, during the recitation of the psalm verse, "The earth and its fullness are the Lord's." For this psalm was especially favorable for making prayers for sustenance.

When Rosh Hashanah arrived, Rabbi Katriel purified himself, and washed his white linen garment, and went before the Ark. He prayed in the presence of the Great and Awesome One, that His Name be magnified in the world. The hearts of his brethren were awakened to the love and worship of God, may He be blessed. After the silent prayer, when they came to the psalm, "The earth and its fullness are the Lord's" a portion of the congregation began to direct their hearts to pray for their own needs, and Rabbi Katriel did so as well. But the Holy One, blessed be He, wished to rejoice in the prayer of that pious man free from any selfish concern. So when Rabbi Katriel began the psalm, "The earth and its fullness are the Lord's," he suddenly forgot all his own needs, and began to focus his concentration on the Holy One alone! May He be blessed!

The same psalm says: "Who shall go up to the mountain of the Lord, and who shall stand in His holy place?" Scripture juxtaposes standing with going up – to teach you that even if a man should arrive at the top, still he must be afraid lest he fall, God forbid. So this pious man, Rabbi Katriel, after he focused all his concentration and intentions for the blessed One alone, his heart began to bother him, that he had not paid heed to the needs of his own household, and he resolved to make the request on the second night of Rosh Hashanah.

Immediately Rabbi Katriel put off all sad thoughts from his heart. For he realized he had not given the Accuser any excuse to speak against him, God forbid. He greeted his wife and children with a blessing, and he recited Kiddush, partook of the holiday meal, and said Grace. Then he studied four chapters of the Mishnah tractate Rosh Hashanah as is customary – for four is the number of letters in the Divine Name, and he recited the Shema, and retired to bed.

There are those who, before going to sleep, recount all dreams that one is obliged to fast over (for if one should have a bad dream, it indicates his sinful thoughts; just as they say in the Talmud: dreams only show a man his inner thoughts), and thereby one does not need to fast. For it is difficult to fast for a dream on Rosh Hashanah. Anyone who fasts on the first day of Rosh Hashanah must fast on both days, for they are reckoned as one long day. And anyone who has fasted on those days once must fast on them all his life. Some men stipulate before going to sleep: "Any dream I might dream I shall not fast over tomorrow," so that the Master of Dreams might not tease or challenge him. Rabbi Katriel followed neither practice, but said that if an evil decree were declared upon him, God forbid, they would make it known to him so that he might examine his deeds and repent. The more so, on the evening of Rosh Hashanah, when the winds wander about in the world to listen behind the scenes for the retributions coming into the world. Sometimes, they make these known to the living through dreams.

While R. Katriel was asleep, he was shown in his dream the following: synagogues and houses of study filled with Jews. And the Jews stood and prayed, and their prayers ascended to the high Heaven, not just to the first firmament but to the seventh, nay, even to the Throne of Glory! And the Holy One, blessed be He, was sitting on His Throne of Glory, and the ministering angels came and stood before Him and asked permission to sing songs of praise. He said to them: "Be silent, all you ranks of angels, until I hear first the sound of the song and praises of My child, Israel!" Immediately, the angels bathed themselves in fire until they were made holy and pure, and they went up amid streams of fire and swayed about in flashes of lightning, and stood trembling and shuddering, in purity, holiness, dread, and humility, to listen to the prayers of Israel. And each and every angel wore a billion crowns of light. They took these off and bound them with each and every letter of the prayers, and placed them before the Throne of Glory, and the Holy One, blessed be He, took them and placed them on His head.

That pious man, R. Katriel, inclined his ears to listen to the sweet voice of Israel, which was so dear to the Holy One, blessed be He. He heard his own voice in song saying: "The earth and its fullness are the Lord's."

The next day, when R. Katriel came to that psalm, he remembered all he had seen and heard in his dream. He grasped the ark and began to recite the entire psalm in trembling and shuddering, in purity, holiness, dread, and humility, with sweet voice and pleasant notes, just like the angels the night before, just as it had been sung in Heaven. Even though the distress of his wife and children did not budge from before him, he did not offer prayer for his own sustenance.

Such is the strength of those who love the Almighty, that they set aside their own distress, for the glory of His Presence.

The Covenant of Love

FOR A WHOLE HOUR the three old men had not spoken a word, but had sat there on the shore, contentedly warming themselves in the evening sun. Drowsy and half asleep, they had suffered the wind to play roguishly through their white garments, whilst the rays of the sun played lightly around their lips like golden keys.

They were three old men who had come, in the evening of their days, out of the tumult of the Exile back to the peace of the Ancient Home. Most of their days had been spent in the toil and moil of small businesses, but at last the "holy memory" had crept into their hearts and taken complete possession. They had locked their shops for the last time and it was as if they had taken on a new vigor and a new life. They had "gone up" to *Eretz Israel.*

It was already some weeks ago since they had prayed at the Wailing Wall, visited the graves the righteous, and performed all the offices of charity and good deeds which are duty of the pious pilgrim. Now they were tired – tired with the scorching sun they had come at last to Jaffa to bathe in the sweet, clear streams of the open sea.

At Jaffa they had put up at a hotel full of fellow-Jews. They would take part in the services, study Torah with the best of them, and recite their due share of song and praise of the Holy One, blessed be He. In the evenings, when the day grew cooler and the sun was setting, they would go out on the beach, sometimes for a bath and sometimes merely to sit for hours on little cane chairs and feast their eyes on the pageant of color. After a time, their shyness would wear off and they would warm towards one another, even though they said not a word. There would be between them a communion of silence, as they sat there watching the waves break into creamy foam and feeling the cool wind brush gently across their faces.

A waiter came out from the hotel and set before them a warm kettle, three cups, sugar and a plate of biscuits. They poured out the tea and started to drink. At once their drowsiness seemed to disappear and they fell to talking.

It was the eldest who started the conversation. "There is no sun," he said suddenly, "like the sun of *Eretz Israel*! Look, it is already going down, yet it still warms the body and enfolds the limbs like a robe." And as he said this he scooped his hand into the sand at his feet and sighed, "*Eretz Israel*" – like a man who calls a thing by its name, uncertain if it is the real thing itself. "Is this really the Land of Israel?"

"Don't worry yourself about that," rejoined his neighbor. "After all, Jaffa isn't *Eretz Israel*. Remember what it says in the Bible: 'Jonah sought to flee from the presence of the Lord' – so he went down unto Jaffa." A broad grin of victory spread over his pearl-white teeth.

"Yes," replied the first speaker, "you say that Jaffa is not *Eretz Israel*. But is *Eretz Israel* itself *Eretz Yisrael*?"

His two companions glanced at him sharply and curiously, as if an ignoramous had just been speaking. "You wonder?" said the speaker, "but I know what I mean. Heaven forbid that I should deny the holiness of *Eretz Israel*, but I ask you, is this *Eretz Israel* which is revealed to us now, the same land as is described in the Bible and in the words of the Sages? Look only at one thing – the way they recite the Priestly Blessing here. Since I came I have never missed a day's service, and every time I saw them go up to give the blessing my whole body was aflame, as if it were a holy day. But now when I hear that they toss out the blessings as a mere routine, like tossing a worn coin at a beggar, I cannot help thinking of all the synagogues and study houses outside the Land, where the thing is a dream to them and they pour out their souls with every note and their hearts with every letter, and the Priestly Blessing is only recited on the Holy days, and each with its special tune. There, they say there is no Torah like the Torah of *Eretz Israel*. But how do they teach it here? Even the study of mystical Kabbalah here is done without savor and without fire. No, my friends, God's Presence is in exile. This *Eretz Israel* is an ark without the scrolls. The little lamp still flickers, but where is the Torah?"

"You are wrong, my friend," replied the second of the three old men "You have lived all your life outside the Land, and have studied Torah and performed all the commandments. You had in your heart the divine spark, shining through the long night of Exile, and you wanted to go to *Eretz Israel*. You thought since you lived Exile while keeping the Commandments and preserving that divine spark, by ascending to the Holy Land you would bring that holy spark with you back to its source. You thought that you would bring back its light with your coming. It is like the candle which shone in a dark place, giving great light, but mistakenly thinking itself comparable to the sun, until it went out into the daylight and the sun immediately melted the little candle."

Then spoke the third of the group. As a rule he used to speak slowly and deliberately. Now the words came tumbling out, as if he were a messenger afraid that he might die before delivering his message. "It is a nice parable, my friend," said he, "but there is no need for parables. I, too, have often felt disquieted and upset at not getting all the joy and peace I had expected out of my life here, but now I have seen it clearly. It is mere folly which promotes such thoughts and which leads a man to sever the bond between God and Israel. Our rabbis have said that settlement in *Eretz Israel* out-weighs all the commandments. Should we not, then, account it an extra grave of Providence, if we do not enjoy it, for so are we accorded the merit of fulfilling this holiest of ordinances for its own sake? And though we are not holy enough to enjoy the meanest part of it, should we not ascribe it to the bounty of Heaven that we are permitted to live in this holiest place? Says the Bible: 'Walk before Me and be perfect.' Our Master Rashi adds: 'Be perfect in all my trial of you. Then I will give you my covenant – the covenant of love and the covenant of the land.' For the upright shall dwell in the land and the blameless shall be left in it."

The Minyan

THERE WAS A CERTAIN WIDOW in Tiberias who had a son of outstanding faith, peerless in Torah, who spent all his life long as does the hart to do with the will of his Father in heaven, but as the flayed pelt of the hart will no longer hold all its flesh, so the body of this lad could not contain his soul, and at last he grew sick to death. They employed every fashion of charm and remedy and summoned every manner of doctor, but to no avail. How shall Man aid if the Holy One, blessed be He, sends no healing from on high?

In those days Tiberias was full of saintly men and men of many a good deed who knew how prayer should be offered to the Omnipresent, and when they heard how near this peerless lad lay to his death they were filled with pity for him. Let us rise and pray for him they said to one another, may it be His will to heal the lad of his sickness. They went to the synagogues and houses of study in which neither Torah nor prayer never cease, and they collected alms and shared the money among seven charities to deliver him from the seven chastisements written in the Torah, so that the verse "and charity will deliver from death" shall be proven with him, and they stood in prayer in supplication all day and all night. Then they went to the graves of Rabbi Meir the Wonder Worker and the graves of all the *Tannaim* and *Amoraim*, and the graves of all the other saints who had chosen to have their bodies buried in the earth of Tiberias, and there they prostrated themselves weeping greatly and lit candles as many as the number of the sick lads years, and as the span of a man's years upon earth, till the whole town was bright with those candles. Yet the lad's breath flickered from him as wick that has no oil. When the saintly men saw that he lay as might one dead they asked one another, "Beloved brethren, say you what more we could have done for the ailing lad that we did not do?" And they answered one another, "Beloved brethren, everything that lay in our power to do we have done." Then they rose, took their prayer books, and returned home in great vexation of spirit.

But the Holy One, blessed be He, still wished to enjoy the lad's Torah, and He set in the hearts of his kin the idea of the sending with him to Mount Meron on the thirty-third day of the *Omer*, at the season when folk come from the four corners of the world to prostrate themselves at the grave of Rabbi Shimon bar Yoḥai, in order that the merit of the holy rabbi might aid him to recover from his sickness. They raised the lad's bed and bore him all the way to Safed. And Safed being filled with doctors who are familiar with the books of remedies in the course of the pulse, they brought the sick lad before them. The doctors looked at him and lowered their heads, sighing and saying, we despair of him and cannot prolong his life by so much as an hour, but this is our council: west of Safed lies an old, old graveyard filled with tombstones in caves, and the *Ari*, our Master Rabbi Isaac Luria of holy memory, used to say that twice as many saints and martyrs were buried there as the number of folks that left Egypt. Take the sick child and make a circuit of the graveyard with him and maybe they will pity him and entreat mercy on his behalf.

They went and made the circuit of the graveyard with tears and entreaty but saw no sign or token of betterment. Then they took him and went up to Meron. And the spirit of life was gone from him when they came thither. They sat down his bed before the cave wept greatly so that all the pilgrims who had come to visit the grave of Rabbi Shimon bar Yoḥai wept with them.

At that very hour came all the sieges of Safed bearing the scrolls of the Torah, dancing all the way in exceeding joy, singing psalms and songs of praise and playing on every kind of musical vessel. The chief Sage, head of all the Sefardic rabbis, strode before them – he was an aged and saintly man whose years were crowned with Torah and good deeds. When he saw the people lamenting he asked, why do you weep? They said to him such and such a widow woman has an only son whom they brought from Tiberias to find healing at the grave of Rabbi Shimon, and when they had brought him here the life was gone from him. The rabbi said, can it be that the day of the great festival of Rabbi Shimon bar Yoḥai will be transformed, God forbid, to lamentation and mourning? He turned to his followers saying, send every soul forth from the cave and the house of study and give heed that no man should enter the cave until I summon you.

They all went out and none remained. Then the rabbi told those who bore the bed to bring the lad into the cave and leave it. They brought him there, set him up on pillows and cushions, and departed. When they were gone the rabbi shut the door of the cave and made the circuit of its walls praying of great prayer until the time came for the afternoon service. Then he opened the door and brought in eight other sages who had taken great care to only pray with a *minyan*, in full assembly of ten men all their lives, and stood with then beside the grave of Rabbi Shimon bar Yoḥai, saying Rabbi Simon, Rabbi Simon, you know full well that our whole adult lives we have never recited a single prayer service other than with the congregation, and now here are we, nine men who are together with this youth lying before you, the requisite *minyan* of ten. We shall not be able to pray as a congregation unless you should beseech mercy for him so that he may revive. And so they stood beside the grave, gazing all the while it the lad, but could see no sign of life. Then each set his hand on the other's shoulder and said, Rabbi Shimon, Rabbi Shimon, it is known to your full well that never have we prayed with less than the quorum of ten men, and now, on the anniversary of your passing, we stand, ten men of Israel, without saying the *Minḥah* prayers with a *minyan* as a congregation. Then the old rabbi without a pause began reciting the beginning of the prayers, *Happy are they that dwell in Thy house, they shell praise the evermore*; and he repeated the psalm verse by verse in awe and dread and trembling; and his companions recited with him verse by verse and word by word. When they reached the verse, *The lord is near to all who call on him, to all who call on him in truth,* they heard a sound from the sick lad. They hearkened and he was whispering the next verse, *He shall perform the will of those who fear Him*; and they knew that their prayer had been acceptable to the Omnipresent, and that the land was alive.

This story is well known in Safed, where I heard it from a certain man that had heard it from an old woman who had been there when it happened. But I cannot remember if the old woman was from Safed or from Tiberias.

– *Translated by I.M. Lask*

Under the Tree

ONCE UPON A TIME I WAS FETCHING saplings to Degania. On the way I got off the donkey in order to rest. Looking round I saw a worthy old Arab lord sitting under an olive tree. I greeted him and he greeted me in return.

Where are you going? said the old pasha to me.

To plant a few trees on our land at Degania, said I to him.

The day, said he, is still long and the sun is hot, sit with me for a while and let us have a chat. I went and sat down beside him. The pasha looked at my sapling and asked: A fresh fruit?

With your permission, sir, said I to him.

The pasha nodded and said, you are training the country well, experiment after experiment, plant after plant, tree after tree, vegetable after vegetable. I shall be surprised if you come to lack anything at all in it.

We do what is possible, said I.

The pasha nodded and said, and the land repays you. It seems to me that the land obeys you alone.

Your kindness opens the heart, said I.

Thereupon the pasha began praising Israel who transform the wildernesses of *Eretz Yisrael* into gardens and groves, and multiply villages and dwelling-places in the country.

Now I nodded in agreement with him and said to myself: When Israel are on the land, even the other nations praise him. Happy is he who devotes himself to the Land and engages in its settlement, for all who devote themselves to the Land and engage in its settlement devote themselves and declare the unity of His Great Name in Heaven and Earth and increase the honor of Israel, like a plant that is put into the ground and flourishes and mounts aloft.

I see, the pasha now said to me, that you are wise and He who made you gave you knowledge. So I shall ask you – tell me, to whom is this land appointed and who will take the ruling of it over in the future?

I considered to myself what answer I should give him. If I were to tell him "The Earth is the Lord's and the fullness thereof," meaning that the Lord had given it to whom He saw fit, then there is the other verse: "And He gave the Earth to humankind," which could be taken to mean that the Lord had given it to those men who dwell therein. And if I were to tell him that he who seizes power therein would continue to be in power – that would be a deceitful answer, since this land is ours and the Holy One is going to return it to us in the future, and no other nation can rule therein save Israel. So I said to him: Do you need me to answer, sir? Why, surely you know to whom it was that the Holy One, blessed be He, gave the Land of Israel, and to whom He has promised to return it.

The pasha lowered his head between his knees and gave no reply. I thought that I might have annoyed him and said, It is not I who said it, but the Torah which declares it.

The pasha raised his head and said: I am one of the few remaining generals of our Lord and King, the Great Sultan, may he rest in peace and blessing. Many a city did I lay waste in his name, many people did I slay in his honor. I taxed whole provinces and earned myself a great name in the name of the pitiful and ever-merciful God, and Allah viewed me favorably and opened His hands and made me satisfied. But when I had come to think that the world was created only to rejoice therein, the sovereign powers attacked our Lord the Sultan and went to war against him. I remembered my victories, with the regiments of soldiers roaring and shouting and trampling. Thereupon my fate sped me to go out to war against the enemy, whether to win or be defeated. I left my home and kissed my children and went to our Lord the King and kneeled down before him and entrusted my soul into his hands, saying: Peace be unto you, my Lord King. May Allah's blessing rise about you. With your permission, O Ruler of the faithful, even a blunt sword in a weak hand can smite the enemy hip and thigh. The King looked at me and said: Ibrahim Bey, Take your hosts and go to wage war against the unbelievers, do not spare them and have no pity upon them and do not rest your head upon the pillow until you have destroyed them under the skies of my country. When I heard this, my heart began to sound like the voice of cornets while my eyes flashed like swords. I set my hand to my eyes and heart and fell to my knees again and said: Allah's shelter and Allah's messenger come to our Lord the King, as Allah hath said and His emissary and the emissary of His emissary, so shall Ibrahim your servant perform and do, O Ruler of all the Faithful. The King gave me his blessing, may Allah's blessing rest upon him, and suffered me to depart in peace. Ere the sun had reached the West all we valiant men had gathered together and set out to make war against the foe.

The battle-field was on the flanks of the desert. We had all that we required of water and food, horses and camels, asses and mules, swords and lances and bows, and all the other instruments of war, so that the desert gleamed with them; and we came to do battle against the foe.

The foe appeared before us with all kinds of weapons. All the instruments of Satan were in his hands. Now the foemen were stronger and now we held sway, and it was almost certain that they would fall into our hands.

But the unbelievers fought bravely for their lives. Some reeled and fell and some rose refreshed, and the war was great and bitter. Swords and lances flashed and iron clashed with iron, lopped heads went spinning while hacked arms flew far and wide, man and beast were trodden underfoot and the whole earth was flowing with blood. The legs of the beasts slipped and they fell away under their riders, they were blinded by the blood of the corpses and went crazy, while the instruments of Satan roared and shrieked and rent and slew. He who fell did not rise up, while he who crouched down was crushed. At the last only vestiges of all the hosts were left on either side.

But we did not turn away from the foes, nor did they turn away from us. They gathered the remains of their soldiers and came against us in a torrent of rage, while we leapt towards them in a fury of vengeance.

The cavalry flung themselves against them first, then came the infantry and all the other troops. There was a vast slaughter on that day. Many fell by the sword and many were swept away in that flood of fire and brimstone and lead. As for those who fled from the fighting, we destroyed them and closed the roads. In that way our armies became divided. Some remained to guard the prisoners and bury the dead while others went forth to destroy those who had fled to the mountains and the wilderness.

For three days we went on slaying. At length we reached a spot we did not know. Our camels and our horses fell and the earth began to give off a stench. The food and water-carriers were three days journey away from us. All we had with us were skins and canteens which did not contain much. The weapons of war were a burden on the men and the skins and canteens did not contain water. The day flamed like an oven and there was no shadow for any creature. Not in the heavens alone was the sun enkindled, but it made the whole earth below seethe likewise. If you raised your head you were burned. If you lowered your face you were scorched. Of the enemies of the faithful there was no vestige, some had been driven off stupefied while some lay as dead carcasses, and Allah alone knows their number, while their corpses and the carcasses of our beasts went on raising more and more of a stench.

As for us, our life was no life either. No food was left and our canteens contained only enough to moisten the mouth. We raised our eyes up. There were only sandhills and stonehills. We turned our faces to the ground. The whole earth was like white fire. There were no trees, there was no spring, no beast or bird. Apart from the desert thorns there was nothing that grew. These thorns are not fit to be eaten even by camels, but as for us, as soon as we saw them each one thrust his head into their midst and sucked at them as a Christian sucking at swine-flesh, until their thorns entered into our tongues which became like cactus leaves.

Then our spirits fell and we cursed the hour that had brought us thither, and we cried: Alas, whither have we come. If Allah does not provide us with water and food then we are lost. Let us pray before Him, for He may accept our prayer and deliver us from destruction. Thereupon we raised our eyes aloft and said: There is no God but Allah and Mohammed is the messenger of Allah. We removed the thorns from our tongues and pressed and embraced the empty water-skins and canteens so that they might give us water, but none came out. We bit the skins with our teeth but there was only air. March we could not, for we had lost the way. We took counsel and climbed up a lofty hill, in case Allah might reveal a spring or tree or plant to us from there.

Yet all the places which we saw were like the place from which we came. No tree grew, no spring gurgled, no bird flew, no kid bleated, hill was entwined with hill and wilderness with wilderness. We flung away our weapons and sat down bitter of spirit. This sitting was worst of all. Our limbs grew rusty and our tongues shrivelled like a water-skin whose waters have dried.

Have we anything to eat? I asked my comrades. Shriveled water-skins, they answered. Cook them, said I, and we shall eat them. So we set the butts of our weapons on fire and roasted the water-skins.

When the water-skins were at an end we roasted our boots. As there was nothing left we went downhill. Yet all our descent was like a mall who leaves one desert for another. The sun reached the west and the day grew dark. We hoped for a refreshing breeze, night came but not refreshment or ease. The moon and stars stood weary in the firmament. The sand had not been cooled and an aimless wind was caught amid the hills. Nor was the night that followed any better. An aimless wind held sway all night long. There was no change whatsoever in the air. That night there was a great fury in our hearts. We had been hoping to moisten our lips at night with the dew and to cool our bones, yet it was as parched as the day. We gazed aloft, and it seemed as though the moon and the stars and the planets were suffering as we did.

The third watch came. Stars and planets sank down in the firmament and a light breeze began to blow. As soon as the sun came out this likewise heated up. At the last it partnered with the whirlwind. We hid our faces in the ground, wrapped up in our robes, and wept for ourselves because of the desert wind. I sat thus for as long as I sat, with my face to the ground and my eyes turned low. I, at whose glance, vast hosts of soldiers had trembled, feared to raise my head against a grain of sand. They had been fine, those days when I had headed my men and all had feared my word. The days had been fine when I had been at home and my men servants and maidservants had stood about to serve me, one raising a glowing coal to light the nargila, and another fanning me, while the fountains in the garden sprayed their water round about like a crown of dew.

I shook myself at length, rose to my feet, removed my coat, raised my voice and said: Come on, stand up. But my words were like a voice falling in a graveyard. My companions all lay dead, and those who had not yet died were as good as dead.

Thereupon I also wished to die. I remembered all the treasures and delights of Time which had formerly assembled together on my behalf. Now all of a sudden I was deprived of everything and was giving up my soul in the heart of the desert where there was no water to purify my corpse nor attendants to bury me. I raised mine eyes aloft and said, There is no God save God, let Him do with me whatever has been decreed for me.

But the Angel of Death had no wish as yet to set his hands on this man who is now talking. While I was still mourning for my household who were left without a master and for my children whom I was rendering orphans, I heard a sigh and saw that several of my comrades were quivering and moving.

O my brethren, said I, Allah has left you so that you should hot perish in the desert. Hold out a little longer and let us mount yonder hill. If our descent serves no purpose, it may be that our ascent will have some purpose.

In this way I stood between the living and the dead, now raising my voice, and now whispering to myself, in order not to disturb my comrades for I had already despaired of their arising, but so that I should feel that I myself had not perished. At last I also grew silent. My tongue still moved convulsively, but my lips were silent.

Yet Allah brought the sound to the ears of my comrades. Little by little, slowly and swayingly, several of them rose to their feet in order to proceed.

Ere we departed we covered the dead with sand, may God's mercies and blessing rest upon them and all the faithful, and we said the prayer for the dead over them. We had no water to wash their bodies. May Allah cleanse them of their transgressions and make their judgment and our own more easy.

That hill was steep and smooth. Even a flea would have slipped and fallen. Ere we had reached the hill-top, my companions had fallen and rolled down and broke their limbs, so that nothing was left of us save myself and three companions.

When we had reached the hill-top we stood looking down at fields and vineyards, and date-palms, flocks and herds. Sweet breezes were blowing and bringing the fine scent and fragrance of spices and springs of water. I raised my eyes aloft and said: Blessed is He who counseled my heart to ascend, all lauds and praise to the Laudable and Praiseworthy who brought us hither. We have only to go down and we are saved.

Yet the descent was twice as hard as the ascent. Even a person who had not seen what befell our companions would have feared lest he became but a heap of bones – and this most assuredly we felt who had seen men rolling and falling down, some with broken heads and some with smashed and broken limbs. And yet those breezes bearing sweet scents restored our spirit for us until the desire of life returned to our soul.

Let us make ourselves legs, said I to my companions, and descend. If we get there alive it will be good, and if not, then better fall in an inhabited place than in a desert. For if we perish amid human beings they will bury us and if we perish in the desert then birds of prey will consume us like the idolaters, may God curse them, who leave their dead to the birds of the heavens. My companions at once agreed, saying, you have spoken well. If we die we shall die among human beings who will bury us, while if we live we shall return to our own places in order to comfort our households and kiss our children. So each one took his soul in his own hand, and we went down on our hands and feet. Within a few moments we found ourselves standing in an inhabited place of gardens and groves, amid date-palms and other good trees and waving grain and a countryside running with water. Yet it seemed as though all our toil had been only in order that we should fall below. For while we were standing there my comrades fell in their tracks, and I also fell without knowing whether I was alive or dead.

I lay there as long as I lay without the strength to move a limb, and assuredly unable to stand up. My eyes closed and my body began to make a hollow in the ground below like a man who digs himself a pit and the earth receives him and holds him entrapped. If this is death, thought I to myself, then there is nothing better. I wished to ask my companions, what do you feel? Yet there was a weariness within me which caused me not to open my mouth.

While I was lying there I heard a little kid bleating from the pasture, not the blast of trumpets nor the sound of people roaring and trampling. My soul returned to me and I slept. It seemed to me that I had returned home from the war and found my household established and my children alive. I greeted them and they greeted me in return. I kissed them and said, All lauds and praises to the Most Laudable and Praiseworthy, here I am with you and I shall not depart from you again until my end comes and I arise to my fate. I sat tranquilly and comforted my household and begat children upon children, and Allah rejoiced my heart and satisfied my desires. Yet all my tranquility did not last long. I heard the sound of warfare and forgot what must not be forgotten and forsook my household to go forth against the enemy. And there I went on slaying until I had raised up a whole hill of dead. While I was standing up to my knees in blood, the earth trembled as though the ground were opening its mouth to swallow me up. I realized that I had departed from the world and was being led away to Gehenna, to be taken down to the lowest hells. I reminded Him on High of the wars that I had waged against the Unbelievers and how many of them I had slain in order that I might achieve merit on the Day of Judgment and ease my transgressions for me, and I cried, God is God…

Ere I had said "and Mohamed is His messenger," two men came who were tall as cedars and the lances in their hands were like date-palms that support the sky. And then I knew that the noise had come only from the sound of their feet. If they have come for peace, said I to myself, they have come only at the command of the Creator in order to deliver me from hunger and thirst. But if they have to do battle, then it is honor for a brave man to perish at the hands of these warriors.

Yet Allah found his believers worthy to have the secrets of the world revealed to them, and gave us strength and courage to remain alive until He His own Lofty Self resolves to take back our souls. I raised my eyes aloft in wonder at His creatures, may He be exalted, but they bent down to us and opened a water jar and moistened my lips and asked me a question. When they saw that we had no strength they picked us up in their hands and took us to their places, a place of tents which was as large about as the expanses of the streets of Damascus and Istanbul. Then they asked us once more whatever they asked us in a tongue that was like your own language. I looked about and saw men wearing cut and dyed garments bearing all kinds of weapons. Then I knew that we were among the tribe of Khaybar, who rule in all those parts and have no sultan over them save from their own midst, and who fear no kingdom save the Kingdom of Heaven. I blessed the Blessed Allah who had brought us to them, since a covenant had once been made of old between Mohammed the messenger of Allah and this tribe of Khaybar. If our companions had held out a little while they would have come hither with us and would have rejoiced their souls with those things that Allah has created in this world. But Allah the Exalted does good to His creatures according to His own loving-kindness, decreeing thus for this one and thus for that one. He had decreed that our companions should fall in the desert, but for us we had decreed that we should live and enjoy His goodness in this world.

While we were sitting they brought us water to drink which tasted like the morning dew upon the mountains. After we had drunk and given thanks to Him who hath created good springs wherewith to restore the souls of His Believers, they set coffee before us. Much coffee had I drunk in my life, but never in all my days had I drunk coffee such as this, although I have often sat with great emirs and he who is set over them, our Lord and ruler the Sultan, may God show him all due mercy. After we had sat a while they brought us a broth, not of the flesh of beast or fowl nor of fish or vermin but of greenstuff – for during those years that they dwelt in the wilderness they did not put out their hands to slay any living animal but were sustained from the earth and the fruits thereof. At the last they prepared soft couches for us. We lay down to sleep and lay all that night and all the following day until the sun set and it became night and it was time to fall asleep again. Then they came and spread a table before us and set all kind of food upon it; today a little, tomorrow more, then after the morrow more and more till flesh grew about our bones and our strength returned. Likewise they clothed and shod us and gave each of us a headcloth and a girdle to set about our heads.

We spent two weeks with them in this way and I saw things beyond the telling of any tongue. Yet I wish to tell you a little of what I saw. They are as many as the sands of the desert, and are dressed in noble garments and wrapped in woolen shawls with fringes and ride upon horses as befits the noble. Their neighbors are subject to them and pay them taxes, yet they hold their neighbors only in the way that the awe of a man is felt within his household. And every one of them is a warrior that is worth ten warriors. There are some among them who can take an Arab in hand as he rides on horseback and fling them both aloft, flinging Arab and receiving horse, flinging the horse and receiving the Arab, without either of them touching the ground. When it is daytime each man goes to his field and vineyard and dates and cattle. When it is night he comes and sits down before the elders to hearken to the Torah of Moses your master. And their wives and daughters sit in their tents and cook and bake and milk the cattle and prepare buttermilk and cheese and spin and weave and sew and roll out bread and do not show their faces without, in order that men might not be led to ill thoughts on their account – for Allah has adorned appearance more than all women and has made them boundlessly beautiful and full of grace. There are women whose bodies are beautiful yet who have no charm and there are women with charm whose bodies are not beautiful. Yet among them the bodies are beautiful and the charm is also great. Some of them are like the sun in its radiance, for whosoever gazes at them is dazzled, and some are like the moon at its full, for whoever gazes at them becomes moonstruck. They do not cover their faces as our women do, for Allah has fashioned them a veil of honor and modesty, and no man looks upon them save their husbands. Each one of them rises early in the morning for prayer and they pray three times a day; and while they pray they turn their faces to Jerusalem. And on the Sabbath they do not leave their tents, but sit night and day praising His Lofty Name who has given them Sabbaths for rest. And they add part of the week-day to the Sabbath, both before and after. And ere the Sabbath begins they take off their weekly clothes and put down their weapons because the Sabbath protects them; and they put on golden array and light oil lamps, two for each; but in their tent of prayer they light twelve lamps, and they welcome the Sabbath as a man who welcomes the King to his home, and they make feasts in honor of it, singing songs and praises at each of these feasts. At the first feast they mention the name of Abraham, may he rest in peace, at the second the name of Isaac, may he rest in peace, and at the third the name of Jacob, may he rest in peace. And at the Sabbath close they all gather together and eat and drink and rejoice, bringing a gold chair and a large golden crown set with jewels and precious stones; and on the seat they set an elder garbed in finest pure gold array with sixty warriors running before him and sixty warriors running behind. And they shout and blow their trumpets and play their musical instruments and cry, "David, King of Israel, lives forever." Thereupon all Israel come out of their tents at once and respond after them, "David, King of Israel, lives forever," while all the women peep out at them from the openings of the tents, and he claps his hands together and says "Kingship is the Lord's." At this two elders come forth, one fetching him a staff and another a pack. Then he descends from his throne and enters the sheepfolds where he feeds the kids and the goats. And he removes the royal robe from about him and the crown from on his head, and swathes himself in his shawl and goes to the elders and says: "My masters, I come but to learn." Thereupon the warriors put down their swords and put on their weekly clothes and go forth to their work. One goes to his field and one to his vineyard and dates, and one to his flocks and cattle, until God brings the Sabbath back to them.

In this way we dwelt with the tribe of Khaybar and saw their strength and bravery and righteousness and generosity and loving-kindness, so that I forgot the arrows of war and all my victories and honor and glory in the lands of the Believers, and rejoiced to have been brought to these noble ones of the people of the God of Abraham. May the Blessed One bless His blessed with His blessings.

Yet one can forget everything except the roof of the house which he saw for the first time when his mother gave birth to him. Ere long the Master of Dreams came and showed me my home and its chimney, and I smelt the scent of food cooked there and desired them with the longing of a pregnant woman.

What befell me also befell my companions. Day by day they desired more greatly to return to their places and drink the waters of their wells and eat the butter-milk of their flocks and teach their children the good qualities which they had learnt in the land of the Khaybar.

Allah looked into our hearts. One day He brought us to a certain tent more handsome than all the others, with three elders seated in it whose faces were bright and shining as the light that was created on the First Day. And their beards were like hanging clusters of dates. We were in awe of them at once, and fell on our faces and kissed the dust at their feet and said, We are your servants. I saw that they did not understand our tongue and I began to talk every language that I knew. The elders shook their beards and I knew that they would sooner hear the talk of beasts and animals and fowls than the tongues of the Unbelievers. Yet it could be seen from their faces that they had nothing against us at heart.

When we saw this, the souls within us were enlarged and we gave thanks to Him who is worthy of all thanksgiving and we kissed the dust at their feet again, and said, God's shelter to His warriors and honor to His elders.

Ere the day was out they set us on swift camels and returned us to our own places. It may be in three hours or in two hours or in one hour that we covered a journey of many weeks and many days. And they parted from us in peace. God's shelter and His peace be upon them.

I entered my home and said, Peace be with you, my children. But my greeting was orphaned. Ere I had come my children had departed and had not returned. Likewise my friends did not come to greet me. My sons and brothers had had the one fate. Both alike had perished in the war. Likewise our Lord the Sultan had returned his spirit to the God of Spirits. Likewise the kings who had waged war against him had died, some of them at their own hands and some at the hands of others. Time had not ended but kings had come to an end. Yet that cry "David, King of Israel, lives forever" still resounds within my ears. Sometimes it is like a flaming fire and sometimes it is as sweet as the shadow of a date palm.

I know for whom *Eretz Yisrael* is set in store. It is intended only for Israel. Yet for whom of Israel – those unto whom the Exalted Creator gave magnificence and honor and strength and bravery and generosity and loving-kindness and who do His Exalted Will out of love, they are the ones who will take over the rule therein in the future. And their rule and kinghood will continue forever and ever.

I rose to my feet and said: Blessed be the Lord God of Israel who permitted you to see what you have seen. Happy are we that you too know for whom *Eretz Yisrael* is intended. It was good for Israel to safeguard their Torah, and esteem it above all things in the land of which it is written, "And ye shall inherit it and ye shall dwell therein and shall observe to do all the statutes," save that the day is short and the work is plentiful. The All-and Ever-Present has imposed many labors upon us. We must plough and sow and harvest and set up sheaves and thresh and winnow, and plant and hoe and pick the vintage and tread the grapes, and prune the tree and beat the olives, we must feed beasts and fowl and shear the sheep and watch over our soil and labor against the destroyers and the thieves. Yet dwelling in the land of Israel is a great deed, equivalent to all the commandments of the Torah. I am now going to take these plants on my shoulder in order to plant them in our land, as it is written, "And they shall plant vineyards and drink their wine and they shall make gardens and eat the fruits thereof and I shall plant them on their land and they shall never more be I plucked away from their land which I have given them, saith the Lord thy God." The Holy and Blessed One has made His planting dependent upon our planting. If we engage in our planting, then it is certain and sure that the planting of the Holy One will last and continue. The whole world belongs to God, and He has shared it out to His creatures according to His will. Esau and Ishmael have taken the fullness of the world and slay one another and destroy one another for the kinghood which they would seize. But we have received this little land from His blessed hand. We have not come to seize kinghood or to hold dominion in it, but to plough and sow and plant.

The pasha did not understand all I had said. He had spent but a little time with the Jews of Khaybar and had not had opportunity to learn much. Yet from his face it was plain that my words seemed reasonable to him.

And so we sat as long as we sat, until day declined and the evening breeze began to blow. The pasha rose and bade me farewell in peace.

As he was about to turn away from me he looked at my sapling and asked: In how many years will it bear fruit?

I told him. He sighed and said: I shall not eat of it, but you and your children and your children's children will eat of them.

By the grace of the Holy and Blessed One, said, I looking upwards.

– *Translated by I.M. Lask*

The Kindling

NEVER HAS A MAN seen rejoicing if he has not seen the rejoicing of the Thirty-third day of the Omer at the grave of Rabbi Shimon bar Yoḥai in Meron, whither the men of Israel ascend in many a festive crowd with song and all manner of musical instruments. From all quarters do they come; from the cities of our God and from the lands of Edom and of Ishmael; and they remain there day and night, studying the kabbalistic texts which tell of the last lesson taught by Rabbi Shimon ere he departed this world; further they study other fitting matters, and pray and chant specially-written hymns. At Meron there is a marble pillar and its top is shaped as a receptacle for oil. Therein they set wicks of silk and fine veils and all manner of precious kerchiefs, also cloth embroidered with thread of silver and of gold; these they set in the oil and then kindle them into a blaze, making the great festival known as the *Hilula* of Rabbi Simon, which marks the anniversary of the day of that Great Saint's passing from this world. They dance round dances before the Holy Presence, as it were, which cometh upon that night to share in the rejoicing of the God-learned sage. And it is plain that the Holy Congregation of the men of Safad, who are closer to the place of Rabbi Shimon than any others, since Meron is accounted within the borders of their territory, have even greater cause than others to rejoice at Rabbi Shimon's festival.

Now by reason of evil and transgression, joy did depart and the entire world seethed with fury because of the kings going forth to war one against the other, the hand of Esau being against Ishmael, the hand of Ishmael against Esau, and the hands of them both against Israel. A man venturing abroad was consumed by the sword; a man staying at home was pierced by the arrows of famine; a man chancing across a few drops of oil never knew whether to burn them in memory of his kin slain in the war, or to use them to sustain his wife and children who were perishing of starvation. The high born, those who had been garbed in silken raiment and had delighted the eyes of mankind by their beauty, now dwelt alone covering themselves with rags and tatters and fearing to go forth; until all the paths and tracks in the land were forlorn and desolated. Mountains once clamorous with Israel were silent. Meron, which had been bright as a wedding-house, now stood darkling and gloomy. Even the Holy Congregation of the Men of Safad, who are punctilious in performing the will of Heaven in joy, now remained concealed and keening in their homes.

The time came when the Holy One, blessed be he, set His head once again in the place whence He had removed it, and saw that which had befallen in His world. Exercising His mercy towards His creatures he entreated with love the remnants from the sword, breaking the rod of the wicked and bringing low the pride of the tyrannous. They lowered their weapons, the use of implements of warfare did cease; and the world began to return to its appointed path. The nations returned, each to its own land and its own home. Now it was a time in which *Eretz Yisrael* was visited as it had not been visited since the latter destruction of the Temple; for those of Israel who had not despaired of the Redemption began to ascend, those of their number who might, to the Land of Israel. They found the land ruined and wallowing in blood, and Israel bleeding and suffering. Thereupon they set their hearts to healing the sick and raising those that had stumbled; and they passed through the entire land, sustaining the people with good counsel, with bread and with garments.

The day they reached Safad was the Eve of the Thirty-third day of the Omer. All Safad gathered unto them, saying, brethren, neither silver nor gold do we desire of you nor any gift; but in the Land of Israel there is a worthy custom of ascending on the Thirty-third Day of the Omer to Meron and kindling oil at the grave of Rabbi Simon bar Yoḥai. Perchance you will aid us in the fulfillment of this commandment; for throughout the years of the war the paths were uneasy with troops, so that we remained in our homes like captives and never ascended to Meron. Now that the Holy One hath pity upon His world we do desire to ascend there to kindle the fire on the day of Rabbi Shimon's *Hilula*.

We too, said the Men of the Exile to the Men of Safad, would rejoice there with you.

They sent and brought jugs full of oil, took some kerchiefs, and ascended to Meron.

When they came as far as the Cave of Rabbi Shimon bar Yoḥai they found Arabs standing there before the cave and rags and tatters steeped in oil were in their hands. Brethren of Israel, said the Arabs unto Israel, blessed be the All-Present; blessed be He who hath brought you here, and blessed be you in sight of the God of our father Abraham for arriving in time. All the years that you never came we kindled the fire upon the grave of the saint; now that you are come, take your own and kindle the fire.

And Israel kindled such a blaze over the grave of Rabbi Shimon bar Yoḥai that the brightness thereof lit up the whole countryside.

The Good Years

In Jerusalem I was the guest of a man who honored me, prepared a feast for me, and seated me next to his father at the head of the table. The old man took pleasure in every dish that was served, saying: "Enjoy it, for it is grown in Israel and is even mentioned in the Mishnah." I was happy to be with such distinguished, God-fearing people. "My friends," I said, "you are blessed. I too am blessed to be able to sit with you – men of good deeds. Of every dish that is placed before you, you remember where it is mentioned in the writings of the rabbis. Of every precept you observe, you recall its source in our laws. Of this the *Ethics of the Fathers* says: 'It is as if they had eaten from the table of the Creator.'"

After we ate and drank, the old man took his cup and said Grace in a clear, pleasant voice. Both the man and his voice pleased me. I saw that he knew how to make the blessing and that it was becoming in him to bless. I noticed also a custom of his. As he blessed the Land he poured a bit of water into his cup of wine in tribute to the strength of Israel's vintage. Rejoicing I said, "Blessed is the land in which, no matter where a man turns, he learns Torah and good manners."

When he reached the part of the Grace which reads, "the good and beneficent," I heard him say: "May the All-Merciful bless my father." I said to myself: I had compared him with the pious and with men of good deeds, but after hearing what he just said, I see that he doesn't even know what almost everybody does. I thought that he knew how to say

Grace, and that it became him to say it, but now I see that he does not even understand the meaning of the words – as if an old man of seventy has a father living and can say of him, "May the All-Merciful bless my father." He is but an ignoramus who doesn't know the meaning of the words, and since "May the All-Merciful bless my father" is printed in the prayer-book, he recites it. Woe unto him who blesses his father at the time he lies in Gehenna, punished because of his son! For anyone who leaves behind him an ignorant son, though he deserves Paradise, is thrown into Gehenna and punished because he did not teach his son Torah.

As the old man finished saying the blessing after meals, another man entered. He was spry and erect. He had the face of a young man and a black beard was about his face in a sort of semicircle. He wore a velvet hat and a white coat that reached well below his knees. A broad sash was folded again and again about his waist, and a velvet cloak, green as the leaf of a leek, covered his coat. His hands were thrust behind the sash. His stockings were white and his feet had leather slippers. He was so light on his feet that his slippers seemed to chase but could not catch him. At the sight of the man, the company rose in his honor. But not everyone's manner of rising was the same. The old man's son half-stood, half-sat. But the old man rose with respect, and after he had completed the Grace he left his seat and offered it to the newcomer. The guest said: "Sit down, my son, sit down."

But the old man continued standing in reverence, took a pinch of snuff so that he should be able to stand (for tobacco relieves fatigue) and patiently waited for the guest to sit down. The guest seated himself in the chair, removed the pillow, and in a tender voice said: "The generations are weaker, the body is frailer, and strength is ebbing. A man sitting in a chair now has to have pillows and cushions. I remember that we used to sit on rocks and no one ever complained to his friend, 'The seats are hard!'"

Then the newcomer asked, "Is there anything to eat?" And they brought him black bread, olives, onions, and a cup of water. I thought: How strange! The table is full of all good things and he asks, Is there anything to eat? They themselves feast on white bread and drink the choice wines of the land and they give him black bread and water.

He stretched out his hand and lifted the black bread with joy and blessed it with a happiness that I had not seen even at the tables of dukes and princes when they sat before delicate meats and the finest wines. He ate with such joy that I myself longed to eat again; and they stood before him with awe and respect like people who pay homage to a great man who has come to sit with them.

What are you doing? I thought. If he is so important to you, why didn't you share your food with him? Haven't you had the best of everything? You are the sons of Abraham, sitting in the place of Abraham, and yet your deeds are not the deeds of Abraham. Our father Abraham slaughtered three oxen for three men, and it is not said that he ate as much as a crumb that day. But my heart spoke up to defend them. I said to my heart, What! Can you find good in their actions? Yes, it answered and said: Blessed is Israel, that they live in the Land of Israel and that they are greater than the rest of Israel in Torah, good deeds and in observance of the Law. Even the poorest among them deprives himself of food, and takes what is meant for his own mouth to give to a poor man. If so, why didn't they offer him what they themselves ate? Because that man is a righteous man and checks his pleasure and eats nothing too much, for while the Creator's Temple is in ruins, should his own table have delicacies?

But my mind and heart did not agree. For the man was eating heartily, did not sigh while eating, and said nothing to ennoble the meal with anything spiritual. In fact, he was enjoying himself. He joked and called the old man, "My son." If he is so pious, I thought, why does he joke? Didn't our Sages, may their memories be blessed, compare the table to an altar? I turned to the old man – the father of the man who had invited me – and said: "With your permission, I'd like to say something."

"Say it," he said.

"I am surprised," I said, "that an old man like you stands before a younger man. Thank God that we are in Jerusalem and not among the sages of Athens. Or perhaps we have become worthy to live in the days before the times of the Messiah as described in the Tractate Sotah: 'Ere the Messiah comes, the aged will stand before the young.'"

They began to laugh and I said: "You are laughing at me."

"God forbid," they answered.

I said: "You laugh at me and say, God forbid, we're not laughing at you, but in spite of that my heart tells me that you do nothing wrong. However, what shall I do, if my eyes and heart do not agree?"

Said the old man: "Will you become angry at me if I tell you a teaching from the Torah?"

"Manners precede Torah," I said, "and what is more, respect your elders is in the Torah."

"He *is* an old man," he said, "and hasn't the Torah commanded us, 'Honor thy father'? If another old man had come, I would also have risen out of respect for him and said, Sit down, if you please. And since he *is* my father, why should I not rise in respect and give him my place?"

I was completely astonished when my host – the old man's son – added: "I see that you didn't know that he is my grandfather. Now that you know that he is my grandfather, say that we act as we should and according to the precepts."

"You are right," I said, "but I should like to ask a question I wanted to ask before but did not."

"What is it?" he asked.

"The respect you give him," I said, "is no doubt proper. However, you ate all sorts of delicacies and drank fine wine but have given your grandfather no delicacies and no wine, and only black bread, olives, onions and water. Would you call that respectful?"

The father of the old man spread out his hands and clapped them together saying: "My son, my son, you too make the same mistake that others make. You think that eating good things is good for you! It is only a punishment. Just as when a sick man is fed all sorts of delicacies and cannot enjoy them. He eats this and wants that. His soul is empty and his face turns green. But a healthy man eats bread and drinks water, enjoys it and is happy. His soul is full and his face shines, and the healthier his body is, the more he despises delicacies and longs for simple foods."

I was astonished and stared at this grandfather who was a youth compared to his own son and thought: Can there be a father who looks younger than his son?

Then the father of the old man said: "How weak have the generations become and how frail is the world! A man of Israel who is not as twisted as a ram's horn and doesn't groan, whose limbs do not tremble and whose bones do not shake, whose hands and feet are perfect, and who is the master of his own body – even though he is older than ten elders they don't believe his age. But the early generations are not like the later ones. The first generations settled in the Land of Israel because of sorrow and toil, because of wanderings and persecution, because of need and lack of food. But they praised God, saying, 'How happy and blessed are we that we pray morning and night in Jerusalem, that we sit before You in Jerusalem and learn Torah in Jerusalem.' And because they were content with their lot and with their living and did not rebel against suffering, their faces gleam and their bodies are of iron, their strength keeps increasing and they live long lives.

"But the later generations toil and never have enough. If they lack but one of all the earth's pleasures, they immediately get so angry that their bodies look rusty. One day they want to go here, another day there, one day to the north, another day south. Comes a wind and they groan, Oh, our legs are tottering. Comes the sun and they soon complain, Oh, our teeth are melting. Woe to us that we are here and have gone from there. If we were there we could have put ice on our heads and covered ourselves with snow. And they don't realize that the land of Israel is better than all other lands, for here every city has its own climate: something that other countries do not have. And Jerusalem is superior to them all, for here you have every climate. In every quarter of Jerusalem you will find a different kind of air, because since the destruction of the Temple the earth has grown smaller.

"Heaven forbid that I should disparage the later generations and give them a bad name. Worthy of their lot are all they who live in the Land. For every one who dwells in Israel is called righteous even though at first glance he is not righteous. For if he were not righteous, the earth would spew him out, as it is written: 'And the land spat forth its inhabitants.' But since it hasn't ejected him, he is righteous, though he may be in the grip of wickedness. Listen, I will tell you a secret. The Holy One, blessed be He, knew that His children wanted to be in His palace, but since they were so few, he gave them the strength to stand up to robbers and troops, evil men and beasts."

I said, "Blessed is He who gave His palace to His watchmen. Blessed are you who are worthy, and blessed is the Eternal Who made you worthy." At that moment I had learned why the old man had said, "May the All-Merciful bless my father." Because his father was alive. And I learned why they ate delicacies and drank wine, and gave him only plain food and water. Because delicacies are a punishment, but a healthy man eats bread in his hunger and drinks water in his thirst. I learned also why the father of the old man looked like a youth. For he was of the first generations, men of great strength who risked their lives and asked for nothing but shelter in His holy courtyard, and He gave them the strength to withstand all. And I learned why the later generations are weak and weary. Because they find no satisfaction in their residence in Israel. I learned, too, why one feels all the world's climates in Israel. Because the earth has grown smaller. And I learned that everyone who lives in the Land of Israel is called righteous, even though he be in the grip of wickedness.

The grandfather ate his bread with joy and his face lit up. He drank water from a clay jug, washed his fingers, and said the Grace after meals with a cheerful voice. Such is the voice of the elders of Jerusalem in praising and thanking His name for even a crumb that He gives them. Anyone who has not heard the voice of the elders of Jerusalem saying Grace has never heard the voice of gratitude.

But lo and behold, when he came to "May the All-Merciful," he shut his eyes and gently said, "May the All-Merciful bless my father." I was dumbfounded and thought: he looks like a scholar but prays like an ignoramus, he blesses but doesn't know whom he is blessing. As if this old man who has grown old and who has grown-up grandsons can have a father living?

However, since he is an old man, I thought, ending his days in Jerusalem, I will sit with him. Perhaps I shall learn something from him. I waited until he had completed saying Grace. After he had finished, I said: "I should like to ask a question but I fear it will trouble you."

"My son," he said, "If you ask well, why are you afraid of troubling me?"

I then said: "I know that you are one of the elders of Jerusalem. I should like to hear about everything that has happened in Jerusalem. Perhaps you remember some of the events that took place."

His face lit up immediately and he said: "Like the slave who is lucky enough to serve at the king's palace and gets his greatest joy out of describing all the wonders that his eyes have seen and what his ears have heard within the palace walls. Blessed is the Creator whose mercies are many in Israel! Though they have sinned against Him, He opens the gates of Jerusalem for them: as it is written, 'Enter His gates with thanksgiving.' If it were not for that explicit verse we never would have dared picture Him as a man who draws people into His house." And he began telling me stories about the pious men who had been in Jerusalem, in whose day no impure thing was seen in *Eretz Yisrael.* And so he went on and his talk was spiced with Scripture and Mishnah, with law and lore.

I said to myself: I will ask him why he said, May the All-Merciful bless my father. For since when is the Grace a memorial prayer? But because he was describing things I longed to hear, I did not interrupt him for fear that he would leap from subject to subject and from incident to incident. And there is nothing harder on the ear than that. In the midst of his talking, he came to an important point but couldn't explain it clearly. "This happened ninety years ago," he said. "I was three at the time and was riding on my father's shoulders. My father slapped my face, saying, 'You don't deserve a slap, but I want you to remember that you were here. You don't know what you are seeing now, but in the future you will remember and rejoice.' If you want to hear more about it, ask my father and he will tell you."

"Excuse me," I said, "please repeat what you have just said. I don't think I heard you well."

He answered: "You will have to ask my father about this, he remembers and rejoices in the telling."

At that moment I thought: how right was Solomon when he said: "Let not your mouth be hasty!" No sooner did I question his saying Grace as a memorial prayer than he tells me his father is alive. I then told him about my own work that takes me from one part of Jerusalem to another.

He said: "Even if you had eagle's wings you could not catch him."

"Why?" I asked.

"Every day after prayers," he replied, "my father goes from one end of Jerusalem to the other in order to fulfill what is written: 'Turn about Zion and go round her.' By the time you reach one place, he is at another. When you reach Mount Scopus he is on the Mount of Olives.

By the time you reach the Mount of Olives he is at the Tower of David. When you reach the Tower of David, he is at the graves of the Small Sanhedrin. And when you are at the Small Sanhedrin he has reached the Great Sanhedrin. We should like to go with him, but what can we do? There is not enough strength in us. If so, how can we fulfill the verse: 'Turn about Zion and go round about her; count her towers'? Come, let us recount the greatness of Jerusalem whom the Holy One, blessed be He, returned to Israel despite the fact that He had entrusted it to other nations."

As we were talking, another man entered. His beard was long and his earlocks were curled. His eyes were like two doves and his face was shining like the Gates of the East. A smile never left his lips. His appearance was that of a king, but his clothes were as simple as those of plain people. At the sound of his feet, they all rose. But not everyone's manner of rising was alike. The old man who had been talking to me rose in reverence, not like his son who half stood, half sat, and who at length wasn't able to stand on his legs. The grandfather drew himself up straight as a snake and bowed his head gently, not like his son whose head drooped after eating.

The newcomer entered and greeted them. "Welcome," they answered. They brought him a jug of water, a cotton towel, and an earthen dish. He rolled up his sleeves and took the dish, ready to wash his hands and eat his breakfast. Seeing that his hands were dusty, he lifted them saying: "These hands that have been graced by the dust of the Holy Land, should I shake them free of this dust?"

"Father," they asked, "Why is today different? Every day you come early and today you have come so late."

He said: "My sons, on my way I reached a place below Jerusalem where a man was ploughing in a field. I thought: I will help him. Not only today, but every single day from now on I will plough and hoe and weed with him until the earth brings forth bread and I will eat my own bread like a babe who thrives at its mother's breasts." The old man saw that his words surprised us and he added: "Do you think that I have forgotten the day of death? By your lives, I have already prepared a grave on the Mount of Olives, higher than the rest of the graves, facing the site of the Temple. There I have left a flask of olive oil for the time when

I give up my soul and you place my bones in my grave." He spread his hands from the top of his head to the ground, measuring his length. "I have prepared a grave," he said, "according to my own height, not a short one where they bend a dead man's legs under him, but a grave to fit me." He spread his fingers on the muscle of his left forearm and pinched the spot where the *tefilin* is placed, saying: "Fortunate are you, my body, that you will be buried in Jerusalem! The place where you have been worthy of living, you are worthy of lying there upon your death." As he spoke, the old man saw me and said: "Peace unto you."

"And unto you, peace," I answered.

He said: "A new face!"

I bowed my head humbly and said: "A new face that likes the old."

Then his son, grandson and great-grandson stood up and indicating me said to him: "He wants to hear the stories of old times from you, for he loves Jerusalem."

His face lit up immediately and he said: "Ask, my son, ask."

Seeing his friendly face, I began asking questions and he answered me. I asked and he answered. And about every occurrence and every event, though it happened fifty, seventy, eighty, even ninety years ago, he said, "I have seen it with my own eyes, may I live to see the Redeemer; I have heard it with my own ears, may I live to hear the Messiah's trumpet." He said this even for incidents that took place three and four generations ago, almost as if the Holy One, blessed be He, unfolded the generations before him like a notebook. I asked him how old he was.

"Do you begrudge me my long years?" he asked.

"May the Lord lengthen your days," I said, "to see the bounty of Jerusalem till your one hundred and twentieth year. Out of the depths of my love and affection have I asked you."

"I am ninety," he said.

"Permit me to say something."

"Speak," he said.

"Then there are two wonders here," I said.

"What are they?" he asked.

"I have never seen a son the senior of his father," I answered, "for your son says he is ninety-three and, what is more, of everything that you have related you say, 'I witnessed it,' even though it took place more than ninety years ago. If so, there are things of which you say 'I saw them,' and you weren't even born!"

The old man smiled, smoothed his beard and said to me: "My son, know that I have spoken the truth and, God forbid, no lie passed my lips."

Then I said: "With your permission, I will say that there is yet a third wonder here."

"Blessed is the Eternal," he said, "blessed is He Who conducts His world in wisdom and order! But, if you have come to seek wonders, there is nothing that is not a wonder. Is there a greater wonder than that you and I are living? But listen and you will know that I have spoken truthfully."

"Respected elder, please continue," I said.

"My son," he said, "Why shouldn't I tell you? It is no secret. When I came to Israel I was twenty-seven, and I have lived here ninety years. But I swear to you by Him who rested His glory in Jerusalem that all the years I lived outside the Land are as nothing in my eyes. Therefore I say I am ninety."

Hearing this, I stood up, moved and shaken. I took his hand in mine and lifted my eyes to heaven and blessed him with all my heart and said: "May the Lord fulfill your years until one hundred and twenty."

He too lifted his eyes heavenward and answered, "Amen," to the blessing. "Amen. So be His will."

Blessed is the Eternal who portions out life to all living creatures! For the sake of Jerusalem my blessing was accepted by Him, and the man remained among the living until his one hundred and twenty years in the Land of Israel were completed. And he passed on at a ripe old age, and as was his strength in days gone by, so was it at the hour of his departing. He really could have lived longer, but out of respect for our teacher Moses, may he rest in peace –as it is written: And Moses was one hundred and twenty years old at the time of his death – he gave up his life and took it upon himself to leave the world and go to his final rest, sound in body and limb and perfect in his senses. And following his bier were his son and grandson and great-grandson, sons of the third and fourth generation, all distinguished elders, even the youngest of them older than your grandfather.

From the day he prepared his grave until the day he died, that area was filled with many graves, for everyone desires burial in the Land of Israel, because the dead of Israel come to life first in the days of the Messiah. When they came to bury the old man they feared they would find no room. Suddenly the flask of olive oil that he had left closed in his grave opened and its fragrance spread. There they buried him: in the choicest of graves, opposite the site of the Temple. The earth, worthy of him during his lifetime, was worthy that he lie in it at death like a babe nestled in its mother's bosom, until the fulfillment of the verse: "Lo, on the hills are the feet of the Herald" and death is forever destroyed.

– *Translated by Curt Leviant*

From Foe to Friend

BEFORE TALPIOT WAS BUILT the King of the Winds used to rule over the entire region; and all his ministers and servants, mighty and stubborn winds, dwelled there with him and blew over mountain and valley, hill and ravine, doing whatever their hearts desired, as if the land had been given to them alone.

I went out there once and saw how lovely the place was – the air crisp, the sky pure blue, the land so open and free – and I strolled around a bit. A wind accosted me. "What are you doing here?" he said to me. "I'm taking a walk," I said. "Ah, so you're taking a walk?" he said. He clapped me on the head and sent my hat flying. I bent down to pick it up. He rumpled my coat, turned it upside down over my head, and made a fool of me. I pulled my coat back off my head. He came at me again, knocked me to the ground and roared with wild laughter. I got to my feet and stood straight. He bumped up against me and shouted: "On your way! On your way!"

I saw I couldn't contend with one mightier than myself, and I went on my way.

I returned to the city and went inside my house. I became restless and went out. Whether I intended it or not, my feet carried me back to Talpiot. I remembered all that the wind had done to me. I took some canvas and pegs and pitched a tent for myself – a refuge from wind and storm.

One night I stayed there. The light suddenly went out. I left the tent to see who had put my light out. I found the wind standing outside. "What do you want?" I asked him. He boxed my ears and slapped my mouth. I went back into my tent. He pulled up my tent pegs and split my rope, turned my tent over and ripped my canvas to shreds. He turned upon me as well and almost knocked me over.

I saw I couldn't possibly match his strength. I picked up my feet and went back to the city.

I went back to the city and remained within its walls. I became restless and yearned for some place with fresh, pleasant air. Since there is no air anywhere in the entire land like the air of Talpiot, I went to Talpiot. And so that the wind wouldn't abuse me, I took some boards with me and made myself a hut. I thought I had found myself a resting place, but the wind thought otherwise. A day hardly passed before he started thumping on my roof and shaking the walls. One night he carried off the whole hut.

The wind carried off my hut and left me without any shelter. I picked myself up and went back to the city.

What happened to me once and then a second time happened to me a third time. I returned to the city and I had no peace. How my heart drew me to that very spot from which I had been driven out!

I said to my heart: "Don't you see that is impossible for us to return to a place from which we have been chased away? And what is impossible is impossible." But my heart thought differently. If I said a thousand times, *Impossible*! my heart replied a thousand and one times, *It is possible*!

I took wood and stones and built myself a house.

I won't praise my house, for it was small; but I am not ashamed of it, even though there are bigger and better houses. My house was small, but there was room enough in my house for a man like me who doesn't desire grandeur.

The wind saw that I had built myself a house. He came and asked me:

"What is this?"

"This is a house," I said to him.

He laughed and said: "I'll be damned if I ever saw anything as funny as this thing you call a house!"

I too laughed and said: “What you have never seen before, you see before you now.”

He laughed and said: “What is it, this house?”

I laughed and said: “A house is … a house!”

He laughed and said to me: “I’ll go and inspect it.”

He stretched out his hand and inspected the door. The door broke and fell. He stretched out his hand and inspected the windows. The windows broke and fell. Finally he rose and went to the roof. Up he went and down came the roof. The wind laughed at me and said:

“Where is this house you built?”

I too asked where my house was. But I didn’t laugh.

At first when the wind drove me away I used to return to the city. Finally things happened that prevented me from returning to the city. Like a homeless animal, I did not know where to go. To return to the city was impossible because of what had happened there; to return to Talpiot was impossible because of the wind who drove me out. I had made myself a tent and a hut but they hadn’t lasted. I had built myself a little house, but that hadn’t stood up to the wind either. But then, maybe it hadn’t withstood the wind because it was so small and frail; perhaps if it had been big and strong it would have stood. I took strong timber and sturdy beams, large blocks of stone, plaster and cement, and I hired good workers and watched over their work day and night. This time I was wise enough to sink the foundations very deep. The house was built and it stood firm and upright on its own ground. When the house was finished the wind came and thumped on the shutters.

“Who is rapping on my window?” I asked.

He laughed playfully and said: “A neighbor.”

“What does one neighbor want of another on a night of storm and tempest like this?” I asked him.

He laughed and said: “He has come to wish his neighbor well in his new house.”

“Is it usual for a neighbor to come through the window like a thief?” I said to him.

He came around and knocked on the door.

“Who is rapping on my door?” I said to him.

“It is I, your neighbor,” said the wind.

"You are my neighbor – please come in," I said.

"But the door is locked," he said to me.

"Well, if the door is locked, it must be because I locked it," I said to him.

"Open up!" the wind answered.

"I'm sensitive to the cold, wait till the sun comes up and I will let you in," I said.

When the sun rose I went out to let him in but I couldn't find him. I stood in front of my house and saw that the land was desolate all around: not a tree, not a green leaf anywhere; only dust and stones. "I'll plant a garden here," I said to myself.

I took a spade and started digging. When the soil was ready I brought some saplings. The rains came and watered the saplings; the dews came, and the saplings sprouted; the sun nourished them, and they blossomed. Not many days passed before the saplings that I had planted became trees with many branches.

I made myself a bench and sat in the shade of the trees.

One night the wind returned and started knocking the trees about. What did the trees do? They struck back at him. The wind rose again and shook the trees. Once more the trees struck in return. The wind lost his breath. He turned and went away.

From that time on the wind has been quite humble and meek, and when he comes he behaves like a gentleman. And since he minds his manners with me, I too mind my manners with him. When he comes I go out to meet him and ask him to sit with me on the garden bench beneath the trees. And he comes and sits by my side. And when he comes he brings with him a pleasant scent from the mountains and valleys, and he fans the air gently around me. Since he behaves like a complete penitent, I never remind him of his former wicked ways. And when he leaves me and goes on his way I invite him to come again, as one should with a good neighbor. And we really are the best of neighbors, and I am very fond of him. And he may even be fond of me.

– Translated by Joel Blocker

Ḥemdat

1

Many have told and many will tell the story of Ḥemdat. Ḥemdat, a young man of good family, was then about eighteen years old. But there's more than that to be said for him. One of his virtues was that God gave him a lyric tongue; another was that his soul was devoted to our holy tongue, and he wrote verse in it. Although in those days the importance of Hebrew had waned and every one preferred to speak foreign tongues, Ḥemdat thought Hebrew was important. Now in this regard, we are inclined to agree with Ḥemdat, that the holy tongue is the most precious of languages. Happy is the man who clings to her. Happy is he who makes much of her.

2

Ḥemdat had already put his studies aside but was not yet in business. By nature he wasn't made to sit in a shop as shopkeepers were wont. There were other livelihoods, like those of doctors and lawyers. But for that one must study in their schools, which lead a man away from the Law. Ḥemdat was the son of a God-fearing man learned in the Law and that was dearer to his heart than all earthly possessions. His father dealt kindly with Ḥemdat and refrained from sending him to such academies. Instead he would sit and study the Law with Ḥemdat. So it was that the Law gave life to its students in the next world but not in this one. So since Ḥemdat put his studies aside and having no other trade, he was at his own disposal doing as he chose. And what did Ḥemdat choose to do? What does a young man know! Sometimes he would go among people to hear their conversation, and sometimes he would seek solitude in the forest or take a stroll by the river bank, or read a book or put into writing the musings of his heart — sometimes in rhyming verse and sometimes in prose. Sometimes he wrote in notebooks, on other occasions his poetry appeared in periodicals circulated throughout the country which formerly was full of thinkers and authors, poets and scholars, and even now a faint but clear voice can sometimes be heard from what is left of the country's authors. So Ḥemdat was one of those few masters of language (some of whose poems and stories appeared in the country's Hebrew periodicals) who preside over the last vestiges of our most coveted possession which has been cut out of our mouths.

As every cause has its effect, so was it said that all the credit was due to his father. For it is taught that the father passes on to his son charm, strength, wealth and wisdom, and certainly the son's poetical talent derives from the father, who knew a thing or two about poetry, and who in his younger days, used to compose metric verse, winning praises from all the connoisseurs of poetry. Even now so hard pressed by the fist of earning a living, still does he steal a while between customers to compose poems of greeting for the New Year or a text for a tombstone — a faithful and living testimony of the poetic spirit within. That which can be said of the father can be said of the mother, in that when Ḥemdat was a baby lying in his cradle, she would delight his sleep with songs and fairy tales, and when he grew older he used what his mother used to tell him and sing to him to compose poems; as for instance the story of the witch who used to milk the moon for her orphaned grandchildren. But there was another who claimed all the credit for himself; that was the tutor who taught him some grammar. If I hadn't taught him grammar, he used to say, he wouldn't have known how to put two words together.

But enough of his father and mother, not to mention the tutor who taught him some grammar. Now we will tell you where in our opinion Ḥemdat did get his talents from. Earthly Jerusalem tends towards heavenly Jerusalem, and the hearts of Israel are tuned to them both. But due to the protraction of the exile and the rigors of oppression there grew a partition between Israel and Jerusalem. Ḥemdat was one who overcame the partition and was privileged to see what was invisible to the ordinary eye. We do not know to which Jerusalem he tuned his heart, but we know that his vision penetrated all partitions. From such vision Ḥemdat betook himself to compose poetry. Some poems he composed about the other kind of love — as that of boy who sets his heart on a girl. But this is neither the time nor the place to speak of that. As a rule we may say that the praises of his poems were mouthed by more than one.

But there was one who doubted the excellence of his poetry. And who might that be? None but the composer himself. Ḥemdat — the fire of God burned within him. And when he saw his words on paper he was like a priest about to make a sacrifice just as the fire on the altar went out. But since the simile is somewhat farfetched, for it is taught, "and rains did not extinguish the altar's fire," so shall we liken him to air which is one of the four elements. Ḥemdat breathed an air of humility, much to his inner dissatisfaction. And now that we have likened him to air we may add that he was more variable and tempestuous than any ordinary flight of air.

3

The prevailing wind suddenly blew favorably for Ḥemdat. Ḥemdat was fit and nineteen and a half years old, so it was plain that they would take him for military service. But in the army a man is liable to eat forbidden food and desecrate the Sabbath. His elders feared that they would make a soldier out of him and that he would transgress some of the injunctions of the Law. They thought it wise for him to be sent abroad. But where? Some said he should go to Switzerland and study at a university in order to become a doctor, and some said he should go to America in order to become rich. It is good for a man to be either a doctor or rich. That may be the case where other men are concerned, but God gave Ḥemdat more than a fair share of understanding for him to want to go to Switzerland or to emigrate to America, for what he desired was to go up to the Land of Israel. Now this was quite unusual. Although one had already heard of the colonization of the Land of Israel, and all the papers used to write about the Land of Israel and so many speeches were made about the Land of Israel, there was no one to be found in and around town who had been to the Land of Israel. And there were already those clever people who said that it was all rhetoric, and that a sensible person should have no part of it. But since the word spread about town that the military commission was due to arrive and as Ḥemdat was not to be held over in town, it was agreed that he go to the Land of Israel. And since his departure was agreed upon, preparations were made for his journey.

This was a secret closely guarded by his family, and even on the day he departed, they revealed nothing to any outsider, lest it become known to the authorities and Ḥemdat be detained. The secret was so well kept that the day before his departure Ḥemdat was out strolling with a friend who reproached him for not raising himself from the swamp of his home town and for not doing anything to get out into the world, saying, Ḥemdat, Ḥemdat, your father will have you married off, and you'll open a shop for yourself and go into business like all the other townsfolk. Ḥemdat heard his reproach and made no reply.

4

It was a spring day between the first and last day of Passover. The swamp was already dry and the sun was warm and pleasant, the gardens fragrant, and trees and shrubs budded and blossomed. We shall not linger in the town nor succumb to the current feeling, for our heart is set on our chosen land — the Land of Israel. And so that day after evening prayers all his relatives assembled to take their leave of Ḥemdat. The small house was immersed in sadness and everyone in the house was melancholy. A tender and pampered youth, it was expected of him to thrive on the Law and bring honor to his family as did his forbears. But no; he leaves his father and mother and goes to a place where no one knows him, and no one knows how he'll make a living there. The country is poor and livelihoods are not readily met with, particularly by a young man inexperienced in the ways of the world. One of his relatives tries to ease the sorrow by making conversation, but seeing Ḥemdat's baggage prepared for the journey, he kept silent and wiped his eyes.

While the members of the household were still moping around, the cart driver who had come to pick up his passenger's baggage, cracked his whip. The members of the household got up and fell on Ḥemdat's neck kissing him and crying over him. There before him lay his ailing mother in her bed gazing at her son. She had raised a son and now he is leaving her, and who knows whether she will ever see him again. With that thought in mind she began to weep. Whoever saw her weep wept with her. But one there was, Rabbi Yakir, Ḥemdat's mother's father who did not. Rabbi Yakir used to say, it won't be long before we will all be going to the Land of Israel so I will be seeing my daughter's son, dear boy that he is.

Who knows how long they would have stood there crying if it hadn't been for the cart driver urging Ḥemdat to get on the cart. Ḥemdat bade all his relatives farewell and mounted the cart. His father went with him as far as the railway station and from there to the town where you change trains. His father fell on his son's neck, hugging and kissing him, telling him, take care, my son, to write to us regularly. Greater is the sorrow of the forsaken than that of the forsaker. And you — you have forsaken your father, your mother, and your brothers and sisters. Many sons have forgotten that and many fathers in their prime of life have been laid low with grief. Thus they stood until the train was about to move. They withdrew their arms. His father returned by another train and Ḥemdat went on his way.

5

We won't tell you much of Ḥemdat's thoughts and of all the people he came across in the train. God created all types of people in his world and many paths stand before each one of them. The paths of all those people do not concern us here — that of Ḥemdat alone is the matter that concerns us. And that matter we already know — Ḥemdat is on his way to the Land of Israel. But he is still far away and will yet experience many adventures before he reaches his destination.

A light spring rain came down. The rain drops thudded against the windows of the carriage. The showers stopped almost immediately and the sky grew pallid. The lamplight in the carriage grew pallid too and a cloudy day peeped in. Out of the clouds emerged Lemberg, the capital of Galicia; and when the train got into Lemberg, Ḥemdat deposited his luggage at the station and went into town.

There are many things one should see in Lemberg, but on that day they were so mixed up, as if they had conspired between them that he should not enjoy seeing them. Hunger began to nag at his stomach. But he did not go into an eating house, neither did he purchase any food at the market, since such as us were unaccustomed to spend money on food. We were kept by our father and fed by our mother. And if we ever came into any money we would buy a book or donate it to the Jewish National Fund. But we were unaccustomed to spend even a penny on food. Shortbread and biscuits, a quantity of which his mother had given Ḥemdat for the journey were in his bag, and his bag was at the railway station.

6

The roar of the big city began to swell. If his father hadn't instructed him to go to a merchant friend of his, Ḥemdat would have returned to the railway Station and sat down there until the departure of the train to Vienna. From there the trains went to Trieste and from there by boat to the Land of Israel. In fact Ḥemdat had a desire not to see anyone but to get away from the bustle of the big city. While on his way, he thought to himself, if I must go and see someone, I had better see the town's scholars and writers.

As he was walking along he heard someone call his name. He turned his eyes and saw a woman close at hand. Ḥemdat tried to avoid her, but she came and stood right in front of him. Now this woman, who came from the same town as Ḥemdat, was the wife of a type-setter at one of the printing houses in Lemberg employed by a Yiddish daily newspaper. Ḥemdat didn't know whether to be happy or sad at this encounter. Had he not left home secretly, apprehensive of being informed upon that he was evading military service? Unexpectedly he had been seen by a woman from his home town. Next she would write to her father and her father would mention it at the Beit Midrash and so all the town would know. As he stood thinking about it she greeted him, her face lighting up with joy. He too was glad to meet a woman in the crowd from his own town and to hear a familiar voice. But the woman did not ask him what brought him to Lemberg, either because she had adopted the manners of the big city or because the joy at meeting someone from her home town overcame her curiosity. Nevertheless she invited him to her home to rest from the journey.

On their way she went into the printing house to tell her husband that so and so was in town. Her husband came out to meet Ḥemdat and ushered him into the printing house and began to inquire what was new in Szybucz. While still inquiring he was summoned to the editor. Ḥemdat was left alone with the pieces of type. Inanimate, lying there, trays of compartments and letters placed in the compartments, each letter a hundred times or more, uncomposed and unconnected, waiting for the compositor to come and put letter to letter, making words, sentences and chapters. As those letters, so were Ḥemdat's thoughts waiting for the Grand Composer to compose them.

After a short while the type-setter returned saying, I told Mr. Grossman that you are here and he wishes to see you. Ḥemdat's face flushed. Such an honor as this, a newspaper editor wanting to see him, he had not expected.

Aaron Grossman hailed from Russia, and during the Russo-Japanese War he found himself by chance in Galicia. He lighted upon Lemberg and became the editor of a Yiddish daily which used to appear there. He was a famous writer who loved writers and what they wrote, and he even thought favorably of Galicia's writers. Once Ḥemdat sent him a story. He had it printed and paid him a writer's fee, and that was something Ḥemdat had not previously experienced. While Ḥemdat got himself ready to go in to Mr. Grossman, Mr. Grossman came out to him and took him to a coffee house.

While they were sitting in the coffee house Ḥemdat whispered to Grossman that he was going to the Land of Israel. Mr. Grossman looked at him and thought to himself, what will such a tender youth do in the Land of Israel? There is no work to be had there, no living to be made there, he has no relatives there, so how will he exist there? He sat down and wrote three letters to three different people living in the Land of Israel, urging them to stand by Ḥemdat lest he stray. And because Mr. Grossman was sorry for such a tender youth who had been banished from his father's table and was going to a place where no one knows him, he exaggerated his praises and showed him the letters in order to raise his spirits. After reading them Ḥemdat began to reflect: I know that all that is written here refers only to the future. In the end Mr. Grossmann put the letters into transparent envelopes so that the address on the letters could be seen from the outside and handed them to Ḥemdat.

7

This is the place to mention the other remarkable personalities that Ḥemdat met in Lemberg, such as Rabbi Eliezer Meir Lipschütz who studied both the Law and philosophy. Every seeker of wisdom in search of truth would rise early to come before him. But since our story is long we shall skip them for the time being. Nevertheless we shall relate how at the Lipschütz home Ḥemdat found a teacher from the Land of Israel who wrote for Ḥemdat letters of recommendation to his friends in the Land of Israel.

We also have to tell that at that time Brenner was living in Lemberg. It so happened that Ḥemdat by chance came by him, and when he heard that Ḥemdat was on his way to the Land of Israel, Brenner said to him, I envy you for having found a place in the world to go to; I can't find a place for myself.

Now we shall go with Ḥemdat to a merchant who had business connections and was friendly with Ḥemdat's father, and whom Ḥemdat had promised his father to visit and enquire how he was.

The merchant was glad to see him and gave him a warm reception. It occurred to him, to that merchant, that the son of his well-wisher had come to do business with him, pronouncing over him a blessing, Blessed be He who has given your father a wise son. But as soon as he heard that Ḥemdat was on his way to the Land of Israel, the merchant was filled with anger and began to speak reproachfully. He said, woe to sons who forsake the works of their fathers and pursue their heart's desire. And since he began in deprecation of sons, he mentioned the works of his own sons, who left his business for the academies. Was there anything they lacked? My business is ever growing and my name well-known in the commercial world, but they would not follow in my footsteps and went after enlightenment. And what did they gain? My elder son is a doctor and what does he earn, a trifle. And his younger brother is no better. He is a high school teacher. The difference between a teacher and a *melamed* is in name only. And my business house which I have promoted and expanded will come to nothing, as if it had never been. And to you I say, as it were, renounce this course you follow and return to your town. Your father grows old and needs assistance, for the strength of youth brings blessing. What is the Land of Israel to you and whom do you have in the Land of Israel? Your aged parent is older than you and he does not go up to the Land of Israel. Retract while you still can.

As long as the merchant spoke of his own sons Ḥemdat shared his distress. But when he told him to return to his home town he jumped up as if bitten by a snake. The merchant, seeing that he was speaking on deaf ears, said to him, I see that you are stubborn like all the other young people, heedless of the advice of older, experienced people. I'll give you a note to some agent in Palestine; and when you need the fare to return to your home town, he will lend you the money. Your Zionists won't stand by you in your hour of need. That agent is a clever Jew. Even in a barren land he knows how to make a living. Ḥemdat took the note and put it among the letters of recommendation he received from the wise men of Lemberg, thinking to himself that he had mixed the mundane with the divine.

We should now relate what we omitted to relate at the outset. A year previously Ḥemdat spent a few weeks in Lemberg as an assistant to Mr. Jonathan Biedermann in editing a Hebrew newspaper. Mr. Jonathan Biedermann was one of the heralds of the revival and published newspapers and periodicals, booklets and tracts which were mouthpieces for Zionism and the Hebrew language. Because of the ills that Mr. Biedermann suffered at the hands of the new Zionists he came to despair and what pleased him at first did not please him in the end. All the same Ḥemdat went round to see him. When Mr. Biedermann heard that he was going to the Land of Israel he began making fun of the Land and its inhabitants saying that they were stirring up the world with false hopes and crying, "Give, give!," adding, When you get off the boat all the local grandees will come out to meet you with extended hands, and they will say "Alms, alms." If you must travel, go to America, for only in America is there any hope for one of our people. Ḥemdat knew that Mr. Biedermann was embittered, remembering his former deeds, and letting his latter-day utterances go by. Bless the Lord that our way is right and all the slanderous things said about the Land and its inhabitants will not deflect us from our path. In the end Mr. Biedermann said to Ḥemdat: I am about to publish a Yiddish anthology. If you have a poem or a story let me have it. Ḥemdat took a story out of his pocket and gave it to him. This story was the last of all his stories that he wrote in the Diaspora and in Yiddish. From then on he wrote only Hebrew.

8

We shall now proceed, tarrying only where necessary. Accordingly we shall stop a while in Vienna, for in Vienna there lives a relative of Ḥemdat a great and famous sage in whom all Galicia took pride. And Ḥemdat had promised Rabbi Yakir his elder to meet their relative and inquire after his health.

That same sage, Rabbi David Zvi Miller studied nothing but Torah until he was nineteen years old. After taking a wife from another city and being supported by his father-in-law, he began to read academic tracts and learn German. Seeing that he was learning the language of gentiles and reading books of gentile wisdom, his brother-in-law become hostile to him, vexing him and chastising his wife, urging her: Seek a divorce from your husband, for it is forbidden to live with a heretic. Now she loved her husband and he loved her. But her brother-in-law roused all of his father-in-law's family against her and they boiled hell over her daily until the poor wretch could stand it no longer. She went to her husband and weeping to his face, asked for a divorce. Realizing the affliction of her soul, her husband gave her a divorce, clearly against his and her will. Since he had divorced his wife and rid himself of all her relations he went to Vienna and entered the University studying there only what he had studied at first in secrecy. It wasn't very long before he was appointed professor at the University. And here we ought to mention the virtues of that sage. After attaining a position of importance he did not overlook his former wife, who married, after her sister's death, that same brother-in-law. In the hour of their need he would give them financial assistance, and when their daughters were born and were ripe for marriage he provided their dowry.

And so Ḥemdat called on his relative the sage. His relative, hearing that he intended going to the Land of Israel, said to him: Settling in the Land of Israel is a great thing, but its climate is hard and much suffering is endured by its inhabitants, and you won't be able to bear the suffering of the Land. You would be better off staying in Vienna and preparing yourself to enter the University, for I will support you. Ḥemdat, whose course was clear did not succumb to the advice of his relative.

9

We still have more to tell and the way is no shorter. Now we shall go up to the railway station and put Ḥemdat on the train to Trieste, and from there by boat to the Land of Israel. It is now night time and the train is full of people. Some were sitting, leaning to one side and dozing, and some trying not to doze off because they had to get off at the next station.

Ultimately all of them left and there remained in the carriage only Ḥemdat and a woman who was sitting restlessly by the window, her head lolling about. She removed her hat and took out a cigarette to smoke; she couldn't find a match so Ḥemdat stood up and gave her a light. She nodded her head to thank him and again leant her head on the window, smoking in silence.

The wind passing through the mountains and the forests came in and blew at the lamp in the carriage. The wick in the lamp flickered as if it would go out. The woman fixed her glance now on the lamp and now on Ḥemdat and said, A dreary night and there's nothing to relieve it. Ḥemdat made some reply, and so a conversation started up between them. They both saw that they were alone there. All of a sudden she closed her eyes and her head was still bumping around as if looking for a place to rest. We don't know how it came about, but we do know that her head dropped on to Ḥemdat's shoulder. Ḥemdat sat still without moving.

Forests and river and streams and mountains drew near and went by. The train went up hill and down hill, up and down. A fine wind blew from the forests, whining as on a dark and stormy night. What might the wind tell us tonight? A tale of yore it tells us. If we transcribe what it tells into human language it is this: Once upon a time there was a young man, well-born, brilliant and studious who went to study Torah, his bag over his shoulder and his staff in his hand. He would skip over the mountains, his heart jumping for joy. O to learn Torah, write books, and may my name endure forever! And then a lass emerged from between the mountain clefts, her hair unkempt and her eyes blazing. The young man looked upon her and followed her. Suddenly there appeared an entrance to a cave through which the lass passed and came into the cave, and so did the young man as he followed her. As he went inside, the cave was sealed and he never came out again.

Ḥemdat's bones began to shiver. He was shocked and taken aback. The woman started from her sleep, raised her head and gave him an odd look. Like the maid of the mountains she resembled all the people who had sought to dissuade Ḥemdat from going to the Land of Israel. But Ḥemdat bore no resemblance to that young man who disappeared inside the cave never to come out, for he succeeded in getting to the Land of Israel.

And now, good friends and listeners to my story, we will take no more time for parables. Now we will sail with Ḥemdat on board the ship until we bring him to the Land of Israel. But before we bring him to the ship, we will accompany him to a citron and citrus fruit merchant from Ḥemdat's home town who lived in Trieste. The latter took Ḥemdat to an inn. The innkeeper wrote to an innkeeper in Jaffa, whose inn was called the Prince of the Sea, saying that on board such and such a ship on such and such a date, such and such a person will come without a travel visa, and the Turk will certainly not let him pass, so he needs someone to intercede in his behalf, etc. Afterwards he took Ḥemdat to buy his passage and some food for the voyage.

Through this man from Ḥemdat's home town Ḥemdat got to know a few young fellows from Galicia and other countries who were living in Trieste and who wanted to go to the Land of Israel. Some of them didn't go, because they didn't have enough money to pay the fare, and others stayed on for other reasons. Now when they heard there was a young man on his way to the Land of Israel, they all got together and went to accompany him, some out of pity, for they knew that there was nothing for a young man to do in the Land of Israel, and if he did find something to do — he wouldn't be able to make a living out of it. In the end Ḥemdat got aboard ship and went down to the hold.

Complete calm at sea — and serenity in Ḥemdat's heart. The water passed by in silence and the sun shone on the face of the water. Time and again Ḥemdat fixed his gaze on the sea and then on the book in his hand. Already a thousand times he has repeated these two verses from the Book of Genesis which God said to Abraham, nevertheless he repeated them again, and we too shall repeat them. "Now the Lord said unto Abram: Get thee out of thy country, and from thy kindred, and from thy father's house, unto the land that I will show thee. And I will make of thee a great nation, and I will bless thee, and make thy name great; and be thou a blessing." Not to Abraham alone did God promise his blessing, but also to his seed and the seed of his seed, till the end of all generations. Now Ḥemdat knew not what would sustain him in the Land of Israel, for he had already spent most of his money on the way. But as he had not asked himself thus far what he would do, so he did not ask himself then. And again he repeated to himself those same verses. So is it taught that the words of the living God live and last for ever and ever, eternal and everlasting, day by day, month by month and hour by hour.

– *Translated by Amiel Gurt*

Nobel Prize Banquet Speech

S.Y. Agnon became Israel's first Nobel laureate in December 1966. Fifty years after receiving the literature prize he remains the sole Hebrew author to be so recognized. The prize was shared with Nelly Sachs (1891-1970), a German-Jewish poet and playwright, who had been residing in Sweden since fleeing Germany in 1940. Her lyrical verse gives voice to the grief of the Jewish people following the Holocaust. Prior to the laureates' speeches, Ingvar Andersson of the Swedish Academy made the following comments:

Shmuel Yosef Agnon, Nelly Sachs – This year's literary Prize goes to you both with equal honour for a literary production which records Israel's vicissitudes in our time and passes on its message to the peoples of the world.

Mr. Agnon – In your writing we meet once again the ancient unity between literature and science, as antiquity knew it. In one of your stories you say that some will no doubt read it as they read fairy tales, others will read it for edification. Your great chronicle of the Jewish people's spirit and life has therefore a manifold message. For the historian it is a precious source, for the philosopher an inspiration, for those who cannot live without literature it is a mine of never-failing riches. We honor in you a combination of tradition and prophecy, of saga and wisdom.

Miss Sachs – About twenty years ago, through the Swedish poet Hjalmar Gullberg, I first learned of your fate and your work. Since then you have lived with us in Sweden and I could talk to you in our own language. But it is through your mother tongue that your work reflects a historical drama in which you have participated. Your lyrical and dramatic writing now belongs to the great laments of literature, but the feeling of mourning which inspired you is free from hate and lends sublimity to the suffering of man. We honor you today as the bearer of a message of solace to all those who despair of the fate of man.

We honour you both this evening as the laurel-crowned heroes of intellectual creation and express our conviction that, in the words of Alfred Nobel, you have conferred the greatest benefit on mankind, and that you have given it clearsightedness, wisdom, uplift, and beauty. A famous speech at a Nobel banquet – that of William Faulkner, held in this same hall sixteen years ago - contained an idea which he developed with great intensity. It is suitable as a concluding quotation which points to the future: "I do not believe in the end of man."

S.Y. Agnon's speech at the Nobel Banquet at the City Hall in Stockholm, December 10, 1966

Our sages of blessed memory have said that we must not enjoy any pleasure in this world without reciting a blessing. If we eat any food, or drink any beverage, we must recite a blessing over them before and after. If we breathe the scent of goodly grass, the fragrance of spices, the aroma of good fruits, we pronounce a blessing over the pleasure. The same applies to the pleasures of sight: when we see the sun in the Great Cycle of the Zodiac in the month of Nissan, or the trees first bursting into blossom in the spring, or any fine, sturdy, and beautiful trees, we pronounce a blessing. And the same applies to the pleasures of the ear. Through you, dear sirs, one of the blessings concerned with hearing has come my way.

It happened when the Swedish Chargé d'Affaires came and brought me the news that the Swedish Academy had bestowed the Nobel Prize upon me. Then I recited in full the blessing that is enjoined upon one that hears good tidings for himself or others: Blessed be He, that is good and doeth good. "Good," in that the good God put it into the hearts of the sages of the illustrious Academy to bestow that great and esteemed Prize upon an author who writes in the sacred tongue; "that doeth good," in that He favored me by causing them to choose me. And now that I have come so far, I will recite one blessing more, as enjoined upon him who beholds a monarch: Blessed art Thou, O Lord, our God, King of the Universe, Who hast given of Thy glory to a king of flesh and blood. Over you, too, distinguished sages of the Academy, I say the prescribed blessing: Blessed be He, that has given of His wisdom to flesh and blood.

It is said in the Talmud (Tractate Sanhedrin 23a): "In Jerusalem, the men of discrimination did not sit down to dine in company until they knew who their companions were to be"; so I will now tell you who am I, whom you have agreed to have at your table.

As a result of the historic catastrophe in which Titus of Rome destroyed Jerusalem and Israel was exiled from its land, I was born in one of the cities of the Exile. But always I regarded myself as one who was born in Jerusalem. In a dream, in a vision of the night, I saw myself standing with my brother-Levites in the Holy Temple, singing with them the songs of David, King of Israel, melodies such as no ear has heard since the day our city was destroyed and its people went into exile. I suspect that the angels in charge of the Shrine of Music, fearful lest I sing in wakefulness what I had sung in dream, made me forget by day what I had sung at night; for if my brethren, the sons of my people, were to hear, they would be unable to bear their grief over the happiness they have lost. To console me for having prevented me from singing with my mouth, they enable me to compose songs in writing.

I belong to the Tribe of Levi; my forebears and I are of the minstrels that were in the Temple, and there is a tradition in my father's family that we are of the lineage of the Prophet Samuel, whose name I bear.

I was five years old when I wrote my first song. It was out of longing for my father that I wrote it. It happened that my father, of blessed memory, went away on business. I was overcome with longing for him and I made a song. After that I made many songs, but nothing has remained of them all. My father's house, where I left a roomful of writings, was burned down in the First World War and all I had left there was burned with it. The young artisans, tailors, and shoemakers, who used to sing my songs at their work, were killed in the First World War and of those who were not killed in the war, some were buried alive with their sisters in the pits they dug for themselves by order of the enemy, and most were burned in the crematories of Auschwitz with their sisters, who had adorned our town with their beauty and sung my songs with their sweet voices.

The fate of the singers who, like my songs, went up in flame was also the fate of the books which I later wrote. All of them went up in flame to Heaven in a fire which broke out one night at my home in Bad Homburg as I lay ill in a hospital. Among the books that were burned was a large novel of some seven hundred pages, the first part of which the publisher had announced he was about to bring out. Together with this novel, called *Eternal Life*, was burned everything I had written since the day I had gone into exile from the Land of Israel, including a book I had written with Martin Buber as well as four thousand Hebrew books, most of which had come down to me from my forebears and some of which I had bought with money set aside for my daily bread.

I said, "since the day I had gone from the Land of Israel," but I have not yet related that I had dwelt in the Land of Israel. Of this I will now speak.

At the age of nineteen and a half, I went to the Land of Israel to till its soil and live by the labor of my hands. As I did not find work, I sought my livelihood elsewhere. I was appointed Secretary of the *Ḥovevei Zion* (Lovers of Zion) Society and Secretary of the Palestine Council - which was a kind of parliament-in-the-making and I was also the first Secretary of the voluntary Jewish Magistrate's Court. Through these offices it was my privilege to get to know almost every Jewish person, and those whom I did not come to know through these offices I came to know through love and a desire to know my brethren, the members of my people. It is almost certain that in those years there was not a man, woman, or infant in the Land of Israel whom I did not know.

After all my possessions had been burned, God gave me the wisdom to return to Jerusalem. I returned to Jerusalem, and it is by virtue of Jerusalem that I have written all that God has put into my heart and into my pen. I have also written a book about the Giving of the Torah, and a book on the Days of Awe, and a book on the books of Israel that have been written since the day the Torah was given to Israel.

Since my return to the Land of Israel, I have left it twice: once in connection with the printing of my books by the late Zalman Schocken, and once I travelled to Sweden and Norway. Their great poets had implanted love and admiration for their countries in my heart, and I decided to go and see them. Now I have come a third time, to receive your blessing, sages of the Academy.

During the time I have dwelt in Jerusalem, I have written long stories and short ones. Some have been printed; most I still have in manuscript.

I have already told how my first songs came out of longing for my father. The beginnings of my studies also came to me from my father, as well as from the Rabbinical Judge of our town. But they were preceded by three tutors under whom I studied, one after the other, from the time I was three and a half till I turned eight and a half.

Who were my mentors in poetry and literature? That is a matter of opinion. Some see in my books the influences of authors whose names, in my ignorance, I have not even heard, while others see the influences of poets whose names I have heard but whose writings I have not read. And what is my opinion? From whom did I receive nurture? Not every man remembers the name of the cow which supplied him with each drop of milk he has drunk. But in order not to leave you totally in the dark, I will try to clarify from whom I received whatever I have received.

First and foremost, there are the Sacred Scriptures, from which I learned how to combine letters. Then there are the Mishna and the Talmud and the Midrashim and Rashi's commentary on the Torah. After these come the *Poskim* - the later explicators of Talmudic Law – and our sacred poets and the medieval sages, led by our Master Rabbi Moses, son of Maimon, known as Maimonides, of blessed memory.

When I first began to combine letters other than Hebrew, I read every book in German that came my way, and from these I certainly received according to the nature of my soul. As time is short, I shall rot compile a bibliography or mention any names. Why, then, did I list the Jewish books? Because it is they that gave me my foundations. And my heart tells me that they are responsible for my being honored with the Nobel Prize.

There is another kind of influence, which I have received from every man, every woman, every child I have encountered along my way, both Jews and non-Jews. People's talk and the stories they tell have been engraved on my heart, and some of them have flown into my pen. It has been the same way with the spectacles of nature. The Dead Sea, which I used to see every morning at sunrise from the roof of my house, the Arnon Brook in which I used to bathe, the nights I used to spend with devout and pious men beside the Wailing Wall - nights which gave me eyes to see the land of the Holy One, Blessed be He - the Wall which He gave us, and the city in which He established His name.

Lest I slight any creature, I must also mention the domestic animals, the beasts and birds from whom I have learned. Job said long ago (135:11): "Who teacheth us more than the beasts of the earth, And maketh us wiser than the fowls of heaven?" Some of what I have learned from them I have written in my books, but I fear that I have not learned as much as I should have, for when I hear a dog bark, or a bird twitter, or a cock crow, I do not know whether they are thanking me for all I have told of them, or calling me to account.

Before I conclude my remarks, I will say one more thing. If I have praised myself too much, it is for your sake that I have done so, in order to reassure you for having cast your eyes on me. For myself, I am very small indeed in my own eyes. Never in all my life have I forgotten the Psalm (131:1) in which David said: "Lord, my heart is not haughty, nor mine eyes lofty; neither do I exercise myself in great matters, or in things too high for me." If I am proud of anything, it is that I have been granted the privilege of living in the land which God promised our forefathers to give us, as it is written (Ezekiel 37: 25): "And they shall dwell in the land that I have given unto Jacob my servant, wherein your fathers have dwelt; and they shall dwell therein, even they, and their children, and their children's children forever."

Before concluding, I would say a brief prayer: He who giveth wisdom unto the wise and salvation unto kings, may He increase your wisdom beyond measure and exalt your sovereign. In his days and in ours may Judah be redeemed and Israel dwell in safety. May a redeemer come to Zion, may the earth be filled with knowledge and eternal joy for all who dwell therein, and may they enjoy much peace.
May all this be God's will.

Amen.

Agnon and Reb Columbus

After receiving his Nobel Prize in 1966, S.Y. Agnon made his only visit to the United States the following Spring—a visit which was abbreviated due to the outbreak of the Six Day War. While in New York he received honorary doctorates from Yeshiva University and the Jewish Theological Seminary, and was the guest of honor at the annual dinner of the American Friends of The Hebrew University at the Waldorf Astoria, in New York on May 23, 1967. On that occasion he delivered the following address to an audience of one thousand guests.

When I was a child, I suffered along with every human being who suffered, whether he was a Jew or a non-Jew. Whenever I heard that misfortune had hit someone, I joined him in his adversity and I would worry along with him, and whenever I heard someone say that he had no place in the world to rest his head, my whole body would shake.

It was through these people sighing and groaning in adversity that I discovered America. How? Here is how it came about. It happened one year, when the snows were melting, that the river in our town flooded the house of a poor man, and he and his entire family bewailed their ruined home, and mourned over the fact that they did not have a place left in the world. My grandfather heard about this, and took them into his home. One day, that poor man got a ticket to go to America. It was on that day that I learned that there was a place in the world called America; that if a Jew had no place left in the world, he went to America.

And I learned that America was bigger than my father's house, for not only had that poor man fixed himself a trip to America, but a number of my townsfolk had arranged to go along with him.

Children are an inquisitive lot. I wanted to know where this America was. And I heard that it was on the other side of the ground under our feet, and that since Earth was shaped like a kind of rolling ball, and it rolled around underneath the sun and the stars, they had night when we had day, and when we had night, they had day. The same went for the trees—they didn't grow in America the way they grew with us: in America, they grew with their roots up in the sky and their fruit down on the ground. And a scholar had already raised the question whether we, in Europe, were permitted to use an *etrog* from America, in view of the fact that it grew upside down.

And not only in this respect did we understand America to be different from all other countries. In other countries, if you had a toothache, you dropped some whisky or oil of cloves on it. If the pain went away, that was fine; if not, you looped a string round your tooth, and tied the other end to the door or bed or table, and you pulled and pulled till the tooth came out. But in America—if a man had a toothache, he went to a doctor, and the doctor pulled the bad tooth and put a gold tooth in there, because in America gold was cheap. They used goldware there the way we used crockery.

After a little while, I added to my store of wisdom; America had been *terra incognita* until Columbus came and discovered it.

I assumed that Columbus had been a Jew and a very holy man, who had seen how people were suffering for lack of a place in the world and gave them America the way grandfather, rest-in-peace, had given a place in his home to that poor man whose house the river had flooded.

What I couldn't understand was that people said "Columbus" without mentioning the title "Rabbi." Such a *tzaddik* who had done such a great thing as to provide a place for people, was worthy of being called "Rabbi Columbus" and not just "Columbus."

The Almighty does not leave children in the dark very long. One Friday, when I was reviewing the Biblical portion of the week—reading each verse, as prescribed, twice in Hebrew and once in the Aramaic translation—I looked at the top of the column of translation and saw the name "Onkelos." I worked it out for myself by *a fortiori* reasoning: if

Onkelos, who translated the Torah by which the Almighty created the world, is called Onkelos and not Rabbi Onkelos, then Columbus, who found America, which is only one quarter of the world (I did not yet know of Australia's existence), must certainly content himself with being in the same class as Onkelos, who is called only by his name, without any title.

Here I should say a few words in praise of Columbus. I remember once, before Passover, hearing two old men talking things over. One said to the other, Here it is nearly Passover and there is so much to buy for Passover, and matzah is so expensive, and I don't have enough money to provide for my family. Said the other, So what are you going to do? Replied the first, I'll buy them potatoes. Not only on Passover do they save us from hunger, but the rest of the year, too. Said the second, If not for Columbus who found America, and found potatoes there and brought them to our countries, a man wouldn't know what to do in order to keep from starving. They say that in olden times, when they didn't know about potatoes in drought years, people died of famine.

America was still a legendary land, a kind of Lost Tribesland, or a land of the class of lands lying beyond the River Sambatyon, except that you cannot get to these lands, because on weekdays, the Sambatyon continuously hurls up rocks and on the Sabbath, when it rests, if you cross over you are stoned for desecrating the Sabbath, whereas America—anybody who had a ship-ticket travelled across the seas and went to America, and made a living provided that he wasn't lazy, because if you're lazy and won't work, America starves you.

One day, a visitor came to our town who was not like the visitors we were accustomed to in our town. He was tall and skinny, and his face was full of wrinkles. The clothes he wore, too, were not the kind we were accustomed to. You couldn't say they were elegant, but you also could not say that they were not elegant; the same went for his shoes, but they were roomy and they carried his body well. From the way he went about, he seemed to be a townsman of ours, because he knew every street and lane, every corner; to judge by his teeth, he seemed to be from America, because whenever he opened his mouth to speak, gold teeth gleamed in his mouth, and when he would laugh, his teeth glinted against his laugh.

What brought him to our town, at a time when half the town wanted to go to America? He came to pay his respects to his dead parents.

When he ran away from our town as a boy, his father and mother had still been alive; now that they were dead, he had come to visit their graves.

He had wanted to come when they were still alive, but the problem of making a living had prevented him. When he saw that he was getting along in years, and that he was no longer able to work in the American style, he picked himself up and travelled to the town in which his ancestors were buried.

He would speak to everybody—to the common folk as well as to the town's notables—the way a man speaks to his good friend, for America is a democratic country, and its people are free men, and everybody in America can say, this is my opinion, without any fear about displeasing anyone. Furthermore, every American is entitled to vote for President, and even to be elected President. Emperor or King in Europe is President in America, but a President in America has more power than all the Emperors in Europe, because they are dependent on the opinion of the Ministers, while the President relies only on his own opinion, and his opinion is the opinion of the people who elected him, and if he doesn't go along with the opinion of the nation he won't be elected again.

That is the way it is with all authority in America. In Europe, a clerk thinks that he has been appointed for his own purposes, and if he feels like it he listens to you, but if he doesn't feel like it he regards you as though you simply didn't exist. In America, every clerk knows that he has been put there to serve the public, so he makes an effort to win their goodwill. Who is honored in Europe? Any idler, just as long as he is rich. In America it is work that brings honor to a man and confers wealth and fame upon him.

And so America emerged from the mists of fable, and was revealed as an object of desire. Whoever could not find himself in our town, set his eyes on America. Whoever had a house or an apartment or anything at all to sell, sold it, and with the proceeds bought a travel ticket. Those who didn't have anything, looked to their relatives in America to help them by sending a travel ticket.

Not everybody who wanted to travel did so. The relatives in America on whom some pinned their hopes could not afford to send a travel ticket, but they sent newspapers—Yiddish newspapers. So they started to read newspapers. Their eyes were opened, and they saw what was going on in the world. Not many days passed, and they began to express their opinions on town affairs, and on public affairs generally, and even on international affairs. America, which had given a place to those who had no place, and had given them the fruit of labor, now also opened the eyes of many to see, and gave them a mouth to speak. America gave us many boons, and this was one of them, one of the greatest of them. Today, with everybody reading newspapers, not everyone can imagine what a great boon this is. Wretched, downtrodden people who had not dared to open their mouths in public, now taught their tongues to speak and what to say.

I also wanted to go down to America, in order to see America, but I went up to the Land of Israel, and I saw our country and our nation built up. It is now some sixty years—with an interruption of a few years—that I have been living in the Land of Israel. Now I have come to America. Why didn't I come before now? Because it was difficult for me to leave the Land of Israel. That is one reason. There is another reason. Allow me to explain it with a parable.

Once there was a young man who had reached marriageable age. The matchmakers came and offered him a wonderful proposition. The young man would not hear of it, and did not even want to have a look at the girl. Said one of the matchmakers: Even if the girl had only a few of the qualities which are spoken of girls, it would be worth your while to see her, and this girl has all of these qualities. Won't you tell me why you refuse to see her? The young man replied, I'll tell you exactly what it is. When a man is standing under the bridal canopy, he has to pronounce the words "*Harei at mekudeshet*... Be thou consecrated unto me according to the Laws of Moses and Israel, etc." I'm very bashful, and I can't open my mouth in public, and I'm afraid that because of my extreme bashfulness I won't be able to utter a word, and I'll make a fool of myself. Said the matchmaker, If that's what it is, then you should have no fear, for the Rabbi and the Cantor and all the relatives and the in-laws will be with you at the wedding, and the Cantor will sing his opening piece, and the Rabbi will recite the Seven Blessings and read the marriage contract, and everybody will say Mazal Tov, Mazal Tov! so what are the couple of words of "*Harei at mekudeshet*" that you'll have to say as compared with all the joyous acclamation.

To apply this to myself: I was afraid to go to America because I was afraid that I would not be able to open my mouth, not knowing English. But my friends came and said to me, If that's what it is, then you have nothing to worry about. What are the couple of words that you will say compared to all the fine things that will be said about you.

So I took myself and my bashfulness in hand and I came. It isn't easy for an old man to go traipsing about, especially an old man like me, who has spent most of his life in Jerusalem.

And although the Western Wall is still in captivity, and Mount Scopus is desolate, and the Mount of Olives—concerning which it is written (Zechariah 14:4-5) "And His feet shall stand on that day on the Mount of Olives," and "the Lord my God shall come, and all the holy men with You"—is humiliated and desecrated, and the sacred remains of the holy of all generations and all countries who came to their eternal rest there, are scattered for beasts to feed on, and their sacred tombstones are used as stones for building, and many other important places into which we pour our hearts, and many other important places which we built, are no longer in our hands—yet how great and sublime is what God has left us for restoring a great populace.

So I have gone out of our glorious Jerusalem and come to America, the biggest and mightiest of lands. And just as America is the biggest of all lands, so is the American Jewish community the biggest of all Jewish communities. There is no Jewish community anywhere in the world as big as the one in America. And America is supreme among all the States in the world, in that America was the first to recognize the State of Israel, and stood by us in the establishment of the State of Israel.

And now I have come from the State of Israel to this country and this City of New York, the biggest city in the world, and here I stand among the notables of the land, may they live with God upon them. May God in His mercy return us soon to His city in Jerusalem.

I have finished my piece. May God complete for us what has to be completed.

Annotations

Original publication data for each story appears below in the individual headings. In most cases those Hebrew stories that had been published in various periodicals during Agnon's life were subsequently revised by him prior to inclusion in his Collected Writings. In almost every case previously published translations appearing here have been revised and annotated for this edition. Stories marked with an asterisk (*) appear here for the first time in English.

1. ***Forevermore***

   "*Ad Olam*," originally published in *Ha'aretz* (April 16, 1954) and collected in *HaAish vehaEtzim*, translation by Joel Blocker in *Israeli Stories* (Schocken, 1962); revised by Robert Alter in *Modern Hebrew Literature* (Behrman House, 1975). "Forevermore" is a story which asks *why* a civilization has been destroyed, causing the reader to consider the degree to which a story written in Jerusalem in the 1950s connects to the events in Jewish Europe just a decade earlier? Alter points out that "Forevermore" shares thematic concerns with Agnon's great posthumous novel *Shira* (Toby Press, 2013), such as the connection between art and disease, or wisdom and disease (lepers feature centrally in both the novel and this story). "Forevermore" should also be read against the background of the novella "Edo and Enam," in Agnon's *Two Tales* (Toby Press, 2014)—another story of a scholar delving into an archaic civilization, similarly containing the curious device of beginning virtually all proper names within the tale with the consonants *gimmel* or *ayin*.

1. Adiel Amzeh / Lit. God's ornament, this people.
2. Guach / Cf. Psalms 22:10, 71:6.
5. Lepers' hospital / Jerusalem's leper hospital, Hansen House, was built in 1887 in the Talbiya neighborhood (diagonally opposite today's Jerusalem Theatre). The facility functioned as a leper colony, and later as an out-patient clinic, until 2000. Today it serves as an artists' colony, housing the graduate programs of the Bezalel Academy of Arts.
5. Existence was a living death / Nedarim 64b; "A leper is accounted as if dead."

21. *Nights*

"*Lailot*" originally published in *Bentayim* (Jaffa, 1913), and collected in *Al Kapot HaMan'ul;* translation in *Prooftexts* 1:1 (January 1981).

One of a series of early love-fantasies, written in highly poetic and romanticized Hebrew, redolent of the biblical Song of Songs, featuring the artist-lover Ḥemdat, recently deserted by Yael Ḥayyut—characters that will re-appear in cameo in Agnon's great novel of the Jaffa period, *Only Yesterday*. Bereft of Yael, Ḥemdat is caught between the imagined Salsibylla and the sister-like Ruḥamah. Compare this tale to the autobiographical story "Ḥemdat" in the final section of this volume.

The meaning of the name Salsibylla is uncertain, although it recalls the sibyls, women that the ancient Greeks believed were oracles, prophesying at holy sites through the influence of divine inspiration from a deity. In the context of the story, she may symbolize the artistic muse Ḥemdat awaits; alternatively there is something that recollects the Hebrew "*bat kol*" (echo of prophecy).

28. Neve Tzedek / Jaffa neighborhood; Agnon settled here upon his arrival in 1908 (in today's southwestern Tel Aviv).
29. Teardrop from the eyes of the princess who must slumber in her hidden cave / Cf. Rebbe Naḥman of Breslov's "Tale of the Lost Princess."

37. *Ḥemdat the Cantor*

"*Etzel Ḥemdat,*" originally published in *Lu'aḥ Ha'aretz* 5704 (1943) and collected in *Samukh veNireh;* translated as "Chemdat" in *Israel Argosy* (Autumn 1952).

It should be noted that the character of the corpulent Cantor Ḥemdat in this story is not to be confused with the young author Ḥemdat, Agnon's most clearly autobiographical literary creation, who appears in a variety of his tales. This Rabelaisian tale of excess, set on the eve of Yom Kippur, takes advantage of the rabbinic edict to eat on the day before the holy fast, in order to enter the day well sated. It also plays off the idea originating in Tikkunei Zohar, which associates (through word-play) Purim and Yom Kippurim—through which a drop of the carnivalesque nature of the joyous Purim celebration can attach itself to the severe and somber Day of Atonement. The power in "Ḥemdat," and the astounding artistry at work in the story, resides in the sharp turn at the end, when the frivolity of excess (the reader is liable to gain a few pounds just by reading what the characters consume) mysteriously and mystically give way to the sacred and transcendental.

37. Jassy / Known in Yiddish as Yas; today Iași, city in north-eastern Romania, formerly capital of Principality of Moldavia.

37. Vasleu / Alt. Vaslui; Romanian city, about 65 km. south of Jassy.

38. Cock at *Bnei Adam* / Opening passage of the Kapparot service, lit., expiations or atonement; ceremony performed on the morning of the day before Yom Kippur in which the sins of an individual are symbolically transferred to a live fowl. The fowl—a rooster for a man, a hen for a woman—is swung around the head three times as biblical verses and a formula of vicarious atonement are recited. Money in the amount of the fowl's value is often substituted for the fowl.

38. Ashtoret Karnaim / City in Bashan, first mentioned in the Bible in Genesis 14:5.

40. Ruzhin / Ḥasidic sect founded by Rebbe Yisrael Friedman (1796-1850), known for conducting his ḥasidic court with pomp and splendor.

43. Mrs. Beadle / I.e., the wife of the shamash, the beadle or sexton of the synagogue and assistant to the rabbi; often a paid official of the community.

44. Yachnes the Physician / Word-play on Psalms 147:23.

44. Shatnez / Forbidden mixture of wool and linen in a garment (as proscribed in Leviticus 19:19 and Deuteronomy 22:11); that a tailor would bear such a name is the equivalent of having a butcher named Treif.

48. Thirteen Attributes of Mercy / Exodus 34:6-7, central passage of the Yom Kippur Confessional.

48. Malbim / Meir Leibush ben Yehiel Michel Wisser (1809-1879), known by the acronymic Malbim, rabbi, Hebrew grammarian, and Bible commentator.

49. Ḥakham / Lit. "Sage"; rabbinic title among Sefardic Jews.
49. Eli, the Priest / I Samuel 2:13.
55. Kittel / White linen robe which serves as a burial shroud for Jewish men, and is also worn on special occasions by Ashkenazi Jews—specifically on the High Holy Days, especially Yom Kippur.

60. *And Solomon's Wisdom Excelled*

"*Vatairev Ḥokhmat Shlomo,*" originally published in *Molad* (August-September 1950) and collected in *Ad Henah*; translation in *Ariel* 71-72 (1988). Arnold Band interprets this story as a retort to the author's critics, "camouflaged as a modern midrash" on a set of puzzling verses concerning King Solomon, a biblical author who hid many of his own writings when he saw them being misinterpreted. According to rabbinic tradition, King Solomon authored the biblical books Proverbs, Song of Songs, and Ecclesiastes.

60. And Solomon's wisdom excelled... / I Kings 5:10-12
60. Some of our rabbis explained... / See Rashi to I Kings 5:12, indicating the phrase "Proverbs of Solomon" appears three times in the book of Proverbs.
60. While others maintain... / Eruvin 21b.
61. And he spoke of trees / I Kings 5:13.
61. Little foxes that spoil the vineyards / Song of Songs 2:15.
61. Left hand beneath his head / Cf. Song of Songs 2:6, 8:3.
61. Flee, my beloved / Song of Songs 8:14.
62. In the cover of your presence... / Psalms 31:20.
62. Before the day cools and the shadows flee... / Song of Songs 2:17.
62. You are fair, my love; there is no flaw in you / Song of Songs 4:7.
62. He put his mouth into the dust / Lamentations 3:29.
62. Solomon had a vineyard at Ba'al Hammon / Song of Songs 8:11; Rashi identifies Ba'al Hammon as Jerusalem.
62. Fifteenth of Av / The Fifteenth of Av is a minor holiday, which is mentioned in the Mishnah as the beginning of the grape harvest. The Talmud (Ta'anit 30b) mentions an ancient custom that the unmarried girls of Jerusalem, dressed in borrowed white garments, would go out to dance in the vineyards, attracting the attention of the young men, leading to marriages.
62. I charge you, O, daughters of Jerusalem... / Song of Songs 2:7.

63. You have ignored my counsel … / Proverbs 1:25.
64. Wisdom cried aloud … / Proverbs 1:20.
64. He who has knowledge, spares his words / Proverbs 17:27.
64. The wise hide their wisdom / Proverbs 10:14.
64. He prepared many proverbs / Eruvin 21b.
64. Vanity of vanities, all is vanity / Ecclesiastes 1:2.
64. If the baker admits his dough is bad / Midrash Psalms 103:14.
64. What profit is there for man in all his work? / Ecclesiastes 1:3.
65. Fear God! / Ecclesiastes 12:13; closing refrain of the book.
65. Then I saw that all toil and all skills … / Ecclesiastes 4:4.
65. My people were immediately angry with me / Song of Songs 1:6.
65. Beware of making many books / Ecclesiastes 12:12.

66. *The Garment*

"*HaMalbush*," originally published *Ha'aretz* (Erev Rosh Hashanah, September 11, 1950) and collected in *Ad Henah*; this translation in *Ariel* 96 (1994) [alt. trans. by Howard Langer, as "The Overcoat," *Shdemot* 14 (1980)].

The symbolism of this tale seems, on first reading, to be fairly simple to decode: The "garment" being equated with the "soul" which the tailor, significantly named "Israel," must prepare (tikkun) to present to the "Lord."

In kabbalistic teaching the "secret of the clothing [or garment]" is a reference to the soul entrusted by God to a human for safekeeping, based on Shabbat 152b: "Our Rabbis taught: 'And the dust return to the earth as it was, and the spirit return unto God who gave it': Render it back to him as He gave it to thee, in purity, so do you return it in purity. This may be compared to a mortal king who distributed royal apparel to his servants. The wise among them folded it up and laid it away in a chest, whereas the fools among them went and did their work in them. After a time the king demanded his garments: the wise among them returned them to him immaculate, but the fools among them returned them soiled. The king was pleased with the wise but angry with the fools. Of the wise he said, Let my robes be placed in my treasury and they can go home in peace; while of the fools he said, Let my robes be given to the laundry, and let them be confined in prison. Thus too, with the Holy One, blessed be He: concerning the bodies of the righteous He says,

He enters into peace, they rest in their beds (Isa. 57:2); while concerning their souls He says, yet the soul of my Lord shall be bound up in the bundle of life with the Lord thy God (Sam. I 25:29). But concerning the bodies of the wicked He says, There is no peace saith the Lord, unto the wicked (Isa. 48:22); while concerning their souls He says, and the souls of thine enemies, them shall he sling out, as from the hollow of a sling (Sam. I 25:29)."

71. Kashipani / A combination of millet and beans with onions and cooked in oil.

83. *The Father of the Ox*

"*Avi HaShor*," originally published in *Davar* (June 1, 1945), and collected in *Ad Henah*; translation in *Israel Life and Letters* (January-February 1958), translator unknown.

In contrast to Agnon's allegory of the origin of the name "Abu-Tor," conventional history records that after Saladin's conquest of Jerusalem in 1187, the area directly south of the Old City walls was assigned to an officer of his army, Sheikh Shehab ed Din el Mukaddasiel, called "Sheikh Ahmed et Toreh" (Sheikh Ahmed of the ox) or "Abu-Tor" (the man with the ox, or the father of the ox) as he was said to have accompanied Saladin riding an ox. Today Abu-Tor is one of the few Jerusalem neighborhoods with a mixed Arab and Jewish population, an irony that would not have been lost on Agnon, as this story was widely interpreted as a parable of the Jewish-Arab tensions of the 1940s.

87. Doxistus the Scribe / The scribe's name is the word for a type of inferior parchment, *dokhsostos*, invalid for use in most ritual scribal arts.

88. Wild Ox Behemoth / Menu item of the messianic feast of Leviathan and wild ox (as described in Bava Batra 75a and expanded in the kabbalistic and ḥasidic literature).

89. Knock knock / Cf. Eruvin 29a regarding the *tukh tukh* sound a pot makes when it reaches a boil.

91. * *Ascents and Descents*

"*Ma'alot uMoradot*," originally published in *Gevulot* (Vienna, 1919) and collected in *Elu veElu*.

The wealthy man who suffers by losing everything is a plot line as old as the biblical Job, yet "Ascents and Descents" appears to lack any hint of theodical speculation—there seems no attempt on the protagonist's part to uncover the source of his suffering or the root of evil. This is particularly remarkable given that the story was studied in a "Hebrew circle" that took place in May 1942 in the Theresienstadt concentration camp! See: *The Terezin Diary of Gonda Redlich* (University Press of Kentucky, 1999), p. 41.

91. The Blessed Holy One sits and fashions ladders / Leviticus Rabbah 8:1. In context, the statement introduces the idea that the exigencies of fate—one's rising and falling in this world—are in God's hands. In full, the quote more sharply underscores the themes of the story: "The Blessed Holy One sits and fashions ladders, he humbles this one and exalts that one; he causes this one to descend and causes that one to ascend."

93. Oniph / Town in central Poland, known as Uniejów in the Lodz region, site of annual trade fair.

95. The machinations of the serpent / Shabbat 55b.

96. Franzensbad / World-renowned spa town in the Bohemia province of Austria-Hungary (in today's western Czech Republic).

96. I'm not going to immerse myself in the mikveh / At the end of her menstrual cycle, and therefore sexual contact with her will be forbidden.

97. The jackal bears offspring… / Ketubot 49b; Rashi explains that the jackal is known for its cruelty even to its own young.

97. The people Israel are not bereft / Jeremiah 51:5, cited to mean: Rescue will come—from some unexpected source.

101. Emperor's jubilee / Franz Joseph I celebrated his jubilee on the throne of the Austrian Empire in December 1898.

101. Like a baby slapped on the mouth by an angel… / Cf. Niddah 30b.

103. He lifteth up the needy… / Psalm 113:7. In *gematria*, which assigns a numerical value to each letter, the lottery numbers would be 40–10–1.

105. The principle of the poor person who was examining a cake…and the principle of the poor person who was gathering olives… / The two cases are examined in Kiddushin 59a and Gittin 59b.

105. Sitting among scorpions / Ezekiel 2:6.

105. The Master of Mercy does not strike first at people themselves / Divine punishment is inflicted first via one's possessions, see Leviticus Rabbah 17:2.

107. And if your brother waxes poor… / Leviticus 25:35.

108. Each one as God's blessings allowed / Deuteronomy 16:17.

109. God maketh poor and maketh rich / I Samuel 2:7.

109. And Joseph recognized his brothers... / Genesis 42:8.
111. Could not restrain himself... / Cf. Genesis 45:1.
113. Salvation comes from the Lord / Psalm 3:9.

114. * *The Death of the Tzadik*

"Im Petirat HaTzadik" appears in Hebrew in *Elu veElu.*

Arnold Band observes that the story begins with the solemnity expected at the death of a tzaddik, a righteous man, leading the reader paragraph by paragraph until it suddenly dawns on him that we are entrenched in a biting satire on human cupidity.

119. Angel entrusted with the souls of the dead / Named as Dumah; Shabbat 152b and Sanhedrin 92a.
119. Three bands of angels... There is no peace... Said God to the evil ones... You shall lie down in pain / Cf. Ketubot 104a; Isaiah 58:22 and 50:11.

120. *The Mother's Voice*

"*Kol HaEm,*" originally published in *Ha'aretz* (July 16, 1941), and collected in *Elu veElu;* translation in *Maggid* 3 (2007).

120. Ḥaim Naḥman Bialik / (1873-1934) Israel's national poet; publisher and pioneer of modern Hebrew poetry, with whom Agnon shared a close relationship.

123. * *Three Sisters*

"*Shalosh Aḥayot,*" originally published in *Davar* (May 14, 1937), and collected in *Elu veElu.*

123. Berl Katznelson / (1887-1944), one of the intellectual founders of Labor Zionism, instrumental to the establishment of the modern state of Israel, and the editor of *Davar*, the first daily, Hebrew newspaper of the workers' movement.

125. *Earth of Israel*

"*Afar Eretz Yisrael*" originally published in *Ha'aretz* (March 16, 1937), and collected in *Elu veElu,* translation in *A Dwelling Place of My People* (Edinburgh, 1983).

125. Lovers of Zion / The *Ḥovevei Zion* (Lovers of Zion) were European Zionist groups, founded in the 1880s to promote Jewish immigration and agricultural settlement in Palestine.

125. Property outside Israel has no blessing / Genesis Rabbah 74:3.
125. Turned his tools into weapons / Cf. Isaiah 2:4.
126. These are the seed, blessed of the Lord / Isaiah 61:9.
126. Barrel of wine from Rishon LeZion / Coastal farm settlement established to the south of Jaffa in 1882; under Baron Rothschild's patronage the Carmel-Mizrahi winery was founded there.
126. The first from Zion is here / Isaiah 41:27; verse from which the town Rishon LeZion take sits name.
126. The rich bought one whole orange... the poor divided / Cf. description of the Paschal sacrifice.
127. That which cheereth God and man / Judges 9:13.
127. Gazoz / Modern Hebrew slang for carbonated beverage; soda pop.
127. Reached the age of his father and he was worrying / Genesis Rabbah 65:8.
128. The earth of Israel atones for His people / Deuteronomy 32:43.
130. Abraham... hid her in a chest in order that the Egyptians might not see her / Rashi to Genesis 12:14.
130. Solomon and Bezalel / Biblical characters known for being graced with wisdom.

136. *Yisakhar and Zevulun*

"*Yisakhar uZevulun*," originally published in *Ha'aretz* (May 30, 1941) and collected in *Elu veElu*; translated in *Jewish Spectator* 47:2 (Summer 1982). The story plays off the midrashic idea about the partnership between the biblical brothers, Zevulun the merchant, who accrued heavenly reward by supporting his brother Yisakhar the Torah scholar (Genesis Rabbah 99:9; cited by Rashi to Deuteronomy 33:18).

136. Gan Eden / The Garden of Eden, Paradise.

138. *Tranquility*

"*Menuḥah*," originally published in *Ha'aretz* (May 21, 1942) and collected in *Elu veElu*, translation in *Conservative Judaism* 21:1 (Fall 1967). The "tranquility" sought in the story is called in Hebrew "*menuḥah*," that which is "created" by God in the vacuum of ceasing to create following the first six days of Creation.

138. Marah / Location of the "bitter waters" encountered three days after the splitting of the sea; Exodus 15:22-27.

140. *Tears*

"*Dema'ot*," collected in *Elu veElu*, translation in *Conservative Judaism* 21:1 (Fall 1967). This short hasidic anecdote relates to the founder of Hasidism, Rabbi Israel (Yisroelki) Ba'al Shem Tov ("Master of a Good Name," c. 1700-1760), who for a time worked as a ritual slaughterer (*shoḥet*). Whether his tears were shed in compassion for the soon to be slaughtered animal or for the Jewish people is left open to interpretation.

140. Rabbi Shmuel Arieh / Galician-born Rabbi Dr. Shmuel Arieh, a friend of Agnon, served as rabbi in Prague before the Holocaust, immigrated to Jerusalem (d. 1950).

141. *The Mill Owner and the Miller*

"*Ba'al HaReḥayim vehaToḥen*" collected in *Elu veElu*; translation in *Maggid* 3 (2007).

141. Rebbe Mottele of Chernobyl / Rabbi Mordechai Twersky (1770–1837), known as the Maggid of Chernobyl, second rebbe of the Chernobyl Ḥasidic dynasty, was renowned for his charitable works.

145.* *Dessert*

"*Kinu'aḥ Seudah*" collected in *Elu veElu*.

145. Rabbi of Apta / R. Avraham Yehoshua Heshel of Apt (1748-1825).

147. *Shabtai*

"*Shabtai*," originally published in "*Sipurei Agadot*," in *Aḥdut Avodah* 2:5-6 (March-April 1931), and collected in *Elu eElu;* translation in *Jewish World* 2 (June 1964).

150. Elijah the Prophet / Biblical prophet; according to Jewish tradition Elijah will usher in the messianic redemption, in folktales he often appears as the hidden savoir of Jews in distress.

150. Elijah won't arrive on Sabbath eve / Eruvin 43b.

151. *The Coin*

"*HaPerutah*," originally published in *Davar* (February 9, 1934) and collected in *Elu veElu;* translation in *Igeret LaGolah* 33-34 (February-March 1951).

154. Melaveh Malkah / The legend of the luz bone, from which one is regenerated at the messianic resurrection (Genesis Rabbah 28:3), is said to derive

its sole benefit from the Melaveh Malkah meal served at the departure of the Sabbath (*Kaf HaḤaim* 300:1-2).

155. *Concerning Those Who Assemble in Laughter and Frivolousness*

"*Keneged Otam sheKoeve'im Yeshivot shel Sḥok veKalut Rosh,*" originally published in "*Sipurei Agadot,*" in *Aḥdut Avodah* 2:5-6 (March-April 1931), and collected in *Elu eElu;* translation in CCAR 23:7 (Autumn 1976).

155. *Tze'enah uRe'enah* / "Come Ye Forth and See" (*Tze'enah U-Re'enah*) contains weekly readings from the Torah and the Prophets in Yiddish, especially adapted for persons not well versed in Hebrew.

156. Not to engage in idle matters on the Sabbath / Shabbat 113b and Zohar II 63b.

156. Women were unwilling... golden calf / This midrashic embellishment of the golden calf story is found in Chapter 45 of *Pirkei Rabbi Eliezer.*

156. Rabbi Yaakov ben Asher / (1270-1340), recorded in his Tur, Oraḥ Ḥayyim, Rosh Ḥodesh 417.

157. * *Introduction to The Tales of Poland*

"*Kedumot,*" originally published in "*Polin: Agadot Mini Kedem*" in *HaTekufah* 5:23-26 (1919), and collected in *Elu eElu.*

157. They stood at the crossroads... / Cf. Jeremiah 6:16.

158. Mieszko / Jews were employed as minters and coiners in the 12th century under Mieszko III the Old, the High Duke of Poland. The inscriptions on the coins were partly in Hebrew and partly in Polish in Hebrew letters.

160. *The Dance of Death*

"*Meḥolat HaMavet,*" originally published in "*Polin: Agadot Mini Kedem*" in *HaTekufah* 5:23-26 (1919), and collected in *Elu veElu,* translation in *Jewish Spectator* (September 1936), translator unknown.

Agnon had been working on the themes in this early, short macabre tale for a number of years, with prototypes of the story having been drafted in Yiddish as early as 1906.

160. Cohanim / The priestly class, under injunction from becoming ritually impure through contact with the dead, do not enter cemeteries—nor did they trample on this hillside out of suspicion the grounds were littered with the remains of the martyred.

161. And he is like a bridegroom... / Psalms 19:6.

165. *Heart and Eyes*

"*HaLev vehaEnayim*," originally published in *Ha'aretz* (September 29, 1943), and collected in *Elu veElu;* translation in *Maggid* 3 (2007).

165. Casimir, King of Poland / Casimir III the Great (1310-1370), ruled Poland from 1333 until his death; encouraged Jewish settlement in Poland and granted generous privileges and protections to the Jews. The legend of his Jewish wife Esther, clearly built on the framework of the biblical Esther in the palace of Ahasuerus, is first recorded in *Tzemaḥ David* by R. David Ganz in 1592. In the Kazimir neighborhood of Krakow, one finds to this day Ulica Estery (Queen Esther Street).

166. So that you stray not after your own heart and your own eyes / Numbers 15:39.

168. *The Great Synagogue*

"*Beit HaKenesset HaGadol*," originally published in "*Polin: Agadot Mini Kedem*" in *HaTekufah* 5:23-26 (1919), and collected in *Elu eElu,* translation in CCAR (Winter 2016).

Gershom Scholem wrote to Walter Benjamin, "I have yet to find anything in his works more beautiful than 'The Great Synagogue,' which I regard as a tremendous masterpiece." Robert Alter describes the story as complex "in its seemingly naïve recuperation of the harmonies of pious tradition."

168. Magical *shamir* / The worm which, according to legend, was used by King Solomon to cut the stones for the Temple altar because the Torah prohibits the use of an iron tool for that purpose (Exodus 20:22); Avot 5:6.

169. Jaslowitz / Village about 16 km. SSE of Buczacz.

170. Voice is the voice of Jacob / Cf. Genesis 27:22.

170. How goodly are thy tents / Numbers 24:5, traditionally recited upon entering a synagogue.

171. In the Depths

"*Bimtzulot*," originally published in *HaTzfirah* (Warsaw, May 13 and June 7, 1917), translated as "Thou Makest Man as Fishes in the Sea," *Zionist Record* (South Africa, September 29, 1967).

171. Asonovki / The village of Ossowce (or, in Ukrainian, Osivtsi), on the Strypa River, 13 km. due north of Buczacz.

171. Count of Buczacz / Througout the 17th and 18th centuries Buczacz was owned by the House of Potocki, one of the prominent Polish noble families in the Kingdom of Poland and magnates of the Polish-Lithuanian Commonwealth.

171. Palm branches… Tabernacles / Ritual of the Sukkot festival; see Leviticus 23:40.

174. Tashlikh / Rosh Hashanah prayer recited by a body of water, in which ones sins are symbolically cast away.

174. Mix his blood in their Passover bread / From the early Middle Ages through modern times, false accusations that Jews murdered Christian children (often in order to use their blood for Passover baking or other such rituals), leading to trials and massacres of Jews.

175. Light is sown for the righteous… / Psalms 97:11, and opening line of Kol Nidrei prayer of Yom Kippur eve.

177. Burying them not in shrouds / Jewish martyrs are not buried in the traditional shrouds, but in their bloodied garments, in order to invoke God's mercy on their souls, and vengeance on their foes (*Shulḥan Arukh*, Y.D. 364:4).

178. *The Goat Which Was Blessed*

"*Al HaSheḥitah*," originally published in "*Sipurei Agadot*," in *Aḥdut Avodah* 2:5-6 (March-April 1931), collected in *Elu veElu*, translation in *Palestine Review* 3 (1938), translator unknown.

Clearly the Passover story, with its sacrificial blood at the doorpost (Exodus 12:7-13), marking where the Angel of Death should "pass over," resonates in this tale.

178. Goats of Rabbi Hanina ben Dosa / Ta'anit 25a.

178. The goat which went through a cave… / Agnon's "The Fable of the Goat" in *A Book That Was Lost* (Toby Press, 2008).

179. Chmielnicki / Bogdan Chmielnicki (1595-1657), leader of uprising against the Polish-Lithuania Commonwealth, and wave of pogroms that swept eastern European Jewry in 1648-49.

181. *The Light of Torah*

"*Or Torah*," originally published in *HaMitzpeh* (December 7, 1906), collected in *Elu veElu*, translation in *Jewish Frontier* 11:1 (January 1944) as "The Light That Is Shed By the Law."

The original version of this story is among Agnon's earliest published writings, written prior to his departure from Buczacz; like most of his works it was reworked prior to republication and collection in *Elu veElu*.

181. "Night-time was only created for the study of Torah" / Eruvin 65a: "R. Yehudah observed: Night was created for naught but sleep. R. Shimon ben Lakish observed: The moon was created only to facilitate study [of Torah]."

183. Hundred blessings of the day / Menaḥot 43b.

186. * *The Tale of Azriel Moshe the Book-Keeper*

*"Ma'aseh Azriel Moshe Shomer HaSe*farim," originally published in *Rimon* 4 (1923, Berlin), collected in *Elu veElu*.

187. Rav Ya'akov ben Rav Yakir / 11th century, studied under Rabbenu Gershom, and was one of Rashi's teachers. See *Sefer Ḥasidim* #128 for a reference to this anecdote.

187. This is my Lord and I shall beautify Him… Beautify yourself… / Shabbat 133b on Exodus 15:2.

190. Shelah /Acronym of rabbinic work *Shenei Luḥot HaBerit* (Two Tablets of the Covenant) by R. Isaiah Horowitz (1558–1630).

190. The year 1847 since the destruction… / 1,847 years after the destruction of the Jerusalem Temple in 70 CE; that is, in 1917 during World War I.

191. Rabbi Gadiel the Infant / See "The Tale of Little Rabbi Gadiel," p. 202 in this volume.

192. *The Messenger from the Holy Land*

"Ma'aseh HaMeshulaḥ MeEretz HaKedoshah," originally published in *HaPoel HaTzair* (July 3, 1925), collected in *Elu veElu*, translation in *Brandeis Avukah Annual* (1932).

193. Withhold thy voice from weeping / Jeremiah 31:15.

194. Voice to Jacob and the hands to Esau / Cf. Genesis 27:22.

194. Because they have sold the righteous for silver / The biblical Joseph; cf. Amos 2:6.

197. He who has not seen the Holy Temple… / Sukkah 51b.

197. For the sake of Zion I shall not be silent / Isaiah 62:1.

198. The best fruits of the land… take double silver in your hands / Genesis 43:11-12.

198. The air of Eretz Yisrael imparts wisdom / Bava Batra 158b.
199. Story of Elisha / II Kings 2:23.
199. The Lord loveth the gates of Zion... / Psalms 87:2.
200. All the synagogues and houses of study which are outside of the Holy Land are destined to be transplanted to Eretz Yisrael / Megillah 29a.
201. Even them will I bring to My holy mountain... / Isaiah 56:7.

202. *The Tale of Little Rabbi Gadiel*

"*Ma'aseh Rabi Gadiel HaTinok*," originally published in *Miklat* 4 (New York, 1920), and collected in *Elu veElu*; translated as "The Tale of Rabbi Gadiel the Infant" in *Gates to the New City* (New York: Avon, 1980), ed. Howard Schwartz.

Arnold Band observes the similarities between this tale, a Judaized "Tom Thumb" story, and "In the Depths" (above), in that "both take place in a feudal atmosphere; both involve a blood libel; both end in a miraculous salvation. In both, furthermore, the reader is immediately introduced into an atmosphere of legend and is willing to accept the miraculous on its own terms." Gershom Scholem was a pioneer in interpreting the kabbalistic sources woven into "The Tale of Little Rabbi Gadiel"; see his *Devarim Bego*, vol. 1.

202. Gravesite of Rabbi Shimon ben Yoḥai on Lag BaOmer / The tomb of R. Shimon bar Yoḥai, where pilgrimage is made on the anniversary of his death on Lag BaOmer, the 33rd day of the period between Passover and Shavuot.
203. But for fear of the authorities... / Cf. Avot 3:2.
204. Begin with the greatest / Cf. Genesis 44:12.
206. Put on garments of vengeance... / Isaiah 59:17.

207. *Rabbi Katriel the Cantor*

"*Rabbi Katirel Shaliaḥ Tzibbur*," originally published in *Ha'aretz* (September 16, 1936), and collected in *Elu veElu*; translated in *Genesis* 1:2 (March 1970), translator unknown.

209. Earth from the Holy Land / According to custom, deceased Jews buried abroad are interred with a satchel of earth from the Land of Israel, sent to the Diaspora from the pious in Jerusalem.

209. The earth and its fullness are the Lord's / Psalm 24, recited as part of the evening service on Rosh Hashanah.
210. Who shall go up to the mountain / Psalms 24:3.
210. Dreams only show a man his inner thoughts / Berakhot 55b. The Talmud teaches of a variety of dreams that serve as bad omens, warranting one to fast the following day in penitence.

212. *The Covenant of Love*

"*Brit Ahavah*," originally published *Davar* (June 1, 1925) and collected in *Elu veElu;* translation in *Canadian Jewish Chronicle* (April 26, 1935). The unknown translator of the story took certain liberties in this lyrical rendering.

213. Jonah sought to flee from the presence of the Lord / Cf. Jonah 1:3.
213. Priestly Blessing / Temple ritual incorporated as part of the daily morning prayers in the Land of Israel (cf. Numbers 6:22-27); in the Diaspora this blessing is only recited on holidays.
214. Walk before Me and be perfect / Genesis 17:1 and Rashi on v. 1-2.
214. For the upright shall dwell... / Proverbs 2:21.

215. *The Minyan*

"*HaMinyan*" originally published in "*Sipurei Agadot*," in *Aḥdut Avodah* 2:5-6 (March-April 1931), and collected in *Elu eElu;* translated as "The Ten" in *The Palestine Post* (May 14, 1933).

215. Hart to do the will of his Father... / Cf. Avot 5:20.
215. Seven chastisements / Leviticus 26:18.
215. Charity will deliver from death / Proverbs 10:2.
215. Rabbi Meir the Wonder Worker / R Meir "*Ba'al HaNes*" (the Wonder Worker), 2nd century leading figure of the mishnaic period; the sobriquet "Miracle worker" is based on a legend recorded in Avodah Zarah 18a.
215. *Tannaim* and *Amoraim* / Rabbis of the Mishnah and Gemara, respectively.
216. Span of a man's years upon earth / Presumably 70 candles, in accord with Psalms 90:10: "The days of our years are three score years and ten."
216. Mount Meron on the thirty-third day of the *Omer* / Near Tiberias, site of the tomb of R. Shimon bar Yoḥai, where pilgrimage is made on the anniversary of his death: *Lag BaOmer*, the 33rd day of the period between Passover and Shavuot.

216. *Ari,* our Master Rabbi Isaac Luria / (1534-1572), foremost rabbi and mystic, resided in Safed, developer of the influential Lurianic kabbalistic system.
217. *Happy are they…* / Psalms 84:5, opening verse to the afternoon prayer.
217. *The lord is near… He shall perform…* / Psalms 145:18-19.

219. *Under the Tree*

"*Taḥat HaEtz*" originally published in *Davar* (February 2, 1934) and collected in *Elu veElu;* translation in *Israel* 6 (April-May 1951). Dov Sadan points out a chronological issue: The narrator is going to modern settlement of Degania; presence of the Pasha seems medieval. This is one of Agnon's few attempts to directly address contemporary socialor political events: in this case the Arab-Jewish conflicts of the 1930s

219. Degania / The first kibbutz, a communal agricultural settlement, founded in 1909 near the southern point of Lake Kinneret, in northern Israel.
220. The Earth is the Lord's and the fullness thereof / Psalms 24:1.
220. And He gave the Earth to humankind / Psalms 115:16.
221. Ibrahim Bey / (1735-1816/1817) Mamluk chieftain and regent of Egypt. The title Bey is a provincial governor in the Ottoman Empire.
227. Tribe of Khaybar / Oasis 150 km. north of Medina, Saudi Arabia. Before falling to Muslim forces in 629 CE this fortress town was inhabited by Jewish tribes.
229. David, King of Israel, lives forever / Rosh Hashanah 25a.
229. Kingship is the Lord's / Obadiah v. 21.
231. And ye shall inherit it… / Deuteronomy 11:31-32.
231. The day is short and the work is plentiful / Avot 2:15.
231. Dwelling in the land of Israel…equivalent to all the commandments / Tosefta, Avodah Zara 5:2.
231. And they shall plant vineyards… / Amos 9:14-15.
231. Esau and Ishmael / Midrashically identified as Christianity and Islam.

232. *The Kindling*

"*HaHadlakah*" originally published in *HaHed* and in *Minḥah LeDavid [Yellin]* (1935), and collected in *Elu veElu;* translation in *Palestine Review* 1 (May 8, 1936), translator unknown. See note to "The Minyan" (above) for background to Shimon bar Yoḥai and Lag BaOmer.

235. *The Good Years*

"*HaShanim HaTovot*" originally published in *Moledet* 9:3 (1927), and collected in *Elu veElu;* translation in *Ariel* 17 (1966-97).

Following the notion that each succeeding generation is less worthy than that which preceded it, Agnon is playing off a literary motif that had already been established by Rebbe Naḥman of Breslov in his "The Tale of the Seven Beggars."

235. It is as if they had eaten from the table of the Creator / Avot 3:3.

236. For anyone who leaves behind him an ignorant son… is thrown into Gehenna / Kohelet Rabbah 4:1.

237. Abraham slaughtered three oxen… / Genesis 18:7-8.

237. Sages of Athens / Known midrashically for disrespecting elders, cf. Bekhorot 8b.

237. The aged will stand before the young / Mishnah Sotah 9:15.

239. And the land spat forth its inhabitants / Leviticus 18:25.

241. Enter His gates with thanksgiving / Psalms 100:4.

241. Let not your mouth be hasty / Ecclesiastes 5:1.

241. Turn about Zion and go round her / Psalms 48:13.

242. Graves of Small and Great Sanhedrin / Burial caves in northern Jerusalem, 1st century CE rock-cut tombs which housed the remains of the judges of the rabbinic high courts.

243. One hundred and twentieth year / Midrashic idea that the outer limits of a lifespan can reach 120, as this was the age at which Moses died (Deuteronomy 34:7).

244. And Moses was one hundred and twenty years old / Deuteronomy 34:7.

245. Lo, on the hills are the feet of the Herald… / Naḥum 2:1.

245. Death is forever destroyed / Isaiah 25:8.

246. *From Foe to Friend*

"*MeOyev leOhev*" originally published in *Ha'aretz* (May 30, 1941), and collected in *Elu veElu*; translation in *Israel Youth Horizon* 5:2 (February 1956), and anthologized in many other publications.

This story, among Agnon's most well-known and most frequently taught in elementary schools, is a parable about the pioneering spirit to settle the Land of Israel on a national plane, and also reflective of various events in

Agnon's biography—including the marauding of his Jerusalem home during the Arab uprising of 1929. Agnon had made his home in the Talpiot suburb, in the southern section of Jerusalem, since 1927.

251. *Ḥemdat*

"*Ḥemdat*" originally published in *Arbaim Shanah* (40th anniversary festschrift of the *Poel HaTzair* newspaper, 1947), and collected in *MeAtzmi el Atzmi*; translation in *Modern Hebrew Literature* 2:4 (Winter 1976). Presented as an autobiographical sketch of the "artist as a young man" in the guise of a third-person depiction of Ḥemdat – Agnon's young poet of the Jaffa period (see, e.g., the story "Nights" above; care should be taken not to confuse the character with the cantor by the same name in the story "Ḥemdat the Cantor").

251. The Law / I.e., the Torah and its commandments.

252. The father passes on to his son … / Eduyot 2:9.

252. The witch who used to milk the moon / Appears in Agnon's early story "*Be'erah shel Miriam*" (published in 4 installments in *Poel HaTzair*, May-July 1909; never anthologized in his collected writings, but reprinted in *Kovetz Agnon*, vol. 2).

253. Rains did not extinguish the altar's fire / Yoma 21a.

255. Rabbi Yakir / The character of the grandfather (referred to here as Rabbi Yakir) aligns with the biography of Agnon's maternal grandfather, R. Yehuda HaCohen Farb, an important town leader in Buczacz and powerful influence on the author's young life. He is depicted in a wide variety of Agnon's stories, from those relating nostalgic childhood recollections to the surrealistic tales of *Sefer HaMa'asim*.

255. Laid low with grief / Cf. Genesis 37:35.

255. Lemberg / Largest city in western Ukraine, center of the historical region of Galicia. Known in L'viv (in Ukrainian) or Lvov (Russian), the city is approx. 165 km. northwest of Buczacz.

256. Jewish National Fund / Founded in 1901 to buy and develop land in Ottoman Palestine (later British Mandate for Palestine, and subsequently State of Israel) for Jewish settlement.

256. Trieste / Port city at the northern tip of the Adriatic Sea (in the furthest northeast point in Italy on the Slovenian border).

257. Mr. Grossman / In Lemberg, Agnon met with Moshe Kleinman (1870-1948), editor of the Yiddish newspaper *Der Yudisher Tagblat* (the name

Grossman, large-man, being a play on Kleinman, small-man). Kleinman provided Agnon with three letters of recommendation to carry with him to Palestine.

257. Rabbi Eliezer Meir Lipschütz / (1879-1946), rabbi, educator, scholar, and leader of the Religious Zionist movement. Lipschütz was among the first to recognize Agnon's brilliance as a writer, and among the earliest to pen a work of literary criticism on Agnon's stories.

258. Brenner / Yosef Ḥaim Brenner (1881-1921), pioneer of modern Hebrew literature, and early champion of Agnon's career; immigrated to Palestine in 1909 where he worked as a farmer, eager to put his Zionist ideology into practice, but unable to take the strain of manual labor he soon devoted himself to literature. Brenner was murdered in 1921 during the Jaffa riots.

259. Jonathan Biedermann / Agnon had spent a number of weeks in Lemberg during the later winter of 1907 as editorial assistant to Gershom Bader in his short-lived Hebrew newspaper *HaEt*. Bader (b. Krakow 1868-d. New York 1953) was an author, playwright, editor, and journalist in Hebrew, Yiddish, German, and Polish. Agnon's final Yiddish publication, mentioned here, was the story "*Toitentants*," later re-worked in Hebrew (appearing in English in this volume as "The Dance of Death").

260. David Zvi Miller / Prof. David Zvi (Heinrich) Miller (1846-1912) was a cousin of Agnon's mother, and professor of Semitics and ancient languages at the University of Vienna.

262. Went down to the hold / Jonah 1:5.

262. Now the Lord said unto Abram... / Genesis 12:1-2.

270. *Agnon and Reb Columbus*

In Hebrew in *MeAtzmi el Atzmi*, pp. 108-112; appeared in *Midstream* (June 1967).

Glossary

AGGADAH / Non-legal exegetical texts in the classical rabbinic literature of Judaism, particularly as recorded in the Talmud and Midrash.

ALIYAH / (1) On Sabbaths the Torah portion is divided into seven sections, and different men are invited to receive an *aliyah* (to be "called up" to the Torah) and recite the blessings before and after each reading. The first two sections are designated for a Cohen and Levi respectively. The third *aliyah* is considered the greatest honor; the seventh is the least. (2) To immigrate (lit. "Ascend") to the Land of Israel.

ASHKENAZIC / Pertaining to the Ashkenazim, Jews of Central European tradition, as opposed to the Sefardim, Jews of the Spanish tradition, from whom they differ in ritual and in their pronunciation of Hebrew.

BEIT MIDRASH / Study house; although prayers are also conducted here it is distinct from a synagogue.

ERETZ YISRAEL / The Land of Israel.

EREV SHABBAT / Sabbath eve; i.e., Friday afternoon prior to the onset of the Sabbath.

GABBAI / A volunteer official who oversees the finances of the synagogue and directs allocation of honors.

GEMARA / Component of the Talmud comprising rabbinical analysis of and commentary on the Mishnah; completed around 500 CE.

ḤASID (pl. ḥasidim) / Adherent of Ḥasidut, mass eastern European Jewish pietistic and spiritual movement begun in the 18th century by R. Yisrael Ba'al Shem Tov.

HASKALAH / 18th century European Jewish Enlightenment movement.

HAVDALAH / Lit. "separation"; ceremony marking the end of Shabbat and holidays, ushering in the new week. The ritual involves lighting a special multi-wick candle, blessing a cup of wine and smelling sweet spices.

HILULA / Synonym for yahretzeit, although usually used to denote the observance of the anniversary of death of a particularly righteous person, one versed in the mysticism of Kabbalah; commemorated specifically through joy and festive celebration.

ḤUMASH / The Pentateuch; Bible, often printed with Rashi's commentary.

KABBALAH / The tradition of Jewish mysticism.

KADDISH / Mourner's prayer.

KIDDUSH / Blessing recited over wine prior to Sabbath and holiday meals to sanctify the holy day; alt. light repast taken following morning Sabbath prayers.

KOL NIDREI / Opening prayer on the evening of Yom Kippur.

KLOYZ / A private house of study, existing separately from the institutions of the community and usually financed by a patron.

MAARIV / Evening prayer service.

MAḤZOR / Special prayerbook for holiday use.

MASKIL / Adherent of the Haskalah (late 18th century European Jewish Enlightenment movement).

MELAMED / Lit. "teacher"; either the instructor in the local ḥeder or meant to indicate a private tutor.

MEZUZAH / Scroll containing Torah passage written by ritual scribe, and attached to doorways.

MIKVEH / Ritual bath.

MINḤAH / Afternoon prayer service.

MISHNAH / First major written compilation of the Oral law, redacted around 200 CE.

MITNAGDIM / Rabbinic opponents to the 18th century ḥasidic movement.

PARNAS / Communal lay leader; usually installed in a position of authority, for a period of time or indefinitely, in deference to his wealth.

PEYOT / Traditional sidecurls worn by orthodox men.

SHAMASH / Sexton of the synagogue and assistant to the rabbi; often a paid official of the community.

SHAVUOT / Pentecost or Feast of Weeks; holiday marking the giving of the ten Commandments on Mt. Sinai 7 weeks after Passover.

SHEMA / "Hear, O Israel"; declaration of Jewish faith and centerpiece of the morning and evening prayer services.

SHTREIMEL / A round, fur hat worn by married men, particularly members of ḥasidic groups, on Sabbath and holidays and other festive occasions.

TALIT / Four-cornered fringed shawl worn by men during morning prayer.

TALLIT KATAN / Ritual knots tied to the four corners of a garment worn under a man's clothing (alt. *tzitzit*).

TALMUD / Central compendium of rabbinic Judaism, comprised of the Mishnah and Gemara.

TEFILIN / Phylacteries; set of cube-shaped leather cases containing Torah texts worn by worshippers on the arm and head as part of morning prayers.

TISHAH B'AV / 9th day of month of Av; mournful fast day commemorating the destruction of both Jerusalem Temples.

TZADDIK (pl. tzaddikim) / Lit. righteous person; can also specifically refer to the Rebbe, or leader of a ḥasidic court.

YAHRZEIT / Anniversary of the death of a family member.

YAMIM NORAIM / Days of Awe; i.e., Rosh Hashanah and Yom Kippur.

About the Author

S.Y. Agnon (1888-1970) was the central figure of modern Hebrew literature, and the 1966 Nobel Prize laureate for his body of writing. Born in the Galician town of Buczacz (in today's western Ukraine), as Shmuel Yosef Czaczkes, he arrived in 1908 in Jaffa, Ottoman Palestine, where he adopted the penname Agnon and began a meteoric rise as a young writer. Between the years 1912 and 1924 he spent an extended sojourn in Germany, where he married and had two children, and came under the patronage of Shlomo Salman Schocken and his publishing house, allowing Agnon to dedicate himself completely to his craft. After a house fire in 1924 destroyed his library and the manuscripts of unpublished writings, he returned to Jerusalem where he lived for the remainder of his life. His works deal with the conflict between traditional Jewish life and language and the modern world, and constitute a distillation of millennia of Jewish writing—from the Bible through the rabbinic codes to ḥasidic storytelling—recast into the mold of modern literature.

About the Editor

Jeffrey Saks is the Series Editor of The S.Y. Agnon Library at The Toby Press, and lectures regularly at the Agnon House in Jerusalem. He is the founding director of ATID—The Academy for Torah Initiatives and Directions in Jewish Education and its WebYeshiva.org program, and an associate editor of the journal *Tradition*.

About the Illustrator

Yosl Bergner was born in Vienna in 1920, was raised in Warsaw, and lived in Melbourne from 1937 where he studied at the National Gallery of Victoria Art School. He left Australia in 1948 and after two years of traveling and exhibiting in Paris, Montreal, and New York City, he settled in the new State of Israel, living first in Safed until moving to Tel Aviv in 1957. A renowned artist and illustrator, Bergner received the Dizengoff Prize for painting in 1956, and in 1980 he was awarded the Israel Prize. He is still at work in his studio every day.

The fonts used in this book are from the Arno family.